"THERE CAN BE NO
HAPPY ENDING FOR US."

Ian went on painfully, "But my memories of you will always be precious...."

Memories. For the rest of her life, Monica thought bleakly, she'd be assailed by memories of this tall, tormented Scot. She could not stand it if those memories remained incomplete....

Certainty came with a powerful rush of emotion. As if drawn by a magnet she moved toward Ian, and his arms reached out to enfold her. Their bodies melted together until Monica was aware only of the strong sweet pulse of desire...and knew that tonight they would belong to each other fully.

Then Ian whispered huskily, "To last us for all time...."

And she was stabbed by the bittersweet reminder that this night was final—a treasure to be hoarded in her memory forever....

MEG HUDSON
is also the author
of these SUPERROMANCES

9 – SWEET DAWN OF DESIRE
36 – LOVE'S SOUND IN SILENCE

These books may be available at your local bookseller
or by writing to:

Worldwide Reader Service
1440 South Priest Drive, Tempe, AZ 85281
Canadian address: Stratford, Ontario N5A 6W2

MEG HUDSON
RETURN TO RAPTURE

A SUPERROMANCE FROM
W🌐RLDWIDE
TORONTO · NEW YORK · LOS ANGELES · LONDON

For Betty Blake, who led the way, and all
the others in the crew who helped make Scotland
such a bright page in our personal memory book.

———————◆—•—◆———————

Published February 1983

First printing December 1982

ISBN 0-373-70053-9

To the Reader

THE SCOTTISH BACKGROUND and history in this story are authentic, but admittedly, some liberties have been taken in the name of fiction. "Monbraithe" is a contrived name, and as far as can be ascertained, has no relationship to any Scottish family. The Mac-Gregors, on the other hand, are very real in the sense that they are one of Scotland's more prominent clans, but the MacGregors depicted in this book are entirely fictitious. Also, the precise area where Castle Monbraithe—fictitiously—is located is in reality "Buchanan Country." "MacGregor Country," although also along the shores of Loch Lomond, is several miles to the north.

CHAPTER ONE

THE PILOT'S VOICE was pleasantly British, his clipped accent laced with a touch of wry humor. "We shall land at Prestwick in twenty minutes, ladies and gentlemen," he announced over the faint static of the intercom, "and I'm afraid I must tell you that the weather awaiting us is typically Scottish. That's to say, wet and windy!"

The voluble lady from Des Moines, who had worn her incredible sapphire velvet hat all the way across the Atlantic, said firmly, "Well, I'm ready for it." She turned to her husband. "You didn't forget your overshoes, did you, Percy?"

"No, but I packed them," he admitted gloomily.

"You should have put them in my tote bag," she told him, then leaned across him to speak to Monica. "You do have rain gear with you, don't you, my dear?" she asked.

"Yes," Monica answered, forcing a smile. The lady from Des Moines, whose name was Mrs. Ewing, had been making motherly gestures ever since they'd left Boston's Logan Airport, and she was not in the mood for them, even though she realized they were well-intentioned. Now, keeping her tone light with an effort, she added, "My coat supposedly is water-proof, and I've a rain hat."

"Good," Mrs. Ewing approved, "though you really should have something for your feet, too."

Mrs. Ewing was sitting in the window seat, her portly, ruddy-cheeked husband was in the center, and Monica had the aisle seat. She had tried to doze as the plane streaked east toward the dawn, but it had been impossible even to approach sleep. A combination of excitement and apprehension was making her so tense that it was difficult to be civil to Mrs. Ewing, even though she knew she must be. The woman was essentially kind, there was no doubt about that, and she was also a paying guest.

Remembering this, Monica warned herself that she really must try to be a bit more pleasant to all the paying guests. After all, she'd been hired to keep the customers on this Magic Carpets Unlimited charter flight happy. That meant it was necessary for her to soft-pedal her own problems and keep a rein on her potentially chaotic emotions in the interests of others. She sighed. She was only beginning to realize that being agreeable just now, and forcing memory into the background, was a far more difficult feat than she'd expected.

She closed her eyes, faced an undeniable fact and nearly spoke the words aloud. *I was a fool to come on this trip. I must be an idiot to think I can possibly come back to Scotland without courting disaster!*

Definitely, she had rushed in where angels fear to tread, clutching at the chance to make the trip as if she were a child trying to grab the gold ring on a merry-go-round. But a gold ring, she reminded herself, not without irony, would have substance, whereas she was doing little better than chasing the proverbially elusive will-o'-the-wisp.

Now that the flight was almost over, it was easy enough to tell herself that if she'd had more time to think about it, she'd never have agreed to take the job in the first place. But hindsight, as always, was something else again! The opportunity to escort a group of older Americans across the Atlantic had seemed fantastic; she'd been thoroughly dazzled by it. The offer had come quickly, unexpectedly, and it had been necessary to make an almost split-second decision. She'd had no chance at all to think things over; nor, she had to admit, had she particularly wanted to.

Scotland again! The mere thought had been sufficiently overwhelming to make her lower the barriers she had raised so carefully in the past months. She had been like a moth lured by the flame of pure temptation. Scotland...and the chance of seeing Ian! She chided herself that she should have no desire at all to see Ian again, but here emotion took over, and logic quickly became the loser. Even the memory of him was overwhelming.

Monica had more than her share of staunch New England pride. Thinking of Ian, she had been appalled at her own reaction, for the surge of feeling that came with even speaking his name was purely treacherous. She had almost convinced herself that she'd got over him, almost made herself believe that she could actually forget the brief space of time a year ago that had so altered her life. She could count the hours that she'd spent with Ian, and if each were a pearl, the total would not add up to a very impressive string. Yet during every minute of each of those hours she had lived in a way that she'd never lived before...and now, she began to realize dismally, was never apt to live again.

Ian had taken possession of her in a sense that was strange when she considered that in the full meaning of the word he'd never taken possession of her at all. During the many sleepless hours since she'd left Scotland she'd wondered how it might have been if their love, their passion, had been consummated.

They'd come very close. If they'd gone on to the heights of distilled rapture, of which she was entirely certain they both were capable, would the ending between them have been different?

There was no way of knowing. No way, certainly, without seeing Ian again. And yet....

Monica had been given very little time in which to take stock of herself and her own emotions. The travel organization sponsoring the trip, Magic Carpets Unlimited, had been in dire need of her services, and they'd pressured her for a decision. She'd said yes almost before she realized what she was saying, and once committed, she'd had all sorts of last-minute details to take care of, plus a hasty instruction session on her duties.

The sponsors of the trip were members of Circle International, a quasi-fraternal organization whose membership was composed mainly of businessmen. Most of them had brought their wives along, although there were two—or was it three—widowers on the list. Monica had met with the group for the first time at Logan not much more than an hour before departure, and her prime concern had been to demonstrate a certain quality of efficiency combined with authority. Fortunately everything had gone well, and thus far she hadn't really been tested!

Almost immediately after takeoff, though, she'd become possessed of a sense of complete unreality; it was as if she were in the throes of a strange sort of dream. Increasingly she'd come to feel that the past had suddenly become present; and even now, as they approached Prestwick, she didn't seem to be able to shake off the mood.

Time had telescoped for her; it had become impossible *not* to feel that this was October a year ago, rather than October now. There were even moments when she found herself imagining Mrs. Ewing was her Aunt Flora, although they didn't look at all alike. For that matter, it was becoming impossible to believe that Aunt Flora really was dead.

A year ago—almost to the day—Aunt Flora had sat in a window seat exactly like the one Mrs. Ewing now occupied. Monica had been in the center seat, and a schoolteacher from Vermont, whose name she couldn't remember, had sat on the aisle. Then, too, a pilot with a British accent had come on the intercom to tell them that they would soon be landing at Prestwick, and he had chuckled and added that the weather was typically Scottish—wet and windy.

Thinking about this, she shuddered, and hoped that Mrs. Ewing hadn't noticed, otherwise next would come the suggestion that, just possibly, she might be coming down with a cold. Mrs. Ewing had already expostulated on the physical dangers of changing climates so quickly, a peril of the jet age.

Mrs. Ewing, however, was busy going through a section of her large, filled-to-capacity handbag, and the bag—to add to the irony with which coincidence is so often laced—was very much like the one Aunt Flora had been carrying a year ago. Monica remembered that bag vividly; there had seemed in it room for almost anything. She remembered Aunt Flora dispensing motion-sickness pills, chewing gum, a needle and thread when required, and even an extra paperback mystery, and now she imagined that Mrs. Ewing could undoubtedly do the same thing, were these demands made of her.

At one point along the way, the schoolteacher from Vermont had mentioned that she had a slight headache, and Aunt Flora had promptly brought forth a bottle of coated aspirin that, she promised, would not upset one's stomach. The teacher had been very pleased about this.

There hadn't been any men on that first trip; that much, at least, was different. Aunt Flora had belonged to the Delphian Sisterhood, an organization of professional women, many of whom were in the field of education. The Scottish holiday had been one of the annual tours booked by their group. The other women had all been much older than she was, Monica remembered, which was perhaps one of the reasons why she'd been so fancy-free when she first met Ian. . . .

Ian. Saying his name, even silently, was like stabbing herself with a sharp-edged knife, and she was afraid she'd moaned aloud from the imaginary thrust of it.

Fool, she told herself again, wishing there was a way she could tell the pilot to turn around and fly back to the United States! But instead she saw the No Smoking—Fasten Your Seat Belt sign flash on, and acting in a unison of which most of them were unaware, the passengers settled back for this last leg of the flight.

Monica's fingers fumbled as she fastened her own seat belt, and she shivered. Then Mrs. Ewing announced, "We're going down! I can feel the pressure in my ears!"

"We should have brought some chewing gum," her husband said, and Monica smiled. Aunt Flora had been one up on them there! She'd had plenty of chewing gum, and they'd both been chewing vigorously as they started the descent toward Prestwick.

Now she, too, felt the pressure and swallowed hastily, which didn't help all that much. Still, the discomfort was minimal, something that could be thrust aside. The growing conviction that she was making a terrible mistake could not be.

How could she have thought that Scotland could possibly be the same again? She asked herself this question with an impatience that verged on desperation. She should have remembered that history, in fact, does not really repeat itself, and that certainly her personal history was not about to do so. She had lived a dream and the dream had died. Now she realized only too well that returning to the scene of her most intense emotional experience could cause nothing but agony. True, there were only ashes left where once there had seemed to be love. Had the fire that had flared so intensely between Ian and herself been pure fantasy, she wondered, as threatening tears smarted. Ian had made his position in regard to her brutally clear; he had left no doubt at all about the fact that she had no place in either his life or his heart, nor would she ever have. How *could* she have been such a fool as to come back?

She glanced at her watch. It was not quite six in the morning, Scottish time, and she couldn't keep herself from wondering where Ian might be at this precise moment. Was he in Edinburgh or Glasgow or at Loch Lomond? Might he perhaps be down in London—or even away from the British Isles entirely?

She imagined that wherever he was he was probably asleep, and it was entirely possible that he wasn't alone. Monica faced this fact, then found herself flinching from it.

Still, an entire calendar year had passed. This was something she must remember, she told herself, something she must continue to remind herself of. There was a very good chance that by now Ian was married. There was a chance, for that matter, she thought bitterly, that he had been married even then! He had told her so very little about himself. In retrospect, he stood before her as a stranger, and she knew she must not categorize him as a beloved stranger, because there was no reason to think of him in that context. No reason at all!

Mrs. Ewing said, "I see yellow lights ahead."

Prestwick. Leaning forward slightly, Monica had a clear view of the airport terminal building. It was starkly modern, made of concrete, chrome and glass, and had the kind of anonymity that links all international airports. There was a restaurant on the upper level called the Tartan Room, if she remembered the name correctly. Beneath it, in the main foyer, there was a gift shop where one could make last-minute purchases of crystal and cashmere and Scottish shortbread. Nearby there was a clock. Ian had told her to meet him beneath the clock, and she had stayed until the last possible moment, her eyes seeking, searching, her heart finally beginning to pound with sheer anxiety.

But he had not come.

MRS. EWING COMPLAINED, "I wish they had one of those caterpillar tunnels, like they do in Boston, so we could walk right out of the plane into the terminal building. They're letting us off in the middle of the field. We're going to be drenched!"

This was a slight exaggeration. They were not really in the middle of the field, but there *was* a fair distance from the plane to the terminal entrance, and the rain was still slashing down. Monica smiled. She'd learned that the Scots could be amazingly impervious to bad weather.

The passengers began to file forward, and she lingered behind to help the stewardesses check that no personal belongings had been left by the group members, either in the overhead compartments or beneath

the seats. She'd already told her charges that first
they would be asked to fill out cards for immigration,
and after that they should move on to collect their
luggage and then go through customs, which, she
assured them, usually involved little more than a
pleasant formality.

Finally she left the plane, dashing through icy rain
propelled by a cold cutting wind. Then, as she neared
the terminal entrance, she heard the sound of bagpipes, and despite the downpour she paused. Just inside the entrance she saw the sturdy figure of a man
dressed in a kilt, his cheeks rosy and puffed full out
as he blew the wailing haunting strains of Scotland's
music.

Again she was plunged into memory. There had
been a bagpiper at Prestonfield. Tears came to blend
with the rain on her cheeks, and she brushed past the
piper, feeling as if her throat were about to close
from the ache that constricted it.

She forced herself to get her mind on business, if
only temporarily, as she caught up with the members
of the tour group. Most of them had finished filling
out their cards and were now filing past the immigration officers, then going through the swinging doors
that led to the baggage area.

Monica had brought only a single large suitcase
with her. She found it quickly, cleared customs and
then went out into the vast airport lobby to look for
the representatives of Magic Carpets Unlimited who
were supposed to meet her. She had been told she
would recognize them by their maroon jackets em-
blazoned with a gold insignia.

As she scanned the people milling through the

lobby, Monica's thoughts turned toward Pamela Flint, who probably had landed in Boston by now, broken ankle and all. Pamela's accident surely had proved what a strange force fate can be!

Although Monica and Pamela had been good friends in school, they'd seldom seen each other since graduation. They'd managed only to meet occasionally for lunch, usually at the Park Plaza Hotel during a period when Pamela was working for one of the airline ticket offices quartered there. Then, a few months ago, Pamela had been offered a job with Magic Carpets Unlimited, one of the larger travel organizations specializing in chartered tours. Thereafter Monica had received postcards from Spain, Germany and Morocco, and then, more recently, Pamela had been assigned to Scotland.

This present autumn tour was the last of the season, and in the normal course of events Pamela would have been here at Prestwick today to meet her new charges. But she had broken her ankle in a fall while negotiating a steep flight of steps leading up to an overlook in the Trossachs, and since it was the policy of the company to have an American representative with American tours they'd been desperate to replace her at once.

From what Monica had subsequently been told, a quick search had revealed that there weren't any Americans available on the scene who could take on the job at what was literally a moment's notice. Then Pamela had thought of Monica and urged Magic Carpets to contact her via their Boston office, in the hope that she might be free.

Obviously Pamela must have remembered that

Monica would have a valid passport, since she had been in Scotland herself only a year ago. She also knew that travel had played a major role in Monica's background, for her father had been an army officer and her early years had been spent in moving from one place to another.

Three years ago her parents had been killed in a car crash. The shock had been tremendous. An only child, she had been very close to her parents and was overwhelmed by the double loss. She still woke up occasionally in the middle of the night, clutched by a terribly vivid dream in which she imagined she could hear the horrible sounds of ripping metal, shattering glass and piercing screams that were not her own.

It was her father's older sister, Flora, who had stepped in at that crucial time and made a valiant effort to fill the gap in her young niece's life. Flora had just retired from the school where she had taught for twenty years, and she wanted to travel. Monica, too numbed by her sorrow to be very enthusiastic about anything, had nevertheless been willing to accompany her. They had taken trips to Portugal, Austria and Mexico, then a year ago they had made what was to be a fateful trip to Scotland.

Amazingly, Flora had never fully realized the effect the trip had had upon her niece. Monica had camouflaged the shadow that sometimes threatened to engulf her entirely, and after their return to Boston, through the rest of the fall and into the winter, she had tried very hard to keep up a cheerful facade for her aunt's sake. Still, it had been the most difficult time of her life. There were moments when she thought she couldn't cope with her grief for her parents, and now that was overlaid by the raw and painful emotional gash inflicted by Ian.

When Flora suggested they go South in search of some sunshine, she had been more than willing to agree. She'd been conscious of the fact that her aunt had not been looking well, though she'd attributed this to the especially cold gray winter Boston had been having. But while they were in Florida the older woman really had become ill. She had always been robust, and the sudden savage intensity of her illness was shocking. By May she was dead.

Monica had returned to Boston possessed by a sense of total loneliness. She was terribly conscious of the fact that she had no one, with Flora gone and Ian out of her life entirely. Although her inheritance from her parents, plus a further legacy from Flora, provided her with enough income to live comfortably, common sense told her that for the sake of her own physical and mental health she should get a job. And she soon found one—as a clerk-typist in a publishing firm.

The job was rather uninspiring in itself, but it was a stepping-stone, and the atmosphere did have a certain glamour. This aura extended to Gerald Strothers, twenty years older than she, a handsome charming man who was as kind and considerate as he was attractive.

One night, when he suggested that he and Monica have dinner together, she agreed. He took her to the Top of the Hub, where they looked out over the brilliantly sparkling spiderweb that was nighttime Boston. Soon she found herself telling him about her parents and about Flora. She almost—but not quite—told him about Ian.

As time passed, Monica continued to see Gerald outside of office hours. He soon admitted, ruefully, that he'd been married twice. The first marriage had ended with his wife's death, the second in divorce. He seemed to think of the failure of his second marriage as something of a mark against him, but this really didn't concern Monica. She found him a delightful thoughtful companion, and she came to rely upon him. In a sense, he filled her world.

Gerald took her to places in Boston she'd never been to before. He was, he admitted, a history buff, and they toured the Revolutionary area around Concord and Lexington, while Gerald told her stories about the country's origin that made the past seem to come alive. Sometimes they'd drive to Cape Cod on a weekend or go in the opposite direction to the mountains in nearby New Hampshire. People often thought they were father and daughter, a situation that Gerald faced with a rather wry whimsy.

"I know I really *am* old enough to be your father," he confessed when, on the Labor Day weekend, they went to the Cape and were walking along a seemingly endless stretch of golden beach. "But if you'd marry me, I think I could make it up to you for the age gap between us...."

Though Monica had realized this time would come between them, she wasn't prepared to face it. She was deeply fond of Gerald, but she didn't love him. Still, she couldn't bear the thought of losing him, for he had become very dear to her.

Her face mirrored her feelings and he said gently, "It's all right, Monica. Honestly, darling, it's all *right*...."

Later they'd gone to a marvelous restaurant near the Cape Cod Canal and feasted on lobster. Gerald had not again referred to his proposal. But back in her apartment that night she knew that there was no way she could continue their relationship, which also meant there was no way she could go on working in the same office with him. It would be deeply unfair to both of them.

She brooded for two days over her resignation, and it took all the courage she could muster to face him with it, then to remain unwavering when he tried to convince her that this was a totally unnecessary gesture on her part. She remained firm, she gave two weeks notice, and when the time was up she stayed in the old Back Bay apartment that had been Aunt Flora's. She stayed there for the better part of a month, as she tried to decide what to do next.

It seemed to her that she had brewed a whole caldron of bittersweet memories, and there were times when she felt as if she were about to drown in them. Then finally she forced herself to face reality, to admit that until she found out why Ian had not come to Prestwick on that October afternoon a year ago, she would never be a total person again. She would never be free to *live*, much less to love.

Prophetically, it was just about then that her telephone rang, and Magic Carpets Unlimited offered her Pamela's job.

CHAPTER TWO

MRS. EWING SAID, "I think that man over there must be with the tour organization."

Monica shook herself mentally and looked up to see a tall dark-haired Scot approaching them. He was wearing a blue-and-green plaid kilt and a maroon jacket with a gold insignia.

She stepped forward, glad of the diversion. "Douglas MacConnach?" she asked him.

"Aye," he responded. "You must be Miss Winthrop?"

"Yes."

"Iris will be right with us," he told her. "We've the tour buses just outside. Nasty morning."

His soft Scottish burr reminded her of Ian. It also reminded her that *everything* was undoubtedly going to remind her of Ian, and this was a thought difficult to face. It would be like constantly having a wound re-opened.

Now a dark-haired woman with a pert merry smile came up to them. She, too, was wearing the maroon jacket with the Magic Carpets insignia and a pleated plaid skirt.

"Iris Kemp, Monica Winthrop," Douglas MacConnach introduced them in a rather offhanded manner. "I should warn you, Miss Winthrop, that Iris is what we call a Sassenach—a Southerner, that is. In other words, she's English."

Iris laughed. "You may not know it," she told Monica lightly, her own accent crisp and British, "but here in Scotland being English is sometimes considered tantamount to a crime!"

The tour group had been assembling and Iris surveyed them. "Well," she said pleasantly, "we're all here, are we? We shall have to count you off like little sheep, you know, to make certain we've not lost any of you. Your luggage has been placed by the exit doors. Identify your bags, will you please, and once you've done so, the driver will put them on the bus. Then I shall ask each of you to give me your name before you go through to board the bus so that we may be certain everything is in order."

"Is there something I can do to help you?" Monica asked.

Iris shook her head. "There will be plenty of time for that later, my dear," she said with a smile. "Just ride along with us for the moment."

Monica was content to do precisely that. She watched as the luggage was handled with quiet efficiency. Then the tour group was directed toward the large Mercedes buses parked just outside. The group made final sprints to them through the pelting rain and gusting winds.

There were two buses, and Monica soon realized that Iris had charge of one of them and Douglas MacConnach the other. As it happened, it was Mac-Connach's bus that she boarded, to find him seated up in the front with a microphone at his side.

He waved her to the seat next to him and smiled at her so reassuringly that she wondered if she looked as uncertain as she felt.

"We'll be off in a minute," he promised, then switched on the microphone and said with an ease she envied, "Do settle in, ladies and gentlemen, and we shall shortly be on our way. I must apologize for this frightful weather, which is in no way akin to Scotland's welcome to all of ye. I note that the windows are steaming up, more's the pity, but perhaps ye can get a wee glimpse of the countryside anyway, so I shall point out various places of interest as we go along."

Next, with quiet expertise he produced a stack of circulars, which he asked the passengers to pass among themselves.

"These describe some of the extra trips we shall be offering whilst ye are in the Edinburgh area," he told them. "The first treat, I might as well tell ye now, begins this very evening with a dinner at Prestonfield House."

Prestonfield. Monica nearly spoke the name aloud.

Prestonfield, a gracious estate now converted into an inn, was totally associated with Ian in her memory. It was a short distance outside of Edinburgh, and she and Ian had driven there for dinner one night. He had ordered a special sort of wine and had toasted her, lifting the stemmed crystal glass on high. His intensely blue eyes, which she already knew were capable of expressing the widest variety of emotion, had been very serious as he added, "May this be forever!"

Despite the denouement between them, which seemed even now to have surely been a total betrayal, Monica couldn't repress the conviction that he had meant the toast—at least when he'd offered it. On that lovely autumn night at Prestonfield, certainly he had been as aware as she that something extraordinarily special had happened between the two of them. There had been nothing hidden about this awareness. They had shared an awe of it, conscious of their personal miracle, and actually revered it even though at times they tried to speak lightly about it.

People with their wits about them, they had agreed, simply didn't fall in love at first sight. That was fantasy. Yet it was also exactly what they'd done. They had taken one look at each other and. . . .

Monica stared out the bus windows, which were indeed "steaming up," and told herself that she must stop this plunging backward; she must, in fact, force herself to do so. She was here in Scotland now, committed for the better part of nine days to helping quite a number of people get the most out of their trip. She couldn't afford to turn to putty every time something came up that reminded her of Ian.

As it was, she had been fighting for an entire year to get over Ian, and the ridiculous part of it was that for a while she'd thought she'd won her battle. Now she knew that her grief over Aunt Flora's illness and subsequent death, and then her involvement with Gerald Strothers had temporarily clouded the issue. She had certainly been deluding herself otherwise if just hearing the name Prestonfield could do this to her!

She shivered, and Mrs. Ewing, who had taken the bus seat directly across the aisle, leaned forward and said, "You should have worn something warmer, my dear."

"No, really," Monica protested. "I'm quite warm enough."

The passengers had finished perusing Douglas MacConnach's pamphlets, and now he spent some time taking reservations from those who wished to dine at Prestonfield. Then he picked up the microphone again to tell everyone that they were passing through Tyre, the town in which the famous David Livingstone, of "Dr. Livingstone, I presume" fame, had been born.

Monica, glancing through a "wee hole" in the steamy window, saw that they were passing a school: children garbed in slickers and knee-length white socks were just turning into its concrete yard. Small stone and stucco houses wearing chimney pots like rakish tilted crowns blended along the soot-colored streets in tones of gray, tan and brown. Most of the houses had tidy front gardens in which roses and deep pink hydrangeas still bloomed in profusion, their lovely colors particularly vivid on this rainy day.

Toward midmorning they stopped at a roadside facility designed for buses, cars and "lorries," and again memory surged like the waves of an incoming tide. She and Ian had once stopped at a place like this. They had eaten sandwiches of savory sausages stuffed into hard rolls, and they had drunk strong tea laced with milk and sugar. There had been a feeling of total rapport between them; they didn't have to touch physically to be totally close, for they had this *consciousness* of each other. They were so entirely attuned; she never before had experienced anything like it.

Was that what love—real love—was like? Despite the shattering effect that Ian had on her sensually, Monica had felt there was something between them that transcended even the tremendous attraction they had for each other. And she had no doubt at all about their mutual desire. The message that day at the lorry stop had wafted unspoken between them. She had known that he wanted her every bit as much as she wanted him. . . .

Now, just remembering, she could feel herself being invaded by a disturbing warmth, and she wondered if she was flushing visibly. She was standing in line with the others, and fortunately it was now her turn to order. She chose coffee and a scone, only at once to have Mrs. Ewing, who was standing just behind her, say, "You really should have something more than that, my dear. You could do with a bit of extra flesh on your bones."

Monica, striving to restrain her impatience, answered a bit testily, "I'm not hungry." She felt reprieved when Iris and Douglas MacConnach asked her to come and sit at their table so that they could discuss a few business matters.

As she settled in, Iris remarked with a laugh, "That one in the atrocious blue hat really does keep an eye on you!"

Monica smiled ruefully. "Yes, she does," she admitted. "Actually, though, she means well."

"I'm sure she does," Iris agreed. "She's a mother hen, that's all. There's one in every tour group. Incidentally, Pamela sent you her love."

"When did she leave?"

"Not till last night. She was so very relieved that you were able to take over for her on such short notice. The Magic Carpets people are frightfully fussy about having an American girl available. They seem to think it gives people necessary reassurance."

"That's true," Douglas nodded, when Monica looked skeptical. "Many of the people on trips like this one have never been out of the States before, and the small things are important to them—the home touches, don't you know? They'll be coming to you for all of that. Iris and I handle most of the patter; you needn't concern yourself too much with it. For that matter, we also put purely local guides on some of the trips. It provides an extra flavor that rather spices things up."

"Then I won't have to give myself a quick in-depth course in Scottish history?" she asked him.

It was Iris who answered. "I should hope not! As a matter of fact, I doubt there's such a thing as a short course in Scottish background. It would take an entire lifetime of tours at least to really get the history of these Scots straight."

"Ye say that because ye are prejudiced, since ye know that the throne of Scotland rightfully belongs to us," Douglas accused her, his Scottish accent suddenly quite a bit more pronounced. He finished his tea and stood up, tall and handsome in his kilt, wearing it so naturally that it was difficult to imagine him wearing anything else. And inevitably Monica found herself wondering how Ian must look in a kilt. He had never worn one when he was with her.

The rain seemed to be slackening as they went back to the bus, and once aboard Douglas suggested to her, "Nap a bit, if you like. You can press the back of the seat down, you know."

She did so, and actually dozed off for a time. After that it didn't seem very long until they were passing the Edinburgh Airport and the Ingliston Fair grounds, where a large open-air market was held each Sunday. Then they were swinging off the highway and going down a ramp, and someone said, "That must be our hotel."

Peering through the front window of the bus, where the windshield wiper was still busy at work, Monica caught her breath.

It had not occurred to her that this group would be staying in the same hotel where she'd stayed last year. No one had mentioned the name of the hotel, nor had she asked about it. She had made out her luggage tags in care of Magic Carpets Unlimited, merely giving the number of this particular charter trip.

Now, though, as she glimpsed the sprawling white building they were approaching, she began to fight back tears. She was thankful that Douglas MacConnach was deep in conversation with the driver and so did not chance to look toward her until she'd had time to compose herself again.

She found herself clenching her fists until her nails

dug into her palms, and she bit the inside of her cheeks in the effort to hold back the tears, succeeding by sheer force of will. Still, it didn't seem possible to her that she could bear to walk inside that building, even though she knew that in just a few more minutes she'd have no choice about doing just that.

This was the worst part of all; there could hardly be a more traumatic moment, certainly. And now Monica told herself that if she could get through this, she could get through anything. Because it was here in this hotel, a year ago, that she had first met Ian.

She blanked out the memory, again by sheer force of will, plunging herself into her work as the passengers began to disembark. Most of them were moving slowly and grumbling at the same time about the wet weather and their various aches and pains, which had been augmented first by the hours they'd spent on the plane, then by the long bus ride.

Monica found that it was possible to lose one's sense of identity, at least temporarily, by staying very busy, so she set about helping people with their luggage and assuring them that she would find out about the ice supply in the hotel and get back to them with this very necessary information. Americans, she observed with some amusement, seemed to bear up under almost anything but a potential lack of ice cubes!

She also set about finding out where postage stamps could be bought, when the coffee shop was open and if the hotel offered room service, and soon she was able to handle most of the questions being directed at her without having to go elsewhere for reference.

Finally, though, there was a lull, and it took only a second for her world to turn upside down. She found it was much too easy to imagine that time really had been turned back twelve months, and that she and her Aunt Flora had just returned from a shopping expedition in downtown Edinburgh, for the hotel was on the outskirts of the city, at a distance of about five miles.

She and her aunt had been about to get on the elevator that long-ago afternoon, Monica remembered, when Flora had decided to go back to the desk in the lobby and buy a few postcards. She had promised to be quick about it, and since there was no one else waiting to use the elevator, Monica had stepped inside it and pressed the hold button.

Ian had come around the corner with a quick easy stride, and he had stepped into the elevator before he even noticed her. Then he smiled, and it was like the sun breaking through the clouds on a damp Scottish day. His eyes were a light yet very definite shade of blue, and as they surveyed her appreciatively she felt none of the resentment she usually felt when men were so quickly and even blatantly responsive with her. She knew, without having any particular conceit about it, that nature had been generous to her. She was slightly above average height, with a slim figure, yet one quite full in the right places. Her hair was naturally wavy, a deep shade of chestnut with reddish glints, and her hazel eyes—sometimes close to clear green—were perhaps her best feature, large and very expressive.

This man before her was noting all of these attributes, she realized. But privately she conceded that maybe the reason she didn't mind was that she was actually staring back at him!

He was tall, considerably taller than she was, with somewhat rugged features that, assembled as they were, made him decidedly handsome. His hair was cut fairly long but not too long, and was sandy in tone, very nearly matching the color of the tweeds he was wearing; yet there was nothing at all monotonous about the color similarity. His suit jacket was beautifully cut to emphasize wide muscular shoulders tapering to a narrow waist that in itself suggested perfect physical fitness. His slacks, in a slightly darker tone, revealed legs that seemed very long yet gave more than a hint of a latent power. As she looked at him, Monica swallowed hard. She had no difficulty at all in leaping to the conclusion that here was the most disturbingly masculine and devastatingly attractive man she had ever seen.

As she stood there, her finger still on the elevator's hold button, his merriment visibly increased, and she came back to reality with disconcerting swiftness. "Oh," she said, the word emerging almost breathlessly, "you must want to go up!"

His blue eyes danced, and he said disarmingly, with a faint tilt of his head, "On the contrary. With such a lovely lady as yourself I would as leave stay here for as long as you might wish."

He spoke with a soft Scottish burr, yet his accent was clear. She had no trouble understanding him, something she couldn't say held true with the other Scots she had met thus far. But now she found herself flushing, and this thoroughly annoyed her. She was behaving like a silly schoolgirl!

"What floor are you on?" she asked, trying to be very matter-of-fact.

His eyes were still dancing as he told her, "Two."

"Very well, then," she answered. "I'll take you on up."

She pushed the proper button, aware that he was watching her much too closely, and the elevator motor began to whir. Then as the door closed he asked, "Have you just arrived?" The way he pronounced "you" was close to "ye" yet not quite that definite.

"No," she said. "We've been in Edinburgh two days."

"We?"

"My aunt and I."

"Then you've not got a husband?"

"No."

His smile deepened. "Good," he declared.

The elevator came to a stop and the door slid open. "Will you be here a few days more?" he asked her.

"Through the weekend," she told him. "Then we go on to Glasgow."

"Surely 'tis fate," he said, and laughed. "I am to be in Edinburgh through the weekend, and then I shall be going on to Glasgow, too, so we are certain to meet again."

With that he left her, and for a moment she stood transfixed, quite unable to move. Then the elevator door began to close. Someone below had pushed the button, Monica realized, and the thought came to her that it was probably Aunt Flora.

And indeed that's who it was. Perplexed, Flora asked, "What happened to you?"

"Someone wanted to go up," Monica said a bit feebly, "so I took him." Fortunately Flora accepted this without further questioning.

The hotel provided continental breakfasts for its guests. Orange juice, jam and crisp rolls were left on trays outside each door in the early morning, and every room was equipped with an electric kettle in which to heat water for coffee or tea.

This sufficed for Monica until Friday morning, when she decided she wanted something a bit more substantial. Aunt Flora, however, already was ensconced in bed with her breakfast tray, munching away while she enjoyed a program on BBC television, so Monica went downstairs alone.

She had ordered scrambled eggs and bacon and was doing some mental arithmetic in an effort to convert the price from British into American money when someone spoke to her. And she knew without even looking up who it was.

"May I?" he asked, and before she could form an answer he pulled out a chair and sat down at her table.

"What a bit of luck!" he said enthusiastically. "It was idiotic of me not even to ask your name. I had about resigned myself to the fate of settling into a chair in the lobby and waiting until you happened by, no matter how long that might take."

She smiled. "My name is Monica Winthrop," she told him.

"Winthrop. English?"

"On my father's side," she admitted. "My mother's name was Riley, which I suppose adds up to a typical American."

"I am Ian MacGregor," he said. "My mother was a Mercier, her family came from Strasbourg, so that I suppose doesn't really add up to a typical Scot."

A stocky little waitress dressed in shiny black brought the eggs and bacon, and toast that Monica discovered was served cold. Ian placed his own order, then asked, "Have you tried the kippers?"

"For breakfast?"

"Yes, for breakfast. We shall have them Sunday morning—if you will join me, that is."

She didn't hedge. "I would like that," she responded.

"Excellent. What about today, in the meantime? I suppose I couldn't possibly be so lucky as to find that you're free?"

She shook her head reluctantly. "Unfortunately, I'm not. My aunt and I are going on one of the side trips. It goes past Linlithgow, the ruined palace where Mary, Queen of Scots, was born, and then across the Firth of Forth to a town where there's supposed to be quite an interesting palace in the process of restoration. Culross, I think it's called."

"Without the *l*," he said. "Oh, it's spelled with an *l* to be sure, but you don't say it. You say 'Cuross' and then you must roll the *r* a bit." The blue eyes were dancing again. "'Tis quite an interesting place, I admit, but must you go?"

"Yes, I really must. There was an extra fee for the trip, and my aunt already paid it."

"And we Scots are supposed to be the thrifty ones," he groaned, teasing her. "Very well, then, what about tonight? Would you dine with me?" Suddenly he was serious. He said, his voice low, "There isn't all that much time, you know."

Their eyes met, and Monica caught her breath. Something unbelievable, something incredible, was happening between them.

He reminded her gently, "Eat your eggs. They're getting cold." Then he paused for a moment, watching her. "Well, Monica, will you have dinner with me?"

"Yes," she agreed. "Yes, I should like to very much, unless Aunt Flora has something else planned."

"Then let us hope she doesn't," Ian said. "I'll wait for you in the lobby. Seven, shall we say?"

That was the night he took her to Prestonfield.

CHAPTER THREE

THERE WAS WORK TO BE DONE in getting the group organized, and Monica accepted it gratefully. Keeping busy permitted her to blot out the past again, at least temporarily. She took her place at the Magic Carpets hospitality desk in the lobby and gradually got to know her customers better as she went over the details of a variety of special tours with them, booking space for those who wished to avail themselves of the extra options.

Clarence Fielding, one of the widowers, was a retired architect. Monica was sure he'd enjoy the restoration work at Culross, and he agreed with her, especially since he'd also be crossing the famous Firth of Forth bridge on that trip. The Sedgewicks were a charming couple from Baltimore, and they liked her suggestion that they see the Trossachs and the Loch Lomond area. Most of the others were equally amenable. Pleasant people, all of them. Monica told herself she was lucky to have drawn such a group.

Iris returned from taking some of the women on a brief late shopping trip into town. Pausing at the desk, she confided in Monica, "I've come down with a frightful headache. Do you suppose you could take over and go to Prestonfield in my place tonight? Douglas will be on hand, so there shouldn't be any problems. It's just a question of having a woman around, really.''

Never before had Monica felt so trapped. Prestonfield was the very last place she wished to visit, yet there seemed no way she could refuse Iris under the circumstances. Certainly she wasn't about to try offering a valid reason for wanting to stay away. Iris was discerning—she'd already realized that—and might guess at the truth easily were she given an opportunity.

Trying not to sigh audibly, she answered, ''Of course. Should I dress up very much?''

Iris shrugged. ''You could wear a long skirt if you like, though any sort of frock would do—something rather soft and feminine, I'd say. It's a pleasant place, and rather elegant. I think you'll enjoy it.''

Monica was tempted to say that she'd been there before, but she suppressed the impulse, and a moment later she was distracted by someone coming to ask the hours in the hotel dining room. When finally she went up to the room she was sharing with Iris, there wasn't very much time to fuss over what she was going to wear, so she chose a simple green wool dress that was cut with disarming simplicity. With it she wore a silver-and-malachite pendant that had belonged to her mother and a pair of matching silver earrings.

She made up with her usual care, brushed her chestnut hair until, obeying her wishes, it curled softly about her shoulders, then dabbed a bit of her favorite perfume, Arpege, behind her ears. Still, the sight of her reflection in the mirror, which should have been gratifying, only made her more aware of the unhappiness that lurked in her hazel eyes, unhappiness that couldn't be erased summarily.

When she returned downstairs, most of the group going to Prestonfield were in the lobby, gathered around Douglas MacConnach. He was resplendent tonight in a dress kilt and a frilled white shirt, and as she walked toward him Monica was aware that his gaze was frankly admiring—as were those of Mr. Ewing and the other men in the entourage, each of them old enough to be her father if not her grandfather. She forced herself to smile back at them, though it was difficult at the moment to keep up a pleasant charming facade. She couldn't wait for this night to be over with!

Once aboard the bus, Douglas again indicated that she should sit next to him up front. She did so, and was relieved when she saw him pick up the microphone and start talking, for she was in no mood at all for a conversation.

He kept up a steady patter, part history, part light-hearted humor, and obviously the tour guests loved him. Monica, though, heard very little of what he was actually saying. It was his tone that reached her, the accent with its soft rolling *r*'s, and low-throated chuckle. She became alert only when they finally turned onto Princes Street. There, to the right, high on its rock, she saw Edinburgh Castle, floodlighted tonight, and she heard the passengers gasp at the sheer beauty of it.

Her own gasp was for quite a different reason, as a purely emotional pain came to stab her. Despite herself she was remembering the Sunday afternoon when she and Ian had explored the castle, walking up the steep cobbled paths that led to the top. The wind had ruffled their hair as they gazed out across Edinburgh, all the way to the Firth of Forth and beyond.

Now Douglas was speaking about the castle, telling his listeners that the oldest building within it was Queen Margaret's chapel, which had been built in the eleventh century and still stood intact, though it was so small it could barely hold twenty people at one time. And again memory came to haunt her.

She and Ian had stood in the doorway of Queen Margaret's chapel, and he had told her a great deal of its story. The castle itself was so old, he had said, that its origin was lost in the maze of history.

"What we know is more legend than fact, until the eleventh century," he'd explained. "'Tis then that Malcolm III—Ceann Mor, that is—married Margaret, who was the sister of Edgar Atheling. Thereafter King Malcolm and Queen Margaret made the castle their residence. Until that time, undoubtedly it had been a fortress. 'Tis a natural site for a place of defense, as well as a retreat in time of danger. It's likely, in fact, that at the very crest of the rock there was a fort guarding this area as long ago as the Iron Age. But this is something that only can be guessed at.

"By the time Margaret and Malcolm came to the castle," he had continued, "'tis thought that the buildings were on the highest part of the rock, and there was probably a wooden stockade around them. One would have climbed up there via a very long flight of stairs. Margaret nonetheless adored Edinburgh Castle, and the king must have adored her. The story goes that in the 'chamber of the blessed Margaret'—in which many future kings of Scotland were to hold audience—there were luxuries quite unknown in this country until then. And 'tis said that Margaret heard Mass daily in her chapel until the very day before her death, which is recorded as of the sixteenth of November in 1093. She had been ill, it seems, at the time Malcolm left for his last raid on England—an ill-fated one. The word of Malcolm's death was brought to her by her son Edward, and shortly thereafter she died herself. Theirs must have been quite a love match. For her exemplary life in Scotland, Margaret thereafter became known as Saint Margaret...."

Ian had looked down at her, a gentle smile curving his lips. He had waved toward the beautiful little chapel and said softly, "'Tis still used sometimes for weddings...."

Astonishingly, Douglas was saying precisely the same thing, and Monica came to with a jolt. This sort of brooding, she warned herself, really was apt to test one's sanity, and again she told herself sharply that she must stop it!

Now concentrating with all the intensity she could summon, she listened to Douglas and found herself agreeing with Iris's earlier statement: it would indeed take a lifetime of "tours" to fully absorb the turbulent history of the Scots!

Despite her concentration, though, her resolutions went flying as the bus made a sharp turn into the long tree-lined lane that led to Prestonfield House. Soft lights gleamed ahead, and she discerned the outline of the familiar three-storied house with a wide pillared portico over its entrance. Chimneys adorned with the ever present chimney pots further heightened each peak of the roof. Monica remembered how Ian had said that someday they'd come back to stay here, for there was limited accommodation available for guests, although usually it was necessary to book rooms well in advance.

Her throat ached with pure longing as she listened to Douglas tell the group that the house was very old, built in 1687 for Sir James Dick, a close friend of the then Duke of York, who himself had become King James II. In 1745, Dick's descendant, Sir Alexander Dick, had received Bonnie Prince Charlie here, and fourteen years later, in 1759, Prestonfield had had another distinguished guest: Benjamin Franklin, who was later to become the American ambassador to the court of Louis XVI.

"Many famous people have come here for nearly three hundred years now," Douglas said, "and they continue to do so. 'Tis said that the visitors' book reads like a world gazetteer. The house is set in the midst of twenty-three acres, which unfortunately you can't see much of at this time of day. 'Tis beautifully landscaped, though, all of it, with sheep grazing about very happily and peacocks strutting around as if they own the place. If time allows, 'twould be nice if you could pay a daytime visit."

The bus was pulling to a stop, and he added with a smile, "Well, now, there's a piper waiting to greet us at the door."

There was indeed a bagpiper at the front entrance. Inside, the formal hall was just as Monica remembered it, the walls dominated by huge oil paintings in ornate gold frames. The floor combined black and white marble in an unusual vertical pattern that led one to focus upon the short flight of steps leading to the reception area.

They went first to the beautiful Tapestry Room on the second floor, and this, too, was just as Monica remembered it. Comfortable upholstered couches were arranged in rather informal groupings. Beautiful antique tables and sideboards were further ornamented by exquisite porcelains, inlaid boxes and figurines, many of which had come from the Orient. There were Persian rugs underfoot, jewel-toned tapestries on the wall, and Douglas now mentioned that the cordovan leather panels were considered priceless.

It was the ceiling that especially intrigued Monica. It was amazingly ornate, the plaster having been worked into an incredibly intricate design. One could easily get a stiff neck, she thought wryly, studying the beautiful ceilings at Prestonfield.

Sherry was served in the Tapestry Room, and Monica assisted in the serving, for which Douglas flashed her a grateful look. Then they went downstairs again to a magnificent dining room with heavy velvet draperies and massive oil portraits lining the walls. And as they were seated at the tables reserved for them, the memory of that earlier evening here became so acute it was all Monica could do to eat.

She barely tasted the excellent barley soup and the succulent crown roast of lamb accompanied by a variety of vegetables. And the dessert tray, when it was rolled in, only reminded her all the more of Ian. He'd tempted her to take two, one with delicious raspberries rolled in a rich pastry, and the other a brandy snap, crisp and lacy and filled with whipped cream. Tonight she settled for a slice of chocolate *gâteau*, which was very good, but still she could eat only a portion of it.

After dinner they returned to the Tapestry Room for coffee, and the bagpiper played a concert for them while two rosy-cheeked girls in brief plaid skirts danced the Highland fling. This, at least, was unlike anything that had happened on that other evening at Prestonfield.

The time came for the women to go to the cloakroom to redeem their wraps, and it was then, while they were slowly wending their way back down the curving carpeted stairs, that Monica looked ahead and saw a tall sandy-haired man nearing the outer door. He was wearing a kilt, but his bearing, his manner, was so achingly familiar to her that she nearly called out his name.

She prayed that he might turn his face so that she could at least glimpse his profile, but he didn't do so. Now she noticed he was holding the arm of a tall young woman with very blond hair, and an older man and a white-haired woman seemed to be with them.

As she made her own way through the entrance hall, with Douglas leading the group, Monica wondered for a heart-stopping moment whether this quartet might be waiting for their car outside, under the portico. As she stepped through the doorway she was almost afraid to look. But there was no one waiting for a car; in fact the tour buses were pulling up in front of the door, and she slowly climbed aboard, intensely disappointed and yet in an odd sense relieved. She couldn't imagine how she would have managed to handle coming face to face with Ian here at Prestonfield, and now she wondered how *he* would have handled it. With his usual somewhat autocratic ease, and that quiet air of self-confidence that was so much a part of him?

For that matter, she reminded herself, she was not at all sure that it was Ian she'd seen. There must be hundreds of tall sandy-haired men in Scotland, nor was it all that unusual for them to wear kilts at dinner. Still, the pattern of the kilt lingered in her mind like a clear color photograph. It had had a bright red background, and there had been green and black in the plaid. She willed herself to remember the pattern accurately and to check on it at the first opportunity.

This opportunity was to come sooner than she might have expected.

When she got back to the hotel, Iris was still awake, propped up in bed as she watched a drama on the "telly."

"There now," she said. "How was it?"

"Prestonfield? Very lovely," Monica replied a bit evasively.

Iris eyed her narrowly. "Things did go off well, didn't they?"

"Oh, yes," she answered quickly. "I think everyone enjoyed it very much."

"Charming place, Prestonfield," Iris went on, and yawned. "Our featured attraction tomorrow will be a fashion show at a woolen shop on Princes Street. After that we take the group to dinner in a downtown restaurant, and later on a night tour of the city." Smiling a bit wickedly, she confided, "They get the greatest delight in having the opportunity to invade a real pub!"

Monica smiled herself at the thought of this. "I can imagine," she said, picturing Mrs. Ewing under such circumstances.

"By the way, love," Iris continued, "our Douglas does seem to have taken a fancy to you. He asked if you might come along for the fashion show, if there's nothing else that needs doing. I told him I couldn't imagine why anyone should simply sit all day long at the hospitality desk when almost everyone's bound to be out. I'm guiding a castle tour that's already booked to capacity, so my guess is you may have a fair overflow for the fashion show, which would mean that Douglas could use the help. If that's agreeable to you...."

"Of course," Monica said, her mind racing ahead. A Scottish woolen shop, she told herself, would undoubtedly have a good selection of tartans.

THE FOLLOWING AFTERNOON she could barely restrain her impatience during the fashion show, although the clothes were quite lovely, and she wished she had enough extra cash on hand to buy one delectable cape in muted shades of mauve and gray. Finally, though, the last model left, after displaying a stunning floor-length skirt, and the tour members were told they had half an hour of free time in which to browse and buy, if they desired.

Monica quickly sought out a clerk and asked to be shown the MacGregor plaid.

"Would you care to see a necktie or a scarf?" she was asked.

"It doesn't really matter," Monica said quickly. "I just want to see the plaid itself."

"Ah, well, then," the young man decided, "in that case I would say a scarf will give you as good an idea as anything."

He reached into a glass case, then laid a length of wool on the counter beside her. Looking down at the soft fabric, Monica froze. The MacGregor plaid was bright red, with green and shadowed black cross stripes!

She tried to convince herself that there were many Scottish tartans with red backgrounds and that she had, after all, seen the kilt the tall man was wearing at quite a distance. So she couldn't, she *shouldn't* be so entirely sure of the pattern. Also, even if the kilt she had seen *was* the MacGregor plaid, Ian was hardly the only MacGregor in Scotland!

But it didn't do any good to try to rationalize just now. In her heart Monica was thoroughly convinced it was Ian she had seen at Prestonfield, and she tried to focus more acutely on her memory of the people who had been with him. There had been the tall young woman; her hair had shone like spun gold when she stepped out into the aura of the light that hung over the front portico. The older white-haired woman had moved with quite a distinguished carriage, and she had been wearing a fur wrap. The gray-haired man seemed relatively anonymous in retrospect. She could remember only that he, too, had an autocratic air about him—at least as seen from her rear vantage point—and had been nearly as tall as Ian.

Now they moved through her memory, four dreamlike figures, and she began to wonder whether she had imagined the whole thing. Had she conjured up a vision of Ian because she wanted so much to see him?

It was drizzling that evening, so the night tour was not as spectacular as it might have been. Nevertheless, as Iris had predicted, everyone thoroughly enjoyed the excursion into a "genuine" pub. They were led upstairs to the section where ladies were permitted and given samples of good Scottish whisky. "The real thing, not the blend most of ye are accustomed to," Douglas said, his eyes twinkling.

Monica was very tired when she got back to the hotel, but she slept restlessly. When she awakened she found that Iris had got up ahead of her, leaving a note behind.

Monica, love, Douglas and I both have an all-day castle tour today, so the hospitality desk must be yours. I suggest you keep it open from ten or so through the lunch hour, and then again from perhaps four until everyone has settled in for dinner. No need to stay chained down any longer than that.

Tomorrow, there's the tour of the Firth of Forth area plus Culross, and some of the country over on the other side of the bridge. If that doesn't appeal to potential customers, you can suggest a tour of a whisky distillery. We've openings for four or five more people on that one. Also, be sure to remind people that we shall be leaving for Glasgow quite early Tuesday morning, going via Loch Lomond.

Loch Lomond.

Monica was not at all sure that she could bear to go near Loch Lomond.

Last night had been bad enough! The night tour, despite the drizzle, had swirled her into yet another whirlpool of memories, especially when Douglas had instructed the bus driver to take them up to the top of Calton Hill. At the top he had urged everyone to get out for a moment despite the weather, and to walk with him past the telescope-shaped Nelson monument and the unfinished national monument, which looked like a ruined version of the Parthenon and was reported to have been largely responsible for Edinburgh's being nicknamed "the Athens of the North."

Ian also had taken her up Calton Hill, but on a star-filled night, pointing out Arthur's Seat, the extinct volcano that rose from Holyrood Park and was such a beloved part of the Edinburgh skyline. He had stood with his arm around her, the city glittering before them, and had told her that although he came from Glasgow—near Glasgow, at least—Edinburgh was his favorite city and he wouldn't mind at all making it his permanent home, were such a thing possible.

She had started to ask him why it wouldn't be possible, but he had interrupted her by drawing her attention to yet another feature of the landscape, and a second later he had kissed her for the first time.

In retrospect, she could see that the kiss had been inevitable, and the setting for it had been absolutely perfect. She and Ian had seemed alone at the top of the world, and she had forgotten everything except the feel of his arms encircling her, and the rough tweed of the jacket he was wearing brushing her cheeks.

First he had said something undecipherable in a low husky tone, and then his lips had come to meet hers in a moment that seemed beyond belief, in the quality of its ecstasy. There had been a kind of sweetness in the beginning, sweetness and wonder, but then it seemed as if everything within her deepened, as if to make way for the surge of pure sensation that came to fill her, every part of her, mental, emotional and physical, as well. There had been no such thing as rationality; she had been beyond herself as she swayed close to him, trembling as his hands searched beneath the folds of her coat in a mission of discovery.

She lost all sense of time and place as their kisses increased in ardor. Her own hands began to move across the back of his head and neck while her body arched toward him, pressing close against him, making her almost inadvertently aware of his very tangible and tantalizing masculinity. Until that moment Monica had never really experienced desire; she had never really known what it was to want a man. But in his embrace she seemed to become a sensual entity, moving without volition as she became possessed of a mounting seething impatience that made her quiver beneath his touch.

Looking back, it seemed ironic to think that it was a tour bus that had interrupted them. Headlights had flared, coming around a bend, and reluctantly they had drawn apart. Monica had been totally shaken, and in the dim light she had seen Ian close his eyes tightly; she had seen him shudder. Then he'd said, smiling slightly and trying to be light about it, "Terrible timing."

"Yes," she'd answered.

He'd drawn a deep breath. "Come along. I should have known better in the first place."

The mood had been broken, and they were silent as they walked, hand in hand, past the observatory and back to the spot along the road where Ian had parked his red MGA.

Last night the Magic Carpets bus had parked close to the very spot where Ian's car had been on that other evening, and it had taken terrific effort—mental rather than physical—for Monica to get off and follow Douglas and the rest of the group around the top of the hill. She had been possessed by the uncanny feeling that at any moment Ian was going to come up and take her by the arm; she could almost

feel the warmth of his hand. Then she'd realized it
was Mrs. Ewing clutching her.

"I can't see a thing," Mrs. Ewing had complained,
and Monica promptly offered to guide her. But there
seemed a chill to the night after that, due not so much
to the drizzle as to the fact that seldom before had
she ever felt quite so cold of spirit, or quite so alone.

CHAPTER FOUR

THE FEELING OF BEING COLD AND ALONE persisted
through Sunday as Monica sat at the hospitality desk
trying to concentrate on answering the questions
various members of the tour group stopped by to
ask. She assured where assurances were needed,
booked reservations for future trips out of Glasgow
to the Trossachs or the Highlands and Loch Ness, or
simply passed the time chatting with pleasant middle-
aged travelers who found themselves faintly home-
sick for the sound of an American accent.

On Monday she presided at the desk again. Back
from yet another castle tour, Douglas stopped by
toward dinner time to confess, out of the hearing of
any of the paying customers, that he was certain he
would have broken an arch had he been required to
approach so much as one more rampart. His voice no
longer reminded her as much of Ian's as it had at
first, for she was becoming increasingly discerning in
the matter of Scottish accents. Still, that soft burr
struck at her heart.

For that matter, Douglas had charms of his own,
and without overstating his case he'd made it clear
that he found her attractive. He was more than wise
enough, she sensed, to put business first; yet he had

managed to let her know that he was from Dundee, he'd had a couple of years at university, and he hoped to go on to study law if he could save enough money from tour guiding. Since he was relatively young and as yet unencumbered, he reasoned—stressing this a bit—there was still time enough in which to pursue a serious career. Meanwhile he readily admitted that, generally speaking, touring was quite a lark.

"And I am coming to dote on Americans despite myself," he'd added with a wicked grin.

Now sitting down for a moment in a chair next to the hospitality desk, he imparted the information that Iris had slipped off to keep a dinner-date in town.

"It's with a fellow Londoner up on a holiday, if I'm not mistaken," he said, "which rather leaves the two of us alone. I wondered if you might like to have dinner with me here in the hotel dining room? 'Tis more or less expected, when there isn't a dinner tour on, that the staff members will dine together somewhat on the latish side," he added. "This is especially so on our last night in a city, and usually they tend to put one on for us. Even produce a bottle of champagne on occasion, if our people have been good tippers!"

Monica was tempted to make an excuse because she had no desire to encourage Douglas falsely. Then she thought of the bedroom upstairs, which would seem very bleak this evening without Iris around. Also, she knew that in the hotel coffee shop she couldn't hope for anything more than a thin cold sandwich and some tea.

Douglas was looking at her with a slightly puzzled frown, and she realized that he'd noted her hesitation and was trying to fathom the reason for it, so she forced a smile. "That would be very nice," she told him a bit primly.

"I'm delighted to hear that," he said with a slightly mocking smile of his own. "I was a wee bit afraid you were about to refuse me. Will nine o'clock suit you?"

"Nine will be fine," she agreed.

Even before eight o'clock, business had slackened off so at the hospitality desk that there really seemed no reason to keep it open any longer. Monica slipped upstairs, wondering whether or not she should change. She was wearing a beige pantsuit that was suitable enough for dinner here in the hotel, yet all at once she decided she wanted to be a bit more festive.

She soaked for fifteen minutes in a fragrantly scented bath and then decided to wear a long wool skirt of a shade of heather green that put added lights in her hazel eyes. With it she wore a simple white jersey blouse with a scooped neck, and a Scottish necklace Aunt Flora had bought her when they were in Edinburgh a year ago. It was a silver circlet ornamented with thistles, and in its center was set a highly polished greenish stone that looked rather like a marble cut in half.

When she arrived in the lobby promptly at nine, Douglas's unconcealed look of approval made her glad of her decision to dress up a bit. With a flourish he gallantly offered her his arm, then led her toward the dining room.

He was wearing a well-tailored gray suit tonight in lieu of a kilt, and he looked quite handsome. It occurred to her that it really was too bad he and Iris weren't more interested in each other on a personal level. She'd thought at first that they might be, and she still wasn't sure just how Douglas felt about Iris, but Iris obviously had a love of her own. Twice now she'd received long-distance phone calls and afterward had seemed very preoccupied.

In fact, Monica had begun to realize that despite her surface blitheness there was something of a shadow hovering over Iris. She put up a very good front, but there was a melancholy not always entirely hidden, and Monica suspected this had something to do with her absent lover, very possibly the fellow Londoner she was meeting for dinner tonight.

On the other hand, Iris and Douglas worked very well together. They were constantly taking small digs at each other in front of the paying customers, making jokes about the high feelings that supposedly ran between the Scots and the English. Much of this, Monica had come to realize, was simply a part of a tried-and-true patter designed to amuse the clients, and they did love it. The tour members also realized that there was a strong spirit of camaraderie between the handsome Scot and the pert Englishwoman, and Monica suspected that some of the women, Mrs. Ewing for one, imagined Iris and Douglas were in love. But then, Mrs. Ewing demonstrated on every possible occasion that she was a hopeless romantic.

Now, as the headwaiter led them toward the table that had been reserved for them, Douglas said,

"There will be just the two of us tonight, and I shall not pretend I'm unhappy about it. Donald Ferguson, the chap who's been driving my bus, has a family in Edinburgh, and so he's taken advantage of his free time to stop in on his mom and dad. Ah, here we are," and he held out her chair for her. "And a good table it is, too. We shall make out, even though they've only a pianist to entertain us tonight, instead of a full orchestra."

Monica smiled. "You weren't expecting me to do the Highland fling with you, were you?" she asked him.

He raised a dark eyebrow. "And why not?" he retorted with a laugh, and for a moment he sounded so much like Ian she felt her heart turn over. "As a matter of fact," he added, "I think you might do the fling considerably better than I could. But we shall see after we've had a wee drop or two."

For the first course they chose a fish mousse, which Douglas assured her was very Scottish and insisted she would like. Somewhat to her surprise, she did. Next came a chicken dish that in Monica's opinion had a strong French influence and was very good. And it was at this point that the wine steward appeared bearing champagne in a silver bucket. The tour members evidently had been good tippers!

Now soft lights were switched on in a previously darkened area at one end of the room where there was a small polished dance floor. A grand piano stood nearby, and as they watched, a slight dark-haired man sat down at it and began to play a pleasant lilting melody.

Douglas raised his champagne glass. "To the loveliest American it's ever been my pleasure to know," he said solemnly.

"Thank you." Monica tried to find words that would match his toast. "To the best tour guide I've ever met," she finally said lamely, and drank.

Douglas's smile was wry. "'Tis not quite what I'd wish you to say in the way of a toast," he admitted, then his dark eyes lingered on her face, sharp and discerning. "Was it another Scot?" he asked.

"What?" she queried in return, honestly perplexed by his question.

"This man you seem to be mourning," Douglas explained. "It would seem to me that he must have been Scottish because every time you so much as look at a kilt I have the impression you are trying to find someone. Am I mistaken?"

She stared down at her plate and briefly, very briefly, shut her eyes. Then she said, her voice small and strained, "You are too sharp, Douglas. Much too sharp!"

"Is that a way of telling me I was right in the first place?"

"I suppose it is," she conceded.

"Where is he now?"

"I'm not sure," she answered, her voice still low. "You see, it's over, quite over. I suppose you could say he gave me up...a long time ago."

"More the fool he, then," Douglas said softly. "Were you here in Scotland before, or did this happen in the States?"

"No. It was here. A year ago. Now, if you don't mind, I'd really rather not talk about it."

He shrugged. "Whether I mind or not really makes very little difference," he pointed out. "I won't be banal and suggest that sometimes confession really *is* good for one's soul. When you want to tell me you will tell me...whatever you want to tell me," he finished somewhat enigmatically, then took another sip of his champagne. "As for right now," he suggested, "would you care to dance?"

Monica was not at all in the mood to dance, yet it offered a temporary escape, so she nodded. She stood and let Douglas lead her to the floor. He was an excellent dancer, his movements smooth and seemingly effortless, and she soon succumbed to the pure sensation of flowing along with the rhythm. It was much too long since she'd danced with anyone.

"We do quite well together," Douglas said with satisfaction, and she had to agree with that. They went on to dance the next number and then the next, stopping only when the pianist left to take a break.

As they went back to their table, Monica was smiling and a little flushed. She nodded agreement when Douglas suggested he refill her champagne glass. She had just touched it to his in a toast to their upcoming trip to Glasgow and was about to take a sip when she paused, her glass held motionless before her lips.

She was sure for a moment that she definitely must be having a vision, for it *couldn't* be Ian sitting at a table across the room, staring at her as if he'd never seen her before. She felt a surge of dizziness; it seemed as if her pulse were about to stop, and her hand tightened on the stem of the champagne glass.

Ian—yes, it was Ian; there was no denying it was Ian—was looking at her directly, but his familiar handsome face was completely without expression, and his features might as well have been chiseled on an old Scottish coin. Only his eyes conveyed anything at all, and they were like blue ice, incredibly cold. She felt herself flinching away from them.

Then she saw the woman approaching his table. His companion for the evening, obviously. Probably she'd gone to the rest room; Ian had clearly been expecting her return. He rose to hold out a chair for her, displaying the casual grace Monica remembered only too well.

The woman had also been his companion at Prestonfield; Monica had no doubt about it. She was tall and blond, and in the moment before she sat down Monica was able to get a very good look at her face. She was not beautiful, but she was lovely in a wistful sort of way.

She's the sort of person I'd like, Monica found herself thinking, *if I'd been able to get to know her under entirely different circumstances.*

Ian said something to the woman and laughed, and it seemed to Monica that his affection for her was obvious, even across this distance. She felt her throat tighten and had the sick sense that she'd been betrayed, then told herself sharply that this should come as no shock. Ian had betrayed her when he'd failed to show up at Prestwick a year ago!

The woman's back was to her now, but she saw the blond head nod eagerly at one of Ian's comments, and for a terrible moment she didn't think it was going to be possible to *sit* here any longer and watch the two of them. She'd heard that jealousy consumed—now she felt herself afire from it.

She started when Douglas said, "Monica, for God's sake, what's the matter? You look as if you've seen a ghost!"

She *had* seen a ghost, she thought miserably. In fact she was still seeing a ghost; a ghost come to life, yet evidently without substance or feeling where she was concerned.

She didn't want Douglas to turn around and glance toward Ian's table, so she wrested her gaze away from the back of the blond woman's head and picked up her half-full glass of champagne.

"I'm sorry," she said. "It was nothing, really. Just a sudden flash of. . .memory."

"Rather a miserable memory, I'd say," Douglas observed grimly.

"Yes, I suppose you could say that," she couldn't help but agree. "Let's forget it and talk about something else, shall we?"

"Very well. Let's get down to business, then. As you know, in the morning we shall have to make sure that everyone's aboard when it's time to take off for Glasgow. Donald Ferguson will be driving my bus, and if he's in a good mood, we'll prevail upon him to sing a song for us about a working man—" Douglas softly rolled the *r* "—who has taken a drop too much. 'Tis called, 'I Belong to Glasgow,' this song, and 'tis almost guaranteed to bring the house down—the bus down, that is. I might even join Donald in the singing of it. Not that I've much voice left—though 'tis true that I sang in a church choir for a time when I was a boy. Would you believe that?''

"No," she said, and found that she actually was smiling.

"Then," Douglas continued, "my voice changed and the world lost a glorious soprano. More's the pity for mankind! You might drink a bit more of that bubbly, don't you think?''

Douglas was being very kind. It made her feel something of a nuisance, but she raised her glass like an obedient child and sipped. Then, out of the corner of her eye, she saw Ian stand up.

He started walking toward her table and she found herself almost paralyzed by fright. She shivered, for this stern-faced Scot approaching her was a stranger. It was as if another being had taken possession of Ian's body...a beloved body that she'd come to know almost too intimately. As it was, it seemed impossible to think that those tightly compressed lips had ever claimed her mouth in a kiss that had signaled a journey into a realm of pure ecstasy.

No, she thought frantically, she couldn't even speak to *this* Ian; she couldn't imagine what she could possibly find to say to him. Then, swiftly, she realized this wasn't something she was going to have to worry about. Ian had veered toward the piano and was talking to the pianist, who had just resumed his place.

Ian was saying something; the pianist was nodding. Money exchanged hands, Monica was quite sure, then Ian was going back to his own table without even glancing in her direction.

A taut moment passed before she heard the first soft chords on the keyboard and caught her breath.

*"By yon bonnie banks and by yon bonnie braes...
where the sun shines bright on Loch Lomond."*

The melody seemed to fill not only the room but her very being. As Monica listened to it she imagined she could hear the words as well as the music, just as Ian had sung them to her when they were driving back to Glasgow with the full moon bright in the autumn sky and Loch Lomond bathed not in sunlight but in pure platinum.

"Where me and my true love were ever wont to gae...."

Monica gulped and put the champagne glass down, her fingers shaking so that it was an effort to set it straight.

Glancing at her curiously, Douglas remarked, "'Tis a bonnie song, I admit. But aren't you over-reacting a bit?"

She said sincerely, "I'm sorry."

"So am I, for more reasons than one. You tell me that this was all a year ago?"

"What do you mean?"

"I'd be dim-witted not to ken that hearing 'Loch Lomond' brings it back to you," Douglas told her. "In fact, if someone were to ask me, I would be inclined to say that it almost seems as if this Scot of yours must be right here in this room...."

Inadvertently she glanced swiftly toward Ian's table—and froze. It was empty, quite empty. In that brief interval since the pianist had started playing, Ian and his companion had left.

"No," she told Douglas, glad she could at least say it honestly. "No, he isn't."

"Then his spirit does come to haunt you," Douglas mused. "I say, shall I ask the pianist to play something else? Is there another song you fancy?"

"No," she replied, relieved because now the last strains of "Loch Lomond" were fading away, and the pianist had begun to play something with a Latin-American tempo.

This was evidently another request because someone at the far side of the room called out, "Olé!"

"Coffee?" Douglas suggested.

"If you don't mind," she said, "I'd as soon not have any."

Douglas nodded, getting her message entirely too easily; she was beginning to feel that he read her as if she were a rather elementary book. A moment later they left the dining room, then, as if by mutual accord, crossed the lobby to stand just inside the glass entrance doors, looking out into the parking lot.

It was drizzling again and Douglas said moodily, "'Tis not weather to cheer one's soul. Though there are those times when a rainy day is very comforting...if one is sitting by the fireside, and especially with a person one loves—"

He broke off to look down at her, and his obvious concern touched her. "I wish," he said, "that this return of yours to Scotland could be an occasion for happiness rather than sorrow."

"Not sorrow, Douglas," she protested. "Nostalgia, perhaps." She tried very hard to believe her own words. Nostalgia...a yearning for something long gone, something precious, a feeling that verged from sweet to bittersweet but dealt entirely with the past.

Ian had proved conclusively tonight that if she was a part of anything, she was a part of his past; otherwise he would have crossed the room to speak to her. As it was, she told herself, he had evoked memory by requesting the pianist to play "Loch Lomond," for reasons she surely didn't understand. But "Loch Lomond" was a part of the past not to be made present, if one could judge by Ian's actions, and where she and Ian were concerned it seemed very clear that there was no such thing as the future.

CHAPTER FIVE

GETTING THE TOUR GROUP TOGETHER to embark for
Glasgow, while making sure that no one left anything
behind in Edinburgh, proved to involve a great deal
of bustle and confusion the following morning. But
to Monica it was a welcome diversion, for idleness
just now bred melancholy.

Iris, too, seemed strained and preoccupied, possessed of an inertia that was unlike her, and Monica
suspected that her dinner-date had not gone well.
This gave her the chance to pitch in with extra vigor
to help the English girl, and Iris said admiringly,
"You are the one! All that American energy."

She said this after they'd finished making their
final head count on the buses—and discovered they
were missing one passenger. Old Mr. Nelson, who
was very deaf but refused to wear a hearing aid, evidently had not heard his alarm clock go off, and so
Douglas was dispatched upstairs to awaken him personally. Now, returning, he was just in time to hear
Iris's remark. He didn't add a comment of his own,
but Monica suspected that he knew quite well her
burst of activity was due not to "American energy"
but rather to the need to plunge herself into work.

Again, Iris boarded one bus and Douglas the

other. Donald Ferguson, the driver Douglas had mentioned the night before, took the wheel. He was a pleasant blunt-faced man who said very little and, when he spoke, had a broad Highland accent. But his occasional comments had a dry humor that never failed to delight the tour group members.

The bus swung out along the Corstorphine Road and on past the Ingliston Fair grounds. Then it took a left turn, starting toward Glasgow, and Douglas busied himself with bringing his passengers up to date on details concerning the hotel where they would be staying. He announced first that there was an automatic ice machine on the second floor for the use of hotel guests—this statement bringing a chorus of approval—and then told them that there were still two tickets available for the tour the following day to the Loch Ness region.

" 'Tis a lengthy ride," Douglas said, "but ye'll see the Highlands with many of the mountains snow-capped this time of year, and with a wee bit of luck ye may see the monster for yourselves."

This remark evoked considerable laughter, but Mrs. Ewing, who was sitting toward the front of the bus, broke in, "I don't think it's all that funny. There must be *something* there. There've been actual photographs taken...."

"Quite so," Douglas agreed solemnly. "Matter of fact, not three weeks ago an army sergeant was driving around the loch when the monster surfaced. He stopped and reached for a camera in his glove compartment, but before he could put his fingers on it our Nessie submerged again. Quite a turn it gave him."

"What had he been drinking?" called out a man in the rear of the bus.

"And what else but good malt whisky?" Douglas demanded. "Scotch, to ye folk."

"Then," Mrs. Ewing challenged, "you don't think there actually is a Loch Ness monster?"

"'Twould never do for me to say such a thing," Douglas said, rolling his *r*'s roundly. "'Twould be sacrilege to deny Nessie's existence."

The passengers began to chat among themselves, and after a minute Monica asked quietly, "How can you? You know perfectly well there's no monster in Loch Ness!"

"Do I now? Actually, I'd be the last to deny such a thing. As your lady in the blue hat said, surely 'twould seem that there must be something, wouldn't you say?"

She shook her head. "Douglas!"

"Well," Douglas went on somewhat wryly, "at least I've brought a smile to your lips, and 'tis the first one I've seen today. Despite all that American energy, you look more than a bit tired out."

"I'm not, really," she told him. "I just didn't sleep very well."

"Bad company last night?"

"Of course not!"

"Bad memories, then?"

"Possibly," she conceded, and was relieved when one of the passengers leaned forward to ask Douglas a question.

This brought their chance for quiet conversation to an end, for Douglas was kept busy all the rest of the way to Glasgow. There, after driving through the city proper, they headed north rather than going toward their hotel, and Monica soon realized their first destination was going to be Loch Lomond, which was just a few miles beyond Glasgow's outskirts.

"A wee bonus," Douglas confided when she wondered aloud about this.

Monica had not been to Loch Lomond in the daylight. She had, in fact, visited the loch on only one occasion, but it was an occasion she would never forget, no matter how old she might live to be.

That evening Ian had taken her to dinner at a country inn in a town whose name she couldn't remember even now. It was a charming place, and she was sure the food must have been very good, but she had barely tasted it, for she'd been aware only of Ian. He was the most delightful of companions, and that night he had been tender, romantic and witty. She had never before been quite so happy.

They had skirted Loch Lomond on the drive back to Glasgow, and it was then that Ian had said, "Do you mind if we stop by at my uncle's place? It's quite near here. He's in London, and he phoned earlier today and asked me to check on something for him."

She would have been willing at that point to go anywhere with Ian, or to do anything he asked of her. In fact, it seemed more than enough simply to be sitting by his side in his red MGA, driving along through the cool autumn night on what would forever seem the wrong side of the road to her. She told him this, and he laughed and responded, "There's a reason for our driving as we do, and a good one, too. It goes well back into history.''

''So do most things in Scotland, it seems to me,'' she teased. ''What is it?''

''Well, in the old days there was always the chance of meeting up with an enemy when one traveled—not that there isn't that chance today,'' he added, his voice very sober as he said this. Then his tone lightened and he continued, ''Most men are right-handed. Thus, in earlier times a man rode his horse to the left of the road so that his right hand would be free at all times to draw his sword should an enemy approach. Carriages, too, held to the left for the same reason. This meant a gentleman was able to leap out into the center of the road, his sword brandished, ready to fight, without a dangerous delay. When finally cars became the preferred mode of travel, 'twas simply a case of no one seeing any particular reason to change.''

''I see. It does make sense,'' she admitted.

''So do most of the things I tell you, you beautiful skeptic,'' he said with a laugh, and there was a caressing note in his voice that further heightened her intense awareness of him.

She sighed, but it was a sigh of complete content, and he seemed to know this. She was paying very little attention to where they were going; she knew only that it was a beautiful moonlit night, and imprudent though it might be, she had fallen hopelessly in love with this man whom she scarcely knew.

Now he glanced toward the full moon and said, ''Hereabouts they call such a moon 'MacFarlane's

Lantern.' In those old days of which I've spoken, 'twould have been a sign for the clansmen to set out on a foray. The MacFarlanes lived at the northern end of the loch, which is itself protected by Ben Lomond. When the moon was full, it would light their way as they went off on their cattle-reiving raids. The loch—and Ben Lomond, I might add—was probably the favorite subject of painters in Victorian times. Even now, if a Scot has a single favorite picture on his walls of any age at all, it's apt to show Ben Lomond rising in the background. 'Twas a real landmark for artists.''

As Ian spoke, he was turning off the main road. They drove down a much narrower one until finally they came to a huge iron gate that, touched by moonlight, had a dark, almost blue black sheen. Ian got out of the car, and Monica saw that he was holding a large key, which he inserted in the gate's massive lock. Then slowly he swung the gate open.

"This won't take long," he promised again as he got back into the car.

But Monica was already leaning forward in rapt attention as he drove down a long tree-lined lane. Ahead of them she could glimpse a mélange of towers and turrets touched here and there by the moon's silver, and she exclaimed excitedly, "Ian! It's a castle!''

He laughed indulgently. "Well, I suppose it is," he conceded, "though we are more apt to call them castellated mansions hereabouts, and the Scottish woods are full of them. Like most of them, this one could do with a bit of fixing up. With the taxes what they are these days, there's usually not sufficient cash available to keep up the trimmings. In fact, I daresay that judging by your American standards, the plumbing is hopelessly outmoded.''

She started to answer, but at that moment he swung the car to a stop in front of a side entrance. "Come along," he said. " 'Twill be colder than the tomb, but we shan't have to tarry. There's no central heating, you know, in these monstrosities.''

Monica could not have cared less about such things as central heating. She stepped out of the car, finding it absolutely incredible to think that she was about to follow a handsome Scot into a castle built along the shores of Loch Lomond. A handsome Scot, whom she loved so much that she. . . .

Instinctively she tried to put a pause to the thought that came to her, and she could feel the warmth surging into her cheeks while a sensation that was purely treacherous swept over her. She wondered, a bit shakily, if Ian had any idea how vulnerable she had become. He would only have to crook his finger to quite literally sweep her off her feet!

"Hold on," he said, as casually as if this were any ordinary thing they were doing. "I've a torch." He switched on a small flashlight and added, "Mind your step. I'd rather not turn on any lights. I'd as soon not arouse the caretaker.''

"He lives in the castle?"

"No, he and his wife live in the lodge, the stone house near the gate. You may not have noticed it as we drove in, you were that preoccupied with this scene out of the age of knights in armor.''

He was laughing at her, she knew, but it was gentle laughter. "Angus and Annie Grewar," he added, "have looked after the place for more years than I can remember, and they're getting on themselves. They sleep in the far side of the lodge, so I doubt if they heard us. But were Angus to be a bit restless tonight, as he sometimes is, he'd be quick to note lights in the castle, overhead ones at least, and then surely he'd come investigating. I don't want to put him to that. He's too old for such night excursions."

"You don't live here, then?" Monica asked him.

"No," he said. "Except on those occasions when I'm required to do so. At the moment I've had business in Glasgow, and I've been staying at a friend's apartment. My uncle, as I think I mentioned, is in London, and my aunt—who does sometimes live here with her son, Walter—has been off visiting in Inverness. So the place is quite vacant."

He was pulling out another key as he spoke, and now the beam of his flashlight focused on a brass lock in a heavy dark wood door. He inserted the key and turned it, and the door creaked as he pushed it open, beckoning Monica to follow him.

They stepped into what seemed to be a rather small anteroom and then into another room and beyond that into yet another. She had a fleeting impression of gray stone and Gothic vastness and felt as if she had stumbled into a feudal bastion.

Ian said, "Careful now. Down one step. There you are. This is the library, and if I remember rightly, there should be a candle around. Ah, here it is."

He struck a match, and the resulting glow of a tall

candle in an obviously antique silver holder seemed
surprisingly bright.

"You'll find sherry over in the corner cabinet," he
said. "Pour some out for both of us, will you? I
shan't be a moment."

Monica nearly protested aloud at the thought of
being left alone here, with just a candle as her single
source of light, but Ian already had vanished beyond
her range of vision. She stood stock-still and shivered, admittedly fascinated yet also possessed by the
prickling sort of sensation so familiar to children at
Halloween. This room, she saw, was lined with bookshelves, liberally filled with impressive leather-bound
volumes in varying colors. At the far side of the room
she could make out a huge fireplace, and there was a
long refectory table flanked by stiff wooden chairs.
But there was also a comfortable couch and several
armchairs; obviously this was a room that was much
used.

Nevertheless, there was an eeriness to being by herself in the middle of this Scottish castle that made
Monica jump when she heard a sound. She was vastly
relieved to see the flashlight's beam and to know that
Ian had come back to her.

"I don't think you've moved," he accused her.
"Nor have you poured the sherry."

"No," she admitted. She laughed a bit shakily.
"I'm sorry," she confessed. "I feel as if some sort of
spell has been cast over me!"

"A good spell, I trust," he said, taking a crystal
decanter from the cabinet he had mentioned and filling two long-stemmed glasses with the wine.

"Yes," she said. "I'm sure it's a good spell."

He laughed. "You would be the perfect one to hear and believe our Scottish legends," he told her, "and I can well imagine that in due time you would be telling them very well yourself."

As he spoke he handed her one of the glasses, and when she took it their fingers touched. For a long moment neither of them moved, as if their hands had been cast in a tableau. Then Ian raised the glass and said, "To you," and she acknowledged the toast with a similar one of her own. But she couldn't escape the feeling that in some inexplicable way Ian had branded her just now and that she never again would be entirely free of him. . . nor did she want to be!

He said, his voice husky, "You are so unutterably lovely!"

Then, as if at a mutual signal, they set their glasses down on the refectory table and in another instant they were in each other's arms, their lips meeting in shared urgency.

As his kiss intensified, it seemed to Monica that every nerve in her body had been touched with a new vibrancy. Never before had she felt so alive. She clung to him, her lips brushing his throat as he whispered strangely hoarse little words of endearment in her ear, and then his tongue came to probe the inner circle of her earlobe, inflaming her further. This was molten, this emotion, as inevitable as the flow of lava from an erupting volcano.

She moaned softly as Ian's hands molded the outline of her body, gently discovering every contour. Finally his fingers reached the zipper that ran down the back of her dress, and he unfastened it partway. She felt his hands warm upon her tingling skin as his arms encircled her, caressing her.

Involuntarily she arched her body so that he was bending over her, and she was scarcely aware of her dress slithering to the floor. They moved to the couch as if motivated by a single force, and in another instant his mouth had found first one taut rosy nipple, then another, sending spirals of a purely flaming desire coursing through her.

It didn't matter in the least that she'd known Ian a very short time and that they were moving very swiftly. She was more than ready to yield herself to him in what would be her first true surrender to any man.

She was only vaguely aware that his need even surpassed her own. Later she would realize the urgency that had possessed him; she would remember the thrust of his male hardness against her, and she would marvel more than ever at the extent of his control. For even as her passion was ascending, even as she knew that they were following the same path and that it was going to lead them into an entirely different dimension, Ian drew back.

His action was so abrupt that she didn't realize at first what he was doing. Then, incredibly, he got to his feet and as she watched through dazed eyes he crossed the room and poured himself another glass of sherry. He stood with his back to her, drinking it at what seemed to be one gulp, and then she saw him shudder visibly. It was as if his entire frame were being racked by a giant sigh.

He said almost sharply, "Do get up and put your dress back on, Monica! 'Tis cold in here."

She hadn't even felt the cold until he spoke, but now it seemed to assail her. She knew, sickly, that it was as much a chill of the spirit as it was of the body, and that everything had suddenly gone very wrong between them.

She groped for her dress and put it on, fastening the zipper with shaking fingers. Desperately she wished that she knew what Ian was thinking, or at the least that she could in some way learn what had prompted his actions.

He went on, his voice still taut, "Can you wait a bit for a powder room? We can stop along the way."

"Yes, of course," she answered. She knew that by the smallness of her voice she was betraying both her hurt and her puzzlement, and she wondered if he sensed this.

If he did, there was no indication. He blew out the candle. "I'll lead the way," he told her. "Just follow the torchlight."

She did so, and he settled her into the MGA again without a word. She, too, was quiet until they'd gone through the gate and were driving up the lane that led to the private road. Then she asked, "Did you get what you came after?"

"What?" he demanded blankly.

"You mentioned that your uncle had asked you to get something for him."

"It wasn't so much to get something, really, as to check on it," he replied. In the light from the dashboard she could see him frown. "As it happens," he went on, "it wasn't there."

It was clear to Monica from the tone of his voice that he didn't want to talk about whatever it was, so she didn't pursue it. In any event, she had enough on her mind. She stared ahead, glimpsing the moon-touched waters of Loch Lomond, realizing how little time she had left in Scotland, and wondering how she could possibly bear to leave him.

"Monica," he said then, suddenly, speaking her name almost peremptorily.

"Yes?"

"What must you think of me!" There was a kind of agony to the exclamation.

"What *am* I to think, Ian?" she asked.

His smile was wry. "Thank you for not being evasive," he told her. "I appreciate that. The fact of the matter is that I've botched things most dreadfully, my darling. I was on the verge of losing all reason back there."

She reminded him very quietly, "You weren't the only one."

"Then let's be thankful that I somehow found the strength to...stop," he said simply. "When tomorrow comes I may call myself a fool—but it would have been entirely wrong just now. When that time comes for us, Monica, I want everything the way it should be for you. And I shall not choose a cold damp dungeon of a place...."

When that time comes for us. The words seemed to echo, and in their wake Monica's heart suddenly became light again.

She said teasingly, "What a way to speak about a castle! It didn't look in the least like a dungeon to me, although I admit I've never been in a dungeon. On the contrary, it seemed tremendously imposing."

"I suppose it is, in its way," he conceded. "We shall have to come back in the daylight so you can see the place properly, and meet my uncle, as well. He won't be in London much longer."

She pointed out softly, "I won't be in Scotland much longer, Ian. Tomorrow the group goes on a day-long trek to Loch Ness, and I really must accompany them. I've been neglecting Aunt Flora, though she's been very good about it. Then early the next day we shall be leaving for Prestwick and. . . home."

Ian covered her hand with his. "We've all our lives ahead of us, Monica. And it would take more than the span of several oceans to keep us apart. Believe me, darling."

She had believed him.

Then, after a time, he had started to sing "Loch Lomond" almost absently, and ever so softly.

"By yon bonnie banks and by yon bonnie braes. . . ."

CHAPTER SIX

DOUGLAS SAID SHARPLY, "Monica!"

"Yes?"

"Come back to us, will you, please?"

Before she could answer him, Douglas reached for the microphone and spoke into it.

"We shall be stopping at Loch Lomond for fifteen minutes," he told the tour guests. "There's a wee gift shop still open, but I want to caution you ladies that on both the trips to the Highlands and to the Trossachs we shall be stopping at woolen mills where the values are excellent. So don't spend all your pence in one place!"

He was addressing everyone on the bus, but his eyes rested on Monica, and she flushed uncomfortably. Douglas MacConnach was proving to be much too discerning.

"In summer," he went on, "this loch is a boatman's paradise. 'Tis twenty-four miles long, and pleasure boats use up every inch of it. There is also a popular paddle steamer, *The Maid of the Loch*, that runs daily and provides a pleasant trip.

"Across the loch, the mountain you see is old Ben Lomond. 'Tis bonnie country, this, and ye are fortunate to be seeing it at the best of times, with the sheep grazing peacefully in the meadows and the bracken turned to gold.''

The bus came to a stop. ''Away to the wee gift shop, ladies,'' Douglas said with a chuckle. ''And whilst they are busy ye gentlemen can mourn the holes in your pockets as ye look at the scenery. A pity there isn't a pub handy.''

Monica got off the bus and stood next to Douglas while the others disembarked. Mrs. Ewing, in passing, said, ''I'd like to find something to take back to my niece in Des Moines, and she's just about your size and coloring, my dear. Would you help me pick out a gift for her?''

''Of course,'' Monica agreed, but Mrs. Ewing was a rather slow walker. By the time they had crossed the parking lot to the gift shop it already was so crowded that there was no chance of entry for the moment.

Mrs. Ewing complained, ''It looks like a department-store bargain basement! Women can be dreadful when they're scouting out a good buy, can't they? I suppose that nice young man will simply have to give us some extra shopping time, that's all. Do you suppose my niece would like one of those mohair stoles they have hanging outside the doorway?''

The stoles looked quite lovely and the colors were delectable. ''I would imagine she'd love one,'' Monica answered, and smiled when Mrs. Ewing swooped forward again with renewed eagerness.

The shop was right at dockside. Beyond it the lake stretched eastward, with Ben Lomond standing guard toward the north. And now, across the brilliant blue expanse of water, set against a hillside on which the grazing sheep, from this distance, seemed little bigger than white polka dots, Monica saw a castle.

"Castellated mansions," Ian had called them, and he'd added that the Scottish woods were full of them. Yet the sight of this particular castle transfixed her.

That night they had been driving on the other side of the loch, traveling along a road that paralleled the water. Then Ian had branched off onto a smaller road that ended at the gate leading to the castle.

She had been too absorbed by Ian himself, too aware of his nearness, to be really conscious of either time or distance, yet it seemed to her now that the distance would be right. In fact, she felt increasingly sure that the castellated mansion she was staring at was *the* castle.

Ian's castle.

IRIS SAID REASONABLY, "No, love, there's no real need at all for you to go on the Loch Ness trip unless you want to. Douglas can manage perfectly well on his own, especially when he has Donald Ferguson as his driver. Donald can be quite a wit when the occasion requires it, as you may have noticed. I shall be taking a group into Glasgow in the afternoon for a bit of shopping and local history, if you'd rather come with us."

They had finished dinner and returned to the room they were sharing. Iris had brewed a cup of tea for herself and had made instant coffee for Monica.

Now Monica asked hesitantly, "Would it help you if I went along?"

"Not unless you want to come," Iris said somewhat abruptly. "I can manage. I suppose you could say I'm used to managing."

Away from the tour group, Iris tended to drop the mask of jocularity that was such an integral part of her professional personality, and it seemed to Monica that she'd become increasingly tense with each passing day. Tonight she was obviously weary, but it was more than that. There was a taut line to her mouth, and her eyes were unhappy.

Now she looked up, intercepting Monica's gaze, and said, "I'm sorry, Monica. I didn't intend to snap at you."

"You didn't really," Monica assured her. "You do seem a bit tired, though."

"I *am* tired," Iris admitted. She paused, then shrugged. "You asked if it would help if you came along tomorrow—well, to be quite honest, love, nothing would help me very much at the moment. I had a bit of a blow the other night in Edinburgh, you see. In fact, were it not for my job I should like nothing better than to go out and get completely sloshed and to stay sloshed for weeks. As it is...." She tried to smile. "It's tea for me," she said. "One might make a ditty out of it, don't you think?"

"Was it...the friend from London?" Monica ventured.

"Ah, so Douglas has been speculating, has he?" Iris countered. "Well, no matter. Yes, it was the friend from London. He's married, as I already knew, but I hadn't realized it was quite so hopeless. If I had a grain of sense, I'd have given him up long ago. As it is, I'm rather mad about him...."

"I'm sorry," Monica said, feeling very inadequate.

"So am I," Iris confessed ruefully. "There are moments when I truly despise myself for being such a fool! You could say that I've smashed three years of my life, and I can't afford to waste years, not with the birthdays mounting as they are."

"You're not all that old, Iris."

"I shall be thirty next time around."

Iris found another tea bag, put it in her cup and added hot water. "There's something to be said for this damned stuff," she observed, "though of course it should be steeped properly, in a pot. Even so, I shan't quibble at the moment. In fact, I've not much of a mind to quibble about anything. He told me this time that—well, that we've got to put a stop to things. Ever since, I've felt quite numb."

Monica said softly, "I know the feeling."

"Your chap was married, too?"

"No. At least I don't think so. I'm not really sure. But it amounts to the same thing. He left me."

"In my case I've only myself to blame," Iris went on dryly. "He never pretended he was free; I knew how things were from the very beginning. I knew he was married, and also that he was very Church of England and all the rest of it in the bargain, with too much at stake to even think of divorce. So... it was a matter of time. I was borrowing time all the way along."

She stirred the tea thoughtfully, then said quietly, "To get back to tomorrow: do take the day, love, and do whatever you like with it. You've a day coming to you, goodness knows! You've done a fantastic job, stepping into Pamela's shoes at a moment's notice as you did. Douglas and I shall both give you top references with Magic Carpets. Do you think you'll want to continue with this sort of job?"

"I might," Monica answered, considering this. "There's certainly a fascination to it, and it gives one a terrific opportunity to travel, to see all sorts of places. As for tomorrow—well, what I'd really like to do is rent a car and take a drive out into the country. I can't help but wonder, though, if I could possibly cope with driving on the wrong side of the street!"

Iris laughed, then asked curiously, "Have you someone to visit hereabouts?"

"No, not really," Monica told her. "Actually, I want to visit a place, not a person. I suppose you could say I want to lay the past to rest. I've heard that if one faces up to a memory, it sometimes fades away. Do you think that's so?"

"Like ghosts?" Iris asked. "I wouldn't know, but I would say it's worth a try. John, the head porter, should be able to help you get a car. I doubt much advance notice would be needed this time of year."

The following morning Monica waited until after the tour bus had left for Loch Ness before she approached the head porter. It was a beautiful day, and the Highlands, she knew, would be gorgeous, with

Ben Nevis undoubtedly snowcapped. She felt a slight pang of envy thinking of the glorious scenery she'd be missing and decided that very possibly Mrs. Ewing might even manage to see the monster.

She had avoided Douglas's eyes as she explained to the Ewings that she wouldn't be making the trip with them, feeling rather cowardly as she did so. Later, she suspected, he would have a few questions to ask her. Now she concentrated on finding John, an affable middle-aged Scot who told her there would be no problem at all in fixing her up with a car.

This he did within the space of an hour, and she set forth with the assurance that she had a full tank of "petrol" and that she should not have too much of a problem driving, since the traffic was relatively light. Nevertheless, coping with other-side-of-the-road driving terrified Monica initially, and she was thankful that the hotel was on the outskirts of Glasgow rather than in the city proper. She was certain she could never have weathered the experience of making a right turn in heavy city traffic.

Once Glasgow's suburbs were behind her the driving became quite easy, though it still demanded concentration. Soon she realized that she was instinctively following the route the bus had taken the day before, which would put her on the opposite side of Loch Lomond from the castle. At the moment, though, she had no clear-cut objective in mind.

It seemed logical, she told herself, to first go out to the dockside shop they had visited yesterday. Then she could look across the loch at the castle and try to decide upon a course of action, preferably with a little less of the emotionalism the scene had engendered in her the first time around.

She had no idea at all of what this course of action might involve. She knew only that she couldn't possibly return to the States without first coming to terms with her feelings for Ian. If this meant forcing an encounter with him, then—well, she would simply have to force one! Despite the lovely wistful blonde who seemed to be very close to him.

There was, she conceded, more than a slight chance she had been wrong in her identification of the castle. And even if it was the right one, what then? What could she hope to do about it? She smiled faintly at the thought of driving up to the front door and storming the place—how *did* one go about storming a castle? She supposed the only course to follow, if she was to go to the castle at all, would be to tell the caretaker at the gate—or whoever answered her summons—that she had come to see Ian MacGregor; and this might result in a literal dead end. Ian MacGregor, so it seemed, had already made it abundantly clear that he had no wish to see her!

In retrospect, he had demonstrated this first by failing to keep their rendezvous in Prestwick, although she still couldn't repress the feeling that he'd had a good reason for doing so. Or was this just wishful thinking on her part? She'd given him her address in the States; he could have phoned later, or written, if he'd wanted to explain why he'd let her down.

Then, of course, he'd proved rather conclusively that he didn't want to so much as talk to her when he'd really cut her in the hotel dining room. There was no doubt at all that he'd recognized her. Now it seemed to her that the least he could have done would be to come to the table and speak to her—even though, at the time, she had cringed at the mere idea of such a confrontation. Nevertheless, they were adults. She'd done nothing to merit Ian's cold hauteur. He'd displayed a kind of arrogance that she never possibly would have associated with him.

Yet he obviously had requested the pianist to play "Loch Lomond."

Why?

Certainly he must have been aware of the effect the song would have on her. In fact, his having requested it seemed to make it evident that the haunting refrain had lingered in his memory even as it had in hers. Or did he connect the old Scottish favorite with his blond companion, as well?

Monica concentrated on her driving, trying—with difficulty—not to become too introspective. Common sense told her that the chasm time had created between Ian and herself was far too deep ever to bridge, and she felt sure he knew this even better than she did. Still, she kept going.

She was now driving through the village that bordered Loch Lomond. She turned onto the road that led past the Bear Park and shortly came to the parking lot with the gift shop on one side and the docks and the loch straight ahead.

There were no tour buses in the lot today, but the gift shop was open, the mohair scarves still hanging by the doorway. Finally, the other day, Mrs. Ewing had bought three of the scarves, a turquoise, a red and a coral. Unexpectedly, she had made Monica a present of the turquoise one because the color suited her so well.

Monica had felt that she shouldn't accept it, but Mrs. Ewing had been so insistent it would have been downright ungracious to refuse her. So to Mrs. Ewing's delight she had draped the scarf around her shoulders as she thanked her. It *was* a lovely thing, warm yet gossamery.

Well, today Mrs. Ewing was on her way to Loch Ness to find the monster, and no doubt she would be asking Douglas to help her with the gifts she would surely want to buy. Monica chuckled at the thought of his being pressed into this kind of service.

So she was still smiling as she entered the gift shop. Although it was small, it was well stocked. There was some very pretty jewelry made with native Scottish stones, ties in a variety of tartans, souvenir ashtrays, boxes of Scottish shortbread and candies, lovely lengths of woolens, scarves and tams—quite a varied and attractive display.

A female voice with a touch of Scottish burr asked pleasantly, "Well, my dear, do you approve of us?"

Monica looked up to meet the amused blue eyes of a gray-haired woman who was probably in her fifties but had a lovely complexion that seemed like a gift of eternal youth. Embarrassed, she said, "I'm sorry if I appeared to be snooping. I was here yesterday, but I didn't have a chance to look around."

"Were you with Douglas MacConnach's bus tour?"

"Yes."

"He's a dear, Douglas is," the woman said. "Brings the Americans here to us even out of season. But there—" this was spoken quickly "—I mean no offense in saying that. I appreciate your countrymen's patronage, believe me. We've a long winter ahead."

"Do you know Douglas well?" Monica asked.

"No, I met him only recently, but he seems a fine lad. And yourself?"

"Myself?"

"Do you know Douglas well?"

"Not really," Monica admitted. "I'm with the tour group. That is, I'm an employee. This is my first trip."

"Ah," the woman said, "then you must have taken the place of the young American who broke her ankle, poor lass. Douglas was telling me yesterday about what happened to her."

"Yes," Monica nodded, "I did take her place."

"I'm Moira Grier," the shopkeeper volunteered. "I can understand, by the way, why you had no chance to come into the shop yesterday. 'Twas quite an eager lot."

Monica smiled. "Yes, they were," she agreed, and added, "I'm Monica Winthrop."

"English," Mrs. Grier said.

Monica laughed. "That's what everyone here says. Actually, my English ancestry is rather remote."

The older woman smiled. "I daresay you've heard a good bit both ways about the English since you've been in Scotland," she remarked. "'Tis an old feud between us."

"But the old feuds are legends now, are they not?" Monica asked.

Mrs. Grier frowned slightly. "I would never say that," she decided finally, "although at least they are seldom bloody feuds these days. We've that to be thankful for."

Monica had come to a window. Through it she could see the clear blue water of the lake and the castle on the far side. She said, striving to be casual, "That's such a picturesque scene. Who does the castle belong to?"

"The earl of Monbraithe," Mrs. Grier told her.

"An *earl*?"

"Quite so. The laird has been dead for a year now, and he was a fine man. He was a member of Parliament from this area, well thought of by everyone. The young laird. . . well, that's another matter."

"The old laird had a son?"

"No. He was childless. It's his nephew who inherited."

"Does he live there now?"

"At Monbraithe Castle? Yes, I suppose you might say that the young laird lives there, as much as he lives anywhere."

"What do you mean?"

Moira Grier shrugged. "Who's to say about the young laird? Sometimes he's here, sometimes he isn't, and then there are those who'd tell you that where he belongs is at the end of a rope twisted around his neck."

Monica shivered, a cold chill sweeping through her. Striving to keep her voice from trembling, she went on, "Does he have another name, this young laird?"

"Another name?"

"I mean, would one call him the earl of Monbraithe, or does he have a name—a clan name, perhaps?"

The storekeeper laughed shortly. "He does indeed have a name," she said. "His name is Ian MacGregor."

CHAPTER SEVEN

IT WAS A CONFIRMATION, of course, but a terrible one, and Monica desperately wished she'd been mistaken about the castle's identity. She would have given a great deal to have this pleasant Scottish storekeeper tell her that the young earl of Monbraithe was anyone other than Ian!

Mrs. Grier said solicitously, "You look pale, my dear. Do you feel ill?"

"No," Monica answered quickly, "I'm all right, thank you. I'm a bit tired, that's all. Instead of driving out here today, on my time off, I should have had the sense to stay at the hotel and take a nap."

She made this statement with the deliberate intent of warding off any further questioning, and it worked. Mrs. Grier said, "Then you're just doing a bit of sight-seeing on your own?"

"Yes." Monica managed a smile. "It's so absolutely lovely here," she added, and meant it. She moved toward the door. "Thank you."

"Not at all, my dear. You're more than welcome here. Do come back again if you have a chance."

"I hope I'll be able to," Monica said. "This is the last tour to Scotland for the season."

"Perhaps another year, then."

"I hope so."

She moved out of the doorway with a final fare-well, and she had the feeling as she was walking across the parking lot that Mrs. Grier's eyes were still upon her.

Well, she supposed it was possible that she had aroused a certain amount of curiosity with her questions about Monbraithe Castle, but she doubted it was a curiosity that would linger. They had not been unusual questions, really; and for that matter, Americans were notoriously curious when it came to castles.

She started the car and was about to drive forward when a service truck swung in from the main road, momentarily blocking her path, then swerved around to come to a quick but expert stop in front of the shop. A dark-haired thin-faced young man wearing garage coveralls got out. He seemed dour looking upon first inspection, but then he glanced in her direction with open appraisal, followed by a grin that revealed totally unexpected charm. *These Scots,* Monica thought, mentally shaking her head as she watched him enter the shop.

Once on the main road again she turned left in the direction of Glasgow, but she had no intention of going back to the city just yet. It stood to reason that there must be a road that wound around the other side of the lake, and finally she found it. It was not the best of roads, but at least it was heading the right way.

This was lovely country. The loch lay to her left, the pines and birches growing almost to the water's edge, the turf still soft and green. In the distance Ben Lomond loomed majestically, a sentinel that had weathered the centuries.

The first turnoff she took onto a side road led to a dead end, but at the second turn she met with success, coming finally to the huge iron gate she remembered so well. It looked even taller and more forbidding in the daylight than it had seemed in the dark, with Ian beside her.

Ian had mentioned the gatekeeper's cottage, which she hadn't even noticed on that first occasion, and now she saw that it stood just beyond the gate itself. Constructed of stone, it looked very old, and charming enough to highlight a photograph descriptive of this region of Scotland. Smoke curled out of the chimney, so evidently the caretaker and his wife were at home, a fact Monica turned over in her mind with more than a slight feeling of apprehension.

Nevertheless, she got out of the car and, facing the iron barricade, looked for a bell to ring or a knocker to clang but could find neither. Finally she moved as close as she could get to the caretaker's house and shouted, "Hello!" Then, after waiting for a few minutes and receiving no answer, she shouted again, using all the vocal power she could muster, and this time she was rewarded.

A grizzled old man lumbered out of the front door of the cottage, hitching up his pants and scowling as he approached her.

Monica had never before felt quite so foolish. It took all her fortitude to face the caretaker squarely and say, "I'm looking for...the earl of Mon-braithe."

"His lairdship's na to home," the old man told her, his accent so thick she could barely understand him.

"Is he expected shortly?" Monica persisted.

"I dinna ken."

Admittedly, she was quick to become discouraged where Ian was concerned, and now her shoulders drooped disconsolately. Suddenly a woman spoke, her voice also thick with the Scottish burr yet relatively understandable.

"If the young lady has come to visit the laird, ye should let her in, Angus," the woman said quietly but with an air of authority.

Monica's eyes swung to focus upon her. She stood in the cottage doorway, small and stout, her dark gray hair nearly matching her shapeless dress in shade, her plump features reminding Monica of a suet pudding.

The man came forward grudgingly, fumbled with the latch and then slowly swung the gate open. "Come, then," he said reluctantly.

Monica very nearly turned away with an apology, common sense telling her that the moment had arrived when she should beat a retreat. But now it was as if some force stronger than herself was propelling her.

"Thank you," she said, and stepped across what seemed a very real barrier.

The woman spoke again. "'Tis quite a trip you must have had," she observed. "I imagine ye could do with a cup of tay."

"Thank you, no," Monica refused quickly. "I don't want to trouble you."

"'Tis no trouble. The kettle's on," the woman pointed out practically. "I'm Annie Grewar and this is my husband, Angus. We're caretakers for the laird."

She stood back so that Monica could enter the cottage, obviously as much a castle to her as anyone's home, for there was a distinct pride to her bearing. Then she led her guest into a long low-ceilinged room that served as both living and dining room. It was spotlessly clean, with shabby but comfortable furniture. Clearly it was a room that had been used and loved for many years, a place through which life had flowed.

"Is the laird away?" Monica asked tentatively.

"For the moment," Annie Grewar answered somewhat indifferently. "But when he'll be back, who's to know."

"Do you think it will be soon?"

"I dinna ken. He's been away the past week; he could be home today or tomorrow or not for a week or month longer. 'Tis as he pleases." She added, "Ye'll excuse me?" and left the room.

Monica looked after her helplessly. She told herself, self-anger brimming, that she had no business at all in being there. She really had played the part of a fool in making such a pilgrimage!

Actually, what she was doing was invading Ian's domain, and what point was there to such a thing? If he had wanted her to come, he would have invited her. That single gesture—still an enigma to her—of asking the pianist to play "Loch Lomond" didn't alter the facts. If he wished, Ian could order a musical salute reminding her of the bonnie banks and the bonnie braes, where he and his true love were ever wont to gae, true—but that was pure romanticism of the rankest sort on her part and surely could be nothing more than a whim on his.

She told herself sharply that it was past the time for her to wake up. She was not Ian's true love. She never had been. She wondered, in fact, if he was really devoted even to the wistful blonde; and she felt almost sorry for the other girl, who certainly seemed to be very much in love—mesmerized, at least—by Ian, if one could judge from two quick appraisals.

Perhaps the blonde, too, was only a casual romance. And Monica was feeling increasingly certain that she herself fell into that category. In retrospect, it seemed that Ian had put paid to their relationship very easily.

Well, people spoke of summer romances. Theirs had been an autumn romance, and she should have realized this instead of continuing to chase mental rainbows woven of pure fantasy. For an entire year she had wallowed in both sorrow and sentimentality, hoping that somehow the threads of her personal rainbow would weave a pattern that could conjure back the charming Scot who had abandoned her. How utterly foolish!

She glanced into the small mirror in Annie Grewar's living room, only to meet her own angry reflection. Facing herself, she said half aloud, "It serves you right! You should have known better than to come out here.''

"You spoke, mum?" Monica swerved to see Annie Grewar coming through the doorway, carrying a heavily laden tray.

"Not really," she said. Then, noting that the tray contained a plate of tarts as well as a teapot and a cup and saucer, she added quickly, "You shouldn't have bothered!"

"'Twas no bother." Annie Grewar motioned to a couch and Monica sat down, feeling like a dutiful child. She noted the single cup and saucer. Annie was not about to join her, which rather tended to put both of them in their places, and Monica was not at all sure she was comfortable in hers.

The tea, laced with milk and sugar, was hot and strong, the raspberry jam tarts freshly made. Monica drank and ate with an appetite that surprised her, for she'd had no particular desire for food. When she had finished, though, she had to admit to feeling both refreshed and revived. Meantime, Annie Grewar had left the room, evidently going back to the kitchen. Monica could hear her talking in low tones, Angus's gruff voice answering in monosyllables.

Setting the tea tray aside, she stood, and as if on signal Annie Grewar came back into the room. Monica hesitated, wondering if it would be proper to offer her some money, yet not quite daring to do so, for she was pretty well convinced that she would be refused. She wished that there was something she could do to show tangible appreciation, but she had to content herself with saying, "Thank you."

Annie Grewar almost smiled. "Ye're quite welcome. Do ye know your way back, then?"

"Yes," Monica answered. Again she hesitated, wondering if she should leave some sort of message for Ian. The Grewars were certain to tell him that an American girl had been there, and once they described her he would surely know without doubt that it had been she. Still, she couldn't imagine leaving him a note, nor could she think of anything to ask either Angus or Annie Grewar to say to him.

She sighed and started for the front door, only to pause midway when outside an auto horn honked twice. Almost immediately Angus appeared in the doorway, and he and his wife exchanged long glances.

" 'Tis the laird," Angus said then.

Monica stared aghast at his receding back, dimly aware that Annie was following him. She felt as if she were a bird suddenly captured, and she sought almost frantically to escape, her hands fluttering as if they were wings. But they were earthbound wings; there was no power to soar left in them.

She wondered if she could make an exit through the kitchen and perhaps go around the house and through the gate. Then she could be off in her car while Ian was yet in the process of entering the cottage himself. She felt sure he would be coming in here once the Grewars told him he had a visitor.

But there was no time for such logistics; even before she could move, her escape route was cut off.

"Monica!" Ian said, and hearing him speak her name she knew that he didn't sound in the least like

Douglas. He didn't sound like anyone in the world but himself.

He stood in the doorway, wearing a creamy Irish knit sweater, as tall and lithe as ever, his sandy hair somewhat rumpled. He said, "So you've come," and she had the odd feeling that he'd been expecting her. Thinking this, she looked across at him with an astonishment she didn't bother to disguise and then, seeing his face, knew a sharp sense of shock.

She hadn't noticed the change in him at a distance. Both at Prestonfield and at the hotel, in artificial light, across a room, it had been imperceptible. But here in Annie Grewar's living room, with the sunlight streaming through the windows, there was a difference about him that made her draw in her breath with dismay.

He had *aged*. Ian, who was not much more than thirty, looked like a man who had suffered, a man who had been harassed, a man who had gone through his own intense sort of private hell in an experience that had done terrible things to him. The light that had danced in his blue eyes a year ago seemed to have been extinguished totally, nor did even a hint of the smile she remembered so well come to curve his lips.

Speaking with difficulty because the impact of this shock was such a profound one, she said, "I'm sorry. I shouldn't have come—I know that now."

"No," he agreed, without those strangely somber blue eyes leaving her face for even a second. "No. You shouldn't have."

She flushed, because his agreement hurt. He had expected her, yet he didn't want her. Without saying very much at all, he was managing to make that quite clear. She went on stiffly, "You needn't worry. I was about to leave. Mrs. Grewar was kind enough to give me a cup of tea, or I would have been gone some time ago."

"Then," he said, "that's your car out beyond the gate?"

"Yes. I rented it."

"You came here alone?"

Her eyebrows rose in surprise. "Of course."

"I should not have taken it for granted," he told her. "The other night you had company. In fact, you rather looked as if you might be on your honeymoon."

"With Douglas?" she asked incredulously.

"Douglas, is it?"

She shook her head impatiently. "He's..." she began, about to explain that Douglas was the tour guide and that their dining together on that particular evening had been a matter of company policy. Then she reminded herself that she didn't owe Ian any explanations about anything.

"Yes?" he asked politely, as her voice trailed off. "You were about to say something about your dinner companion?"

"If you're speaking of the young man I was with at the hotel—it was a business arrangement," she answered lamely, and immediately was vexed at herself for sounding as if she were making excuses.

He laughed shortly. "Interesting business," he observed. "Champagne, dancing and the lot."

"Why should it matter to you?" she flung at him.

"Why, indeed?" he agreed.

His tone cut her. She would not have believed that he could be so cold. In a horrifying moment she could feel tears start up, and surely the very last thing in the world she wanted to do was to cry in front of him.

She said, forcing herself to speak coolly, "Ian, I'm sorry I've intruded. I shall go now. Mrs. Grewar seems to have stepped out, so would you please give her my thanks for her hospitality?"

She turned toward the door, forcing herself to restrain her pace so as not to hurry visibly. But in an instant he was across the room, grabbing her elbow roughly as he swung her around.

"Not quite so fast!" he warned.

He seemed to tower over her, his face tense and tight-lipped. This was an Ian she had never seen before, and she flinched from his fury even as she fought to remain calm.

"Please," she said, her own tone icy now. "Let me go!"

"Not until you explain to me why you took the trouble to come out here," he said roughly.

She faced up to this one. "I've no intention of explaining anything," she told him. "There's no reason why I should. There are personal reasons. They don't concern you."

"In other words, I don't deserve to hear them, is that it?"

"If you wish to put it that way, yes."

His glance was mocking. "Are you trying to tell me that you went to all the trouble of hiring a car and driving to Monbraithe on a matter that doesn't concern me?'' he demanded, his Scottish accent more heavily pronounced than it usually was. He shook his head, as if chastising a recalcitrant child. "You must know, Monica, that I can't be put off so easily," he told her.

"No," she answered slowly, "I don't know."

He was still clutching her elbow, but now he dropped his hand. "Exactly what do you mean by that?"

"I don't really know you at all, Ian," she said simply. "I've never known you; I can see that now. I was a complete idiot to come here, and I can't wait to leave. Does that explanation satisfy you?"

"I cannot believe it."

"It's true," she insisted, and for the moment it was. But the moment was short-lived.

Their eyes locked, and he said, his voice heavy, "I cannot blame you for anything you think, or anything you do. It is I who have been entirely at fault— and believe me, I know it all too well. It is a lesson I have learned over and over again. I've lived with it every day, every moment, of this past year. I thought, in the course of things, I had also learned how to get on without you, but it would seem that I was mistaken about that, too. Now, though, you have come to me of your own free will. . .as, I suppose, you might say that I prayed you might. But to have you standing here beside me, telling me I have no right to expect anything from you. . . ."

Ian's voice seemed to break as he shook his head, and he looked so incredibly weary that it was all

Monica could do not to reach out to him. But instead it was he who reached out to her, and she went into his arms as easily as if she had never left them. She felt his lips, his beloved lips, come to claim hers, and then his kiss enveloped them both in a touched-with-gold moment that blotted out everything else in the world.

He pressed her close against him, and she could feel his heart thumping, and she knew that her own pulse was more than matching it, beat for beat. Time was no longer a factor; there *was* no such thing as time where she and Ian were concerned, or so she thought as she clung to him, entirely his if he wanted her.

The kiss seemed eternal and yet finally it ended, and she buried her head against his shoulder as his grip tightened. He said huskily, "The other night at Prestonfield House I thought I saw you, at the far end of the hall. Then other people came between us and I told myself it had only been a vision, a memory. I convinced myself that you could not possibly have been there. But later, at the hotel in Edinburgh, I looked up and you *were* there but with someone else. I very nearly went to you. It took all of my will and more to remind myself that I had no right to approach you, no right at all. But it tore me apart, Monica, can you understand that? I felt I had to send you a message, so like a romantic fool I asked the pianist to play 'Loch Lomond.'"

"And when I looked up you had already left," she reminded him.

"Yes," he said sadly.

"Why, Ian? Why couldn't you come and speak to me?"

He smiled faintly. "Jealousy, perhaps," he responded, and she realized he was thinking of Douglas. "That, at least, was a factor, but there were other reasons, as well."

"What reasons?" she persisted.

He shook his head. "'Twould do no good to burden you with them. They are entirely too complicated."

She wanted to shake him, yet there was something she had to know, and now seemed the moment to ask him about it. She forced herself to bury her pride, then demanded bluntly, "Why didn't you come to Prestwick?"

He drew back, and Monica felt as if a distance had suddenly been created between them; it was as if he were looking at her across a gap of miles. He told her slowly, "I was not able to come to Prestwick. Had I been able to, nothing would have stopped me. You will have to believe that."

"Don't you think I deserve a better explanation, Ian?" Her nerves felt as if they were rubber bands stretched taut. "Even if for some valid reason you couldn't come to Prestwick as you said you would, you could have phoned or written later."

He turned away from her. "Ah, Monica, Monica, I cannot answer your questions," he sighed. "Perhaps one day I'll be able to do so, but I can hardly expect you to wait until that day, especially as it may never come at all. It is far better that you should go back to your young man in Glasgow—"

"Douglas is not my young man!" she protested furiously.

A faint hint of his old smile crossed his lips. "Well, then," he said, "I am forced to admit that is good news. To do so is very selfish of me, but I would be a liar to pretend otherwise. Still, 'tis back you must go, and that's something there is no doubt about."

CHAPTER EIGHT

MONICA STARED AT IAN as if she had suddenly been given new vision. She knew that she was only beginning to realize the magnitude of whatever had happened to him, and this daunted her severely. She saw for the first time that all these months she had been thinking primarily of herself and her own wounded pride.

Now her entire attention, her entire concern, became focused upon this handsome haunted man who stood before her. She said quickly, with more than a hint of desperation in her voice, "Ian, I had a chance to take a job with a tour organization. That's why I'm in Scotland. It was a last-minute sort of opportunity. A friend of mine was working with the group, and she had an accident. She broke her ankle. They needed an American, and I agreed to give it a try. Then, once I'd committed myself, I felt that I'd been every kind of a fool to take the job. I was not at all sure I could bear to come back to Scotland."

"Yet you came," he pointed out softly.

"Yes," she admitted.

"So," he said, "your curiosity must have been stronger than your romantic fears."

Monica stiffened. "Curiosity," she responded

tautly, "was not a part of my reason for coming back to Scotland, Ian."

"Ah," he taunted, "are you saying, then, that it was a love for my country and its people? You do seem to become easily captivated by Scots; I'll agree to that."

"I presume you're referring to Douglas?"

"Yes. Are there others?"

"No, there are no others," she retorted, trying to suppress her growing anger at his attitude. "I've already told you it was a business matter with Douglas. He works for the same tour organization, and usually all the employees have dinner together on the last night in a city. It's often rather festive, which was the reason for the champagne. As it happened, there were only Douglas and myself to share it. The others were engaged elsewhere."

Ian nodded. "I believe I've said you made a handsome pair," he observed. "You danced well together, too, but then I am sure you could dance well with anyone. Now...." He stared at her, a bleakness in those blue eyes that once had been so full of life. "When do you go back to the States?" he asked her.

"In three days," she said. "Saturday. The trip was for nine days inclusive."

"So...." Ian hesitated. "You can tell me it's none of my affair, but I do wonder what you plan to do once you've returned home."

"I've no real home," Monica answered, without stopping to think about making such an admission.

"No?" He raised a questioning eyebrow. "You no longer live with your aunt?"

"Aunt Flora died several months ago."

It seemed to her that his gaze softened. "I am sorry to hear that," he said. "If I remember correctly, it would mean you are very much alone where family is concerned."

"That's right." She forced herself to speak emotionlessly. "As for what I am going to do after I get back to the States—well, I'm not entirely sure as yet. I've been told the travel organization may offer me a permanent job if they're satisfied with my performance in this initial venture. If so, there will be tours going to warmer places in the winter and spring."

"Then," he queried, "'twould be another year before you would come back to Scotland?"

"I don't know about that," she answered slowly. "At the moment I don't intend ever to come back to Scotland again."

She was sure he winced at this, yet he recovered so quickly that she told herself the spasm could have been entirely a matter of her imagination. He said gravely, "I can't blame you for feeling that way, Monica. Tell me—today you had time off?"

"In a sense. The group, most of them anyway, was going on a trip to the Highlands and Loch Ness. They didn't really need me—"

"So you decided to hire a car and see if you could find my uncle's house by yourself?"

"Yes," she said, and faced him squarely. "Only it isn't your uncle's house anymore, is it? It's your house...your castle, rather. I understand that you, too, had a loss in the family this past year, and now you're the—the earl of Monbraithe, are you not?"

He raised his eyebrows. "'Twould seem you've been busy ferreting out information from some source," he told her. "Very well, then. Yes, I have inherited."

"I suppose," she suggested, "that I should curtsy and say, 'your lairdship.'"

His face darkened. "Don't be a fool, Monica," he said sharply, and he looked so angry that she was almost frightened by him again. But even more alarming was the aura that seemed to hover around him, composed of more than a hint of tragedy, so that she felt as if a shadow had come to cloud the room. Then he scowled and told her with definite finality, "'Tis best now that you get back to Glasgow."

It was a dismissal, and it stung.

She flushed. "Very well," she agreed. She picked up her handbag. "Once again," she said, "thank Mrs. Grewar for the tea, will you?"

He didn't answer, but said only, "I'll see you to the gate."

They were silent as they walked outdoors, the autumn sun slanting down around them. Monica felt as if she were aching in every inner fiber of her being, for she sensed that this was indeed to be their real parting. Never before had she felt so miserable.

Something had happened to Ian during the course of the past few months, something terrible that had wreaked havoc with him. But she had no idea of what it might have been. She knew only that he was still a tormented man and had no place at all for her in his present way of life.

There was to be no ardent farewell, she soon saw.

Ian held the car door open for her, and she slid into her place behind the wheel, her fingers trembling as she turned the key in the ignition switch—only to be greeted by first a rasping sound and then silence. To have the car fail her now, she thought grimly, would be the ultimate embarrassment. She pressed down the accelerator, turned the key again and could feel her cheeks getting hot with pure chagrin when nothing happened.

"Here," Ian said finally, exhibiting a streak of what she could only consider pure male chauvinism. "Let me have a try at it."

She had the feeling that if she didn't get out of the car he would yank her out of it, and so she complied, then stood by as he tried to start an engine that seemed to have died completely. After the first few attempts he was swearing under his breath—and then he emerged to rake her face with an intensely sardonic glance.

"What have you done to it, Monica?" he demanded.

She couldn't believe she was hearing correctly. In fact, it took a long moment before she realized the extent of his insinuation, and then she was furious.

"Do you actually think," she challenged, "that I would fool around with the car just so I could stay here longer and be insulted by you?"

"I do not know," he said, sounding very Scottish.

"You've much too great an impression of yourself," she assured him coldly. "I've no intention of becoming a hindrance to you, I can promise you that. If the Grewars have a telephone, I shall call the nearest garage and get someone to come out and solve the problem, whatever it may be. In the meantime, I shall simply sit here in the car.''

''Shall you, now?'' he asked, and to her amazement she saw a hint of amusement in the form of the slightest of smiles, come to twitch his lips.

''Yes.''

'' 'Twould not be practical,'' Ian pointed out. ''To begin, there's no phone in the cottage. They've only an intercom connecting with the castle.''

''Oh,'' Monica said, deflated. She had already decided that she definitely was not about to ask him if she could go up to his castle and use his telephone. No, she'd have to find another way of handling this.

''The castle is occupied at the moment,'' Ian continued, ''and I would prefer not to take you there. We can, however, phone from the nearest Royal Auto Club booth, and they will take care of the matter. Go along to my car, will you, while I speak to Angus.''

For the first time Monica noticed the familiar red MGA parked inside the gate along the private driveway. Just looking at it brought back a surge of memories that she knew only too well could be very treacherous to dwell upon. Holding her chin high, she declared, ''There's no need for you to drive me anywhere. I can walk to one of the booths you mention myself.''

He actually laughed. '' 'Twould be a longish stroll,'' he told her, ''and even were you to find a booth it would do you no good. The Royal Auto Club gives keys to the booths to their members, and no, Monica, I will not lend you my key so that you can prove your independence. Get along now, and I shall be with you directly.''

She marched the short distance to the red car and clambered in, damning Ian for his autocratic air. Still, her pulse was thudding as he came to take his place beside her, and she tried not to watch his long capable hands as the MGA's engine purred into instant action, and he swung around to go back to the main road. She was too intimately acquainted with those hands; she knew their potential for tenderness, as well as for provoking ecstasy of the most intense sort. . . .

She shuddered, fighting back such thoughts, and forced herself to stare straight at the road ahead, trying to pretend that Ian was anywhere but at her side.

THEY STOPPED AT THE RAC BOOTH and Ian made the phone call about the car, but once at the wheel of the MGA again he did not turn back toward Monbraithe. Instead he took a country road that led them away from Loch Lomond and ultimately into a village with an old cross-timbered inn bordering the main street.

Ian consulted his watch. '' 'Tis not quite time for the pub to open, but the owner is a friend of mine. We shall ask if we may borrow a private parlor.''

''Oh? Why?''

''Because I want to talk to you,'' he said simply.

A few hours earlier this statement would have been an occasion for joy, but it wasn't now. Monica told him, ''I don't think we've anything to talk about,'' fully believing this statement.

"Don't you?" he questioned. "I do. You've come all this way to Scotland; it would seem to me the least I can do is to tell you why I failed to meet you at Prestwick."

She shook her head. "It's too late for that, Ian. You've already warned me you can't answer my questions. In fact, I'd say you've made your position very clear."

"I don't think so."

"I do," she contradicted. "You hedged around, there in the Grewars' cottage, but your message was clear nevertheless. It's long over between us."

"Did the kiss—there in the Grewars' cottage—mean nothing to you, Monica?"

"The kiss belonged to the past, Ian," she said steadily.

"Rubbish! The kiss was *now*, as present as you are and as I am. Do you deny our feeling for each other?"

"Past, too," she insisted.

He mumbled something under his breath that she was glad she couldn't make out, then swung angrily into the parking lot at the side of the inn. "If you don't mind," he said with exaggerated politeness as he came around to open the car door for her, "please come and have some tea and scones with me."

He stood waiting for her, and again she had the impression that if she didn't move, he would lift her out of the car by force. Although he was quite thin just now—he had definitely lost weight these past months—there still was a kind of taut strength about him. She had no doubt at all of his capability to physically put her exactly where he wanted her to be.

As they walked together toward the inn's side entrance, she stole a glance at him. His profile seemed chiseled, it was so set, and his face at the moment was expressionless, yet these very factors gave her the opportunity to see him exactly as he was. The resulting impact of his attractiveness had never been more forceful: it was a jolt, bringing her to an awareness entirely too sensual.

He knocked on the old weathered wooden door with that air of authority that was such a part of him. After a moment a crack appeared and a gruff voice said, "Sorry, but 'tis not time yet."

Ian shook his head impatiently. "Come along now, Bert," he insisted. "Open up!"

Hastily the door swung inward and the innkeeper stood in the entryway. He was a big heavy man with graying hair and a friendly ruddy face. "M'laird," he protested, "I did not know ye. I spied the young lady first."

"Yes," Ian said, and added whimsically, "and she's a better sight than I am, is she not?"

Without waiting for an answer, he pushed Monica in front of him, and they entered a hall with a low ceiling, heavy wood paneling and wide floorboards. There was a snugness, a warmth, a feel of centuries about the place that instantly appealed to her.

Ian introduced her, "This is Miss Winthrop, Bert."

"I'm pleased to meet ye, miss," the innkeeper nodded. "Ye are more than welcome. Any friend of Laird Monbraithe's—"

"Might we use that small back parlor of yours, so as to have a bit of privacy?" Ian interrupted. "Miss Winthrop and I haven't seen each other for a year, and we've a lot to catch up on."

"The parlor is yours," the innkeeper said solemnly.

"Could you manage tea and scones?" Ian persisted. "Or," turning to Monica, "perhaps you'd like something a bit stronger."

"No, thank you," she answered. "Tea will be fine."

"Ye know the way," the innkeeper told Ian. "I shall be along directly with your tea."

Ian nodded and led Monica down a long corridor, past a public room in which a plump dark-haired girl was polishing the top of a dark wood bar. At the far end of the corridor, a door opened into a small parlor with a piano in one corner and a red-and-black plaid rug on the floor. Worn but comfortable couches and chairs, and tables of uncertain vintage completed the decor.

Monica smiled. "It's delightful," she said.

"That it is. A good place, and Bert is a friend. A very discreet man."

"Is discretion needed, Ian?"

"Would that it were not," Ian responded wryly. "As it is, will you kindly go sit down in that chair over there before I forget myself entirely?"

There was a hint of laughter in his voice, and she could almost imagine that in a moment the merriment would come back to curve his lips and put sparkle into his eyes; that he would become the Ian of a year ago. But this was not to be. He sat down in a chair across from the one she chose, keeping a good distance between them, and asked with a frown, "How did you learn of my inheritance?"

"Does it matter?"

"It may, more than you might think," he said enigmatically.

"Very well, then. We—the tour bus, that is—stopped at a gift shop on Loch Lomond yesterday. It's run by a Mrs. Grier—"

Ian nodded. "Yes."

"I...well, I was looking out across the lake, and I saw the castle," she went on.

"The loch," he corrected.

"Oh, very well, then!" She glanced at him suspiciously, but he looked quite serious. "The loch. In any event, I saw the castle."

"And you recognized it from that distance, even though you'd been there only at night?" he asked skeptically.

"Recognized it? I don't know how to answer that. I suppose I didn't really *recognize* it, but I had a feeling...."

"Intuition, eh?"

"Make fun of me if you must, Ian," she retorted bitterly.

"Ah, but I am not making fun of you, Monica," he said, and his gaze was so intent that she felt like wriggling. "I do not discount intuition, and God knows that if thought waves could have played their part, you would have been led toward Monbraithe."

"Now you *are* making fun of me!"

"Not at all. I told you, didn't I, that I'd hoped you'd come."

"That's a bit difficult to believe," she told him. "It seems to me you could hardly wait to get rid of me."

"True," he agreed, "but that had nothing to do with my personal feelings. It was for quite a different reason."

She leaned forward, exasperated. "Surely you must know that you're being most contradictory," she accused. "You seem to be playing word games with yourself."

"Yes," he conceded, "I suppose I am. But my life has been complicated this past year, entirely contradictory in itself. I did not wish to involve you in any of it, believe me."

"Oh, I believe you." Her tone was heavy with an irony that was unlike her.

Ian shot a quick glance in her direction that was a blend of many things, and because of this quite impossible for her to analyze on the spur of the moment. She had at least pricked his shell, that much was clear, and she supposed it should give her a sense of satisfaction, but it didn't.

Her thoughts turned backward, and she remarked, "It seems strange to think that you really are the earl of Monbraithe."

Now there was no need to try to analyze his expression: it held pure suspicion.

"I suppose I should have realized, the night you took me to the castle, that your family must be titled," she explained. "But you never really told me anything about your family, and just then I wasn't thinking about—"

"No," he intervened, as if avoiding dangerous ground. "I never did say very much, I realize that. Would it have mattered to you if I had? Does such a thing as a title make a difference to you?"

"I don't know," she admitted. "It does set you apart in a way."

He shook his head wearily. "Not you, too, Monica," he pleaded. "For God's sake, don't be American when it comes to such things as lords and ladies and castles and all the supposed romance of it. If you indulge too much in fantasy, it will be that much harder for you to wake up!"

CHAPTER NINE

IAN LEANED BACK, stretching his long legs out in front of him, and regarded her levelly. "There are more important things to talk about than my having a title," he told her, "though I daresay that does enter into it. As a matter of fact, I don't know where to begin if I'm to make you understand...anything at all." His blue eyes were moody as he added, "It is not a pleasant story, Monica, and though it may seem strange to you, I can best begin by telling you a bit about Scottish history."

"A bit?" she echoed, remembering Iris and her comments on the history of Scotland. "As I understand it, there is no such thing as a 'bit' of Scottish history. I gather it would take a lifetime to know very much about it at all."

"That's so," he conceded, "but I need only give you some background." He sighed. "Scotland," he began, "as you doubtless know, has a most turbulent history, a very violent history. Through the centuries life in Scotland has been built around the clans, and in the earlier days there was great feeling amongst them. There was rivalry, enmity and constant warring. Today, true, 'tis no longer like that, but there are still feelings, passions, emotions, and sometimes they are easily aroused. Then, there is something else to deal with, a growing spirit of nationalism. There are those in favor of devolution, as we call it—a plan that, if carried to the fullest extent, would make Scotland an independent nation. I would say in this area there is in fact a wide range of sentiment, from those who are purely fanatics to those who would merely like to see Scotland belong more fully to the Scots. So, as you might expect, in some quarters there is also quite a bit of feeling against the English because some think we are too much a part of their system of government.''

''Iris—she's a guide with the tour and she *is* English—and Douglas often speak about that, but I've always thought they were joking,'' Monica interjected.

''Well, perhaps they have been, but to many this is an extremely serious matter. Some of those in Scotland today who feel that we should be completely independent from England stress that they are ready to strive to gain that independence at any cost. I would say they are in the minority. There are many more who feel that we should merely have a stronger voice, more independence than we do now; and then there are also those who feel that we are best as we are now, a part of Great Britain, subject to England.

'' 'Tis rather like a tapestry,'' Ian continued. ''A tremendous tapestry that is still in the process of being woven, with a background that is part feudal and part modern. 'Tis a tapestry colored with all kinds of likenesses and differences, and the clans and the bagpipes and tradition—for tradition is a strong thing here—provide a varying part of the theme. It is against this tapestry that my own bit of family history is being acted out...."

There was a rap on the door, and Ian said, "That will be Bert."

He rose to admit the innkeeper, who came in carrying a tray laden with the makings for tea and a plateful of freshly baked warm scones.

"If there is anything else, your lairdship, you have merely to ring," Bert said.

"This will be fine, thanks," Ian told him, and when the man had gone he turned to Monica with a smile.

"You can pour," he suggested. "Since this is something I don't think you've ever done for me before, I take a spoon of sugar and a bit of milk, if you please. I don't like my tea overly white."

She was tempted to say, "Yes, your lairdship," but could imagine the reaction this would provoke, so she set about pouring the tea with a mounting sense of unreality. It didn't seem possible that she could really be here in this pleasant sheltered room with Ian.

The tea was hot and strong, the scones warm, the butter sweet, and the jam homemade and rich in flavor.

Ian went on between bites, "To begin, I shall have to go back to the end of the Second World War, when my father married my mother while he was still in the British army. She was French: she came from Alsace—the town of Strasbourg, to be precise—which has had its own share of upheaval. It has been

French or German many times during the course of
its history. As a matter of fact, when my father
brought my mother home with him his relatives considered her more German than French. Needless to
say, they were not too happy with the marriage.

"My father was Donald MacGregor, second son in
his particular branch of the clan. My uncle, Terence
MacGregor, was the oldest son. My grandmother
came from Northern Ireland, which accounts for his
first name. 'Twas Terence who inherited when my
grandfather died.

"Another brother, Keith, who was a year younger
than my father, was killed in the war. Although he
was not much more than a lad at the time, he had
married before going across the Channel. My Aunt
Jane is his widow and he left a son, Walter, who is
quite a bit older than I am.

"In Britain, however, the law of primogeniture
still holds, and this applies to Scotland as well as
England—although in many respects, as you will
learn, our laws are not the same at all. In any event,
the eldest son always inherits, and then the title and
the estate are passed to his son and so on. For a long
while my Aunt Jane hoped that her son, Walter,
would be the one to inherit. My Uncle Terence didn't
marry until fairly late in life, and then he chose a
younger woman who finally ran off and left him for
someone closer to her own age. They were childless,
and he became a bitter man. 'Twas he who brought
me up for the most part."

"Your parents died?" Monica asked.

"Yes. Not together, that is, but...."

Ian held out his teacup, and as she refilled it he said, "You see, my mother was quite delicate, and she and my father were married for several years before she gave birth to me. My father didn't want to risk her having a child, and I can only think that perhaps she was more mindful of the title than he was. If so, she died because of it, which is to say that she died in childbirth. Afterward, so I've been told, my father was brokenhearted and wanted no part of me. He traveled a great deal. We had a house in Edinburgh, which I still own. When I was very small I lived there—"

"Who took care of you?" Monica asked.

"Governesses," Ian said tersely, and it seemed to Monica that she could feel a knot of pain forming in her heart. She could envision a cold gray stone Edinburgh mansion, and a little boy who knew from the very beginning of his life that he was unloved. She told herself that there was good reason why such sadness was etched just now on Ian's face. A sadness that made her want to go to him, to put her arms around him, to comfort him.

But Ian a year ago had not seemed at all sad. He had been such a light and laughing young man, full of fun, brimming with a zest for life. Which, she wondered, was the real Ian?

His voice was low, his tone calculatedly level, as he continued. "When I was nine," he told her, "my father was killed in a hunting accident at Monbraithe Castle. Maybe that's why I have always hated hunting so, which is considered quite un-Scottish of me. They brought his body back to the house, and I was there, in the entrance, when they carried him in.''

Monica shivered, moved by both horror and pity for him. She said, her own voice low, ''How terrible for you!''

He went on as if she hadn't spoken. ''Upon my father's death I became the heir to the title, and thenceforth I was very much under my uncle's aegis. I was sent to the proper school and I finished at Oxford, but frankly, nothing at all meant very much to me. There wasn't anyone I truly cared for, so I suppose you might say I decided the best way to live was to burn one's candle at both ends and make the best of it.'' His blue eyes were very direct as he said this. ''I got quite a reputation for myself carousing around, if you wish to call it that. I burned my candle not only at both ends but sometimes in the middle, as well. I know my uncle was often disgusted with me, but once I was through university there wasn't very much he could do about it. As far as money was concerned, I'd received an ample inheritance, including the house in Edinburgh, from my father. I had no need to ask favors of Uncle Terence.

''I visited Monbraithe Castle as little as possible. I despised the place, especially after my Aunt Jane and Walter moved in—by my uncle's dispensation. Terence was not a generous man, but he was a Scot to the bone, loyal to the clan, with everything that implies.

''He made Jane his hostess, and he began to entertain again. 'Twas not on the scale that had been customary at Monbraithe in earlier years to be sure, but he did have his dinner parties and such, and Jane was in her glory. He was good to her, actually; I feel quite sure that she hoped eventually he would ask her to marry him, but obviously he had no intention of doing so. Still, he made life pleasant enough for her, and it was only once, at Christmas two years ago, that I ever saw him become really angry with her.

"Uncle Terence had been persuaded to stand for Parliament from this area and he had won his election, so he was deep into politics. He insisted that I come over from Edinburgh for the Christmas festivities that year, and I had enough family loyalty to wish to please him. I had taken a position with a bank in Edinburgh, but I already knew that I wasn't apt to stay with it. I was drifting; I had no idea at all what I wanted. But Christmas *is* a time for family, so I came across to Monbraithe Castle.

"Jane, Walter and I were in the drawing room awaiting our dinner guests, and I'd already had my share of whisky, when my uncle came in, dressed in his kilt. He cut a fine figure in it, too. He seemed quite mellow at first, and then his eyes fell upon my aunt's neck and he stormed, 'Take that off, woman! Where the hell did you get it in the first place, and what makes you think you might possibly have the right to wear it?'

"Aunt Jane went deathly white, and then I saw that she was wearing the Jacobite medallion."

"The Jacobite medallion?"

"Yes," Ian nodded, "which brings me back to Scottish history once again. You see, in 1603 James Stuart ascended to the throne of Great Britain and became the first king of *both* England and Scotland.

It was more than a century later, in 1745, that our Bonnie Prince Charlie fought to regain the crown for the Stuarts, and he was defeated. Those who followed Prince Charlie were called Jacobites—from the Latin Jacobus, or James. Charlie was the grandson of James II. His father, whom they called the 'Old Pretender,' had also aspired to the throne.

"The Camerons, whom many call the bravest clan of all, were one of the first to join forces with Charlie. 'Twould take me hours to tell you of the intrigue and the fighting that went on during this period in our history. But in the course of it a beautiful medallion was given to one of my ancestors in appreciation for her part in helping Prince Charlie find refuge on a certain occasion. She was a Cameron, and the medallion was given to her with the injunction that she was to pass it on to her daughter, who would pass it on to *her* daughter, and so on. In the event that there wasn't a daughter, it was to be given to the heir at the time, to be presented to his wife.

"It was an odd sort of legacy, but it has been preserved throughout the years, and finally the medallion came into the possession of my Uncle Terence. Fortunately, his wife did not manage to make off with it when she left him. Now, since there are no daughters in the present generation, the medallion rightfully will be given to my wife—that is, if I ever marry. Regardless of whether I do or not, though, Aunt Jane has no right to it for as long as I live. If I were to die, it would become Walter's. Then, if he chose, I suppose he could let her wear it.

"In any event, when my uncle saw the Jacobite medallion about Jane's neck I felt that he over-reacted rather terribly. It seemed to me it was unreasonable for him to become so incensed about a bit of vanity on his sister-in-law's part. She told him she had thought she would enjoy wearing the medallion for the evening, and so she had taken it from the glass case in the small parlor where it is always kept with various other family trophies. Terence told her to put it back at once, and she did so. But she was so chastised that I couldn't help but pity her.

"Until then, I hadn't realized the extent of my uncle's contempt for both Jane and Walter, despite the fact that he was letting them live at Monbraithe. It was quite a revelation."

Ian stood and stretched. Bringing his empty cup across to her, he asked, "Is the tea still hot?"

"Yes," she nodded, and filled it for him, adding a spoonful of sugar and a dash of milk.

She thought for a moment that he was going to sit down at her side; it was almost as if he were visibly wrestling with this idea. But then he gave a slight shrug and moved back to the chair he had been occupying.

"You know, it's very strange," he went on, "the way things sometimes happen. After that Christmas, for no particular reason that I could see, my uncle seemed to look upon me more favorably than he ever had before. We met frequently in Edinburgh for lunch or dinner, and he was a surprisingly pleasant companion.

"That next summer he asked me to come to Monbraithe Castle for a brief vacation, and for the first time in my memory I actually looked forward to going there. One evening we had a long talk. I confessed I wasn't happy with my position at the bank in Edinburgh and had about decided to make a change. In earlier days he would have frowned upon this, and not without reason, either. I'd made a number of changes by then. That night, though, he actually urged me to give up the bank position and to move to Monbraithe on a permanent basis. He said the estate would be mine one day, after all, and he felt I should learn something about running it.

"Frankly, I rather sidestepped the issue. I had no desire at all to settle down in the country, especially at Monbraithe. There is vast acreage at Monbraithe. God knows how many sheep are raised—for their wool, rather than their meat, incidentally. I'd never been able to see myself in the role of managing the estate, whereas my uncle was one of those individuals who could do well at anything he chose to handle.

"He had done a good job of managing Monbraithe, but taxes, as you may have heard, have become incredibly high in Scotland. Terence had no desire to make his properties a part of the tourist trade, which today is actually Scotland's biggest business. He didn't want to open Monbraithe to tour groups, or to get to the point where the castle would be available to paying guests, but he could see that this was precisely what was going to happen unless he could think of some way of forestalling it.

"Certainly he sensed my reluctance in making a commitment that night, so—to my surprise—he dropped the subject. But early the following autumn he met me in Edinburgh one day. We lunched together, and he told me frankly what it was he wanted of me.

"He pointed out that I was in my late twenties, and he said he felt he'd been more than liberal in permitting me to sow my wild oats, as he put it. Now he felt that the time had come for me to think of the future and settle down. He asked me to come to Monbraithe the following weekend to meet a young lady. He said he had invited this young lady and her parents to be his guests for a week of grouse shooting. He told me her father was the owner of one of the biggest whisky distilleries in Scotland—a millionaire. Terence's idea of the solution to Monbraithe's problems became quite obvious."

"Did you go for the weekend?" Monica asked.

"Yes," Ian confessed. "I thought it would be amusing, but it wasn't."

"Wasn't she beautiful enough for you?" The question was inadvertent, but as she spoke she felt a twinge of jealousy that actually made her shift her position.

"Not beautiful, no, but attractive enough," he said rather impatiently. "Quite charming, in fact. However, she was vastly uncomfortable, poor thing. She knew as well as I did why she was there. I felt sorry for her, despite myself, and so I was nicer to her than I'd intended to be. This, of course, only served to encourage my uncle about the whole enterprise.

"The young lady in question lives in Edinburgh.

No sooner was I back in town than she called to ask me for tea at her home the following Sunday. I went, with the intention of making it clear that there was no romance involved on my part, because this seemed the only fair thing to do. However, there were others there, as it turned out. It was impossible to talk alone with her, so I let it pass. I didn't call her; I hoped that would be message enough. But a few days later she wrote to ask if I would accompany her to a charity ball. I wrote back that on the particular weekend in question I planned to be in London; I even *went* down to London, so that no one could accuse me of prevaricating.

"Then, a friend who had been at Oxford when I was there came to Edinburgh unexpectedly. He was to be in the city only briefly, and he called and asked if I would stop by at his hotel for a drink. I agreed to do so, and I walked into the elevator . . . and you were there."

Now Ian's eyes met hers, and they were so intensely blue, she was reminded of Loch Lomond on a clear day. He said, "It was an unforgettable moment, Monica. Don't you agree to that?"

"Yes." The word was wrung from her because this was a question she would have much rather avoided.

"When I realized I didn't even know your name, let alone how long you would be in Edinburgh, I was frantic," he admitted. "I went back to the hotel the next day praying that I would find you again, and I *would* have found out who you were if I'd had to steal the guest register to do it! Nevertheless, I was so afraid you'd left I could hardly believe my own luck

when I saw you sitting in the coffee shop. You know
very well that I spent every hour you would let me
spend with you in those next few days. And I began
to wonder what in God's name I was going to do
about you. I was painfully aware of the fact that in
no time at all you would be leaving Scotland, and
that if I were not careful I would lose you...as in
fact I did," he concluded, the light gone from his
eyes again; and she could find no answer to this.

He finished his tea and set the cup aside. Then he
continued, "The night came—the night before you
were to go to Loch Ness with your aunt—when we
went to dinner, and I stopped off at the castle."

"Yes," she said, her pulse thudding.

Ian seemed to be staring into space, and she realized he was using all the control he could muster not
to look in her direction. "The reason I went to the
castle—as I believe I mentioned at the time—was that
my uncle wanted me to check on something. A bit
more than that, really. He was in London, you may
recall, and he'd asked me if I'd go to Monbraithe and
get the medallion."

"The Jacobite medallion?"

"Yes, and I was puzzled by such a request," he
answered thoughtfully. "I knew the medallion was
valuable in its way, but still it is hardly one of the
crown jewels. I asked Terence if he was thinking of
getting married again, but he saw no humor in that
suggestion at all. He said, rather testily, that it was
merely that the damned thing had become something
of a symbol, and he wanted it out of the castle and
into a bank vault, for safety's sake.

"When I left you in the library, I went to the small parlor and looked in the case where the medallion was usually kept, but it was missing. I thought possibly Jane had taken it to Inverness to wear at some function she planned to attend. It seemed likely she'd thought she could do so without being found out by Terence, and the entire matter really didn't seem all that serious to me. Later that night, though, Terence telephoned me, and when I told him I hadn't found the medallion he was extremely upset. He asked me to meet him at Monbraithe the next day.

"I told him that with Jane and Walter away the castle had been closed up for more than a fortnight and was colder than the grave. I suggested that we meet here, at the inn, in fact that we stay here. He agreed that it would at least be wise to have a bite of lunch here first, and then drive on out to Monbraithe in either his car or mine, and that it would also be a good thought to stay here, were it necessary to remain in the area overnight.

"I called Bert and made the arrangements. When I arrived here the next day, my uncle was waiting for me in the pub. He was in an extremely ugly mood. He'd been drinking, and although usually he held his whisky better than any man I've ever known, it wasn't sitting well with him that day. He started to quarrel with me, first by accusing me of trifling with the affections of the young lady in Edinburgh to whom he'd introduced me. I, in turn, accused him of smelling her father's money a bit too keenly for my comfort.

"Then all at once his face got beet red. He thundered out, 'Who is this American you're fooling around with?' So help me, my mind went blank. Surely I didn't consider that I'd been 'fooling around' with you, nor did I think of you simply as an American. Rather, you were someone entirely unique to me. Terence took my silence to mean that I was evading the issue, so he took pains to inform me that I'd been seen with an American girl in Edinburgh at Prestonfield House and elsewhere, and then again in Glasgow. For that matter, he said he knew we had been at the castle only the evening before.''

"How could he possibly have known that?" Monica demanded.

"He was not about to tell me. I wondered if Angus or Annie had seen us leaving and had told him—though I couldn't fathom why they should have. I've asked them since and they deny it. At the time I accused my uncle of having set spies on me, and to my surprise he didn't deny it. I tried to ferret out his purpose for being so concerned with my actions, but I got nowhere at all. Rather, he accused me of having found the Jacobite medallion in its proper place the evening before and of having given it to you.

"To *me*?"

Ian smiled bleakly. "Quite so. I was infuriated, and I told him he was behaving like an idiot. We'd both become so loud at this point that Bert came over to the table to soothe things—he's an expert at handling ruffled feathers. We settled down and had lunch, and by the time we'd finished coffee my uncle was sober, and I decided that it had been the whisky speaking earlier. He became downright mellow, in fact, and even apologized a bit—as much as he ever could apologize to anyone about anything.

"After a time we drove out to the castle in his car, leaving my MGA here with Bert. I remember that it was a magnificent day, mild for the season, with a sky as bright as our bluebells. I thought of you at Loch Ness, with your aunt, and wished I were with you.

"At the castle, Terence soon saw for himself that the medallion was missing, and he was inclined to agree with me that Jane had probably taken it with her to Inverness to show off. He told me that he'd had quite enough of Jane, and of Walter, too, and he'd about decided that he'd let them stay at Monbraithe through the Christmas holidays, and then he was going to see to it that they moved somewhere else. He said Jane had relatives at Inverness, and he saw no reason why she couldn't go there.

"With the business of the medallion over, we still had the better part of the afternoon before us. Terence suggested that we do a bit of shooting. As I've told you, I despise hunting. In fact, I hate it as much as Terence loved it, and his asking me annoyed me because I knew he was well aware of how I felt. Nevertheless, I didn't want any further problems with him at the moment, so I agreed to go along.

"We set out through the meadows to the back of the castle. The bracken was golden, the heather still in bloom, and I—well, I was lovesick. I couldn't get you out of my mind. . . nor what had happened in the library the previous evening. It was never my intention—''

''Ian,'' she broke in. There was a warning note in her voice as she spoke his name, so that he looked up at her sharply.

''All right,'' he said, ''I won't get into it. There's enough else to go into first, God knows. You see, Uncle Terence went on ahead, and I was happy enough to let him go. I tarried behind; in fact I sat down in a quiet little knoll and had a cigarette. I *think* I heard a shot ring out, but that part is still muddied—I've never been entirely sure. I don't remember anything else. I blacked out entirely, and when I came to again there were rescue people working over me.''

''Rescue people?''

Ian nodded. ''I was in Terence's Bentley, and the Bentley had crashed into a tree. They took me directly to hospital in Glasgow.''

Monica blanched. ''Dear God!'' she whispered. ''Then that's why you didn't come to Prestwick!''

His blue eyes were very sober. ''Yes,'' he said, ''that is why I didn't come to Prestwick. . . and a part of the reason why I made no attempt to find you later.''

''Were you badly hurt?''

''Yes, I was,'' he admitted. '' 'Tis a miracle, as a matter of fact, that I wasn't killed outright. I was in hospital until well into the new year. My back was injured. For quite a time they thought I wouldn't walk again.''

"And your uncle?" she asked, almost afraid to hear his answer.

"When I recovered my wits sufficiently to understand anything, they told me my Uncle Terence was dead and that I was now the earl of Monbraithe. But they said all of this in an odd manner, though at the time I was still too befuddled to question it.

"Also, I could well imagine how you had felt when I didn't appear at Prestwick...yet I was beginning to realize it was for the best. There was a very good chance that I was going to be a helpless cripple, confined to a wheelchair for the rest of my life, and I couldn't imagine asking you to share such an existence. So I tried, those weeks I was in hospital, to force you out of my mind.

"Ellen," he continued slowly, "the young lady from Edinburgh, came to see me frequently. In the beginning I used to pretend that it was you who was visiting me, then I made myself stop that and accept Ellen for herself. I admit, I welcomed her company. It was a very lonely time, and hers was just about the only friendly face.

"Fortunately, there was a surgeon at the hospital who decided to take a chance on me. He operated, and 'tis thanks to him that I can walk today. But my injuries were only a part of it all."

Monica frowned. "What do you mean?"

"It was whilst we were hunting that afternoon—or whilst I was pretending to hunt—that my uncle was killed. I had assumed that we'd both been in the car crash. On the contrary, as I've told you, I thought I heard a shot, and it seems that I must have, and that it was this shot that killed him. As I've said, I remember nothing else except that one fleeting impression of a sharp sound. So you can imagine the shock it was to be told that my uncle had been murdered—and that it was I who was accused of having murdered him!''

CHAPTER TEN

MONICA STOOD UP without even realizing that she was doing so, and in an instant Ian was at her side.

She was shaking; the shock of his statement had triggered a series of reactions that mounted one upon the other. From the moment of their first encounter today she'd known that Ian had been living through some sort of private hell. But she'd had no idea of its magnitude.

No wonder he looked older, bitter. No wonder that dancing light that had so intrigued her had faded from his eyes.

Ian accused of murder!

She said, her teeth chattering as she formed the words, "How could anyone possibly accuse you of such a thing!"

His smile was wry. "Thank you," he responded quietly, "for assuming my innocence so easily."

"It's not an assumption!" she fumed indignantly. "I *know* you're innocent. I know it...deep down inside myself."

He was watching her intently, and she saw his face contort as if with a spasm of pain. Then he said sharply, "Oh, my God, darling!" and in another instant she was in his arms.

There had been moments when she'd wondered whether her feelings for Ian included love—real love—or whether she'd been swayed primarily by the intensity of her profound physical reaction to him. Now she knew that she was a victim of the deadliest combination of all. She loved him as much as she desired him, and her desire for him was like a cresting wave.

Their mouths locked, suppressed passion surfacing to make of their kiss a kind of torture because it was only a prelude. She felt the probing thrust of his tongue, and instinctively she pressed close to him, possessed of the age-old urge to make herself one with this man who held the essence of life itself for her. There was no doubt about his own arousal, and for a tense moment they clung together, each fully knowing the other's need. Then, as it had been that first time at the castle, it was he who broke away; but this mood was an entirely different one.

"We can't," he sighed. "Just now we can't." He shook his head, as emotionally drained as she was and every bit as dazed; she could see that. He went on, "Look, my dearest, there's still so much I must tell you. I owe it to you to tell you everything."

She shook her head. "No," she said. "No. You don't *owe* me anything."

"I think differently." His sigh was almost a shudder. And the strain on his face was painfully evident as he added, "I only wish others felt as you do. Many of the people hereabouts believe I killed my uncle."

She stared at him, horrified. "You can't be serious!" she protested.

"Ah, but I am. You see, he was shot with my gun. And the gun was found in the wreck of the Bentley...with me." He added very slowly, "I've never really been able to explain it away, Monica, and the bad part is that that whole time is entirely blank to me. I was totally out of it. There's no doubt, I might add, that it really was the gun in the Bentley that killed him. There were ballistics tests that proved it beyond a doubt.

"Of course, at Monbraithe my uncle had a whole cabinet full of guns. That afternoon he chose his favorite and picked out another for me. The choice was of little importance to me. However, it was the gun I supposedly had 'chosen' that fired the fatal shot.

"The police investigated, and determined that there were only two guns missing from Uncle Terence's collection. Angus testified to that. Angus, as it happens, has been serving the MacGregors his entire life, and Terence's death was a tremendous shock to him. Actually, Angus is something of a distant cousin. His name is Grewar, which comes originally from MacGregor. His family belongs to the same clan.

"To go back to the murder—Uncle Terence was shot in the back. I can only assume that someone must have knocked me out from behind...so swiftly, so expertly, that I never knew what happened. Then they must have stalked Terence and killed him. After that, I think I must have been carried, or dragged, to the Bentley and then driven out along the road that leads to the loch. The car must have been set in the right direction, and the murderer must have managed to jump out after wedging the accelerator down in such a manner that the Bentley plummeted into the tree."

"Are you sure that's what happened?" she asked him.

"As sure as it seems possible to be," he shrugged. "I hired investigators of my own to go over everything. As a matter of fact, I've been trying ever since this happened to prove my innocence. But I wasn't able to convince the court."

"The *court*?"

"Quite so," Ian said stiffly. "I was taken to trial, late this past spring. I was still on crutches; some said I was using them deliberately to gain sympathy, and I rather wish they had taken them away from me in the courtroom. Without them at that time I would have fallen flat on my face."

"But I don't understand," Monica said, puzzled. "You must have convinced the court of your innocence. Obviously you weren't convicted. You're free."

"No," Ian told her. "Not free. Not in the true sense of the word. As I've mentioned to you, in Scotland the judicial process is quite different. We've a different brand of law here from the common law used in England and the rest of the British Commonwealth, and in your country, as well. Our law is based on Roman law. Under it, three verdicts are possible in a court case: guilty, not guilty or not proven. In my case, the verdict was 'not proven.' This is considered a complete acquittal, and so in a sense I am free, if you can call it freedom."

"But that's so wrong!"

"Right or wrong, that's the way it is, and it means that I live with a cloud of dark suspicion still hanging over me; hanging very heavily, I might add. It is something I shall have to continue to live with until either I manage to prove my innocence—or the man who killed my uncle succeeds with his scheme and murders me, as he intended to do the same day he killed Terence."

"Ian, what are you talking about?" Monica demanded sharply.

"I am a target," he said simply. "I've no doubt someone wanted to do away with me, just as he did Uncle Terence, for reasons that may be personal, political or both. So, knowing this, I long ago became determined that you would in no way be involved with me, for the sake of your own safety. Do you think I could have stayed away from you for any other reason?"

She could only stare at him.

"All the while I was convalescing," he went on, "I thought about everything that had been done and said between Terence and myself, all the words and events that had led up to the shooting and my supposed subsequent accident. It seemed to me that I could hear my uncle speaking again of the 'American' who, he charged, had claimed my affection to the point where I would give her the family medallion, and I knew that to have you associated with me could only mean danger for you. If you were close enough for me to have given you the medallion, you can see, can't you, that you, too, might become an obstacle to a fanatic killer?''

"No," she said. "No. I can't see any such thing at all.''

"Then believe me, Monica. Accept it. Realize that for months now a major concern of mine has been to keep my unknown enemy from learning of your identity. Had it been up to me, I would never have let you come back to Scotland of your own accord. Yet you came, and when I thought I saw you at Prestonfield I was so torn between fear for you and joy for myself that I think I became a bit irrational. I told myself that I must have been dreaming, that I must have seen a girl who looked like you and so it had all been a trick of memory.

"But in the hotel dining room there was no chance of playing such games with myself. You were there... with another man.''

"You were with another woman," she pointed out.

He nodded absently. "Ellen," he said. And he added slowly, "She has become very dear to me.''

Very dear to me. Monica had the feeling that the words had been wrung out of him, that he hadn't wanted to say this but had been forced to by an inherent sense of loyalty. Loyalty to the wistful blonde? The thought gave a new dimension to their relationship, opening up something she shied from learning too much about.

Ian, still speaking almost absently, continued, "I can't tell you what seeing you did to me. My instinct was to go and speak to you immediately, and it was very difficult not to do so. But I would sooner have killed myself than place you in danger, so I yielded to a childish gesture. I asked the pianist to play 'Loch Lomond.'"

She swallowed hard. "You must have known that once I heard it I couldn't possibly go on as if. . . as if nothing had happened."

"Yes," he nodded, "I should have realized that. But—"

He was interrupted by two sharp raps on the door. "That must be Bert," he said, his tone almost one of relief.

The big burly innkeeper was frowning. "Did ye phone to the castle from here?" he asked Ian.

"Phone? No," Ian answered.

"I didna think so," Bert said slowly. "But just now Angus called from the castle; he said your cousin Walter had fetched him to tell him there'd been a call—from here. Walter said ye wanted to know if the young lady's car had been tended to. Angus's message was that it took a time to reach the garage in Balloch, but Bobby Grier is on his way to Monbraithe now."

Ian scowled. "Who would have known I was here?" he demanded.

Bert shook his head, bewildered. "I canna imagine," he said, "and that's the truth. Unless ye were seen coming in."

"The street seemed deserted," Ian reflected. "Still, who's to say?"

"Who indeed?" Bert echoed, a bit too grimly.

"You'd best put the tea on my bill, and we'll be on our way," Ian told him.

Bert nodded and looked across at Monica. "It's been a pleasure to meet ye, miss," he said.

IAN FROWNED as he slid behind the wheel of the red MGA, turning the key in the switch as if he more than half expected the car to refuse to function.

As the engine purred into action, he said ruefully, "Each time I turn the key, I wonder if the whole damned thing is about to blow up. I wish I could set all this to rights by going to a psychiatrist and having him tell me the whole thing is in my head. 'Twould be nice, wouldn't it?"

Monica was dismayed by the expression in his eyes. It was as if he were testing her reaction to this statement. "Ian, don't be ridiculous!" she said impulsively. "You act as if you actually think you're flaky."

He smiled briefly. "Flaky," he mused. "I love your American slang. Well, as a matter of fact, someone *has* accused me of being more than slightly off. My Aunt Jane—she insists that I've developed a persecution complex."

"What about your cousin Walter?"

"What about him?"

"Well, how does he feel about you? He's the next in line for the title, isn't he?"

"Yes," Ian conceded, "which makes him such an *obvious* suspect, if indeed there is any dire plot afoot against me. True, I might very well be the only one to suspect Walter, since almost everyone else has been so busy suspecting *me*. But even though he stands to benefit, I can't imagine Walter actually plotting out a nefarious scheme and going through with it. It isn't his style, as you'll see for yourself if you meet him. Also, it would have taken someone reasonably strong to drag me back to the Bentley. Walter is big enough, but he's on the flabby side.''

They drove through the village in silence, then turned onto the road that paralleled the loch. With Loch Lomond ahead of them glistening in the sunlight, Ian said softly, " 'By yon bonnie banks and by yon bonnie braes. . . .' Every time I see it I think of you.''

She was watching him intently, and it seemed to her that he stiffened suddenly. Then he went on, almost under his breath, ''But that, of course, was all in the past.''

Monica felt as if she had been placed in a cold draft. His words cast a chill over her, and she didn't know how to answer him. But before she could say anything he asked abruptly, ''What are your plans?''

''My plans?'' she echoed.

''Yes,'' he responded a bit impatiently. ''You've said that you have a job with a travel group.''

''Oh,'' she said, for she'd forgotten completely about Magic Carpets Unlimited and about Douglas and Iris and all the members of her tour. ''Well,'' she told him slowly, ''tomorrow those who wish to do so are going on a half-day trip to the Trossachs. Then some of the group will be visiting a whisky distillery; at least I think that's the plan. Friday they're to tour Glasgow, with time to shop. And we leave Saturday morning.''

"Two and a half days more," he said thoughtfully. And then added, "'Tis as well it isn't any longer."

Now the chill was real and she actually shivered. There was a note of finality in Ian's voice; she knew without being told that he was convinced there was nothing ahead for them. The bleakness of his expression frightened her—she felt as if a distance had come between them, for at this moment he seemed very unapproachable. He might as well have donned a suit of armor.

Why had he brought her here with him? Why had he bothered to explain? As far as she was concerned it only made the whole situation all the more agonizing. Yet it would have been even more cruel to let her leave the Grewars' cottage without saying or doing anything further; although this, she reminded herself, was evidently what he had intended doing until they'd discovered her car wouldn't start. He had been angry about the car's failure. He had even accused her of tampering with the engine....

He broke into her thoughts. "See—there at the bend? That's the tree the Bentley crashed into. You can still see where the bark was scraped off the trunk...."

The scars were plainly visible. Monica looked at them and shuddered. She said, her voice small, "To think you might have been killed! And if, God forbid, such a terrible thing had happened, I would never have known. I would have gone on thinking that you didn't come to Prestwick that morning because...."

"Because?"

"Because knowing me had been only a...relatively unimportant incident in your life."

He didn't answer her immediately. The road to the castle, she saw, was just past the bend, and now he swung into it. Only then did he say, "You may think worse of me than ever, Monica, when I finish saying what I must say to you. I am not going to promise to meet you at Prestwick this coming Saturday, when it's time for you to leave Scotland. In fact, I am going to bid goodbye to you now, before we reach the castle. When we *do* reach the castle, please take whatever I may say at face value. If I seem to disclaim any relationship, simply accept it—because that is the way it must be."

She shook her head. "I don't understand you," she told him.

"I can't expect you to," he said flatly, "and I dislike being so blunt. However, we both must face the fact that you *are* an American, after all."

"What do you mean by that?" she demanded, stung by his tone.

"In part, that I realize full well you are captivated by the mystique of a title, the history, the romance...just as you were captivated originally by your first sight of the castle. But all of that—well, it is so much dross, Monica."

"Oh?"

"Yes," he said. "The days of the knights clanking around in armor, whether Scottish or English or whatever, are over. Chivalry is dead, for all practical purposes. Yet those of us whose inheritance dates back to those age-old times must also exist. . . for all practical purposes. What I am trying to say, though I don't enjoy phrasing it in this way, is that it is essential I marry a rich woman—an heiress, in fact—if I am to keep up Monbraithe. Do you fall into that category?''

He flung the question out to her, and she shrank back, staring at him in disbelief. ''No,'' she told him. ''No, I don't. You know very well that I don't. I've never pretended to you to be anything other than I am. And I am not one of those Americans whose antecedents discovered oil wells or invented automobiles or started cereal factories.''

''Very well, then,'' Ian went on coolly. ''Despite my *personal* feelings, the conclusion that must be reached is an obvious one, wouldn't you say? You are not for me.''

She sagged back and closed her eyes, staggered mentally and emotionally by his words, knowing that when she emerged from this she was going to feel far more battered, more bruised, than she would have had he slapped her physically.

The car slowed, and she saw that the gates of Monbraithe Castle were just ahead of them. Mustering all the dignity she could manage, she declared coldly, ''If my car is ready, I shall start back to Glasgow immediately. There is no need for me to go on to the castle with you, as you seem to have intended me to do.''

She peered ahead anxiously, her spirits falling even further when she saw that her little rental car was no longer parked by the gatekeeper's cottage.

Following her gaze, Ian suggested, "Walter probably has it. He fancies himself quite a mechanic. We shall go see," he added, and as he touched the horn Monica saw Angus Grewar slowly coming toward them.

CHAPTER ELEVEN

VIEWED BY DAYLIGHT, the castle was even more imposing than she'd expected it would be. In fact, it was an architectural gem built of gray stone and perfectly proportioned, with towers, turrets, everything but a moat filled with water.

The rental car was parked in front of the main entrance, and there was a service truck just beyond it. Two men were working over the car, and one of them was wearing white overalls, evidently having come from the garage in Balloch. The other, a plump tawny-haired man wearing brown corduroy pants and a rust-colored pullover sweater, straightened and turned to face them.

Ian brought the MGA to what Monica considered a needlessly screeching stop. "Well, Bobby, I see you've finally arrived," he observed. "Have you helped him diagnose the problem, Walter?"

Walter MacGregor, who looked to Monica like an oversized teddy bear, said mildly, "I was only trying to help out a bit, Ian. Bobby said he could use a hand."

"Bobby is being paid to use his own hands," Ian pointed out in a voice so cold that Monica flinched at the sound of it.

The man in the white overalls now stood up, and she saw, to her surprise, that he was unexpectedly familiar. He was thin faced, dark haired, and she recognized him at once as the driver of the truck that earlier had swung across her path in the gift shop's parking lot.

Simultaneously, she noted the flicker of recognition in his dark eyes, but he said only, "Mr. Mac-Gregor wished to help me, m'laird."

"Very well," Ian said with a haughtiness that made Monica realize fully, for the first time, that he was indeed the earl of Monbraithe!

He got out of the MGA, then walked around and opened Monica's door for her, all but sweeping her out of the car and through the entrance to Monbraithe Castle without even pausing to introduce her to his cousin. Then, over his shoulder, he called back, "When you've finished, come and fetch us, Walter." And without even seeing him do so, Monica was sure that Walter was nodding obediently.

A second later she was transfixed, despite herself, as Ian led her into the castle's vast main entrance hall. It was in actuality a rotunda, with a sweeping stone staircase at the far end. Recessed alcoves held busts of earlier MacGregors, while tapestries vied for position with formidable family portraits, these done in dark-hued oils. Oriental rugs, undoubtedly priceless, were scattered across marble floors. Spears of a significance she couldn't fathom, except to realize that they must be connected to the clan warfare of earlier days, were grouped around in clusters. A huge crystal chandelier dominated the vaulted ceiling, and it was easy to imagine how the hall must look on formal occasions, with the chandelier blazing, the men stalwart and handsome in their kilts, the women entrancingly lovely in long, beautifully colored gowns, and the champagne flowing.

Now a tall slim woman with dark hair and a gardenia-white complexion came toward them. Ian introduced them, "Monica Winthrop—my Aunt Jane."

Monica felt that she should curtsy, or certainly that she should do *something*, but before she could do anything at all Jane MacGregor said, "I'm delighted to meet you. We've heard a good bit about Ian's American friend."

Monica did not so much as glance at Ian, yet she could feel his warning as clearly as if he had voiced it. Immediately she responded, "It's kind of you to welcome me, Lady MacGregor, but I imagine Ian has a number of American friends." And she could sense at once that he had relaxed.

She had not intended the "Lady MacGregor" as a slight; in fact she was not at all certain, at this point, just who of Ian's family merited a title and who didn't. His explanation, in a way, had made things even more confusing to her. But now she knew at once that she had made a mistake, and the frostiness of Jane's tone confirmed it.

"Mrs. MacGregor," she said simply, then added with a glance at Ian, "Possibly Ian does have more than one American friend...."

Ian broke in lightly, "I've told you that I'm quite a

cosmopolite, dear aunt. But no matter—'tis Miss
Winthrop we are entertaining now. Would you like
to have a whisky, Monica?''

Although normally she didn't care much for
Scotch, Monica knew only too well that she needed
all the fortitude she could get right now, even though
she'd never had much confidence in the kind of
strength that comes out of a bottle. ''Yes, thank you,
I would,'' she said quickly.

She followed Ian into a relatively small room, a
drawing room of sorts, which was furnished very formally with gilt-framed chairs and couches upholstered in beautiful tapestry. The small bar to one side
was the only modern note, and now Ian busied himself with bottles and glasses, asking at the same time,
''Will you join us, Jane?''

''I'll have a sherry, please,'' his aunt said.

''Very well. Monica, do you want ice?''

She did, most definitely. In fact, she wanted a lot
of ice. But she thrust this particular Americanism to
the background and answered stoically, ''Just water
will be fine, thank you.''

She thought she noted a faint flicker of amusement
pass over Jane MacGregor's face, but the older
woman said only, ''What brings you to Castle Monbraithe, Miss Winthrop?''

There was something decidedly supercilious about
the question. Jane MacGregor's inference that she
undoubtedly didn't belong in such a place as the castle was patently clear. Monica could feel herself
bristling and knew that it would be more than easy to
be goaded into a sharp reply. But all at once the en-

tire matter became a game to her, perhaps, she conceded, because of the unreality of the setting. She'd visited her share of castles, true, both as a tourist and, more recently, as a tour guide; but being *here* was like living in a fantasy. It was as if she'd suddenly been dropped into an entirely different era, and would wake up either back in Boston or, at the least, in her hotel bed in Glasgow.

She flashed a pleasant smile, immersed in her own playacting, and said brightly, "To tell you the truth, I came here purely to ask a favor. I work for a tour group, and when I was in Scotland last year I met Ian briefly. Naturally, I was intrigued to find he actually lived in a castle."

Ian handed his aunt her sherry, and Monica had no problem in reading the glance Jane sent him. It was more than a bit superior, and definitely amused. She might as well have asked aloud, "Where did you ever find her?"

Now she saw Ian frown, and before he could speak she went on hastily, "When I came back to Scotland this year I realized, of course, that the members of the tour group were dying to go through a castle. I mean a really private castle, like this one. So I thought that just possibly—"

Jane MacGregor raised her eyebrows. "Do you mean that you thought you could make arrangements for your group to tour Castle Monbraithe?" she interrupted.

"Yes," Monica said a bit breathlessly. "I know that our customers would be absolutely delighted, and I'm rather new at the job, you see."

"So it would enhance your future prospects with your company, is that it?" Mrs. MacGregor persisted.

"Yes, you might say so."

"Well," Ian's aunt said firmly, "we don't do that sort of thing. I should think Ian would have told you so."

"I hadn't actually got around to asking him," Monica confessed.

"Your whisky," Ian said, and handed her a glass. As she sipped it she nearly gasped aloud at its strength, and shot him an involuntary glance of reproach—only to see that he was smiling.

He explained smoothly, "Monica and I met a year or so ago in Edinburgh, Aunt Jane. She was on one of those whirlwind tours Americans seem to favor so—I mean no offense by that, Monica. In any event, I told her at the time that should she ever return to Scotland I hoped she would get in touch with me. Now she's done so, but I fear it's been to see my house, rather than myself."

"My house, rather than myself." *Oh, you liar,* Monica thought, forcing the words to remain silent. *You consummate liar!*

From the doorway Walter MacGregor announced, "Ah, there you are! The car is ready, Ian. A valve problem, but Bobby and I have fixed it, at least temporarily. That motor needs a good going over. It does seem that the place shouldn't have hired out a car in that condition."

"Miss Winthrop can point that out when she returns it," Ian suggested. "Monica, I don't believe I introduced you to my cousin Walter."

"How d'you do?" Walter said, and added, "I would offer to shake hands, but I fear mine are more than a bit dirty at the moment."

Walter, Monica saw now, was nearly as tall as Ian, but she imagined that he must weigh at least thirty pounds more than Ian did. He was ginger haired, almost as pale as his mother and, as Ian had mentioned, definitely flabby. Monica felt a pang of pity for him, and she replied sympathetically, "I imagine it's grease from my car, isn't it?"

Walter smiled, a surprisingly pleasant smile. "Yes," he admitted, "but 'tis no matter. I enjoy fooling around with car motors when I have the chance."

Ian broke in sharply, "You are quite sure the car is in good enough condition for Miss Winthrop to drive it back to her hotel, aren't you, Walter?"

"Oh, definitely," Walter told him. "Bobby took it for a spin along the lake road, and at the moment it's running like a charm. 'Twill do fine for transportation into Glasgow, but I think I would ask for another car at that point if I were you, Miss Winthrop."

"I won't be needing another car," Monica responded.

"Monica will only be in Scotland a short time longer," Ian explained, when Walter looked somewhat puzzled. He added almost rudely, "If you've finished your whisky, Monica, you can be under way. I know you're anxious to get back to Glasgow."

She had barely touched her whisky, but she agreed hastily, "Yes, I am," and this certainly was the truth.

She stood. "I'm so pleased to have met you, Lady—Mrs. MacGregor," she said. "And you, Mr. Mac-Gregor."

Jane managed a remarkably regal nod. "It has been my pleasure, Miss Winthrop," she answered coolly.

Walter, his light blue eyes definitely appreciative, hesitated for just a second and then volunteered, "I can drive you to Glasgow if you've any hesitation about handling the car yourself. I can always find someone to bring me back to the castle."

She was touched by his offer. "Thank you very much," she said, "but I'm sure I'll be able to manage."

"Monica's a most competent driver," Ian cut in, as if that finished the matter, even though he actually knew nothing at all about her driving habits.

She left the castle with Ian literally at her heels, feeling as if he were pushing her out the door. Her little rental car was still parked at the entrance, but Bobby Grier had left with his service truck. Ian's red MGA also had disappeared; she imagined Angus Grewar must have garaged it.

Ian, having closed the door behind her, lingered to ask, "Are you sure you know the way back to Glasgow?"

"Yes."

"Keep straight to it," he said. "No detours, mind you. I'd suggest you not take any more detours for the rest of your stay in Scotland."

She looked up at him directly, forcing him to meet her eyes. "Is that an order, m'laird?" she asked mockingly, and was satisfied when she saw a dull red stain edging its way into his cheeks.

Briefly, there was pure misery in his blue eyes as he told her huskily, "I hate this! Oh, my God, Monica, it tears me apart knowing how you must feel! If this were another time, another place. . . ."

"But it isn't, is it?" she demanded, her anger flaring. "Never mind. You've not the slightest cause to worry. I should say that you've accounted quite satisfactorily for your American friend. Or perhaps it would be more accurate to say that she accounted for herself—for you!"

She turned the ignition switch, thankful to hear the engine roar into action, then started off without another glance at him. But her own cheeks were burning, and she would have sworn that she literally could feel his eyes boring into her back as she drove on down the driveway. The gate had been left open, but neither Annie nor Angus Grewar was in evidence, which was just as well. Right now she wanted nothing to do with anyone even remotely connected with the MacGregors of Monbraithe!

As she turned out onto the main road she was painfully conscious of Loch Lomond ahead of her, its waters darkening now with the approach of night. She bit her lips, the words coming unbidden into her mind: "By yon bonnie banks. . .and by yon bonnie braes. . . ."

"The hell with the bonnie banks and the bonnie braes!" she said aloud furiously, and then tried to put everything—and everyone—behind her as she headed back toward Glasgow.

DOUGLAS SAID EXPLOSIVELY, "Well!"

Iris put in more softly, "We're not asking you for any explanation, love. I know I told you that you could have the day to yourself. Still, we've been back and had dinner and—"

"I had car trouble," Monica explained. "It was near that town at the end of Loch Lomond—Balloch, isn't it? You can check with the garage there if you like."

"Love," Iris protested, "you needn't get your back up so! You act as if you think we're trying to spy on you, and that's not the idea at all, believe me. It's just that in a group situation such as this one—"

"The fact of the matter," Douglas interrupted gruffly, "is that Iris and I both have been worried about you, thinking about you driving around by yourself on 'the wrong side of the road' and all that. But you're here now, so it's all right. Did you have dinner?"

"No. But I'm not hungry."

"Then," Douglas suggested, "how about a sandwich in the lounge and perhaps a gin and bitters? Would that suffice?"

"You've a love," Monica told him, and meant it. At the moment Douglas seemed like a tower of strength to her.

True, he was a Scot even as Ian was, with all of that same overwhelming history in his background. Yet just now he seemed so much more *human*. Possibly, she thought grimly, that was because he was not a titled nobleman. For Ian, as he himself had made quite clear, very definitely belonged in a society that she had always considered somewhat archaic. Although he had professed to despise grouse shooting and sheep raising and all the rest of it, he *was* the earl of Monbraithe; he had his own castle, his own estate and everything else that went with such a position...including, she decided, a full measure of arrogance!

In Ian's scheme of things there was no place for this particular American, Monica reminded herself once again. No place at all! His uncle, wise man that he had been, had known that a year ago.

Douglas said now, "Come along. I'll take you to the lounge. Will you join us, Iris?"

"No, thank you," Iris refused. "I believe I shall turn in, since I doubt anyone will be wanting any of our services for the rest of the night. Everyone was quite exhausted after the Highlands jaunt," she added to Monica.

Monica managed a smile. "Did Mrs. Ewing see the Loch Ness monster?" she asked.

"I imagine she thinks she did," Iris told her. "God knows how many pictures she took on the scene. Perhaps she fancies the monster will loom up in at least one of them! But even she was tired tonight. Most of the group," she continued, returning to business, "have had dinner and have gone to bed, though I believe a few are having a nightcap in the lounge. In any event, as I've said, they won't be wanting us. You've a key to our room, haven't you, love?"

"Yes," Monica said.

"Very well, then, I shall lock the door behind me."

Iris left them with a brief wave of the hand, and almost immediately Douglas said tersely, "Where *are* you, Monica? Miles and miles away, I should say. Back on Loch Lomond, perhaps? By yon bonnie banks and by yon bonnie braes? Who *is* he?"

She stared at him, momentarily unable to answer, and he challenged her, still curiously angry, "Don't you realize that I knew there must be someone across the room the other night? Someone who meant a great deal to you? You and I had been having a good time together, and then all at once you were lost to me; your eyes kept straying. Yours is a most expressive face; your eyes can talk for themselves when they wish. I knew just then that they were saying volumes, but it was not to me. Then the pianist started to play 'Loch Lomond,' a rare enough song to hear in such a smart restaurant. 'Twould be rather like someone playing 'Swanee River' in one of your supper clubs in the States." Douglas shook his head. "Did you really think we Scots are all that dense?" he demanded.

"No," she said, not knowing whether to laugh or to cry, and caught somewhere in between. "I don't think you Scots are dense at all. Would that you were a bit more so!"

For an answer Douglas took her by the arm. "'Tis that gin and bitters you are needing just now," he told her, and Monica walked dutifully by his side into the lounge.

Almost at once she was engulfed in what at first

seemed to be a cloud of turquoise. It turned out to be Mrs. Ewing, enveloped in the long mohair stole she had given Monica as a gift only the day before.

"We've missed you, dear," the older woman declared promptly. "Also, I'm afraid you're going to think I'm the most dreadful kind of an Indian giver!" She held out a swath of the stole. "As you know, this was a present to you. I intended to give the coral one to my niece and to keep the red one for myself—it will be perfect for Christmas parties. Tonight, though, when I put on this dress I realized your stole would match it almost exactly, so I asked Iris if she thought you'd mind very much if I borrowed it back just for the evening. She said she was sure you wouldn't, and she went and got it out of your room for me. I hope you *don't* mind?"

"Of course not," Monica assured her.

"Well, I'm glad," Mrs. Ewing admitted. "I've felt like a regular thief." She smiled, the matter solved. "Good night, then."

"Good night," Monica said. "And please keep the stole for as long as you wish. You may want to wear it again with that lovely dress."

As they crossed the lounge, Douglas remarked, "She's a funny old duck but most likable, I admit, when she isn't talking one's ear off. You Americans do tend to be chatty!"

"Don't start knocking Americans," Monica advised him. "I'm in danger of becoming downright anti-Scottish as it is, and I *surely* shall be if I hear any more slurs against my nationality."

Douglas grinned. "You'll have to explain that

statement," he warned her. "It sounds as if some of my countrymen have been acting out of character, if it's true. But how could a Scot worthy of the name be other than thoroughly conscious of your considerable charms, Monica?"

They found an empty table and settled into the comfortable armchairs on either side of it, and Monica frowned slightly because there was something that wasn't quite right about the way Douglas was talking to her. Then she realized what it was. "You know, Douglas," she said, "I find that your accent varies tremendously. Sometimes you're full of 'thee' and 'ye' and all sorts of little folk touches. Other times you sound as if you've just come down from Oxford."

"Do I now?" he mused, eyeing her speculatively. "Well," he said then, after a moment's contemplation, "whatever your suspicions about me, I am pure Scot. I swear it."

"With nary an English drop of blood in your body, I suppose?"

"Nary," he insisted staunchly.

"Oh, come off it!" Monica was more than a bit weary of Scottish pride. "No one is totally pure-blooded, and what difference does it make anyway?"

"It can make a great deal of difference to a Scot," Douglas assured her solemnly.

Monica suddenly felt very tired, and she found herself wishing that they actually were at the eve of Saturday. It was time for her to leave Scotland!

She admitted slowly, "I suppose I don't really understand Scots. It seems to me you have too much history to contend with, too much violence, far too much intrigue. We Americans are ever so much simpler."

Douglas beckoned to a waiter hovering nearby and ordered, "Whisky for me and gin and bitters for the lady—with a liberal amount of ice, if you please. And a sliced-chicken sandwich for the lady, too."

Monica smiled faintly. "Thank you, Douglas."

"You're quite welcome. 'Tis glad I am to be of service."

"Are you?"

"Just what do you mean by that?"

"Only that I don't quite believe in your 'thee's and 'ye's," she told him. "I admit that they're perhaps a necessary stock in trade—or that you think they are because you feel this is what Americans expect to hear. But even so. . . ."

"Yes?"

"There's something that doesn't ring true about you, Douglas," she said frankly.

He frowned. "Monica," he began, but she held up her hand.

"Not tonight," she told him. "I'm not up to explanations tonight. Forgive me—I shouldn't have brought it up."

His gaze was entirely too discerning. He said softly, "You must have had quite a day at Loch Lomond."

Was she reading a hidden meaning into this statement? At the moment Douglas didn't seem like the friendly good-natured Scot she'd become accustomed to.

She was spared an answer because their drinks came, followed shortly thereafter by the sandwich. And when she had finished both, Douglas said firmly, "Well, 'tis up to join Iris for you! Will you be coming to the Trossachs with us in the morning?"

"Yes," she answered, and had the odd feeling that he was relieved, though she couldn't see why he should be.

CHAPTER TWELVE

THE GOOD WEATHER HELD, and the tour group going to the Trossachs left the hotel promptly at nine o'clock. Monica realized almost at once that they were traveling in the direction of Loch Lomond, and when they came to Balloch it was as if she were gripped by a purely physical pain. She didn't think she could bear to go on past the road that led to Castle Monbraithe, and when Donald Ferguson, at the wheel of the bus, took a turn to the right, she breathed a sigh of deep relief. Loch Lomond was nearby, she knew, but at least she couldn't see it.

Today the sun seemed to be finding new dimensions in the gold of the bracken, and the cloudless sky was an incredible shade of blue. It was not right or even remotely fair for her heart to ache so on such a glorious day, Monica told herself, and resentment of Ian came like a piercing shard. She could almost imagine just now that she hated him.

For that matter, thoughts of Ian at all, placed in the context of her experience yesterday, had a grimness about them, a total nightmare unreality. Yet yesterday had happened, she reminded herself soberly. And at the end of it Ian had showed her the door... or the gate... or whatever one wanted to call it. He had made it very clear that he wanted to be rid of her.

She forced her thoughts away from the misery of introspection and concentrated upon Douglas, who had picked up the microphone and was addressing the passengers.

"So," he was saying easily, "today we shall be visiting Scotland's 'bristly country.' 'Tis a land full of spiky trees and steep hills, and it seems to be cobwebbed with roads that twist and turn, each of them tossing out to ye a view of breathless beauty at every bend."

Monica smiled, for Douglas was back in full form today. His speech, she knew, was going to be laced with "thee" and "ye," and he was rolling his *r*'s roundly. He actually was a professional Scot, she found herself thinking with some amusement, and at that very moment he looked across at her and met her eye.

Obviously he couldn't resist a slight smile, but then he continued imperturbably, "Strictly speaking, the Trossachs are a wooded gorge running from Loch Achray to Loch Katrine. I shall direct ye especially to Loch Katrine when we come to it, for 'tis the loch Scott chose to immortalize with his famous poem 'The Lady of the Lake.' Loch Katrine has a more practical function, as well. For well over a century, this loch has provided Glasgow with its water supply. I might add that many of the lochs today are under use by the Scotland Hydro-Electric Board to provide water needed, especially in some of the newer, industrial communities. 'Tis a credit to the authorities that they've managed to achieve progress without marring the beauty of our glorious countryside.''

Douglas rolled the *r* in ''glorious'' with a definite roguishness, and this time when his eye caught Monica's he actually winked.

''Now,'' he said, ''there is a bit more to be said about the lochs and such in this region, some of which I've already told ye. For example, many of ye can see the River Clyde from the windows of your hotel rooms, and ye know that 'tis along this river that the famous *Queens*, and many of the most important ships ever to be used for transatlantic trade, were built. 'Tis a sad thing, to my mind, that they no longer rule the seas.

''The Clyde, as ye know, twists southward, the Firth of Clyde leading to the sea. And from it sea lochs strike north. Loch Long, deep enough for the passage of great oil tankers, probes out to adjoin Loch Lomond, which now lies not far to our left. 'Tis Loch Lomond and the Trossachs themselves that we think of when we contemplate this very beautiful region of Scotland, and to my mind 'tis one of the loveliest sections of all in a country that surely, for its size, was more than abundantly blessed by nature,'' Douglas added with obvious satisfaction.

''Also, as I explained to those of ye yesterday who took the Highlands trip, the Loch Lomond area and the adjoining Trossachs are actually a district of the Highlands, though obviously not nearly so stark and overwhelming in contour as the countryside ye passed through on your way north. 'Tis a district just as dramatic in history, though, and again we can give

credit to Sir Walter Scott for making this corner of
Scotland famous for all times. 'Twas this area that he
used as the setting for his novel, *Rob Roy*, and now
this section is often called, 'Rob Roy's Country.'

"So," Douglas continued, "ye may ask me exactly
who *was* Rob Roy, and whether or not he was a real
person or a creation of a writer's mind. I will answer
by saying to ye that he is as real as Robin Hood, whom
ye may ken a bit better. Rob Roy, that is, was our
Scottish Robin Hood. There are the same legends of
great courage and chivalry surrounding him. Like
Robin Hood—who, of course, was a Sassenach—he
was on the side of the oppressed. He knew deprivation
on a personal basis because his own clan had suffered
under the hands of more powerful neighbors and for a
time had known banishment, becoming landless, for-
bidden to use even their own name or to claim their
royal inheritance. Thus Rob Roy, like Robin Hood,
became what would be called today an enemy of society. He robbed the rich and gave to the poor. He
belonged, incidentally," Douglas went on, an odd
deliberation to his words, "to the clan MacGregor."

The clan MacGregor! As she heard this, Monica's
head snapped upward, and she found herself staring
at Douglas, realizing that he was watching her closely,
his expression unfathomable.

"The MacGregors came to fare considerably better
later on," Douglas continued, still with that delib-
erateness that she suspected was intended to make her
attend his words. "As a matter of fact, some of ye may
remember that the other day when we were at the gift
shop on Loch Lomond there was quite an impressive

castle to be seen on the opposite banks of the loch. 'Twas Castle Monbraithe, home of the earl of Monbraithe, who is a MacGregor.''

"Does the family still live there?" a member of the tour group asked.

"Aye," Douglas said. "Last year the old laird was killed in a hunting accident. Now 'tis the new, young laird, his nephew, who has taken over."

"Is he tall, dark and handsome?" one of the women asked, with a slight giggle.

"I wouldna ken," Douglas said briefly, and as their eyes clashed Monica shivered.

Douglas knows, she told herself. *He knows, at least he surely suspects, that Ian is the Scot in my life. I'd say he even knows Ian himself!*

It was an astonishing revelation. Only last night, in the lounge, she remembered, she had accused Douglas of faking a part of his Scottish accent, of at times making himself sound more provincial than he really was. Now doubts came to merge with her curiosity about him, and suddenly he looked away, almost as if he feared her ferreting out his secrets.

What *were* his secrets, she wondered. Was Douglas merely an attractive young man, with the gift of gab and a knowledge of his local history, who had taken up tour guiding because it offered a reasonably decent living? Or did he have an alter ego? Did his tour guiding tie in with some other, much more important work?

TIME PASSED, and Monica tried to get her thoughts in order, for she could feel herself on the very verge of personal chaos. The tour group had become entranced

with some of Douglas's stories about the legendary
Rob Roy, and now Douglas assured them that Rob
had indeed been a "real" person. He promised that he
would show them Glen Gyle, where the Scottish Robin
Hood had been born in 1671. This glen stretched from
the head of Loch Katrine back to Ardlui, which was at
the very head of Loch Lomond.

He also regaled them with stories of Helen Mac-
Gregor, who had been Rob Roy's wife and was re-
puted to have defeated government forces in the pass
of Loch Ard. This, as it happened, proved to be an
especially scenic place.

"Ye should come back in the spring, when the
rhododendrons are in full bloom along the shores,"
Douglas observed when the bus stopped so that they
could gaze out over the sapphire waters of the loch.
"'Tis the most glorious of sights. As to Helen
MacGregor's victory," he continued, "'tis said that
her husband was away at the time, and so it was she
who led the clan. Some say 'tis true, others claim this
a bit of fiction," Douglas conceded.

"What do you say?" Mrs. Ewing challenged, and
Douglas chuckled.

"'Tis not something I'm about to get into an argument over, especially with a woman," he said good-
naturedly, and several of the men laughed.

They stopped for lunch at a delightful restaurant in
Aberfoyle, then continued on through this "bristly
country" where, as Douglas had promised, each
bend in the road offered a new and unexpected vista
of pure beauty.

"'Twas a time of war hereabouts, in the days of

Rob Roy,'' Douglas told the group rather gloomily. '' 'Tis difficult to believe that, for it is so intensely peaceful, would ye not say?''

There was a chorus of agreement, and he continued, "Each season has its glory; nature's colors merge, blending palettes. Ah, 'tis carried away I get when I think of it," he added, sounding more than a little theatrical in Monica's opinion. But then he went on softly, in so mellow a voice that even she was captivated, "In his novel Scott has Rob Roy say, 'Were I to lose sight of my native hills, my heart would sink, and my arm would shrink like fern in the winter's frost.' And then he concludes, 'The heather we have trod on while living shall sweetly bloom over us when dead.' And Helen MacGregor herself cries, 'Quit the land of my sires—never!'

"There are many among us Scots," Douglas said, this very solemnly, "who still feel exactly that way today...."

Toward midafternoon they stopped at a woolen mill. It was a tumbled barnlike place at the edge of a stream, but since Douglas had told them there was an end-of-the-season sale going on, it became an obvious Mecca to the women on the tour. They hurried out of the bus, almost falling over one another in their eagerness to get into the ramshackle building, whose wide doors were invitingly open to display garments in all sorts of colors, as tempting as the candy canes on a Christmas tree.

Standing by the bus, Douglas lighted a cigarette and shook his head as he looked after them. "They'd stay the rest of the day and all night if I didn't blow the whistle on them,'' he said. ''What about you, Monica? Don't you want some scarves or mittens, or perhaps a Shetland sweater to take home with you?''

''No,'' she told him. ''Not this trip.''

''Oh? Did you buy your fill of tartans when you were here before?''

She noticed that once again he had reverted to saying ''you'' rather than ''ye'' when he was alone with her. Or at the least the ''ye'' was almost closer to ''you.'' His accent under such circumstances seemed very much like Ian's. Scottish, to be sure. . . but hardly provincial.

She answered a bit stiffly, ''As a matter of fact, I didn't buy much of anything when I was here before.''

''Were you too busy with other matters to tend to shopping?'' Douglas persisted.

She looked him squarely in the eye. ''Why don't you tell me what you really mean by that?'' she suggested.

''Nothing in particular,'' he said, flicking the ashes off the end of his cigarette.

She hesitated for only a moment, then decided that she had nothing to lose in getting down to essentials. Absolutely nothing to lose!

''Douglas,'' she asked him, ''who are you?''

His eyebrows shot upward. ''Who *am* I?'' he echoed. ''Have you suddenly had a touch of amnesia, Monica? I am Douglas MacConnach, remember? The tour guide.''

''Who else are you?''

''What makes you think I might be anyone else?'' he evaded.

"Oh, don't dissemble, Douglas," she said impatiently. "I know perfectly well that you're far more than a tour guide. And you're really a bit too old to be a student...."

He flinched, or at least pretended to. "That's rather a nasty blow, isn't it?" he asked. "I hadn't realized that my years were showing, and as a matter of fact I am not too old to be a student, Monica. As I believe I've told you, I'm interested in pursuing the law, when I've amassed sufficient funds to do so—"

"Maybe," she interrupted. "But you already have a career, don't you? And I don't mean spinning tales about Rob Roy in that delightful phony accent of yours."

Douglas's mouth twitched in the briefest of smiles, then he said, "You do know how to wound a man, don't you? Monica, love, 'tis necessary sometimes to be a bit of an actor."

"Isn't it, though!" she agreed caustically.

"It doesn't become you to be so cynical," Douglas said soberly. "And I mean that."

"What do you expect me to be?" she demanded bitterly. "I feel as if I've fallen into a caldron brimming with intrigue, and I'm apt to drown if I don't get out of it soon!"

He eyed her narrowly. "Isn't that a bit dramatic?"

"*You're* accusing me of being dramatic?" she flung back. "My God, Douglas, it seems to me you're playacting half the time."

"I think I've said it's part of the job," he pointed out levelly.

"Part of which job?" she prodded in a nasty voice.

"Monica," he began, but she held up a deterring hand.

"Please," she said, "no more evasions, no more hedging. If you can't tell the truth, don't say anything!"

His face was expressionless and his voice very quiet as he asked, "Just what do you want to know?"

"You know Ian MacGregor, don't you?" she accused. "The earl of Monbraithe?"

Douglas didn't answer immediately, and she saw his face twist, almost as if it had been contorted by pain. Then he stared down at the ground, his conflicting emotions so obvious to her that they seemed almost tangible.

Very slowly he said, rather then asked, "Then it *is* he!"

"What do you mean?"

Now he looked at her again, and there was distinct anger in his eyes. "A laird, no less," he said, and the way he said it stung her.

She retorted swiftly, "I didn't even know he was titled, and I couldn't care less. In any event, he didn't have a title when I first met him."

Douglas's face was a study in mockery, and the smile that resulted after a moment was purely infuriating. "Are you suggesting that it's possible for an American not to be impressed by a title?" he asked skeptically.

"Yes," Monica said. "Yes, yes, *yes*!"

"All right now," he told her hastily. "Keep your voice down, for God's sake, or the paying customers will be hearing you. The last thing I want is to arouse their curiosity about much of anything. Certainly, not about this. It's not something to be bandied about, I assure you.''

''Then you do admit that there *is* something?'' she challenged him.

''Let me ask you a question before I answer that,'' he countered. ''Are you trying to tell me that the situation would be the same between you and Ian MacGregor if he were not a laird?''

''I don't know what you mean by 'the situation,' '' she replied, her voice tight, ''but certainly matters would not be at all the same between Ian and me if he were not a laird. They would be much, much simpler!''

He stared at her for a moment, so intently that it was hard to meet his eyes, and then his next question came so suddenly, so abruptly, that she was totally unprepared for it.

''What do you know of the Jacobite medallion?'' he asked her.

She stared back, pricked suddenly by caution. Mixed with it was fear for Ian, which came on her without any warning at all; that was much more difficult to understand.

She turned away from Douglas, walking over to a small stand outside a tiny grocer's shop, which stood at the edge of the mill premises. She stared down at the array of paperback novels she saw displayed on it, picking one up and fingering it as if it had attracted her.

She was remembering yesterday's encounter with Ian with a new sort of vividness, and suddenly she knew she couldn't accept what he'd said to her. It was totally out of character for the man she had known. No one, she told herself, could change so completely in the space of a year, no matter how terrible the things that might have happened to him.

Ian had said that he must marry money if he was to keep up Monbraithe; and he had pointed out that the castle, after all, was his inheritance. It followed naturally enough that he would consider its upkeep a prime responsibility, so perhaps what he'd told her in essence was true enough. Perhaps the simplest solution to at least one of his problems was to marry a rich woman. But Ian had been brazen in the way he'd spoken about this—insulting, actually, both in stating the facts of his situation and in giving his reasons for not seeing her again. And she'd been so stunned by his attitude that she'd slipped into a kind of mental fog, which only now was beginning to lift.

Her lips lightened. Whatever else he might be, she chastised herself, she should have known that Ian MacGregor was no fortune hunter. Nor could he possibly have become the cruel callous person he was now pretending to be.

She shuddered, and felt a twinge of something close to fear—but for Ian, not for herself. Dear God, his uncle had been *murdered*, and for that matter he'd very nearly been murdered himself! He'd made it plain enough that one of his reasons for not contacting her was that he wanted to keep her out of his problems. Now she had no doubt that he really *was* concerned for her safety should she become involved with him, although she couldn't understand why.

Nevertheless, Ian still had enemies; he had been open about that. And certainly he had a grasping aunt. There seemed no doubt that Jane MacGregor wanted to be the chatelaine of Castle Monbraithe more than she wanted anything else. And she could be, Monica realized anew, if Ian were to die and her son were to inherit. With Walter the earl of Monbraithe, Jane's position would be firmly established.

As for Walter...it seemed difficult to believe that he could be Jane's son, yet there was often truth to the old cliché about appearances being deceiving. Though it was hard to imagine such a thing, the possibility had to be faced that beneath that placid teddy-bear exterior Walter could be devious and grasping.

Douglas, at her shoulder now, picked a book off the rack himself and pretended to study it. Then he said softly, "In a sense you've answered my question, Monica. The Jacobite medallion obviously has meaning for you."

"Suppose it does?" she challenged.

"I should like to know a bit more about the kind of meaning," he went on, his voice still low and his eyes on the book in his hand.

Monica hesitated for only an instant. Then she said firmly, "And I would like to know more about *you*, Douglas. I think I've made that fairly clear."

His smile was a shade too placid. "And what would you like to know about me, Monica?"

"Who are you, Douglas?"

Douglas put the book he'd been holding back on the rack. "I think some of our party are tiring of the woolen shop," he observed. "At least, some of the men are clustering in the doorway. We'd best go back to the bus."

"I refuse to go *near* the bus until you answer my question," she told him staunchly.

"Very well," he gave in. "I shall tell you 'who I am,' though that isn't precisely the way I would put it. Rather, it's a question of what I do." He sighed. "The fact of the matter is that I am a government agent," he said heavily.

"A spy!"

"No," Douglas explained wearily, "not a spy. I've no liking for that word, nor do I consider that it applies to me. I see skepticism in your eyes. Very well—take a quick glance at this, will you please, without being too obvious about it."

Glancing down at the small leather folder he thrust out at her, she scanned its contents hastily. She felt her fingers grow cold as she handed it back to him. There was a definite shock value to knowing that Douglas was official—very official indeed.

"Now, perhaps, will you tell me what the Jacobite medallion means to you?" he persisted.

She said slowly, "I know only that it's a treasure of sorts, and that it has been passed along in Ian MacGregor's family for a long time. I think it dates back to your Bonnie Prince Charlie."

"Did you know that it had been stolen?"

"No. I know that a year ago it was missing. At least, it wasn't where it was supposed to be, which, as I understand it, was in a cabinet at the castle. I assumed it had been found, though, long since."

Douglas shook his head. "Now you're dissembling," he told her. "Do you have it yourself by any chance?"

She stepped back as if he had struck her. "Do *I* have it?" she echoed, furious.

"Please," Douglas said hastily. "Keep your voice down, will you, Monica?"

"You expect me to be sweet and calm when you've just accused me of being a thief?" she demanded.

"It was not my intention to accuse you of anything."

"Then you and your intentions don't match with each other very well. I don't know how else you can expect me to take it, Douglas. Do I have the Jacobite medallion? My God, what do you think I would be doing with it? I don't give a damn for your Scottish heirlooms! In fact, I can't wait for Saturday, so that I can get out of this country forever and ever and ever—"

"Please," Douglas said insistently. "In another minute you'll be breaking into tears, and that wouldn't do at all!"

"Then," she suggested, "you'd better explain yourself, and you'd also better tell me who you are! If you don't, so help me, I'm going to start screaming!"

"Will you *please* keep your voice down," Douglas warned, between clenched teeth. "For heaven's sake, can't you see that this is not something to be broadcast? All right, it is my fault, the whole thing, I admit it. It was poor timing on my part to bring the subject up here, in the middle of a tour. On the other hand, you'll have to admit that I've had few opportunities to speak with you alone lately.''

''What about last night?'' she asked him.

''You were too tired last night to get into anything like this. Monica. . .I think you should understand that I am on your side in this matter, insofar as the earl of Monbraithe is concerned.''

''What is that supposed to mean?''

''A number of us, both in government service and out of it, consider it highly important to find out whether or not Ian MacGregor really *did* kill his uncle,'' Douglas answered slowly, his voice low as he kept his eyes on the entrance to the woolen mill. ''That much I can tell you. A 'not proven' verdict in such a case is hardly satisfactory. I think it goes without saying that this type of verdict primarily benefits the guilty. If, in fact, Ian MacGregor is innocent—and, like many others, I hope he is—then he has suffered a great deal in a way in which he shouldn't have been made to suffer at all. Certainly his name should be cleared so that he can go on to live a life free of suspicion. If, on the other hand, he is guilty, then that fact should be established without doubt, and he should be punished for his crime.''

''And what is your part in all of this, Douglas?''

''I have been asked to get at the truth,'' he admitted.

''And you're playing tour guide in order to do so?''

''It seemed a reasonably good cover,'' Douglas responded, with a faint smile. ''I'm not unfamiliar with the work; in fact I did quite a bit of this sort of

thing while I was in college, to help with expenses.
That's one reason why we decided upon handling
matters this way: I'd had the experience, and it was
easy enough to slip back into the role.''

"Even to the elaborate accent?" she mocked.

"Even to the elaborate accent," he agreed calmly.
"The job was arranged, obviously. The Magic Carpets Unlimited people were entirely cooperative. I
would say that this is something that surely gives me
a perfect opportunity to do what I need to do. As a
tour guide I can wander around quite freely without
raising too many suspicious eyebrows.''

He looked down at her, his face grave. '' 'Tis a risk
I am taking, telling you this,'' he told her seriously.
"You realize that, I'm sure. On the other hand, it
seems to me it would be almost more of a risk to have
you go around shouting questions I can't answer, at
the worst possible times. So, not for my sake alone
but for Ian MacGregor's, as well, I am asking you to
keep my confidence. You mustn't say a word about
this to anyone, not even to Iris.''

"Iris isn't in league with you, then?"

There was a hint of bitterness in Douglas's smile.
"No," he said, "Iris is not in league with me at all.
In any way. . . more's the pity.''

CHAPTER THIRTEEN

THE TOUR RESUMED, and for the rest of the afternoon Douglas outdid himself, detailing bits of Scottish history, pointing out the local flora and fauna and making jokes in a broad yet remarkably comprehensible dialect that delighted his customers. He seldom so much as glanced toward Monica.

That was just as well, for her mind was whirling, her confusion intense. She tried to sort out things a step at a time, but inevitably the steps seemed to telescope. It was difficult to get used to the thought of Douglas as a government agent, on a mission to establish Ian's innocence—or to prove his guilt! Further, Douglas had said that a number of people "both in government service and out of it" were involved in this effort. Fortunately, most of them at least seemed to be on Ian's side.

Ian. Remembering the fatigue in his beloved face, the misery in his eyes, and his recital—almost toneless at times—of the hideous events at Monbraithe a year ago, Monica found herself moved even more deeply than she'd been yesterday, and she had to fight back brimming tears. Ian had stated very plainly that he wouldn't be coming to Prestwick Saturday. His goodbye had been so final, so ultimate, that she flinched at the memory of it. In the end he had been totally cold and cutting.

Why? With the drone of Douglas's voice in the background as he spoke to the passengers, she tried to separate emotion and logic and to concentrate on logic just now . . . but it wasn't easy.

There was a chance, to be sure, that Ian wanted her to go back to America because he felt that associating with him could actually put her in danger. But it was even more likely, she felt dismally, that he considered her a stumbling block in the solution of his problems. In the harsh light of reality, she had to concede that there really *was* no place in the life scheme of Ian MacGregor, earl of Monbraithe, for Miss Monica Winthrop of Boston, Massachusetts.

Monica had a sudden vision of the tall young woman with sleek blond hair and a decidedly wistful quality that was definitely appealing. Ellen. The woman who, it had to be faced, was undoubtedly perfect for Ian in many ways. Even that glimpse of her at Prestonfield had given an impression of quiet confidence despite the wistfulness; an impression that had been reinforced in the hotel dining room the other night.

Further, she was remembering now that Ian had told her Ellen had visited him while he was a patient in an Edinburgh hospital, over the course of long and undoubtedly weary months. In fact, he had mentioned that he'd pretended to himself, in the beginning, that it was she, Monica, who was visiting him. Then later he had welcomed Ellen for her own sake.

True, he must have been lonely at the time, lonely and bewildered, so that almost any visitor would have been welcome. Monica tried to tell herself this, but it didn't really wash. No, by the end of Ian's hospital stay there was a good chance that Ellen had been standing totally on her own with him. And even though he'd insisted they weren't in love with each other, he admitted she was very dear to him. Now the nagging memory came, too, that Ellen's father was a wealthy man. Added to this was the obvious fact that she and her family had stood by Ian in his time of trial—literally. The "not proven" verdict had caused no alienation; that was obvious. The recent dinner at Prestonfield House surely indicated a decided bond of some sort.

Well, Ian had said that Ellen's father owned a whisky distillery; and Ian, after all, *was* a laird, a member of the Scottish nobility. In the social scheme of things, this surely would mean a step upward for the daughter in the family.

Monica sighed deeply. It was too much, it was all too much, and she was beginning to have a throbbing headache. She became aware that Douglas had stopped talking, and glancing out the window, she saw that they were on the final leg of the trip, almost back at the hotel.

The bus pulled in at the entrance, and there was the usual flurry of activity as the passengers reached for the numerous bags containing the purchases they'd made at the woolen mill and elsewhere. As she watched the group get off the bus, Monica couldn't repress a rather wry smile. No wonder shopkeepers were so happy to see American tourists loom up on their local scenes!

Douglas, lingering behind, asked quietly, "Will you join me for dinner?"

"Thanks, but no," Monica told him. "Not tonight. I think I'll opt for a hot bath and a rest, if I'm not going to be needed for a while."

"'Twill do you no good to go without eating," Douglas pointed out, and she sensed he was about to become adamant about this.

"Well," she conceded, "maybe I'll stop in at the lounge later and have a sandwich."

"Very well," Douglas said. "I'll meet you there. Take your time; there's no hurry. It's Iris's turn to be on duty at the desk through the dinner hour."

Once upstairs, Monica did take her time, luxuriating in water that fortunately was really hot just now, the bath beautifully augmented by one of the vials of scented bubbling oil she had brought along with her. She forced herself to blot thoughts of everything out of her mind, simply to relax for the moment—and was reasonably successful. Finally she dressed in slacks and a bright patterned blouse, and shortly after nine o'clock she went back downstairs.

A number of the tour members were still at tables in the dining room. She could hear them laughing and chatting with one another and had to admit, strictly to herself, that her fellow countrymen en masse did tend to be a bit loud.

Douglas was waiting in a corner of the lounge; he stood and beckoned when he saw her. She went to join him a bit reluctantly, because she wasn't nearly as sure of him as last night, when she'd been so appreciative of his consideration for her comfort. Now he was no longer simply a friend; he was much more of a stranger. A government agent. It remained difficult to accept this fact.

As she sat down in the chair he held out for her, he asked, "Whisky?"

"Thanks," she said, "but I'd rather have gin and bitters again. With lots of ice."

He shook his head over this, but nevertheless he went in search of John, the head porter, who took care of such matters as food and drink served in the lounge after hours. Returning, he told her, "I took the liberty of ordering some sandwiches and coffee for both of us, to be served later."

"Thank you."

Douglas offered her a cigarette and she took it. Although she seldom smoked, anything that might steady her nerves, if only for the moment, was fine tonight as far as she was concerned. As he lighted the cigarette for her, however, Monica found that her fingers were trembling, for it was hard to remain on an even keel with Douglas looking at her in such a cool and appraising fashion.

"What is it?" she asked finally, and he frowned.

"I'm sorry," he said. "What I mean to say, actually, is that I'm not about to pretend to you I don't wish we'd never had that conversation this afternoon. I shouldn't have said nearly as much to you as I did. It was. . . unwise of me."

"You mean unprofessional, don't you?"

"Very well, then, unprofessional. You've not said anything to Iris?"

"I haven't even seen Iris since we got back,"

Monica replied impatiently. "I think she's taking a dinner group somewhere."

"How does she seem to you?" Douglas asked unexpectedly.

"Iris?"

"Yes, Iris."

"Are you asking for professional or personal reasons?" she queried suspiciously.

"Gad, you do mistrust me, don't you?" Douglas shook his head ruefully. "For personal reasons, if you must know. Iris has a lot of...very good qualities. But of late she's been difficult."

"I think you know as well as I do that things haven't been going smoothly for her," Monica pointed out.

"Yes, I know that," Douglas admitted gloomily.

He hesitated, evidently trying to decide how much more he should say, and then was spared from saying anything at all by a sudden commotion out in the lobby.

"Well," he observed as they heard voices raised against the sound of decidedly American laughter, "our friends have finally finished with their dinner. Now I suppose some of them will be coming in here for a bit of something or other to lull them to sleep."

From their vantage point in the lounge, they had a fairly clear view of a large section of the lobby. Looking out, Monica saw a number of the tour members engaged in animated conversation, Mrs. Ewing among them.

Mrs. Ewing had taken her at her word about keeping the turquoise stole for as long as she wished. She was wearing it again tonight; in fact she had draped it over her head mantilla-fashion.

Now several people started for the lounge, while the rest headed for the elevator. At the last moment Mrs. Ewing said something to her husband, waved to some of the others and turned away, going in the direction of the front entrance.

Douglas said, "She must have left something on the bus. Well, Donald is probably still around, and if she doesn't find him, I shall go to her rescue."

"Will she need someone to rescue her?" Monica asked.

"She'll need someone with a key to help her get anything out of the bus," Douglas pointed out. "We keep the buses locked when they're not in use. See here, now," he added, glancing toward her drink. "Your gin will do you no good at all if you leave it sitting on the table. Your blasted ice will melt."

"True." Monica raised her glass.

Douglas beckoned to John, indicating that he wanted another whisky, and then he went on thoughtfully, "Tomorrow is our last day. I'm doing the Glasgow tour, incidentally. In the morning we'll be going to Clydebank, where the *Mary* and the *Elizabeth* and so many of those great ships were built. After the port of Glasgow we shall stop at the Kempock Stone, which dates back to prehistoric times. It used to be a custom for couples intending to marry to encircle the stone, in order to get a very special sort of nuptial blessing.

"Glasgow is a fascinating city," he continued. "It grew up around its great cathedral, which is dedicated to St. Mungo, and of course we'll stop there. We'll see the rood screen, which depicts the seven deadly sins, and then St. Mungo's tomb, where a light is always kept burning. We shall also visit Tolbooth Steeple and the factory overlooking the green, which was constructed in the style of the Doge's Palace in Venice. Then, of course, there is George Square, with its many magnificent statues, and the City Chambers, an excellent example of the Italian Renaissance style. After all of this we'll stop for lunch—''

Douglas broke off as he became aware of Monica's expression. "I really didn't mean to ramble on so."

"If I didn't know otherwise," she told him, "I would say that you're completely dedicated to your career as a tour guide."

Douglas had the grace to look a bit shamefaced. "I suppose I was trying to sell you, shall we say, on the idea of accompanying me," he confessed.

She shook her head. "You outrank me, Douglas, remember? All you have to do is tell me my services are required."

"I've not felt the inclination to do that with you, Monica," he said somewhat stiffly.

"No," she admitted, and now it was her turn to feel slightly ashamed. "I'm sorry, Douglas; I suppose I'm just not in a very good mood. Yes, of course I'll go on the Glasgow tour with you tomorrow, if you want me to."

"Only if you wish to," he said. "I refuse to make it an order, Monica. I've no right at all to give you orders anyway. As it is scheduled, however, Iris will stay here at the hotel. There are always last-minute details to attend to when a group is so close to departure, and she is very good at handling such things. I *can* do the Glasgow tour by myself, of course, but I would welcome having you with me, and I could use your help. Also, I think you might enjoy it.''

And also, she thought silently, *if I'm with you there won't be any problems for you in keeping an eye on me.* This idea came to her unbidden, and she found it very disturbing.

''Very well,'' she agreed, ''I'll come.''

''Good. After lunch the afternoon will be free, so that those who haven't purchased their full share of Scottish souvenirs will have the chance to do so.''

''I can't imagine how we'll be able to get everything they've already bought on the airplane as it is,'' Monica said wryly.

''They always manage,'' Douglas assured her. He hesitated, then went on, ''Tomorrow there is to be a rather gala farewell dinner for the group. I hope you will permit me to be your escort.''

''I suppose I'm expected to attend?''

He winced. ''You really don't believe in flattery, do you?''

''No,'' she said honestly. ''Not under the circumstances.''

''And what do you consider the circumstances, Monica?''

''I've come to realize that your interest in me is primarily professional, Douglas,'' she explained, ''and frankly I don't find that at all to my liking. There's absolutely no reason for you to have that sort of interest in me. I don't know exactly what your assignment involves, but I'll say it again: I play no part in anything you might touch upon.''

''You're so sure of that?''

''Yes, I am. I should imagine that a good bit of what you're engaged in involves politics, and I know nothing at all about your Scottish politics, nor do I have any desire to suddenly start studying it.''

Once again Douglas was watching her with an intentness that was disconcerting. ''Are you quite sure of *that*?'' he persisted. ''In your meetings with Ian MacGregor, has he said nothing to you about Scottish politics?''

''Very little,'' she replied. ''Anything that he has told me has merely been part of an effort to try to help me understand something of this country's history and background. And you should know better than I how complicated and involved that is!''

''Did he say nothing to you of devolution?''

Devolution. The word rang in her mind, and now she remembered that Ian had indeed used it. She only hoped that her expression, obviously much too transparent where Douglas was concerned, did not give this fact away.

''Independence,'' Douglas said now. ''Independence from England.''

''Don't you mean revolution?''

''No. *I* don't,'' he said, ''although some people might.'' He toyed with the glass of whisky the head porter had just brought him. ''In recent years, as you must be aware, nationalism has been a rising force all over the world, Monica, sometimes to good effect, sometimes to bad. Scotland has not escaped the trend. There has been a rising tide toward nationalism here, too. Especially since oil was discovered in the North Sea just off our shores, there have been more and more thinking Scots who believe we should have considerably more control of our own affairs than we do. Members of the Scottish National Party are increasingly being sent, in representation, to the English Parliament."

"Are you saying that Scotland wants to be free? A country entirely to itself?" she asked him.

"There are some that do," he said. "There are many more who are considerably more conservative. To them the concept of devolution is actually much closer to what you Americans might call 'home rule.' Under such a policy, Scotland would run a good ninety-eight percent of her own affairs, and yet we would still belong to the United Kingdom. It would mean that substantial powers would be transferred, say, from Parliament in London to a kind of subnational assembly in Edinburgh. There would be a delegation of central government powers without a relinquishing of sovereignty, if you follow me."

He smiled apologetically. "I rather fear my soapbox is showing."

"No," she told him, "as a matter of fact I find all of this very interesting, Douglas. You're right—Ian MacGregor did tell me something about it, but until he did so I thought that all your bantering about the Sassenach came under the heading of rather wellworn jokes."

"Joking often hides deeper feelings," Douglas

said quietly. "As Ian MacGregor also probably told you, it is impossible to understand all of these things in a minute. The fact is, though, that for a long time Scotland has been more than a bit under the British thumb. At moments it has caused quite a blister."

"And yet you yourself wouldn't favor all-out independence?" she asked.

"You mean I wouldn't be in favor of precipitating the sort of conflict you Americans engaged in?" he asked, obviously teasing her, then quickly sobered. "No. I should think not, unless efforts toward devolution failed totally. To be sure, there are those who think that the entire concept of devolution is a misguided one, but my personal feeling is that unless it has indeed become hopelessly strangled by the many complications involved, we could be on our way toward gaining the kind of a democracy I think Scotland should have.

"I," he said, "am something of what you'd call in your country a middle-of-the-roader, I guess. There are also, of course, those conservatives who believe that our national interests lie in thinking first of Britain and then of Scotland. And then there are the radicals."

"The true revolutionaries?"

"Yes. Whenever there is a major governmental movement there are radicals. Fanatics, perhaps, is a better word for such people. Unfortunately, they tend to give anyone interested in any sort of change at all a bad name."

"And that is true here?"

"Yes, that is true here."

She hesitated, then asked, "How did the late earl of Monbraithe stand politically?"

"Well," Douglas said slowly, "to the time of his death he had not yet supported the Scottish National Party, but I think, from what I have learned, that he was becoming something of a fence sitter. He was a man who tended to wait until he was reasonably sure how things were going before expressing an opinion of his own."

"In other words, he was primarily concerned with his own interests?"

"Yes, I suppose I would have to agree with that."

"And what about Ian MacGregor?"

His glance was sharp. "I was hoping that you would be able to tell *me* something about Ian Mac-Gregor's thinking," he admitted.

Monica shook her head. "You're completely off base, Douglas," she told him. "You couldn't be more wrong in all these things you've been surmising. You've really been leaping to conclusions, as I've already tried to tell you. I've never been Ian Mac-Gregor's confidante, and I can't imagine why you should think that I ever might be."

Now it was her turn to look across at him sharply. "Where does the Jacobite medallion enter into all of this?" she asked.

"Well," he said reluctantly, "we've come to think that it may be some sort of symbol."

He seemed about to say more, but those particular words were to remain forever unvoiced, because at that exact moment a woman screamed. They glanced quickly toward the lobby to see one of the members of the tour group pointing toward the entrance. At once Douglas was up and heading toward the door, muttering something indecipherable under his breath. Monica quickly followed him.

By the time she reached the lobby there seemed to be people coming from every direction, and then, in the entrance itself, she saw Mrs. Ewing, still swathed in the turquoise mohair stole. She was swaying and there was blood streaming down her face. And as Monica watched in horror, the voluble little woman from Des Moines quietly slumped to the floor.

CHAPTER FOURTEEN

DOUGLAS SAID CRISPLY, "Go fetch John, Monica, and ask him to see if there's a doctor about. If there is someone here in the hotel, 'twill be much quicker than putting in a call."

There was a doctor in the hotel. He was English, up from London to visit Scottish cousins, and once she had regained consciousness Emily Ewing was thoroughly delighted with him.

She had rallied with surprising swiftness, and fortunately the cut on her head, once the blood was washed away, was not nearly as severe as it had looked at first glance. In all, Mrs. Ewing was a tough old soul, and Monica couldn't help admiring her. Also, there was something very endearing about her, despite the fact that at moments she did tend to fall into the nuisance category.

Now, with her husband hovering close at hand and both the English doctor and Douglas hanging on every word she said, Mrs. Ewing actually seemed to be enjoying herself. Yet there was already a lump the size of an egg on the side of her head, and the resulting ache, Monica suspected, would surely have daunted a less stalwart person.

After first aid at the scene, the doctor, the Ewings,

Monica and Douglas went to the third-floor room the Ewings were occupying. Monica helped the older woman get into her nightdress, a voluminous pink affair, and then tucked her into bed.

As she was doing so, Mrs. Ewing said regretfully, "I'm sorry about the stole, dear. I'm afraid it must have got torn."

"It doesn't matter in the least," Monica said quickly, amazed that she could even think about such a thing under the circumstances. "Look, Mrs. Ewing, the doctor is going to give you a shot so that you can get some sleep."

"I don't want to go to sleep," Mrs. Ewing protested. "Not just yet. We should call the police first, don't you think?"

"The police?" Monica stared blankly at Mrs. Ewing. Then she realized she'd surmised the injury had been purely accidental, probably the result of a fall outdoors in the dark. Now she asked slowly, "Why the police?"

"Because," the older woman answered smugly, "someone tried to run me down out there in the parking lot!"

Monica had noticed before that Mrs. Ewing had quite a streak of the dramatic in her nature, more pronounced at some moments than others. Her "impressions" of the Loch Ness monster had been one indication of this.

Now she said patiently, "Mrs. Ewing, are you sure?"

"Yes," Mrs. Ewing responded, "of course I'm sure. I hadn't realized that the buses were kept locked, and I went out to get a package I'd left on board, a woolen evening skirt I bought at the mill today. Mrs. Fenton—she's the lady from Albany with the purplish hair—wanted to see it because she thought maybe she could find something like it in Glasgow tomorrow.

"When I found I couldn't get into the bus, I started back, intending to get Douglas or that nice Donald Ferguson. I was sure one of them would have a key. But as I started across the lot this car came out of nowhere. It was like something you see on TV, Monica. It simply rushed toward me, and I didn't think I had a chance in the world. I didn't see how I could possibly avoid being hit."

"But you weren't hit, were you?"

"No, of course not, or I'd be in considerably worse shape than I am," Mrs. Ewing said practically. "I flung myself sideways, as I've seen them do on TV, and the car went screeching by. But in doing so I fell, and I guess I hit my head on the curb. I must have been unconscious for a time...."

"Dear God!" Monica exclaimed.

"Yes," Mrs. Ewing continued, "it *is* scary, isn't it? I think whoever was driving the car must have thought he'd hit me in the first place, when he looked back and saw me in his rearview mirror, lying in the street—at the edge of it, actually. Otherwise he could have circled back—"

"Mrs. Ewing!" Monica protested, sick at the thought of such a thing. "Look, I'll get the doctor, and Douglas...."

She did so, and at this point Percy Ewing joined

er two men. Once again Mrs. Ewing told her
giving it a few embellishments this time. Still,
Douglas pressed her for facts, there was very
e could tell him. She'd noticed nothing about
itself; she could give no clues as to size, shape
r.

I saw were those two headlights bearing down
ne," she said, "like a pair of giant evil

nis had to suffice. Douglas said quietly that he
ould, of course, get in touch with the police, and
that he'd also like to have another talk with Mrs.
Ewing in the morning, when she'd had some rest.
The doctor insisted upon giving her a shot that would
ensure that rest, and he was sufficiently charming
about it that she bravely bared her arm for him.

Finally the doctor left, and Douglas said to Monica
in an undertone, "Wait outside for me, will you? I'll
be with you directly."

She nodded, and stood outside the Ewings' door in
the corridor, hoping that no one else from the tour
group would come along. At the moment she didn't
want to have to make explanations of any sort.

Douglas took so long, despite his promise to be
with her "directly," that Monica was on the verge of
leaving when at last he came out, quickly closing the
door behind him. He said at once, "Let's go to your
room and get our stories straight, because there will
certainly be questions asked about this. Mrs. Ewing
agrees that 'tis best for the moment to say simply that
she stumbled and fell and hit her head in the course
of things."

"I can't imagine her sticking to that story fo
long," Monica pointed out.

"Nor can I," Douglas agreed, "but that is wha
will tell people for tonight at least, so should you
counter anyone I'd appreciate it if you'd say the san
thing."

"I don't think I'm about to encounter anyone,'
Monica told him. "As a matter of fact, I've had it,
Douglas. I'm played out, and I'm going to take two
aspirin and go to bed."

They rode the elevator to the fourth floor, where
she and Iris had their room. As Douglas walked
along the corridor beside her, she said, "There's no
need for you to stay here, Douglas."

"On the contrary," he insisted, "I have no intention of leaving you until I've first checked things out
for myself. Give me your room key, will you?"

"Really," she began, but his expression silenced
her. There was no mistaking the authority in his
voice.

"Give it to me, please, Monica," he said firmly.

Even so, she was grumbling as he unlocked the
door and said, "Wait a minute. I shall go in first."

He did so, only to call out shortly, "All right."
But as soon as she had entered the room, he closed
the door behind her and locked it. "I do not intend to
take any chances," he told her quietly.

She stared at him, puzzled. "What is this all about,
Douglas?" she demanded wearily. "Must you play
your cloak-and-dagger games just now?"

"I don't find that comment very amusing," he
said coldly. "You're being foolish, Monica. I should

think you might be able to consider what happened here tonight and reach some conclusions of your own about it.''

She shook her head. "I haven't the vaguest idea what you're talking about," she confessed.

"It doesn't occur to you that the attack on Mrs. Ewing was meant for you?" he asked her.

"For *me*?" There was no doubting her incredulity.

"Yes. Because of the scarf, don't you see?"

"The scarf?"

"That bluish green whatever-you-call-it," Douglas explained.

"The mohair stole?"

"Yes, then, the mohair stole. Mrs. Ewing bought it for you the day we stopped at the gift shop by Loch Lomond, didn't she, and then borrowed it back? Iris was quite amused by that."

"Yes," Monica admitted slowly. "Yes, she did."

"Mrs. Ewing is not one to keep matters to herself," Douglas said. "I think she told everyone on the bus about buying a gift for you, and then I'm sure she had a great laugh with a number of the others about borrowing it back. The bit about borrowing, though, was strictly within our own group. Anyone else—anyone who happened to be around the gift shop the other day, let us say—would have known only that you were the recipient of that particular stole. So they very well could have thought it was you walking out into the parking lot tonight. As a matter of fact, it would make more sense for someone your age to do such a thing than it did for Mrs. Ewing."

"Are you suggesting someone could possibly mistake Mrs. Ewing for me?" Monica demanded.

"In the dead of night, 'tis possible," Douglas responded. "She is just about the same height as you. Her figure, of course, is entirely different, but the stole was enough by itself to camouflage that. Primarily 'tis the color that would have been seen by anyone who happened to be about the lot in a car just then. The color would have shown up under the outside lights.

"God knows there should be more of those lights," Douglas went on. "And as it is, those that are there are entirely too dim. 'Twould be easy enough for our man to make a mistake. Yes, I've no doubt at all, Monica, that Mrs. Ewing was mistaken for you."

"I can't believe it!"

"I think you had better believe it," Douglas told her ominously. "Our man must have considered it a rare bit of luck when his intended victim simply wandered out the door. He must have been planning to approach you in another manner."

She shivered. "Douglas, please!"

"Not so funny, is it, when you picture the scene?" he asked her, and before she could answer he continued, "In any event, he made his move, and it would seem that he thought he'd succeeded. Now, of course, there is a good chance he may already know he had the wrong person, and in that event there is no guaranteeing he will not come back and try again. Which is why I wanted to search your room before you entered it by yourself."

Monica frowned. "I wonder where Iris is. . . ."

"I don't know," Douglas answered abruptly. "She came back with her dinner group; they'd gone to some country inn. I glimpsed her talking with Donald Ferguson, but then in all the excitement revolving around Mrs. Ewing I lost track of her. I'm not trying to alarm you, but I would suggest that you put the bolt on the door, and when she comes up she can call out to you."

"Douglas—"

"Monica," he said testily, "will you kindly stop arguing with me?"

"I wasn't arguing with you."

"You were about to," he told her shortly. He seemed very somber as he crossed the room to sit in a small armchair by the window, and she surveyed him helplessly.

"What now?" she asked.

"I'm not about to stand guard for the night, if that's what is worrying you," he told her coolly. "I shall go along in a few minutes, but first there are a few matters I would like to set straight in my mind. You would be doing Ian MacGregor as much of a favor as you'd be doing me if you simply answered my questions."

"Is that an official order?" she asked somewhat nastily.

"Damn it, no. Merely a request. You seem to doubt it, but I am trying to be helpful, Monica."

Was he trying to be helpful? Monica went over and sat on the edge of her bed, feeling alone and forlorn and, for the first time since she'd been in Scotland, like a stranger in a foreign country. Until now she had been welcomed wherever she went, and she had come to thoroughly admire the rugged character of the Scottish people and their wonderful humor. But it was as if she had suddenly been cast adrift; literally, she was on alien shores.

Douglas had gone into a great deal of explanation about Scottish politics; the presumption was that the whole matter involving Ian and his uncle's death had political overtones. But even though Douglas had told her he was on Ian's side, she realized, bleakly, that there was no way she could be absolutely sure of this.

He was watching her narrowly, and now he said, "You will have to trust me, at least to an extent."

She nodded. "Yes," she conceded, "I suppose I will."

"Then, tell me—you did go to Monbraithe Castle yesterday, did you not?"

"Yes."

"Were you invited there?"

"No, I wasn't."

"You went to the castle to see Ian MacGregor purely of your own accord?" he asked, and she sensed his surprise.

"Not exactly," she answered. "That is, I didn't set out with the idea of going to the castle at all. When we were at Mrs. Grier's shop at Loch Lomond the other day—"

"Mrs. Grier?" he interrupted. "How is it that you know her name?"

"I went back there yesterday," Monica said wearily, "and she told me her name."

"You went back to the gift shop?"

"Yes. That's what I just said, didn't I? You see, when we were there the other day I saw the castle across the lake and I . . . well, I was almost sure it was Ian's castle."

"Ian's castle, eh?"

"Yes." She could feel her cheeks growing hot.

"When did you meet him, Monica?" Douglas asked her softly.

"Last year, in Edinburgh," she told him reluctantly. "I was on a tour with my aunt, who has since died. Ian and I met . . . quite by accident. We went out together a few times, and later, when I went on to Glasgow with my aunt—the tour was very similar to this one—I saw him again. One night we stopped by at the castle on our way home from dinner. Ian was doing an errand for his uncle—"

"Involving the Jacobite medallion?"

"I think you already know the answer to that," she challenged.

"Very well, I do," he admitted. "Go on. You stopped at the castle . . . ?"

Now her cheeks were flaming, for she certainly wasn't about to tell Douglas what had happened at Monbraithe Castle! Even touching upon the memory evoked a surge of feeling that she'd been trying for months now to keep suppressed. Her body was the traitor, she thought bitterly. When she remembered lying in Ian's arms, the world around them lighted only by a single candle that seemed to flicker as their passion mounted, it was all she could do to bear her body's treachery. And, seated there on the side of the bed, she plaited her fingers together in her lap like a bashful teenager, feeling the need to cling to something, if only her own grip.

"I sense that I'm touching upon something painful," Douglas said softly, "and I'm sorry, Monica. I wouldn't willingly hurt you."

Something painful! She nearly laughed aloud, because Douglas was indeed touching upon something painful. He had no real idea of the torment he was inflicting upon her. Her memories were a mixture of raw emotion and shame; the aftermath of that night at Monbraithe would forever haunt her. At this point, it had become impossible to put the past in any sort of proper context...to say nothing of the present! She loved Ian. Yes, there was no denying that love, for it far transcended volition. Yet reason told her that he did seem to have been able to cast her away with a surprising lack of regret. Or was it a case of stoicism, a case of concern for her rather than for himself? Had he really been so afraid for her all along that he was willing to sacrifice their mutual chance for happiness?

She sighed, and Douglas said sharply, "Monica!"

"I'm sorry." She clutched her hands even tighter. "There isn't much more to tell you, Douglas. Last year Ian told me he would come to Prestwick to see me off, but he didn't show up. That was the end of it. I didn't hear from him again."

"Until you came back to Scotland?"

"I didn't hear from him when I came back to Scotland," she admitted. "The night the tour group went to Prestonfield House for dinner I thought I saw him there. After that, on the last night in Edinburgh when you and I were having dinner together, he was in the hotel dining room with...a friend. He saw me with you, and he thought we were involved in some sort of romance—''

''Hah!'' Douglas snorted explosively.

''Well, I doubt he would have approached me anyway. But he did send me a message of sort. Now he considers it a rather foolish gesture on his part, but he did ask the pianist to play 'Loch Lomond,' which has a...a significance for us. He left immediately after that. I suppose that probably I should have left it at that, but then yesterday I felt compelled to go back to Loch Lomond, even though I realize *that* was a foolish romantic gesture on my part. Nevertheless, I rented a car and drove out to the gift shop. It was Mrs. Grier who told me the castle across the lake *was* Castle Monbraithe. She also told me that Ian's uncle had died and that Ian had inherited the title.''

''I see.''

''After that,'' Monica went on slowly, ''I had a— well, I guess I'd have to call it a compulsion. I drove around and found the gate to the castle, and the gatekeeper came out and met me. He and his wife assumed I was a friend of Ian's, and she offered me tea. Before I'd finished it, Ian returned.''

''How did he react to seeing you there?''

''I'm not quite sure,'' she said. ''He indicated that he had more or less expected me to appear, and yet he seemed very anxious to get rid of me.''

Douglas raised a skeptical eyebrow. ''No joy at the reunion?'' he asked her.

"A very transitory joy," she said quickly. The memory of Ian's kiss returned now to make her lips feel as if they were burning. "We talked for a bit," she went on hastily, before Douglas could ask anything else, "then I started to leave, but my car wouldn't start. Ian didn't seem to want to take me up to the castle just then, so we drove along to one of those Royal Auto Club booths, and he phoned for help."

"To Balloch?" Douglas asked.

"Yes, I think so."

"And after that?"

"Well, after that we drove to a very pretty little town where there was a lovely old inn. It was too early for the bar to be open, but Ian knew the owner, and he served us tea and scones in a private parlor."

"I see. I suppose it would be invading your privacy if I asked what you discussed while you were having your tea?"

"You've been invading my privacy all along," Monica retorted grimly, trying to shut out the memory not of what she and Ian had said but of what they had done during the course of that tea. It was far too easy to imagine the feel of his arms around her, the passionate warmth of his mouth pressed against hers. Her cheeks flaming, she said stiffly, "I'm sure you won't give me any peace until I tell you what you want to know, so I might as well say that Ian told me of his uncle's death and his own accident. Then he said that he had been tried for murder but that the verdict was 'not proven.' This, it seems, is one of three verdicts permitted under your

Scottish law, but I can't say that I think much of it.''

"That depends," Douglas told her. "As I've already mentioned to you, if a man were guilty, he'd surely feel in rare luck to come off with such a verdict.''

"You're not suggesting that Ian is guilty?"

"No, I'm not suggesting anything. To return to yesterday...."

"Ian and I went back to Monbraithe, and this time Ian took me up to the castle with him. There was a man from the garage fixing the car, and Ian's cousin Walter was with him. It seems Walter has an aptitude for mechanics. Ian took me inside and I met his aunt. Then Walter came to tell us the car was fixed, and so I came back to Glasgow...."

"Just like that?"

"Yes," she said. "Just like that."

"And are you to see Ian MacGregor again?"

"No." Monica shook her head as if to emphasize this. She hesitated, then added with a note of desperation that reached out to Douglas, "Don't you think maybe there's a simple explanation about Ian's uncle's death? Couldn't it have been a hunting accident? Isn't it possible that Ian might have shot his uncle accidentally and then blacked out and wrecked the car when he was in the grips of a kind of amnesia, because he has such a horror of guns?"

Douglas stared at her. "He told you he has a horror of guns?"

"Yes. His father was killed in a hunting accident at Monbraithe Castle when Ian was very young. He's never forgotten it. He was at the castle when they

brought his father's body back into that vast hall."
She shuddered. "Last year he only agreed to go hunting with his uncle because they'd been disagreeing
previously, and he was making an effort to please
him."

"I didn't know that," Douglas said, and smiled
wryly. "Despite his solicitor, and the barristers who
represented him in court—all of them excellent—his
lairdship made a rather poor showing in his own defense," he told her.

"He was just out of the hospital," Monica retorted hotly.

"So he was," Douglas allowed. "To go back a
bit—did he tell you that this disagreement he'd had
with his uncle involved the Jacobite medallion?"

"I think he did, actually, yes," she admitted.

"And yourself?"

At first she didn't realize what he meant by this,
then she said reluctantly, "I suppose so. His uncle
questioned him about an American he had been seen
with."

"And indicated that he had given this American
the medallion?" Douglas persisted.

"Yes."

"Did he, by any chance, give you the medallion?"

"No!" she said angrily. "I've never even seen the
blasted medallion!"

"It is not so much a question of the medallion
itself but of its significance," Douglas explained.
"From what I understand of it—and I've not seen it,
either—the medallion is not all that valuable. No
crown jewel, in other words. It is, however, priceless

historically, and a lovely piece of jewelry in its own right, and people have been killed for much less. But 'tis the significance of it, as I've said, that is so important. The fact that it goes to the reigning lady of the house of Monbraithe in each generation. Where you come into the matter is that there is reason to think enemies of Ian MacGregor's suspect you are to become that reigning lady.''

"Oh, my God," Monica exclaimed, "I've never heard anything more ludicrous! Why don't you ask Ian about that directly?''

"Perhaps I shall," Douglas responded. He stood gazing down at her, looking tired and more than slightly unhappy.

"Am I right in assuming that you would yourself do a great deal to help establish his innocence?'' he asked her.

She didn't hesitate on this, no matter what sort of revelation it might involve. "Anything," she told Douglas fervently.

She caught a fleeting expression that translated as admiration in his eyes, but he only nodded. Then he seemed to shake himself mentally. "Once again," he warned her, "let no one in except Iris, and make quite sure it is Iris you are admitting!"

CHAPTER FIFTEEN

THE PHONE RANG, a jangling disturbing noise. Having napped and awakened, Monica was just now beginning to undress; she stood stock-still in the middle of the room, feeling her pulse thud against her chest as the sound broke the stillness.

Douglas had said that the man—the unknown terrible man who had struck down Emily Ewing—might come back again. Now a fear without reason gripped her as she concluded that it must be he at the other end of the line.

Then logic took over. Thoroughly impatient with herself because one couldn't, after all, be harmed through a telephone, she forced herself to be very calm as she picked up the receiver. "Hello?"

"Love," Iris breathed across the wire, "I was about to ring off. I thought you must be out."

"No," Monica told her, then glanced at her watch. It was nearly one in the morning, more than two hours since Douglas had left her with yet another final admonition to bolt the door behind him. She had slept much longer than she'd realized.

"Where are you?" she asked Iris.

"At the Albany, in Glasgow," Iris said. "I'm calling from a phone in the lobby. I know Douglas will be quite furious with me, but Donald Ferguson was coming into town and he gave me a lift. You see, he is in Glasgow. . . . ''

"Donald Ferguson?" Monica asked.

"I must have awakened you out of a sound sleep," Iris observed, her chuckle faintly exasperated. "No, not Donald."

Monica silently berated herself for being so stupid. She should have known, of course, that there was only one "he" in Iris's life.

"He came up on a late train from London," Iris explained. "I'm staying the night here. We've had a drink or two and he keeps saying he has something terribly important to tell me. Oh, Monica, pray, will you, it's something that will mean we can be together?"

"If that's what will make you happy," Monica agreed, wondering at her own hesitancy because there didn't seem much doubt that this would be exactly what would make Iris happy.

"Oh, love," Iris said, and laughed. "But then, you wouldn't know about things like this. There's such an innocence about you. One day, though, when you truly fall in love. . . ."

One day, when you truly fall in love. . . .

These words came back to haunt Monica after she had hung up the receiver, and they tended to have a shattering effect. She felt that her composure at the moment was as tenuous as a fine thread, and this dismayed her. It would be so easy to dissolve into hysteria, or dementia, or whatever people tended to dissolve into once they'd slipped over the edge of reason.

Brushing her hair in front of the mirror, she studied her face and tried to relate what she saw in Iris's comment about her having "such an innocence" about her. True, with her chestnut hair curling down around her shoulders she did look especially youthful; and her eyes, more green than hazel tonight, seemed very wide and almost too large for her piquant face. But innocent. . .? She smiled wryly at her own reflection. In one sense of the word, she had lost her innocence a year ago, in a Scottish castle. There had not been a true culmination, to be sure. But she could not deny that her passionate need and her emotional intention had been—

The phone rang, once again a jangling intrusion. She sighed, hating to answer it because she was sure it must be Douglas this time. Very probably he'd discovered that Iris had not yet returned to the hotel and was checking up on her.

But it was not Douglas at the other end of the line.

"Monica," a man said, and there was only one man in the world who could say her name in exactly that way.

Her voice caught in her throat, making speech temporarily impossible, and he said again, "Monica?" Then, "I beg your pardon. May I speak with Miss Winthrop, please?"

"This is Monica," she said quietly, and now it was his turn to be silent until she added, "Ian?"

"I didn't mean to wake you," he said, his tone curiously strangled. "I'm sorry."

"I wasn't asleep," she told him. "But it wouldn't matter if I had been."

She winced at the bittersweet tone of his laugh. "Thank God you're willing to even speak to me after yesterday," he said then. And added, after a pause, "MacConnach was out here."

"Douglas?"

"Yes. Had you told me his full name I would have known who he was. As it happened, you said only 'Douglas,' and so all I was aware of was a severe pang of jealousy."

"Ian—"

"I'd not seen him before tonight, you see," he explained, "although I've known of his activities on my behalf. He has been in contact primarily with my solicitor, Basil Ingram." He hesitated. "MacConnach told me that you are very...loyal in your convictions about me," he went on, his voice low. "Monica...I cannot even begin to tell you what hearing him say that did to me. It was like being given an infusion of pure strength."

"Because I told Douglas I believe you are innocent?"

"Don't say it so lightly," Ian told her. "How many people are there, do you think, who truly believe in my innocence?"

Ellen, for one, she nearly answered, but she bit back the name.

The tension between them was a vibrant thing. It was as if it were being transmitted through the telephone wires to run like an electric shock through Monica's veins. Ian laughed, a short tormented laugh. "This is selfish as hell of me, but I must see you," he admitted. "I can't let you go back to the

States with only the memory of the way I left you at the castle yesterday. I've got to see you tonight!''

"At the castle?"

"No," he said, "not at the castle. I'm at a friend's house in Glasgow; Basil's house, as a matter of fact. I've a key to it, because he knows how I feel about staying at Monbraithe. There are moments when the place tests what sanity I have left! Basil is in Edinburgh tonight, though, so I am quite alone. All I ask is that you come for a drink. I want to talk to you, and to feast my eyes on you. But I promise that I will not touch you. . . ."

Her own laugh was small and very shaky, for this was not at all the sort of promise she wanted to hear from him. True, there would be a new sort of safety in their relationship if they could sit in a room with each other and not so much as touch. But. . . .

She grasped at reason. "Ian," she said, "it's half-past one."

"I know that. I know the entire idea is completely insane, too, but I've stretched logic to the breaking point where you're concerned. There are those times, damn it, when one has to let the heart rule, if only temporarily. Otherwise one is apt to end up with a stone where the heart should be."

He was as much as telling her that there could be no permanence, that this was an impulse he was acting upon, she thought dully. In fact, he might as well have come out and said that with the dawn they'd be back to the old basis, he going his way and she going hers.

He said, "Monica?" and she sensed the withdrawal in his tone. "You are quite right to hesitate," he told her, "and I am a fool. Had MacConnach not come to Monbraithe tonight I would not have thought of suggesting such a thing to you. But once he had left, I couldn't get you out of my mind."

There was silence, but it was a fraught silence. She not only sensed his struggle, she was totally embroiled in a struggle of her own. Being with Ian could end only in further pain for her; every vestige of common sense that she possessed warned her of this. And yet if it were destined that she was never to see him again after she left Scotland, there was nothing that she would not do in order to be close to him...just one more time.

His voice deepened. "Whatever happens," he said, "there will always be a glory to my memory of you. Someday, perhaps...."

"Let's not wait for someday," Monica suggested, and love's wings carried off the final shreds of her caution. "Tell me, Ian, how one gets from this hotel to Glasgow at this hour of the morning."

"Only one way for you... I'll come up and get you."

CHAPTER SIXTEEN

MONICA DRESSED WITH SPECIAL CARE, choosing slim slacks of a deep amethyst shade with a matching velour top that had a snugly knitted neckline. Yesterday, at one of the shops they'd stopped at on the tour to the Trossachs, she had yielded to impulse and bought a short pale gray woolen cape, and now she slung it around her shoulders after once again checking her makeup.

She had used a bit of camouflaging cream where there were definite dark shadows tonight, caused by pure fatigue, and she had highlighted her expressive eyes with a lovely shade of emerald smoothed over the lids. Aside from that, she'd used only a touch of lipstick and a bit of blush. While it was impossible to dispel the impression of weariness entirely, cosmetics were, when the occasion demanded, a remarkable camouflage, she thought, pausing at the last instant to spray on a bit of Arpege.

It was only as she actually was letting herself out of her room that the full knowledge of what she was doing swept over her. Douglas had warned her so thoroughly about not letting anyone in. Now it seemed a bit incongruous to think that, rather, she was letting herself out; and she could well imagine how Douglas would react!

The corridor stretched beyond her door, empty all the way to the elevator, and the elevator responded promptly, whirring its way upward. She stepped into it quickly, relieved when the door clanged shut and the elevator started downward. And once in the lobby she more than half expected that she would stumble upon Douglas in the flesh, and she prepared herself for his ire.

The lobby, though, was completely deserted; not even the head porter was in evidence. There was something very lonely about the expanse of empty chairs in groupings, and the unmanned registration desk seemed surprisingly vast.

She waited just inside the glass entrance doors. Then, as the red MGA came into sight, she ran out, climbing into the front seat next to Ian and collapsing against the soft upholstery, her breath coming fast.

"You seem as if you've been running a marathon," he observed, a note of quiet amusement in his voice as they drove off. "Did I pressure you that much?"

She shook her head. "No," she said. "It was just rather spooky in there, that's all. The lobby was deserted—there wasn't anyone around. I don't usually scare easily, but after the episode with Mrs. Ewing...."

"What episode with Mrs. Ewing—and who, for that matter, is Mrs. Ewing?" Ian asked her.

She stole a glance at him, thankful that he was concentrating on his driving, for it was drizzling and the road, she realized, must be slippery. He was wearing dark slacks—she saw in the light cast from the dashboard that they were a brown so dark in tone as to be close to black—and a thick matching turtleneck. The sweater emphasized the breadth of his shoulders and his muscular arms. . .his beautiful muscular arms. It was the sort of casual garb that not only became him tremendously but seemed to reveal a facet of his personality usually kept hidden behind a facade that could be austere and aloof when the mood struck him, or so urbane that she was made to feel very unsophisticated.

Now she was conscious primarily of his masculinity, a vibrant quality that seemed to simmer between them, and she swallowed hard. The very scent of him, somehow such a totally male scent, was enough to send her senses reeling, and she wondered how she could possibly hope to handle being alone with him in his solicitor's apartment. Probably, she conceded, Ian had enough stamina in that direction for both of them. Obviously he had an unassailable sort of discipline when discipline was demanded; she was painfully aware of that fact.

He reminded her, "You've not answered my question."

"Oh?" she said, wishing she could throw herself into his arms and communicate to him her own mounting need. Then surely something within him would rise to meet it, and—

"Mrs. Ewing," he prodded. "Who is she, and what happened to her?"

"She's a member of the tour group, from Iowa," Monica told him. "She's quite a nice old thing, and tonight—last night it is now, I guess—she evidently was mistaken for me. At least Douglas said so."

"MacConnach?" Ian frowned. "He didn't mention anything to me about a Mrs. Ewing."

No, Monica said silently, *and I shouldn't have, either! It will only alarm you...maybe to the point that you'll turn around and take me back to the hotel.*

"Is she really an 'old thing,' or is that merely a phrase?" Ian demanded.

"Well, she's past middle age, I'd say."

"Then how could she be mistaken for you? Never mind; tell me first what happened to her."

"A car tried to run her down in the parking lot," Monica said briefly. "She'd gone outside to get a package she'd left on the tour bus. She didn't realize the buses are kept locked at night."

Ian swore under his breath and then, to her consternation, pulled the car over to the side of the road, braking to a stop. He turned to face her, his eyes very intent. "Why was it presumed that she was mistaken for you, and who presumed it? MacConnach, you say?"

"Yes. It was Douglas's idea."

"How could an elderly lady be taken for you, for God's sake?"

"Because we're about the same height, and Mrs. Ewing has a—well, she has quite a good figure for a woman her age, although she's heavier than I am. Mainly, though, it was because of the stole."

"*What* stole?"

"When we were out at Loch Lomond the other day she bought me a turquoise stole in the gift shop there. Then she borrowed it back, because it matched a dress she had. She was wearing it tonight; she had it draped over her head like a mantilla. Douglas thinks the person—whoever was at the wheel of the car, that is—saw the stole and assumed it was mine, and so...."

"I see." Ian sat for a moment contemplating the rivulets of rain running down the windshield. There was a bleakness about him that made Monica shiver.

"It may have been entirely an accident, Ian," she suggested.

"MacConnach doesn't think so, does he?"

"No. But Douglas tends to be dramatic at moments...."

"Douglas—" Ian emphasized the name "—is a well-trained professional. I suppose he can be dramatic enough when he's dipping into his sack of Scottish lore to enliven things for his customers on their trips about the countryside. But in a matter like this I would say he wouldn't tend to stretch reality at all. MacConnach doesn't seem to be one to press a panic button, as you Americans say."

"I hate it when you refer to me that way," she said.

"What way?"

" 'You Americans'! You make us sound like creatures from another planet."

"There are those moments when you seem to be," he told her, and then, unexpectedly, he grinned. "Never think I would have you otherwise," he added, and to her surprise he reached out to place his hand over hers.

He did nothing more than this. He simply let his

hand touch hers, but at once there was a tangible communication between them. His palm became the source of a current that pulsated through every part of her body. There was a strength, an assurance and a quality of endearment to his touch, as well as a large measure of pure sensuality. If she had wondered whether the horror of the past year had in any way weakened Ian, now she became convinced, simply by this hand-to-hand contact, that it had not. No, actually, he was stronger, much stronger, than the blithe and handsome young man whom she had met in an Edinburgh elevator. There was added resolution and new character to his beloved face, and as she looked across at him tears came to smart her eyes. She had never loved him quite as much as at this moment, even though she had, in a sense, loved him utterly for a long, long time now. And she would never be over him. Even if she never saw him again after today, she was as committed for life as if she'd taken vows. There could never be anyone else for her. Never.

The softness of his Scottish burr did alarming things to her already faltering emotions as he told her, "You have never been lovelier than you are just now. I should be keeping my head on my shoulders, and yet you must know that it is all but falling into your lap. Ah, Monica...."

Involuntarily she plunged toward the sanctuary of his arms, only to have him say, with a rueful laugh, "Damn these bucket seats! Back in your place, my beauty, because despite the urgings of my common sense I am going on to Glasgow with you."

She felt a pang of pure exultation and it was very hard for her to subside quietly. Now she welcomed her body's treachery; she let waves laden with the most tantalizing sensations wash over her as she kept her eyes on Ian's profile, memorizing every line of it.

They drove through a series of housing projects on the immediate outskirts of the city, and then she was aware only vaguely of the city center, of streets and buildings. They traversed a bridge across what, she supposed, must be the River Clyde, and finally Ian pulled off into a street that seemed to be a sort of crescent. They came to a stop in front of an imposing gray stone house, one of several of its type in that particular block.

"'Twas a town house, formerly," he explained as they mounted the wide front steps. "Now it has been converted into flats. Basil's is on the first floor."

He was turning a key in the massive front door as he spoke, and he let her precede him into a vestibule. Then, to her surprise, he indicated the staircase that ran up the inner wall.

"I thought you said the flat was on the first floor?" she questioned.

"So it is," he answered, his voice amused. "In Scotland 'tis the ground floor we're on now, and the floor above that is the first. Remember?"

He was thinking of their initial encounter in the elevator, she knew, for she'd been mixed up about the floor numbers even then.

She smiled. "I won't forget again."

"Mind that you don't," he chided with mock severity as they made their way up the stairs together.

The same key that had opened the front door was used to open the door to the flat itself, and once inside Ian busied himself with switching on lights. Monica found herself standing in a small foyer; just in front of her was a large and rather formal room that served, she suspected, as a combination living room, study and library.

The furniture was a bit too heavy and the decor too somber for her taste; the dark wood and the deep wine-colored brocade curtains at the window set the general mood. But the room was impressive in its way, opulent and very comfortable. Bookshelves lined one entire wall, filled with books that she could see at a glance were well used.

"Shall we have a whisky first," Ian suggested, "and then I'll make some coffee. 'Twouldn't do to get you drunk," he added, smiling down at her.

When she agreed, he went to get their drinks while she wandered across to the wide front window. This crescent-shaped street was really a cul-de-sac, charming in its arrangement; a quiet backwater where, Monica suspected, one could find remarkable peace in the heart of a major city, and time in which to think.

At her shoulder, Ian observed, "Very Scottish, isn't it? Gray stone and wet pavements and drizzle. Do you find Scotland bleak, Monica?"

"Oh, no," she said quickly. "Every corner of Scotland I've seen, whether by day or by night, has a charm for me. I've loved all of it."

"Even Castle Monbraithe?" he asked softly.

Taken aback by the question, she took the whisky

he handed her before answering. "Castle Monbraithe is very impressive, Ian," she said carefully.

"And very cold." The word had any number of meanings. He turned away and went to sit in an armchair, and she had the feeling that he had deliberately avoided choosing the couch for fear that she would come to sit next to him.

She chose a chair herself, settling into it primly, and took refuge in a sip of the whisky as she tried to gather her wits. Being so close to Ian was disturbing beyond belief, yet if he could keep his hands off her, she told herself resolutely, she could damned well keep her hands off him! She had never been the aggressor between them and she had no intention of trying to play such a part now, for she knew very well that to be rebuffed would kill everything left in her spirit.

She glanced at him to see that he was eyeing his whisky moodily, twirling the glass between his fingers. He said slowly, "I cannot quite understand this Mrs. Ewing business, and it bothers me."

"I still say that Douglas may be a bit too inventive," she insisted.

He shook his head. "Not MacConnach," he told her firmly. "Basil Ingram, my solicitor, has known him for quite some time and has great faith in his ability. What I can't understand is why he didn't mention the incident to me."

Maybe, Monica thought, *because he knew that if you knew about Mrs. Ewing you might not seek me out. Maybe it actually fell within Douglas's plan to have you call me tonight.*

It was an arresting idea. Yet Douglas had been so firm about her staying in the room and keeping the door bolted. . . .

"You're not drinking your drink," Ian accused her.

"Scotch still has a rather strange taste to me," she admitted as she slowly took another sip. Then she, too, stared broodingly into the amber liquid, her nerves growing tauter with each second because it was impossible to be so near him and not. . . .

"Ian," she asked suddenly, "what are you going to do?"

He looked up, startled. "What do you mean? Do about what?"

"Yourself," she said. "Suppose they never do find out who killed your uncle? Suppose it *was* the man who tried to run Mrs. Ewing down at the hotel last night, because he mistook us and wanted to be sure I didn't get the medallion."

"*What?*" Ian demanded.

"The Jacobite medallion," she explained.

"And why should anyone think you might be 'getting' the Jacobite medallion?" he asked icily.

She flinched at his tone, but she said only, "Douglas seems to think the medallion is involved—and that I am, too, evidently because of some misapprehension on your late uncle's part."

"I see." Ian sighed deeply. "'Tis not exactly the moment to tell you this, but such assumptions are groundless, and they will be proven so very shortly. My engagement is to be announced within the next few days; there will be a story in the newspapers about it, the proper pictures, all the rest."

Ice came to claim her veins, taking possession with cold brittle fingers. "To Ellen?" she asked.

"To Ellen," Ian nodded.

"So," she stated, the words coming only with great difficulty, "she, too, has faith in your innocence."

"Yes, bless her." There was no doubting the warmth in Ian's voice. "She has always believed in me, as have her parents. I'm very grateful to them."

"I see," she managed.

Silence thudded between them. Then she couldn't repress the next question, even though she knew it would be impossible to erase the obvious agony from the words. "Why did you ask me here tonight?" she demanded.

"For my own selfish reasons," he said. "I told you that in the beginning."

He put the whisky glass aside and stood up, looking very tall and surprisingly powerful despite his present slimness, for she realized again that he'd lost quite a bit of weight since she'd first met him. His blue eyes were grave.

"Think me a bastard if you must, Monica," he said with a helplessness that was odd to him, "but I cannot possibly keep the promise I made to you. I told you I wouldn't touch you, and that was my intention. But when I'm with you my intentions and everything else to be considered seem to go to hell. Nothing matters except *you*—do you understand that? I think you do, because I think, God help us, that you feel the same way about me! Your eyes show me what you so desperately try to conceal when you're with me. Can you say the same?"

She tensed, unaware that those eyes he spoke of had become emeralds set in a taut white face. "That isn't something I should answer, Ian," she told him levelly.

He groaned. "Monica, this is no time to play games!"

There was scorn in her voice. "Ian, what kind of man are you?" The question was like a gauntlet flung down. "You've just told me that you've become engaged. I saw your fiancée, remember, at the hotel in Edinburgh the other night. Your affection for each other was very evident. Do you deny it?"

He stood statue-still, without speaking, and the moment that passed seemed eternal. Then he said, as if the words had been wrenched out of him, "No, I do not deny it."

"And yet. . . yet you are asking me to let you make love to me?"

"What a monster you make me seem!" Ian responded bitterly. He turned away and busied himself with refilling his glass with Scotch. Then, as she watched him, he tossed the drink down in one gulp and shuddered, his face darkly brooding.

"Come," he said. "I shall take you back to your hotel."

"Ian. . . ."

"There is no sense in prolonging the agony, Monica."

She shook her head. "I don't want things to end like this between us."

"Why not? 'Twould seem as if there can be no happy ending for us; you know that and so do I. And my memories of you will not be distorted by this final scene.'' A near-physical spasm of pain crossed his face. ''They will be as wonderful as they've always been,'' he finished slowly.

Memories. For the rest of her life, Monica thought bleakly, she would be assailed by memories of this tall tormented Scot. Yet those memories would forever be incomplete unless....

Ian seemed to be reading her mind. ''Let's go now,'' he said harshly, ''while we're both capable of doing so. I warn you: no matter what it may cause you to think of me, I cannot keep this distance between us much longer.''

Certainty came with a rush of emotion so powerful she was rocked by it. It was not even a question of considering her actions but of responding to an age-old instinct. She moved across the room as if drawn by a magnet, and his arms reached out to enfold her. There were no further words between them. His lips moved to brush her forehead, her eyelids, her cheeks, then went on to claim her mouth; and his probing tongue became an incendiary force. Their bodies melted together as the tempo of his lovemaking intensified, until Monica was aware only of the strong sweet pulse of desire, and she soared past a point of no return.

Ian began to undress her, and each button, each hook, became an obstacle to be surmounted by love, by ardor, by the blend of a mutual yearning that spiraled them upward. He pressed her body even closer to him after first pulling off his sweater, and then he gently moved her fingers to his belt buckle, and she began a task of her own, trembling when at last he stood before her, his masculinity a proud and awesome thing.

The bed in Basil Ingram's bedroom was very large, and Monica felt lost in the depths of it. But then Ian came to lie beside her, his hands caressing her breasts, her waist, then finally touching her with an intimacy such as she had never known before. He rained kisses upon her as his fingers explored, and she in turn stretched out her arms to entwine them around him, for he could never be close enough; she could never have enough of him.

And then they began a final voyage, a voyage that seemed to take Monica to the deepest parts of all the oceans of the world, to drown in unfathomable depths of love and passion. These forces, blending, mounted to a tidal wave of ecstasy—cresting, peaking, then past crescendo, ebbing slowly, to leave her totally spent.

For a long time Ian held her close to him, as tender and gentle toward her now as he had been demanding just a few minutes before, in a way that was the essence of maleness. And as she laid her head against his shoulder, tears that were like a distilled essence of love came to trickle down her cheeks.

After a time he stirred, and when she finally looked up he had put his trousers back on and was pulling his turtleneck over his head. She saw that there was an unexpected grimness to his expression.

"'Twill be dawn if we don't watch it," he said, almost curtly. "I'll make us some coffee while you dress."

She watched him leave the room, her heart aching, because she sensed fully from his attitude that anything between them from now on, leading to their inevitable parting, would be purely anticlimactic. Tonight, she knew, they had belonged to each other as fully as it was possible for two people to belong to each other, and yet she also knew that there had been a finality to their lovemaking. There was a bittersweet sorrow in the thought that this night was something to be hoarded in her memory for the rest of her life. In fact, she was almost certain that in those moments when they were, both of them, coming back to reality, Ian actually had whispered, "To last us for all time. . . ."

CHAPTER SEVENTEEN

IT WAS NEARLY DAWN when the red MGA drove up in front of the hotel again, but it seemed to Monica that the lights in the lobby were blazing more brightly than when she left.

She and Ian had said their goodbyes at the flat, and they had agreed that at this last moment she would walk away from him without looking back. Now she did so, though the effort required her to summon up the very last vestiges of a crumbling will-power.

As she entered the lobby she knew primarily that just now she wanted no contact with anyone. She was glad Iris had opted to stay in Glasgow overnight and only hoped she wouldn't be too early in returning.

I need to be by myself. . . to lick my wounds, she thought bitterly.

This, however, was not to happen. As she walked through the glass entrance doors Douglas descended upon her like a malevolent genie escaped from his bottle: it was obvious he was furious. The night porter, a thin gray-haired man, was on duty at the desk, and Monica was only too aware that he was watching them with a curiosity he obviously couldn't conceal; nor could she blame him. Douglas's voice was thunderous as he demanded, ''Where the hell have you been?''

She was in no mood for questions, accusations, explanations. ''Would you mind not shouting?'' she said angrily.

''Yes, I would mind not shouting,'' Douglas told her, but he did lower his voice. ''Come into the lounge.''

''I don't want to come into the lounge, Douglas.''

''I don't really give a damn about your wants, Monica.''

''Look,'' she said, ''obviously you're used to having people take orders from you, but you've picked the wrong individual this time. I don't intend to have you tell me what to do.''

''A sudden assertion of independence?'' he asked her. ''It seems to be catching. I might ask you if you know where Iris is, too?''

''And suppose I do?'' she countered. ''What makes you think I'm going to tell you?''

''Ach,'' Douglas grumbled between clenched teeth, ''I would like to take the back of my hand to you.''

''I might like to return the compliment,'' she retorted, and added, ''You had no right to go and see Ian behind my back.''

Douglas swore so violently that she winced. ''Is that what he told you?''

''Not precisely,'' she admitted. ''I do know, though, that you were at Monbraithe since I saw you last.''

''I shall come upstairs with you,'' Douglas decided

suddenly, and as she looked at him she knew there was no point in arguing. He was a lot stronger than she was!

They maintained a chilly silence on the ride up in the elevator and the walk down the corridor to her room. There, once again, Douglas took the key out of her hand, opened the door and went in, and after a moment, in a voice that was decidedly dour, he gave her permission to enter. Nevertheless, she had the feeling of a rather overwhelming déjà vu, bringing in its wake the unreal sensation that perhaps she'd dreamed the whole thing about being in Glasgow with Ian.

Dreamed it? Once again her body proved itself a traitor, making her only too aware of the fact that she had indeed been with Ian tonight! She turned away from Douglas so that he would not see the color stealing into her face, tossing off her cape and putting her handbag on the floor beside her bed.

"Now," Douglas began, with a determination that made it clear he was not about to brook any nonsense from her, "let us take things one at a time. First, Iris. Where is she?"

"She is at a hotel in Glasgow with her lover," Monica told him bluntly.

"What a damned fool she is!" he exclaimed. "The man is clearly using her."

"Perhaps," Monica conceded. "But she is in love. One day, if you really fall in love yourself, Douglas..." she said, unconsciously echoing Iris.

"I shan't look forward to the event," he told her stiffly. "For that matter, I cannot afford to fall in love. In my work a man needs to keep his wits about him, rather than to have them addled by a perverse female.''

She couldn't help but wonder if he was thinking of her when he referred to a ''perverse female.'' In his book, though, Iris undoubtedly fell into the same category, so possibly he was thinking of both of them.

''Well,'' he said, ''does Iris intend to join our group again, or is she about to elope with this Casanova?''

''I'm sure she'll be back anytime now,'' Monica promised, and at once wondered if she might be wrong. Iris's return, she suspected, could depend very much upon what the important news was that the man in her life had wanted to tell her. If it included her, as she had hoped it would, she might very well abandon her job and just about everything else!

''All right.'' Douglas evidently took her at her word. ''We shall await Iris's return and see what she has to say for herself.''

Monica laughed. ''You sound like a frustrated school principal,'' she accused him.

''Indeed?'' he retorted, evidently miffed by this sort of reference. If so, though, he quickly shrugged his personal feelings aside. ''To go on to the earl of Monbraithe...I definitely did not go behind your back, Monica.''

''No,'' she conceded, ''I suppose you really didn't. But I do think you might have mentioned that you intended to visit Ian when you left me here.''

''The idea had not come to me yet,'' Douglas told

her. "'Twas a bit later that I decided I wanted to talk to him, so I went directly out to the castle, hoping that he would receive me. And he did.''

"And?"

"It was a satisfactory interview," Douglas said. "Did he not indicate that to you? Oh, yes, I can tell by your face that you've seen him again, Monica. You are most transparent where he is involved.''

"I think you've already said I lack a poker face when it comes to just about everything," she reminded him.

"And you do. I've no wish to discuss your face just now, pleasant digression though it would be. You don't deny, do you, that you've been away from the hotel for several hours?"

"Of course I don't deny it," she said impatiently. "You probably started camping on my doorstep five minutes after I left here and had some sort of warning system going so that you were alerted when I returned.''

"I was downstairs," Douglas replied coldly, "and I saw MacGregor's car drive up.''

"Then why the inquisition if you know all the answers?" she asked.

"I don't know all the answers. Where did he take you, Monica?''

"That," she told him, "is none of your damned business!''

To her surprise, Douglas smiled faintly. "Very well, then; for the moment I shall accept that. To get to other things: I doubt that Iris will be fit for much of anything today...if she does come back, of course. Possibly if she can get enough of a rest during the morning, she can open the hospitality desk in the afternoon and take care of all those last-minute details I've mentioned to you. We shall have to see about it.''

''I could stay at the desk,'' she volunteered.

Douglas shook his head. ''I think not. I would prefer to have you on the Glasgow tour with me.''

He offered no further explanation, nor did she ask him for one. She knew only too well that a good bit of his reasoning stemmed from the fact that he intended to keep an eye on her. This time around he had no intention of letting her escape him!

At the door he said, ''I hope when daylight is fully with us 'twill seem a bit brighter. I've had enough of dismal weather for the present. . . .''

As it happened, though, the morning was not at all brighter. Clouds glowered above the Clyde, casting dark reflections onto the smooth steel of the river; and as she stood at the window, looking out over this famous stretch of water, Monica felt virtually convinced that it would again be raining the following morning when it came time to leave Scotland.

If I believed in omens, she told herself, *I would say it must mean something.*

She had nearly finished dressing when the phone rang. Thinking it must be Iris, she answered quickly, only to hear an unfamiliar male voice with a decidedly Scottish accent. ''May I speak with Miss Winthrop, please?''

''This is Miss Winthrop,'' she answered.

"Walter MacGregor here," the man said, and she barely repressed an audible gasp of surprise. "I'm calling to ask if there's a chance we might meet? I'm anxious to talk to you. Would you be free to have lunch with me?"

Such an invitation was the last thing Monica had expected, and she felt a prickle of something akin to fear. Despite his teddy-bear appearance, Walter *was* next in line to the title of earl of Monbraithe, and very likely had more than a little interest in the disposal of the Jacobite medallion.

It seemed ludicrous to think that she could actually be in danger from him, yet equally foolish to deny that this was no ordinary situation. Douglas's warnings crossed her mind and she hesitated. Douglas was a professional, as Ian had pointed out. Also, she knew very well that if Douglas were to learn about an engagement with Walter MacGregor, he would take definite steps to forestall it. Yet everything would take place in broad daylight, she told herself, and there was the chance that by meeting with Walter she might learn something of benefit to Ian.

"I should love to have lunch with you, Mr. MacGregor," she said quickly, before she could think further about it. "As it happens, though, I'm scheduled this morning to go with the tour group I'm working for into Glasgow. Then after lunch there I'll be expected to accompany some of the ladies while they shop."

"Could you not get away from them for perhaps an hour?" Walter suggested.

"I can try."

"Well, then, are you familiar with the statues in George Square?"

"No, though I've heard of them."

"There are quite a number of them. I shall wait for you near the Sir Walter Scott statue. You can't possibly miss it. The statue itself stands atop an eighty-foot column. 'Twas intended originally to have a statue of King George III—the square was named for him, you know—but Scott won out."

"I'm glad he did," Monica responded. "George III is not the most popular of monarchs where Americans are concerned."

"Because of your revolution, of course?"

"Yes," she said with an inward smile, "because of our revolution."

"Ah, yes." Monica could imagine Walter shaking his ginger-colored head in solemn agreement. "In any event, I will wait for you near the Scott statue. Come any time after three, why don't we say?"

"I'll do my best. If I don't come, you'll know it's because I really couldn't get away," she added, thinking of Douglas's very long potential leash.

"Then I shall call you later," Walter promised.

As she hung up the receiver, Monica was intensely curious. Somehow, she pledged, she would have to break away from the others, even if it meant arousing Douglas's fury once again. Also, it certainly would be better to meet Walter MacGregor in the heart of Glasgow's George Square than in the hotel lounge, where they could hardly have a conversation without a number of people—including Douglas, no doubt—becoming fully aware of it.

But why did Walter want to see her?

Her conjectures were interrupted by a knock at the door, and she remembered Douglas's instructions in time to call out, "Yes?"

"It's Iris," she was told; the Englishwoman's voice was unmistakable. "Let me in, will you? Have you shot the bolt?"

Monica was at the door in an instant, pulling back the bolt and opening it—only to stare, appalled, at Iris. She stood sagging on the threshold, her deep-shadowed eyes like coals in a gaunt gray face.

"Why the security measures?" Iris indicated the bolt.

"Douglas's idea," Monica said briefly. "Iris—"

"Don't tell me; I've seen a mirror," Iris cut her off. "Speaking of Douglas, he said to tell you he's waiting for you in the lobby. It seems you're to go on the Glasgow tour with him?"

"Yes. He wants me to. But if you need me—"

"At the moment," Iris told her, "I need sleep, and I've a couple of pills that will take care of that trick for me. Later...."

Iris was already turning away, and after a moment of hesitation Monica said, "Very well, then; I'll be on my way."

Iris didn't even answer her, and as she went down the corridor to the elevator Monica could imagine that the finale of last night's encounter between Iris and her lover had, in some ways at least, rivaled her own experience with Ian.

Douglas was waiting for her directly in front of the elevator. He quickly steered her toward the coffee shop, where he ordered tea and breakfast rolls with ham for each of them.

"You look well enough," he observed, casting an appraising eye over her, "especially for someone who got very little sleep. But I can't say the same for Iris: her rendezvous must have ended in a disaster."

"She didn't want to talk about it. Do you know how Mrs. Ewing is this morning, by the way?"

"Yes. She's amazingly chipper. I stopped by to see her, and it took a bit of persuasion on both my and her husband's part to get her to stay in today. We succeeded only when we pointed out that she will want to be fit for the gala farewell party tonight."

Monica had forgotten all about the farewell party, and now she sighed even as Douglas asked, "You'll go with me, won't you?"

"I'd rather get some sleep," she admitted.

"You wouldn't sleep, Monica," he told her. "And even if you would, there will be time enough for sleep later, when you get back to the States."

That, she thought dolefully, was true enough. She had a ghastly vision of endless years looming ahead of her when there would be more than enough time for sleep. . . and for reliving memories that for a long time would remain as smoldering embers.

Breakfast finished, they joined the other members of the tour group in the lobby. Despite the weather the paying customers were in good form this morning. They climbed aboard the bus grumbling slightly but good-naturedly about Scotland's fondness for rain, and Monica again took her place up front next to Douglas.

He gave her a long look before he picked up the microphone; then, his Scottish burr rich and thick, he said, "Good morning again to all of ye, ladies and gentlemen. Now, as we roll along, I shall tell ye a bit about Clydebank, where those great ocean queens were built...."

Monica found herself quite impressed by Glasgow, although Edinburgh, she knew, would always remain her favorite Scottish city, in part because it was so inextricably associated with Ian.

She was also pleased when the tour bus drove along one side of George Square, and she was amused when Douglas pointed out that "as recently" as 1745, at the time when Bonnie Prince Charlie's troops had come to occupy the city, this central area had been a marshland surrounded by meadows. In a way, Monica was reminded of her own Boston, where the famous Back Bay area had once been nothing more than an extensive fen, long since reclaimed. Boston was old in terms of American history, and yet the "recent" time of which Douglas was speaking anteceded the famous Boston Tea Party by something like two decades.

"Originally Glasgow Cross was considered the center of the city," Douglas told the group, "but now 'tis George Square, no doubt about it. As ye will see, the square is surrounded by imposing buildings of all types. On the east you will see the City Chambers, on the south the principal post office, and on the west the Merchants Houses. Here ye'll find the Glasgow Chamber of Commerce, which happens to be the oldest not alone in Scotland but in all of Britain. Also, ye will find here the office of the National Trust for Scotland. On the north, ye will see the Queen Street railway station...."

And right in the center, Monica added silently, *you will note the column that displays the statue of Sir Walter Scott.* Walter MacGregor could hardly have picked a more visible spot as the site for a rendezvous.

They stopped at a restaurant not far from the square. It was within easy walking distance; having got a good grip on her sense of direction, Monica was sure it wouldn't take her more than ten minutes to negotiate the few blocks in between. With lunch over, Douglas turned his passengers loose to shop to their hearts' content, as he had promised. Many sections of the city had been turned into "pedestrian precincts" with shoppers in mind, and he predicted that none of them would come back to the bus empty-handed. He also set an appointed time and place for them to rendezvous for the return trip to the hotel, and then they were off.

Monica trailed along with a group of the women. It was only two-thirty, so there was still half an hour before Walter would arrive at Scott's statue or, at least, before he would expect to find her there. Feeling a bit guilty because she was about to abandon them so soon, she paid special attention to her charges, and they warmed to her, asking her advice about colors and tartans, and whether or not a girl her age would like a sweater or might prefer a jaunty tam.

She gave each question due consideration and was

pleased that the women seemed happy with her answers. Her one concern was that the shopping expedition seemed to be going farther and farther away from George Square, and she knew that at this rate she might have to try to find a cab to cover the distance back.

Finally, at about a quarter past three, she confided that she had an engagement. Possibly it was the way she said it, but the women were immediately convinced that her date was with a man—which, of course, was true. However, she knew that they were giving it romantic overtones, and that if this got back to Douglas, he would immediately surmise she had gone to meet Ian.

It couldn't be helped, though. She was not about to give up her appointment with Walter because of Douglas's possible annoyance; let the ladies think what they might. But as she was about to leave the thought struck her that Douglas had told them to meet at four o'clock on the corner near the restaurant where they had lunched, and there was, of course, no possible way that she could have any sort of real talk with Walter and get back in time to meet the bus. She sighed, imagining what Douglas would have to say about this, then warned the women that she just might not make the appointed deadline.

"But be sure not wait for me," she cautioned. "I'll find my way back to the hotel in plenty of time for the dinner-party."

CHAPTER EIGHTEEN

It was still drizzling as Monica walked across George Square toward the Scott statue, and she was glad that she'd worn a raincoat with a hood. At least in part because of the weather, she was sure, the square was surprisingly deserted. To her chagrin, she saw no one at all in the vicinity of the great column atop which stood Scott's statue.

Douglas had pointed out the information bureau at one end of the square, and she supposed that she could walk across to it and take shelter there. But she might miss Walter if she did so. Seconds ticked by, and she wondered if something had happened to hold him up. Possibly Jane had got wind of his intentions and put her foot down on the meeting; she seemed a person entirely capable of doing such a thing.

On the other hand, there was always the chance that Walter wasn't quite as docile as he appeared to be. For his own sake, Monica found herself wishing that he wasn't; and then felt almost as if she were seeing a vision when she saw him approaching from the direction of the information bureau. Evidently he'd gone to take shelter there himself.

He was wearing a cinnamon-colored mackintosh with a tweed cap pulled down squarely over his ginger hair. With a slight change of chapeau, Monica decided, he could almost masquerade for a very large version of Paddington Bear.

"Miss Winthrop," he said, and she realized that he had covered the distance between them with surprising speed for a man of his build.

She found herself looking up into his bland pinkish face. His blue eyes were not at all reminiscent of Ian's; they were smaller and of a much lighter shade.

"Nasty day," he remarked. "I'm sorry to be dragging you out in it like this."

"That's quite all right," she told him. "As I mentioned, I had to be in Glasgow anyway."

Walter fingered the small ginger-colored mustache that made him look more than ever like someone's pet plush bear. "I say, shall we cut across to a pub I know? They've a ladies' lounge. Or would you prefer to go to a tea shop?"

"The pub will be fine," she assured him.

"Good," he beamed. "'Twill give us more privacy there."

He took her arm, leading her across the square in an opposite direction from the restaurant Douglas had chosen earlier. This confirmed, Monica reflected absently, that it would be impossible for her to meet the tour group in time to go back to the hotel with them.

The pub looked as if it must have been in Glasgow since the time of Bonnie Prince Charlie, with its leaded windows, the panes made of yellowish glass that appeared to be hand blown. There was a staircase to the right immediately inside the entrance, and Walter told her, "This way, please," then let her precede him.

The ladies' lounge was surprisingly modern, with a bar all of its own and comfortable lounge chairs grouped around large coffee tables. Walter led her to a table in the farthest corner—there was no doubt about his desire for privacy, she decided—and then went back to the bar to return a moment later with two whiskies. He had brought along a glass of water as a concession to her taste, Monica saw, but ice cubes were singularly absent. She also realized that it would never occur to Walter that someone might want something to drink other than good Scottish whisky.

He lifted his glass in a somewhat automatic toast, then sighed rather deeply and brushed off his mustache with the back of his hand.

As she watched him, as covertly as possible, Monica sensed that he didn't know how to begin saying whatever it was he wanted to say to her. The contrast between Walter and Ian was more than a little startling when it came to social graces; Walter didn't seem at all the sort of man who had spent a good bit of his life living in a castle and was, like Ian, the nephew of a Scottish laird—now the cousin of one, as well. He appeared to be an essentially simple person, probably much more at ease among men that he was with women. In fact, she could imagine him being quite bluff and hearty as he drank his whisky with compatriots after, say, a stint of grouse shooting.

She wished that she could help him now in breaking the conversational ice, but she had absolutely no idea how to do so. The subject of the weather had been fairly well exhausted as they'd walked to the pub, and try as she might she could think of absolutely nothing else they had in common.

Except Ian.

Yes, they had Ian in common—but she couldn't bring herself to mention Ian's name. So it seemed more than a little uncanny when Walter began rather abruptly, "Miss Winthrop, I shall be frank and tell you I don't know how to start. You see, 'tis my cousin I want to talk to you about."

He frowned unhappily and continued, "I think you should know that Ian was not at all himself at Monbraithe on Wednesday. 'Tis not like Ian to be rude. Bobby Grier was the first to mention it to me, and 'twas not bad enough that Ian acted a frightful snob to Bobby, but he was cutting to you, as well."

Walter shook his head ruefully. "You must excuse Ian, Miss Winthrop."

She was astonished. "Are you *apologizing* for Laird MacGregor?"

"Yes," he said, looking at her with surprising directness, for until now Walter had been evasive in his glances. "I guess you might say I am. You see, Ian mentioned that you leave for the States tomorrow, and 'tis not fair, in my opinion, to have you go carrying the kind of impression of Ian you surely must have. Perhaps if you were to know. . . ."

He hesitated, and she couldn't resist a bit of prompting. "Yes?"

"Ian has had more than his share of tragedy," Walter resumed soberly. "All of his life, actually, he has lived with a pall over him because of his father's feelings first, and now this terrible business involving our uncle. Ian, you see, never knew his mother, and when he was only a wee one he lived with her shadow forever coming between his father and himself. Then there was that dreadful time when his father was killed. My mother has told me of it. Ian came out into the great hall at the castle just as they were carrying in his father's body. He was but eight or nine at the time. 'Tis not a sight a lad would be likely to forget.''

She shuddered. ''No,'' she agreed. ''No, it isn't.''

''Then,'' Walter continued, ''there was Uncle Terence's death last year.'' Again the light blue eyes came to dwell upon her face with surprising intentness. ''If it is of any account to you, Miss Winthrop,'' he said, ''I would like you to know that I, for one, never believed that Ian shot him.''

This was the last thing she had expected Walter to say, and she couldn't mask her surprise. But he didn't seem to notice particularly. In his rather unhappy way he continued, '''Twas enough, as far as I am concerned, that Ian was so severely injured himself. 'Twas months before he could really get around again, and he will never be able to do the things he used to do. Ian skied very well, and among other things he was an expert at playing tennis. He has had to give up all such activities.''

Monica frowned. She realized now, that in telling her of his uncle's death and the events that followed it, Ian had passed over his own injuries as lightly as possible.

"Are you saying that Ian actually is...crippled?" she asked his cousin. "He surely doesn't seem to be."

"No," Walter said. "He is not crippled—not in any visible sense, anyway. Alex MacDuff, who is an old friend and our family doctor, says that as long as Ian is reasonably careful he should have few problems. When he forgets himself, though, and overextends, he has to wear a brace for a time until his back mends again." Walter smiled faintly. "Ian tends to be impatient," he told her. "Such things are hard for him to become reconciled to; he considers them a dreadful nuisance, but for all of that he is not one to fret. I have not heard a single complaint from Ian during the course of all of this...and believe me, he has had a great deal to complain about. It was enough to have to go into court accused of murder while yet on crutches and barely able to hobble. Then to have the verdict one of 'not proven' rather than 'innocent'...."

This time when Walter looked at her directly she was for a fleeting instant reminded of Ian. And his voice was almost like Ian's as he said, "You must wonder why I have asked you to meet me here, only to chat on about Ian and his problems."

"You've said that you didn't want me to leave Scotland with a...misapprehension about him," she pointed out.

"True, but there is another reason, a most important one." Walter looked so miserable that she felt more sorry than ever for him. "I have come to ask you if you will consider returning the medallion to Monbraithe."

Monica felt as if this friendly-teddy-bear-become-a-man had suddenly dashed ice water into her face, and Walter flinched before the expression in her eyes.

"Please," he said quickly. "You must not take this the wrong way. I am not accusing you of anything!"

"Well, I shouldn't think you would be!" she told him icily. "As I understand it, it's your own mother who has the Jacobite medallion. I presume that's the medallion you are referring to."

"But she doesn't have it!" Walter protested. "That is why I felt so impelled to get in touch with you. Wait, please! I know it must seem to you that I think you guilty of thievery, but that is not the case. As I've said, I am not accusing you of anything. After all, if Ian gave you the medallion in the first place, then 'tis natural that you should not feel obliged to return it."

"Oh, come now," Monica said impatiently. "Why should you think Ian would have given me the medallion? And if that *is* what you think, why haven't you asked *him* about it? Never mind, Mr. MacGregor; you don't have to answer that. Let me assure you instead that I definitely don't have the medallion! For that matter, I've never even seen the blasted thing!"

"You've never seen it?"

"No!"

"Then," Walter said, his face oddly pale, "that night last year when Ian took you to Monbraithe Castle, it really was missing?"

Monica's eyes snapped. "How did you know Ian took me to Monbraithe Castle?" she demanded.

"You were seen there," Walter replied unhappily.

"By whom?" she asked suspiciously.

"By Brucie Grewar."

"And who might he be?"

"He works about the place, tends the sheep and helps Angus. He is a distant cousin of Angus's, a nice lad but not too bright, and something of a loner. He lives in a cottage on the castle grounds and he doesn't bother anybody. Some say he's a bit daft, but if so he's harmless, Brucie is. He has a great touch with nature and I would swear he talks to the animals and they talk back to him. Also, he has a way about him, Brucie does. He can walk silently around the countryside without so much as stepping on a twig. He's a great walker, Brucie. He walks everywhere."

"So it would seem," she observed bitterly.

"Ah, you must not blame Brucie because he saw you and told Angus, and Angus told me," Walter said. "Brucie meant no harm. I daresay he'd been at a pub in the village that night and was on his way home. He says he got a glimpse of your face and then he heard you speak to Ian, and he knew you were an American."

"Very astute of him!"

"As I've said," Walter told her, "he meant no harm." He finished his whisky. "Would you care for another?"

"Thank you, no."

"Would you mind if I . . . ?"

"No," she responded. "Go right ahead."

"Do you have transportation back to your hotel, Miss Winthrop?"

She glanced at her wristwatch. It was well past four o'clock; she had definitely missed the tour bus. She shook her head. "Don't worry about it," she said. "I can get a cab."

"There is no need for that," he insisted. "Bobby Grier will be stopping by for me in half an hour or so."

She remembered the thin dour-faced mechanic with the unexpectedly charming smile.

"He's the son of the woman who owns the gift shop across the lake from you, isn't he?" she asked.

"Across the loch?" Walter repeated, but with no obvious intent of correcting her choice of words. "Yes, that he is."

"And he's some sort of a distant cousin, too. I mean, the MacGregors and the Grewars and the Griers are all more or less related?"

"Distantly, yes. The others all belong to the MacGregor clan."

"I see. Why is Bobby Grier stopping by here for you?"

"I've been having a bit of trouble with my car," Walter explained, "and Bobby has an angel's touch with motors. 'Tis his day off, and he suggested he drop me off at George Square and then spin around a bit so that he could diagnose the problem. He will be taking me back to Monbraithe, and your hotel is on our way, really. I should be delighted to give you a ride."

"Very well, then," she said, none too graciously. "I'll accept."

Walter nodded. " 'Tis sometimes difficult to get a

cab when it is drizzly, especially late in the afternoon,'' he pointed out, and then went to get himself
another whisky.

Settled by her side once again, he told her, ''I owe
you an apology, of that I'm sure, but the medallion
has been a real thorn to me. Would you mind if I tell
you why?''

''Not at all.''

''Well,'' Walter began, ''a year ago, you see, I
went to Inverness with my mother on a visit. She has
relatives there, and we've visited them when we can
these past couple of years. There is, I'll admit,
another attraction for my mother: a man, a widower,
to whom she has become quite attached. He is of a
suitable age for her, and well-fixed financially.''
Walter hesitated. ''I should like very much to see
them married,'' he admitted.

Monica could well imagine that he would like to
have his mother off his hands. Jane, she suspected,
could be a very demanding woman, and surely she
was an ambitious one.

''You see,'' Walter added slowly, ''she has always
had a dream of my becoming the earl of Monbraithe.
'Tis not that she would wish Ian any harm; I swear to
that. It's just that—''

Monica came to his rescue. ''I think I understand,'' she told him.

He nodded gratefully and then went on, ''Well,
you see, recently when we were once again at Inverness, this man proposed marriage, and my mother
has accepted him. Thus far they have not announced
their engagement publicly, but they will do so at

Christmas. Now my mother seems impelled to set everything to rights before she leaves Monbraithe so that the castle will be in readiness for Ian's bride in every sense of the word,'' he added.

Ian's bride! She couldn't bear the thought of it!

"The medallion has come to be an obsession with her,'' he explained, "and she would do a great deal to see it returned to its rightful place before she leaves the castle, even though she herself had nothing to do with its disappearance. There was a time, though, when my Uncle Terence made some very dark accusations against her because of the medallion, and she has never forgotten this. He openly denounced her for daring to wear it, and this hurt her dreadfully.

"A year ago, when Ian told our uncle that the medallion was missing—after he had gone to the castle with you—Terence telephoned my mother in Inverness and accused her of having taken it there with her. She was furious; I've never seen her so angry. She swore that she would confront Uncle Terence and make him take back his accusation, but of course she never had a chance to do so. She never saw him alive again.

"Now you see,'' Walter said, "that is why I thought that if Ian *had* given you the medallion, it would be a very generous thing of you to return it, if only temporarily. It would mean a great deal to my mother... psychologically, I suppose you would say?''

"Even though your uncle is dead?''

"Yes, even so.''

"Then I'm sorry," she told him, and meant it. "I truly am sorry. I wish I did have it."

"So do I," Walter conceded morosely.

HE FINISHED HIS WHISKY, and they talked casually of safe things like, once again, the Scottish weather. Monica suspected he was as glad as she was when the time came to go downstairs and meet Bobby Grier.

The dark-haired mechanic was prompt. At exactly the appointed hour he pulled up to the curb in Walter's car, an English make of dubious vintage. Before Walter could hold the door open for Monica, Grier had got out from behind the wheel and made it around the hood to perform this task himself, bowing elaborately as he did so.

There was a boldness to his gaze that made her uncomfortable. Bobby Grier was a different breed of Scot, she realized; she could well imagine him riding out on a clansman's foray in the old days, under the light of a full moon. She also had the impression that he had an excellent opinion of himself where his prowess with women was concerned, and she didn't return the smile he flashed in her direction.

On the drive to the hotel the two men talked mainly about the car's internal problems. Bobby Grier had a heavy Scottish accent that Monica found very difficult to understand, and she soon gave up even trying to do so. When he was talking about things like automotive parts, he became virtually incomprehensible to her.

Walter "saw her to the front door" at the hotel with rather touching gallantry, and he was obviously sincere in his thanks to her for having spared him a couple of hours on her last afternoon in Glasgow.

"And so you shall be going back to the States tomorrow," he said, looking down at her. He actually seemed regretful, although she would have imagined he'd be glad to see the last of her.

"Yes," she told him.

"When you return to Scotland, I hope the circumstances will be happier ones for you," he finished.

When she returned. . . .

As she made her way toward the elevator, thankful that Douglas was not in sight at the moment, that doubtful "when" had a very empty sound.

CHAPTER NINETEEN

MONICA DRESSED for her final evening in Scotland with a great deal of care, even though there seemed no good reason for doing so. She needed something at the moment to build up a sagging morale, and so she chose to wear a wool dress in a lovely burnt orange color that had touches of intricate gold embroidery at the neckline and on the sleeve edges. The tight bodice fitted snugly at the waistline, then flared into a fanfare of tiny pleats.

The only jewelry she wore was a lovely antique gold pendant, set with a single deep-toned carnelian, that had belonged to her mother. She used a bit more blush than usual because she was very pale just now, but she was careful to keep her eye makeup discreet—she knew that too much of it would only make her look even more tired than she felt.

Finally, after adding a touch of Arpege, she took a long look in the mirror—and she knew that the best thing she could do to enhance her appearance was to take a good long nap. Would that there were the time for one! She realized now that she'd had virtually no sleep at all the night before. She'd almost literally gone from Ian's arms onto the Glasgow bus tour, and the short interval of troubled slumber had done more to tire her than refresh her, for the dreams that had plagued it had not been good ones.

Now she pocketed her room key and took the elevator down to the lobby, only to find Douglas waiting for her, as she had feared he would be. He practically pounced on her, scowling as he demanded, "And what sort of rendezvous was it this time? I happen to know that you were not with Ian MacGregor!"

"Have you set your spies out everywhere?" Monica asked coldly.

"No. Oh, the ladies told me that you had a 'date,'" Douglas responded, mimicking a female voice and an American accent in a dual act that showed he did indeed have talent in such areas. "They had no doubt, bless them, that there was a man in the offing, nor did I, for that matter. How many do you keep dancing the fling in attendance upon you, Monica?"

"I don't find that very funny, Douglas," she said stiffly.

"Nor do I," he assured her. "Are you going to tell me who it was you were with this time?"

"There is no reason why I should," she retorted, "except that I don't want to be pestered by you all evening. I met Walter MacGregor and had a drink with him."

Douglas stared at her, obviously astonished, and this pleased her, rather perversely.

"Well, I'll be damned!" he said.

"Go right ahead," she suggested pleasantly.

"Monica, I—"

"Do keep your voice down, Douglas," she said sweetly. "The paying guests are assembling, and you wouldn't want them to think there is any dissension between us, would you? On our very last night together!"

"Monica, I swear—"

"Don't, Douglas. It doesn't become you."

"The hell it doesn't!" he said. "Look, to change the subject for a moment, is Iris still up in your room?"

Monica frowned. "No, she isn't. I haven't seen her since I got back from Glasgow, as a matter of fact."

"She wasn't here when we returned," Douglas told her. "She had been at the hospitality desk. I checked with the head porter—John, that is—and he told me she stayed till nearly four, but then she went off. Do you suppose she's gone back to her lover?"

"I wouldn't think so," Monica answered. "She didn't go into details, but I had the impression this morning that this time it's definitely over."

"Ah? And how was she taking it?"

"Not well at all," Monica admitted.

She caught the expression that flickered across Douglas's face before he could camouflage it. Completely surprised by what it had revealed, she exclaimed, "Douglas! You're in love with her, aren't you?"

He shook his head. "'Tis entirely too discerning that you are, Monica," he told her.

"Being in love is nothing to be ashamed of, Douglas," she answered, almost adding, *as I should well know!*

"But 'tis fruitless when it is not returned," Douglas said ruefully. "Iris does not even *see* me; she sees only a robot performing a function."

"Give her time."

He raised a questioning eyebrow. "Are you telling me you think there's a chance for me?"

"Yes, if you're patient. Iris has had a tremendous letdown, and she's going to need someone to stand by her...."

"I'm not particularly anxious to catch someone on the rebound," Douglas complained.

"If you let matters take their course, it may not be on the rebound at all. Just *be* there for a while, Douglas, and let her realize it. Then later...."

"'Tis an advice to the lovelorn column you should be writing," Douglas said with an attempt at briskness. "Possibly Iris has gone off with Donald Ferguson. He has family nearby, and the two of them seem to get on well together."

"I thought Donald had family in Edinburgh."

"He does." Douglas grinned. "'Tis a large family."

Douglas was attractive when he was in this mood, and the matchmaker instinct stirred in Monica. But then he sobered to ask, "Why did you go meet Walter MacGregor?"

"He phoned this morning. He was anxious to see me."

"What about?"

"Honestly, Douglas!"

"You might as well tell me, Monica," he said, and she knew only too well that this was so.

"Well," she answered, "he thought that Ian had given me the medallion, and he was hoping that if I had it, I'd return it."

"I see." To her surprise Douglas didn't seem inclined to pursue the matter. But then he went on, "Before you go dashing off anywhere again, do me the favor of letting me know where you're going and whom you plan to meet, will you? I would like, at the least, to get you out of Scotland safely tomorrow."

She glared at him, thoroughly annoyed but said only, "Very well."

"I'm serious, Monica," he told her. "I really mean it."

She nodded. "I think you've made your message clear." Then, glancing toward the desk, she saw that she was being waved at vigorously.

Mrs. Ewing was standing near the desk with her husband and several of the other tour members, beckoning in a rather violent gesture of invitation. She was dressed in an outrageous shade of shocking pink, her gown trimmed with feathers of a lighter hue, but somehow she managed to get away with wearing such a costume, just as she got away with most things. Although she looked rather pale, she also looked entirely capable of proceeding under her own steam, and Monica had to admire her. Despite last night's terrifying attack, Mrs. Ewing was clearly prepared to enjoy her final evening in Scotland. Such a positive approach to life on the part of an older woman *had* to be admired!

She crossed the lobby swiftly, Douglas following close behind her, and clutched Mrs. Ewing's arm with genuine affection. "It's really good to see you up and around," she said.

Mrs. Ewing smiled. "Well—" she let the words have a certain added significance while not overplaying them "—I must say that it's good to be here!"

"You're all right?"

"Quite all right," she responded, and patted Monica's arm as if she felt the need to console her. Well, Monica admitted, maybe she did need consolation at that. She felt terrible to think that Emily Ewing evidently had suffered from being mistaken for her, and clearly the woman was aware of this.

Now Mrs. Ewing turned one of her best smiles loose upon Douglas. "Ah, good evening, Mr. Mac-Connach."

"Good evening to ye," Douglas said. "I am more pleased than I can say to see ye about."

"You didn't think I'd miss the party on our last evening in Scotland, did you?" Mrs. Ewing asked archly.

Percy Ewing, at her side, gave a laugh that sounded like the rustle of dry leaves. "Couldn't have kept her in that bed tonight if I'd had a concrete block to put on top of her," he confided, his voice a mixture of pride and despair.

"And more power to her!" Douglas said gallantly. "Mrs. Ewing, I do hope this nasty experience ye've had will not be leaving ye with a bad feeling about my country?"

"Not at all," Mrs. Ewing declared staunchly, and added, "After all, people get mugged, whether by hand or by automobile, just about everywhere these days."

Douglas and Monica exchanged glances, and Monica was very tempted to say, "Do they, now?" But at this precise moment Iris appeared from the direction of the dining room.

"Our tables are ready, everyone," she announced. "Shall we go in?"

Douglas was standing so close that Monica could feel his start of surprise, and she heard him murmur under his breath, "I wonder where the hell she came from."

"Why don't you ask her?"

"Don't think I'm not about to." He was surveying the English girl narrowly. "I'd say she's had one or two already," he opined. "With Ferguson, I'd wager."

Iris's color did seem a bit on the high side, Monica agreed, but this could very well be the effect of makeup. In any event, Iris looked stunning in a bright red dress of a clinging material that emphasized the curves of her body and was a perfect foil for her striking brunette coloring.

Monica said, "I don't think I've ever realized it before, but Iris is beautiful! I've always thought she was very attractive, but it's a lot more than that."

"She has the potential for beauty," Douglas corrected, and at that moment Iris looked across the room and saw them. Briefly, the set smile she'd put on so carefully faded from her face.

She came across to them immediately, and before Douglas could speak she said quickly, "Douglas, I'm sorry. I really wasn't trying to make things difficult for you, but then you should know I wouldn't really let you down. I closed up the desk a bit early and dressed, and then I went off with Donald for a couple of hours to visit some of his relations and have tea with them. I had a long talk with a great-aunt of his who is nearly ninety, a remarkable woman, and it's done me a great deal of good. So don't quibble, will you, please?"

"No," Douglas responded, strangely meek. "I shan't quibble, Iris."

"Thank you," she said, and the smile she gave him was a genuine one. "Come on, now—let's get everyone into the dining room and get things started!"

THREE LONG TABLES had been set aside for the tour group, and each featured a lavish floral centerpiece. There was also a rose wrist corsage at each lady's place, and as soon as they were seated the champagne began to flow.

The gala evening indeed promised to live up to expectations. The group had been a convivial one from the very beginning, and except for Emily Ewing's misfortune—even this having a happy ending—there had been nothing to mar their pleasure on the trip. Actually, Emily was becoming something of a heroine among them, and her "accident" was bound to make potent conversational material once they were back in the States. Everything that had happened was the stuff of which memories were made, and Monica could imagine how the various events would be rehashed again and again.

Tonight the atmosphere was especially congenial; everyone was in a holiday mood and Iris, despite her personal problems, certainly was proving herself an excellent hostess. She had told them lightheartedly that they were to have a six-course dinner, and promised that she would rotate among the three tables, spending two courses at each one.

Now, as they were partaking of succulent thin slices of smoked salmon as an appetizer, a small combo started to play for dancing. Emily Ewing at once insisted upon waltzing with Percy, even though he protested that she wasn't up to such goings-on. Emily thought otherwise, however, and soon proved her point: she went on to whirl around the floor with Douglas midway during the soup course, a clear herb-seasoned lamb broth with barley in it.

As champagne glasses were raised in toasts the laughter became a little bit louder; but this could be forgiven tonight, Monica thought, because everyone was so clearly happy, and it was such a *good* group when you got right down to it. She danced with some of the men herself and decided that they were dears, all of them, even though most of them were terrible dancers. And she made no protest at all when Douglas refilled her wineglass again and again.

It was while the musicians were taking a brief intermission that a sudden hush fell upon the room. Monica, conscious of the fact that people had stopped talking and that heads were turning, turned her own head, looked and then gasped.

Ian was just entering the dining room—or, rather, was being ushered into it ceremoniously by the headwaiter, who was all but bowing backward as he made his way across the floor toward a choice table for two.

Tonight Ian *was* the earl of Monbraithe; he could have posed for a palace portrait. He was wearing a dress kilt in the predominantly red MacGregor tartan, with a ruffled white shirt and a magnificently tailored black cutaway coat. As he walked across the room with an arrogant grace that, Monica knew, was quite unconscious, he was devastatingly handsome. So handsome, in fact, that as she looked at him desire's tempting fingers came to clutch at her like tentacles that could not be pried loose, and she felt herself flushing.

There was an older man with Ian, gray haired and very distinguished in appearance. He, too, was wearing a kilt, and as the two men were seated waiters came to hover about their table. But Ian waved aside menus with an imperious gesture and spoke briefly to the maître d'hôtel. A moment late two glasses of whisky, looking disconcertingly plain under the circumstances, were delivered on a silver salver, and Monica smiled despite herself.

Emily Ewing, sitting next to her now, asked raptly, "Who *is* he?"

Monica, her emotions in whirling conflict, could not possibly have answered, but Douglas said, "He is the earl of Monbraithe, Mrs. Ewing."

"An honest-to-goodness lord!" Mrs. Ewing exclaimed softly. "Only you say 'laird,' don't you? He looks every inch of it, doesn't he?"

"Yes," Douglas said quietly. "Yes, that he does."

The musicians started to play again. . . and then it happened, before Monica could even begin to come to grips with herself. The earl of Monbraithe rose with a kind of indolent suavity that suited him astonishingly well, and with the eyes of virtually everyone in the room upon him, he crossed to Monica's table and very gravely bowed before her.

He nodded toward the dance floor with no visible change of expression, except that suddenly his blue eyes seemed to be laughing. She winced inwardly, reminded almost more than she could bear to be of the Ian-of-the-elevator and then, inevitably, of sunlight sparkling on the waters of Loch Lomond.

Scottish lochs and Scottish legends, Scottish castles and Scottish lairds. This particular Scottish laird crooked an inviting elbow and asked politely, "May I?"

Because there was nothing else that she could do without creating a scene, Monica stood. Her legs were rubber, so uncertain beneath her that she clutched at Ian's arm, and together they walked toward the dance floor.

CHAPTER TWENTY

SHE WAS IN HIS ARMS, her awareness of him so direct, so acute, that the rest of the world receded, vanished, thrust out of sight by the wave of a magician's wand. They clung to each other, and Monica felt as if she were drowning in a sea of rich sensation; she was much too close to the edge of something she knew she couldn't cope with.

Ian whispered huskily, "Oh, my God, darling, this isn't easy! Just to touch you...."

"You shouldn't have come," she whispered, the truth of her own words choking her. She realized that she'd been dancing with her eyes closed, and now she opened them to find, to her horror, that they were alone on the dance floor. She said miserably, "You'd think some of the others would get out here and dance, too. They're acting as if this is some sort of command performance."

"So they are," he agreed mildly, and managed a smile. "Don't glare so, Monica," he chided. "People *are* beginning to dare to come out and dance now, so you can relax a bit."

"All right." She forced a smile so taut it emerged as more of a grimace.

"Monica, my love," he urged, "do try a bit harder, will you?"

"I can't," she responded, and was afraid that if she didn't watch it, she'd be crying instead of smiling. "Ian, why did you come here?"

"Because you're leaving tomorrow," he said calmly. "Isn't that reason enough?"

She knew that she was glaring at him again, but she couldn't help it. "You are going to drive me utterly insane!" she cried. "Twice now we've gone through the throes of a final farewell. I don't think I can bear another one."

"Perhaps there will not be the need for another one," he suggested.

"What's that supposed to mean?" she asked suspiciously.

"What would you think of staying in Scotland?"

"Is that an invitation?" she asked. Then anger surged at the thought that he would dare suggest such a thing when he had made it very plain that his engagement to another woman was to be announced formally within the next few days.

"Keep your invitation!" she said violently. And before he could answer she continued, her voice low and angry, "What sort of a person are you, Ian MacGregor? Being an earl doesn't give you the right to—to make chattels out of people. Not in this day and age!"

"Chattels?" he echoed, with a politeness she would have questioned under any other circumstances. "I'm afraid I wouldn't know quite what to do with a chattel, Monica. In any event, that has nothing to do with whether or not you'd want to stay in Scotland, does it?"

"I should think you'd be able to answer that question yourself!'' she told him. ''Dear God, how dense can a person be? I wouldn't stay in Scotland if it were the last place in the world!''

''I see,'' he said quietly. She glanced up at him quickly, only to see his mouth set so firmly that there was a thin white line around his lips.

''I doubt you see much of anything at all where I'm concerned,'' she told him bitterly. ''And you haven't really answered my question. Why did you come here tonight?''

''You seem to think it was to make you miserable.'' A rueful smile twisted his mouth. ''On the contrary, it's just as I've told you. It was because you are leaving tomorrow, and because MacConnach and I had another talk this afternoon. . . .''

''This afternoon?''

He nodded. ''We met at a club I belong to in Glasgow while you ladies were shopping.''

''This lady was not shopping,'' she retorted, before she thought better of it.

''No? What were you doing, then?''

She sighed. ''I suppose if I don't tell you, Douglas will. I met your cousin Walter, and he took me to a pub near George Square. We had a drink together.''

Ian stopped dancing and stared down at her, as astonished as Douglas had been. ''You had a drink with *Walter*?'' he demanded.

''Watch it, m'laird,'' she said, enjoying herself for this moment at least. ''People will be noticing.'' She mocked his accent as she spoke.

It was his turn to glare, but he did start dancing

again. "How did you happen to meet Walter?" he asked in a low voice.

"Because he asked me to," she replied. "I'm surprised Douglas hasn't told you all about it, except that there hasn't been time. He didn't know himself until shortly before we came in here for dinner, but I'm sure he'll fill you in as soon as he has the chance to do so. The two of you have quite a grapevine going, don't you? You're in such...such cahoots!"

"MacConnach and I are not in anything like... like whatever it was you called it," he said loftily.

"I beg your lairdship's pardon," she retorted, curtsying vocally.

He looked down at her, and the blue eyes that could be so merry, that could remind her so totally of sunlight dancing on the waters of Loch Lomond, were thoughtful and more than a little sad. "Knock it off, will you?" he suggested softly.

Her body was playing traitor again, and with an impishness she wasn't feeling she told him, "That's American slang."

"I don't give a damn what kind of slang it is," he responded. "I know what it means, and I mean it." He paused, catching his breath, then continued, "I've nothing against kilts, in fact I'm proud of them, but I got dressed up like this tonight and came here to make a damned spectacle of myself for a specific purpose, as I should think you might guess. I've never been an exhibitionist; you must know that. But I persuaded Basil—my solicitor, you remember—to come here tonight with me for a purpose."

"Do you call dancing with me being an exhibition-ist?" she hedged.

"No," he told her shortly, "and you know damned well that's not what I meant!"

The tune to which they had been dancing came to an end, and now the tempo of the music changed. Monica had no idea how many pieces they'd danced to nor could she possibly have told one from another, although normally she had a good ear for music. But now, curtsying ever so slightly, she said, "Thank you, your lairdship. If you don't mind, I'd like to go back to my table."

His mouth tightened; she could feel his anger. "I would like nothing so much as to turn you over my knee, damn it! For God's sake, Monica...."

But she had already started to leave the floor, so with a shrug he followed her.

They had nearly reached her table when she saw Mrs. Ewing, evidently returning from a visit to the ladies' room. Now, touched by a sudden mischiev-ousness, and also because she knew that this truly would mean a lot to Emily Ewing, she took Ian's arm and pressed him forward. "Mrs. Ewing, may I pre-sent the earl of Monbraithe."

Mrs. Ewing seemed to imagine herself being pre-sented at court. She essayed a swoop of sorts that managed to be surprisingly regal, and Ian, bowing low, kissed her hand as if she were indeed a lady in the queen's court.

For a moment Monica was afraid that Mrs. Ewing—who had done so well at getting over an ac-tual attack—was now going to swoon right in front of them all. She glanced suspiciously at Ian, who was surely holding the hand of the lady from Des Moines considerably longer than he needed to. She wondered if he shared her fear and might be prepared to offer first aid should the older woman need it.

But once again Monica had not reckoned with Mrs. Ewing's considerable fortitude. Now the older woman rallied and said almost demurely, "This *is* a pleasure, your lairdship."

Ian, not to be outdone, returned in his softest Scottish burr, "'Tis my pleasure entirely, Mrs. Ewing."

He turned to Monica, his face a mask of politeness as he told her, "Thank you for the dance. And good evening. I trust you will have a safe and pleasant trip back to the States."

And with that he left them.

Mrs. Ewing didn't move for a long moment. Then she whispered, "Where did you ever meet him?"

"I'll tell you some other time," Monica promised as she steered Mrs. Ewing back to their table.

Douglas, standing to hold her chair out for her, said sourly, "That was quite a spectacle."

"Don't let Mrs. Ewing hear you criticize it," Monica warned him. "She was in heaven for a moment there. And anyway," she added tartly, "don't go getting the idea that I engineered it."

"I hope you don't think I did?"

"I wouldn't know," she retorted.

The headwaiter appeared, beaming at them. "His lairdship has ordered champagne for everyone in your party," he announced.

"How generous of him," Monica responded coolly. She glanced toward the table Ian had been occupying and was not too surprised to find that he and his solicitor had left.

Mrs. Ewing, following her gaze, sighed, "Oh, dear, now we can't thank him. I shall have to get his address and write him a letter."

But Monica scarcely heard her. She turned toward Douglas, instinctively keeping her voice low. "What *is* this all about?" she demanded. "What's the real meaning of Ian's coming here dressed to the teeth and acting like some marionette in a royal opera, then suddenly leaving—"

"Please—" Douglas kept his voice equally low "—be patient just a bit longer! There *is* a plan, and I shall tell you about it as soon as I'm able to, but I can hardly say any more at the moment. Eat your *gâteau*, will you?"

Her glance was venomous. She said, "I rather hope you choke on yours. As for Ian MacGregor...."

"Don't judge him quite yet," Douglas said surprisingly, and though she glanced quickly at his face she could read nothing from it.

Mr. Ewing came to ask Monica to dance, a twinkle in his eyes, and this was a kind of reprieve. As she let him waltz her about the floor in a delightfully old-fashioned manner, she realized that she'd become really fond of the Ewings. The Sedgewicks, Clarence Fielding, old Mr. Nelson and a number of others in the group had definitely stirred her affections, too, and it would be hard to say goodbye to them in Boston.

Mr. Ewing said, "It was kind of you to introduce

Emily to your friend the lord. I don't think I have to tell you it will be the highlight of her whole trip.''

"Well," Monica answered, "after last night I'd say she deserved a pleasant experience. She's really remarkable, and she's been a wonderful person to tour with. I wish I had half her spirit."

He smiled. "It *is* quite a spirit," he admitted. "I know. I've had fifty years of experience with it."

"Really?"

"That was the main reason for this trip," he confided. "We've been celebrating our golden, though it doesn't seem possible. The years have gone too quickly, and I've enjoyed every one of them with her...even though we've had our downs as well as our ups. Then last night, when I thought I might lose her...."

He grinned before Monica could respond to this, and added, "Emily would be the first to say that you don't get rid of bad pennies all that easily!"

CHAPTER TWENTY-ONE

THE GALA EVENING finally came to an end. Iris rapped on a table for order and then warned the group that they faced an early start in the morning. She smiled at the chorus of groans that arose when she told them their luggage should be in the corridor outside their rooms by seven o'clock at the latest, and that they themselves should be in the lobby ready to leave by eight-thirty.

"Please do be prompt about this," she urged them, then added with a teasing note in her voice that took any sting out of her words, "and be sure you don't leave anything behind you!"

Iris concluded, "So, we had best call it a night. But for a topper, and so that none of you will forget Scotland, I am going to ask our bus driver, Donald Ferguson, to do us a special favor. He has been hiding from many of you the fact that he has a really glorious voice, and so now I am going to ask him to sing an old Scottish favorite."

The pianist struck a chord, and as Donald started to sing, something seemed to twist within Monica, and she gasped from the pain of it.

" 'By yon bonnie banks and by yon bonnie braes . . . where the sun shines bright on Loch Lomond. Where me and my true love were ever wont to gae...on the bonnie, bonnie banks of Loch Lomond....' "

Donald's voice soared pure and true.

Mrs. Ewing exclaimed anxiously, "Monica, my dear! You're as pale as a ghost. Is something wrong?"

"No," she said, struggling for self-control. "Nothing, really; I'll be all right in a minute."

She felt an oversized handkerchief thrust into her hand. Douglas whispered, "Take this, and pretend to sneeze."

She didn't need to pretend. She did sneeze, almost as if Douglas had prearranged it.

Donald came to the end of his song, and there was an appreciative round of clapping and cries for an encore. He responded with a rousing local drinking song.

" 'I belong to Glasgow,' " he began. " 'Glasgow is my town.' " Then, with a wry face, " 'But something's wrong with Glasgow, for it's going round and round....' "

Under the cover of laughter, Douglas urged, "Come with me; you need to get out of here for a breather." And as Monica nodded agreement he turned to say in an aside to Mrs. Ewing, " 'Tis that last bit of champagne. It went down the wrong way. Some fresh air will do the trick."

Mrs. Ewing, intent on the song now, nodded and whispered, "Take good care of her, Mr. MacConnach."

"Would that I *could* take care of you," Douglas muttered grimly as he led her out of the dining room and into the lobby. He drew her into a secluded corner and whispered, "Pretend to be wiping your eyes as if you really did choke a bit. At the same time, kindly don't argue with me. Just listen to what I am about to say."

There was a deadly seriousness to Douglas's tone, and because of this it was not at all difficult for Monica to become an instant actress. She sniffed and pretended to choke and blew her nose until Douglas, patting her on the back none too gently, said, "There, 'tis enough of that. Don't overdo it. Monica, not long ago you told me you would do anything in your power to help prove Ian MacGregor's innocence. Does that still hold true?"

Her eyes widened as she stared up at Douglas; it was impossible not to be daunted by the grimness of his expression. Somehow she knew, without being told, that the answer she was about to give him was crucial, though she couldn't understand why it should be.

But would she do anything in her power to help Ian? Regardless of everything that had happened between them, both the positive and the negative, she had no doubts at all when it came to this of all issues. Her love for Ian was so transcendent that when it came to the bottom line she knew only too well she would do anything for him. Anything at all.

She wanted to say a resounding yes to Douglas. But instead she hedged for a moment to ask, "What are you getting at?"

"I think you may be able to help him," Douglas told her, "though he'd have my hide if he knew what

I was about to suggest to you. However, before I make the suggestion I must ask you if you realize his reason for coming here tonight dressed in full regalia.''

"No," she answered honestly. "No, I don't."

"It was not to torment you, if that's what you think," Douglas assured her, reading her mind with disconcerting ease. "What he hoped to do was draw attention to himself."

"If that's the case," she said, "he certainly succeeded!"

"It was attention from certain quarters that he was thinking about," Douglas went on. "He was not seeking the limelight for his own glory."

"My," she responded bitterly, "you *have* become his champion, haven't you?"

"I believe him innocent," Douglas said, "and in my opinion 'tis wrong for any innocent man to have to live under a shadow of suspicion for the rest of his life. He himself detests the thought so much that he is willing to take any sort of risk in order to prove himself. That is why he came here tonight, Monica."

She sighed. "I must be very obtuse. I'm simply not following you, Douglas."

"We've reason to think that the person who attacked Mrs. Ewing will return tonight," Douglas explained. "We think that it was his intention to come back to make a second attempt at you, but it stands to reason that if Ian MacGregor himself could be his target, 'twould be a much more effective accomplishment. You *can* understand that, can't you?"

"I find it unbelievable," she said, "but then I've found everything about this unbelievable."

"You must admit that the attack on Mrs. Ewing was not fantasy, Monica," Douglas chided.

"All right," she answered wearily. "I do admit that. But I can't imagine why Ian would be so foolhardy as to deliberately set himself up in this way."

"For two reasons," Douglas said tersely. "Because, as I've said, if we can force the person behind all of this out into the open, he feels, as do I, that we will have his uncle's murderer. Also, his motivation was increased a thousandfold when he realized himself that there is apt to be another try at you before you leave Scotland. For all our man knows, you will be taking the medallion with you, Monica. And he would do much to stop that from happening. Acquiring that medallion would be the next best thing to getting rid of Ian MacGregor entirely, and 'tis my thinking that our man believes he can accomplish both tonight. He believes that an attack on you may enable him to retrieve the medallion, for he's certain to think that if you have it, you must carry it around with you, even though you haven't dared to wear it publicly. And he knows that such an attack will also smoke Ian out...."

"Is Ian supposed to be psychic?" she asked cynically. "Is he to know, via some sort of seventh sense that will come to him out there at Castle Monbraithe, that I'm being run down?"

"He isn't at Castle Monbraithe," Douglas said abruptly. "He is here in the hotel. Actually, he is in my room, but the impression has been given that he is in yours.''

''What?''

"Think it out, Monica," Douglas said impatiently. "To our man's way of thinking, Ian MacGregor is here for a last rendezvous with you before you leave Scotland—taking the medallion with you. According to his lairdship's plan, he will leave after this rendezvous supposedly has culminated. His intends to go across the parking lot to his car by himself—it's parked at the far side, near the tour buses. Every opportunity has been given our man to keep well out of sight, until he's ready to make his move.''

She frowned. "I suspect that you're not entirely thrilled with Ian's plan," she accused him.

"It is intensely dangerous," Douglas admitted, "even though there will, of course, be a number of us watching and waiting and ready to move in. But if our man elects to use a gun again, there is a good chance we will be too late. And in my opinion that is exactly what he has decided to do. He is an excellent shot; he has already proved that," Douglas pointed out ominously. "There would be no point to an attack upon the earl of Monbraithe unless it has a final conclusion. And on the other hand, he would have no wish to kill you. . . .''

"Oh?" she asked. "What makes you so sure of that?"

"There would be no point in it," Douglas said simply. "He does not want your life; he wants the medallion. We are convinced now that after he struck down Mrs. Ewing he paused long enough to go back and examine her, and that is when, certainly, he discovered his mistake. He also discovered, of course, that she did not have the Jacobite medallion."

"You think he actually *stopped*...?"

"Yes," Douglas said, "I think he actually stopped. There wasn't anyone about at the time; he made sure of that before he made his move. We shall make sure that the premises seem equally deserted tonight. We will give him every chance to carry out his plan, short of actually letting him execute it." He paused. "Ah, you're looking at me as if you don't believe me. But you must remember, Monica, that we are dealing with a political radical, a fanatic. Think of the things that such fanatics have been doing in other countries, whether or not they are caught in the act. Men like this are willing to sacrifice themselves for their causes—more than willing. There is a glory to it. They have gone beyond reason."

She nodded slowly. "Yes," she conceded. "I have to admit you're right about that."

"Well, then," Douglas continued, "don't you think it would be folly to let Ian MacGregor walk out to an almost certain doom?"

"Need you ask such a question?" she cried. "Of course I think it is folly; in fact 'folly' is a very weak word for what I think it is! But you forget, Douglas: I know Ian. How do you think you are going to stop him?"

"By your going first," Douglas answered softly, "if you are willing to do such a thing."

She found that she was holding her breath, and Douglas, watching her closely, said abruptly, "Forget it, Monica!"

"I will not forget it!" she exclaimed indignantly. "You've staggered me a bit, that's all. Do you wonder at that?"

"No, I can see that I have," he said grimly, "and 'tis more than foolish of me to suggest such a thing. As I said in the beginning, his lairdship would have my hide if he knew about this."

Monica swallowed hard. "Well," she said then, "he is not going to know of it. By the time he finds out, it will be all over. Just what is your plan, Douglas?"

"My plan *was* to walk out of here with you, and for the two of us to get into a fair argument once we were just outside the door," he confessed. " 'Twould not be difficult for us to simulate an argument, God knows! I would tell you that I know Ian MacGregor has left a car for you, and that you intend to go to a final rendezvous with him at Castle Monbraithe. And I would profess great jealousy, of course. As I've said, there is indeed such a car parked directly across the way, but you would have no need to go near it at all. As a matter of fact, I would want you to retreat almost at once. You would be aware that someone is going to try to run you down with a car—I feel certain that same approach will be used where you are concerned—so there would be no element of surprise, as there was with Mrs. Ewing. You could run directly back into the hotel. Meantime, there are police officers in plain clothes all around this place.

They are watching us now, and they would be watching you every second, of course, fully prepared to go into action. Still, there is considerable risk.... In fact, I'm convinced as I speak of it that there is entirely too much risk. We shall have to find another way to smoke our man out.''

Monica smiled faintly. ''What you actually intended to ask was that I be your pigeon, then?''

''I beg your pardon?''

''In old-fashioned American gangster parlance, that means you've been planning to set me up,'' Monica told him. ''Well, consider it done, Douglas. I am going to walk directly across the lobby and out that front door!''

''I forbid it.'' Douglas reached over to lay a restraining hand on her arm.

''There is no point in your forbidding it,'' she insisted. ''If you try to keep me from going, I shall make an absolutely horrible scene and blow the whole thing open for you. As it is, we certainly look like we're quarreling already. I don't think it will take much more acting on our parts to make our dissension thoroughly convincing.''

''Damn it, Monica,'' he hissed.

''Come on, Douglas!'' And with her chin held high she started away from him.

She pushed open the heavy glass entrance doors and stood shivering in the chill of the October night. It was drizzling very slightly, and she wished that she had a wrap of some sort with her to sling around her shoulders.

Douglas, immediately behind her, said furiously,

"Damn it, Monica, get back inside! You'll catch your death of cold, among other things."

"I am going to him," she declared distinctly, and heard Douglas curse violently, not entirely under his breath.

"What makes you think he is at Monbraithe?" he asked then.

"Because while we were dancing he told me he would wait for me there," she fibbed, and was a bit surprised at her fluency in such a department. "He's had more than enough time to get back."

Douglas's laugh was harsh. "What do you think?" he demanded. "That he is going to receive you with his aunt and his cousin in attendance?"

"No," she responded, searching for an inspiration, then clutched at the first thought that flew in her direction. "I am to meet him at Angus Grewar's cottage. Angus and Annie will stay at the castle tonight. Ian arranged that."

"So," Douglas said in a voice that was dangerously calm, "it is to be the perfect rendezvous?"

"Yes," she told him defiantly. Now she let fantasy take over, only wishing in this particular instance that it was fact. "We shall not see each other again until he comes to the States for the wedding," she said, and her words seemed to ring out into the night with crystal clarity.

"Monica," Douglas began, and as he reached out to her, she knew that in another moment he literally would be dragging her back inside.

"No!" she cried, so peremptorily that he stiffened. "This is what I want—you must understand that! Go back to the others, Douglas. I know what I'm doing.''

"You *think* you know what you're doing," he thundered. "Can you seriously believe that the earl of Monbraithe is going to marry a penniless American?''

"Yes," she said, and only wished to God it was true. "Yes, I can seriously believe it!"

She had reached the first of the streetlights that encircled the parking lot, and although it was dim she could see Douglas's eyes clearly as he looked down at her. It seemed to her that they held a curious mixture of apprehension, admiration and a third ingredient that, she knew, was going to prove to be her trump card. Uncertainty.

Douglas wanted her back into the hotel for her own sake. Yet he also wanted her to continue with this perilous experiment because he knew it was their one chance of proving Ian's innocence, without a danger far more terrible to Ian than any peril she possibly could face now.

She seized the situation, turning it to her advantage as she started forward. "Go back, Douglas," she told him. "Even if you stop me now I shall only start out later, and you can't stand guard over me every second of every hour until it's time to leave for Prestwick.''

She saw him shrug ever so slightly, and she knew that she had won. "Very well, Monica," he answered quietly. "But take care."

There was something particularly ominous about this understated warning. A feeling that was quite a stranger to her came to clutch her throat, and she recognized it as fear.

She stood waiting under the streetlight until Douglas turned on his heel and went back into the hotel, and she heard the glass doors clang behind him. Then she tensed and touched her hands to her shoulders, hugging herself to ward off not just the chill of the steady drizzle but also the danger that was lurking out there beyond her range of vision. And in the cold quiet of this November night, she knew that she'd never before been quite so alone.

It didn't do to think. She forced herself *not* to think at all as she started out across the lot toward the car parked just beyond the shadows. And then all at once it seemed to her as if the lights of the entire world had been switched upon her.

The roar of the car engine was a thunderous thing; surely no sound had ever been louder. And the headlights bearing down upon her were the evil eyes of a malevolent giant. Douglas had said there would be no element of surprise this time, but she had time to think to herself, in fact almost to say aloud, that he'd been wrong about that. Despite the fact that she had known what was almost certainly going to happen, the element of surprise was strong, and she stood rooted to the spot.

Only when she heard a shout somewhere behind her did she manage to move, but it was too late. She felt as if she were being clamped into a vise and then thrown into space like a sack full of flour.

Her head seemed to burst as she collapsed onto the concrete. She felt the wind roaring past her as she heard shots fired, brakes squealing and the climactic finale of a crash. The horrible ripping crunch of metal and the brittle explosion of shattering glass were the last sounds to reach her.

Then she fainted.

throp," Walter insisted, and then smiled. "Come to think of it," he observed to the room at large, "had Ian not gone to the rescue as he did I should hardly have been able to get a clear aim. So I would say we rather worked things together, Ian," he finished, seeming very pleased about this.

Monica's head was spinning. She sipped Walter's whisky, then coughed violently. It was straight Scotch, and it tasted to her like concentrated peat.

Regaining her breath, she asked in a small voice, "Could someone tell me what has happened?"

"Later," Ian promised.

She shook her head, then winced because it hurt. "No," she said, her voice gaining strength. "Not later. Now."

"If you don't mind, your lairdship, I shall fill her in on a few details," Douglas suggested. "Mr. Mac-Gregor, I rather think you'd better give your cousin a bit of that whisky, too."

Walter nodded, filled another glass and passed it to Ian, who tossed it down neatly and said, "Thanks."

"And how about you, Mr. MacConnach?" Walter offered.

"Yes, if you please."

Monica felt as if her nerves would surely begin screeching aloud in protest as Walter carefully measured out whisky for Douglas and handed the glass to him, then poured a drink for himself. Douglas sipped with aggravating slowness, and it was only then that he began, "You already know, Monica, that I'm in government service?"

"Yes."

"Well, forgive me if I seem to be telling you things you already have heard, but 'tis necessary to take it all in order."

"I'm sure it is," she replied.

Douglas glanced at her suspiciously, then continued, "For the past few months I have been on loan from my usual post so that I might have a fairly free hand in looking into the matter of the late earl of Monbraithe's death. As you may know, the gentleman you saw his lairdship with earlier this evening is his solicitor, and from the beginning he has been thoroughly convinced of his lairdship's innocence. So convinced, that when the 'not proven' verdict was handed down some strings were pulled, as you might say in the States. Since I'd had a bit of success in similar matters, I was assigned to the case.

"Now," Douglas went on, "as you already realize, the Jacobite medallion plays an important part in the background of all of this. It is a venerable piece, it has a tremendous history, and 'twould be easy for it to become a symbol of sorts."

"What kind of symbol?" she managed.

"Well, if it got into certain political hands—radical hands—'twould be easy for it to become a symbol indicating that the Monbraithes, a great Scottish family, stand prepared to fight for separation from England at any cost. You can imagine the widespread impact this could have.

"The old laird realized this, but when the medallion proved to be missing he preferred to think first that either Jane MacGregor had taken it to Inverness or his nephew had become involved with an attractive

American and—in a burst of international generosity, let us say—had given it to her.''

Monica closed her eyes. ''I can't believe you are serious,'' she protested weakly.

Ian's voice rang out peremptorily. ''MacConnach, she's exhausted! Let this wait until she's had some rest, will you?''

''No,'' Monica insisted, shaking her head again despite the pain this caused. ''I want to hear all of it now!''

''Well,'' Douglas continued, without waiting for a verdict in the matter from Ian, ''after the old laird's murder, and with the medallion still missing, it became vital to know the truth. This is when I was assigned to the case, and—if I may resort to an Americanism again—I found an excellent 'cover' could be arranged through my acting as a tour guide. It was work with which I was familiar, and it was a simple enough matter to set up.

''I was hired, and I started making trips throughout this region. I made it a point to take the tour groups to certain shops, to frequent certain inns for lunch or dinner, so that I could become better acquainted with the people hereabouts and they with me. Finally I began to wonder myself if his lairdship had given you the medallion, Monica, perhaps as a token of an engagement between the two of you.''

''Douglas,'' she bristled, ''don't be ridiculous!'' She didn't dare look at Ian.

''Very well,'' Douglas said, ''I was wrong. And as a matter of fact, the medallion has been recovered in these past few days.''

Her eyes sparked dangerously. "And you didn't tell me so?"

"No, Monica, I did not tell you so," Douglas admitted.

"Douglas—"

"Don't blame him, Monica," Ian broke in, his voice so weary that her own breath caught in her throat as she looked at him. "He wasn't trying to deceive you, but it was essential that we keep the medallion's recovery a closely guarded secret."

"As indeed you did," Walter said reproachfully. "Ian, you know, damn it, how upset my mother has been about the medallion. Couldn't you have told her at least?"

"No," Ian interrupted, "I couldn't have. In this situation too many walls have had ears, Walter. It isn't that I mistrusted either you or your mother, and certainly I have never mistrusted Monica, but—"

"Where was it?" Walter demanded coldly.

"Brucie Grewar had it," Ian said.

"Brucie Grewar?" Walter's astonishment was obviously genuine.

Brucie Grewar. Angus's distant relative—and Ian's, too, Monica supposed—who was a shepherd of sorts and perhaps a bit retarded, from what Walter had told her. Brucie Grewar, who lived alone in a cottage on the grounds of Castle Monbraithe.

Walter shook his head disbelievingly. "What would Brucie have wanted with the medallion?" he asked. "You can't be right about this!"

"He is right about it, Mr. MacGregor," Douglas told him. "Brucie Grewar's motive for taking the medallion was to keep it safe. The theft, if it is to be called that, was accomplished the same night his lairdship and Monica visited the castle, after your uncle had asked his lairdship to be sure the medallion was in its proper place. The old laird suspected that someone might have a go at stealing it—''

''And he thought it was my mother,'' Walter interrupted bitterly.

''I doubt that,'' Douglas said. ''I think he realized full well the sort of political use to which the medallion could be put. And I would say that he had made up his mind, from what he told a few of his confidantes, to come out and state his position at the next session of Parliament so that there could be no doubt about where the Monbraithes stood on the issue of devolution. I would assume that actually he made this clear to too many people, with the result that he was killed before he could take action. Then an accident was arranged so that the present laird would become the scapegoat.

''On the night of which we are speaking, however,'' Douglas continued, ''Brucie Grewar had been at a pub in town, and he overheard conversations that made him think there was going to be an attempt at stealing the medallion. So he went to the castle himself—like Angus, he had a key—and he took the medallion and was leaving when his lairdship drove up with Monica. This is how he heard her American accent so clearly, and later he told Angus about it.

''At the time, Angus was not suspicious. Angus's wheels turn slowly, but they do turn, and eventually he began to wonder about Brucie's having been so close to the castle that night. There was no reason at all, though, to suspect Brucie of a politically motivated theft. Nothing could interest the lad less. But he is a member of the clan and loyal to it, and he was acting in an age-old instinct of preservation.''

"You don't have to make a hero of him, MacConnach,'' Walter said sourly.

"Well,'' Douglas responded, "I don't doubt that in his own mind he was a hero at the moment. Later he began to have second thoughts, and after the murder he was terrified. He didn't dare come out and say he had the medallion, and he kept it hidden in his cottage, surely the last place anyone would ever look. The months passed, and as a matter of fact I believe Brucie when he says that he more or less forgot about the medallion. Angus didn't give it any particular thought, either, until the day when you appeared at the gate, Monica. Then he remembered the old laird's accusation about your having been given the medallion by his nephew, and he started to wonder. Only two days ago, he approached his lairdship and asked him outright about it. . .and was given a direct answer. And 'tis then that his thoughts turned to Brucie.''

"And so Brucie confessed.''

"Not quite that easily,'' Douglas said. "Angus, in fact, was afraid that Brucie would try to get rid of the medallion even to the point of throwing it into the loch, and that is one reason why I made my trip out to Castle Monbraithe that night, Monica. We talked to Brucie, all of us. . . .''

"And you knew *then* that the medallion had been recovered?" she demanded incredulously.

"Yes, we did."

"And you, Ian, can still say that Douglas didn't deceive me?" she accused scathingly.

"It was a necessary deception," Ian insisted. "It was not MacConnach's intention to keep the truth from you, but for the moment we couldn't tell anyone. I even held my breath about Angus, much as I trust him, and about Brucie, for that matter. MacConnach put the fear of God in Brucie in regard to what would happen if he discussed the matter with anyone."

"I can imagine," she said bitterly.

"Monica—" a note of desperation edged through the fatigue in Ian's voice "—I would not knowingly have kept any of the truth from you if I'd had a choice; surely you must realize that. Any more than I would have countenanced your being lured over here as you were, had I known anything about it in time to stop you."

"Lured over here?" Now she actually managed to sit up, even though her head at once began to throb as she did so. "What do you mean by that?"

Douglas said slowly, "Well, you see, despite all of our efforts during the months past, neither the Jacobite medallion nor any evidence that would support his lairdship's innocence came to light. So it became apparent to us that in order to complete the cycle we must in some way lure back the American girl who—though entirely inadvertently—had stepped into the very midst of the situation on her first trip to Scotland.''

Monica's eyes narrowed. ''Are you telling me that Pamela didn't really break her ankle?'' she demanded.

''I am afraid I must admit that she didn't,'' Douglas answered reluctantly. ''You see, by then we had traced you via the tour you took with your late aunt. We'd established your identity—with no help from his lairdship, I might add—and we knew that you came from Boston. We confided in Pamela that we were trying to locate you, though we didn't, of course, tell her why, and to our amazement, considering the size of your country, she actually knew you personally.''

''It isn't so amazing when you're dealing with New England,'' Monica said grudgingly.

''Regardless, we couldn't believe our good fortune,'' Douglas went on. ''We had to take Pamela into our confidence to a limited extent at that point, and she agreed to go along with us. So we arranged the 'accident,' and we were vastly relieved when you were persuaded to step in as her substitute.''

Monica sighed deeply. ''I shall never again believe in anything or anybody,'' she stated. ''What about Iris? Was she in on the whole thing, too?''

''No,'' Douglas said. ''Iris is quite what she appears to be. She knows nothing of any of this. She believed that Pamela broke her ankle because Pamela did an excellent acting job when we took her to the airport. Of course, we had her leg in a cast and all the rest of it.''

"Suppose," Monica said, "I hadn't agreed to come here voluntarily. What would you have done then?"

Douglas had the grace to look sheepish. "We would have attempted to think of something else," he admitted. "It was most important that we get you back to Scotland. But you did come, and so no further invention was needed."

"And," she said bitterly, "I imagine that I exceeded your wildest expectations! I even made a sufficient fool of myself to go right out to Loch Lomond at the first opportunity. What an innocent little fly I was, walking into your web!"

"Monica!" Ian protested.

"Oh, *please*!" she said, weary and aching and disillusioned. "You were in it up to your neck with the rest of them, Ian, so don't try to pretend otherwise. All you were interested in was clearing your own name and getting back your precious medallion. Now you can go about your life and marry your whisky heiress and live happily forever after, and frankly I don't give a damn what you do!"

She was conscious that all three men were staring down at her, and that Douglas and Walter, at least, looked thoroughly appalled. She couldn't even begin to read Ian's expression.

Wanting this over with, wanting to get away from all of them, yet possessed at the same time of an almost desperate need to know, she said, "Now, suppose we omit past history for the moment and get down to the present. Could one of you please tell me what happened tonight?"

THE KNOCK CAME, loud and authoritative. A voice called out, " 'Tis Alex."

Walter said quickly, "I'll let him in." And he opened the door to a tall angular Scot with tousled brown hair, a craggy face and pale gray eyes that even now seemed to hold a hint of humor.

Ian, Monica saw, had tensed to the point where he looked as if he were about to snap apart. "How is he?" he demanded hoarsely.

"He'll live," the newcomer answered. "In fact, he undoubtedly will make a complete recovery. If I may speak as a human being and a friend of yours, rather than a physician, he doesn't deserve that much." His eyes fell on Monica. "So," he said. "I am delighted to meet you, Miss Winthrop."

Walter broke in hastily, "This is Alex MacDuff, Miss Winthrop. Our friend and, heaven help us, also our doctor."

Alex MacDuff nodded pleasantly enough, but his eyes just now were on Ian. "You look like hell," he observed, "and for good reason, I understand. I've been told that you felt a sudden great inclination to do some gymnastics?"

"So I did," Ian agreed casually.

It was too much! Monica, thoroughly irritated, blurted, "Must you all act as if you're at some sort of cricket match, or is that purely English rather than Scottish? I'm leaving Scotland in the morning, and I can assure you I won't be sorry to go; but before I depart from this charming country of yours, I'd like to know a few of the facts if it's possible for any of you to get down to essentials."

Ian and Douglas started to speak simultaneously, and at once Douglas said, "I'm sorry, m'laird."

Monica, disgusted with both of them, said, "Don't be so damned subservient to him, Douglas! He doesn't deserve it."

She saw Ian wince, and he said, "She's right, Mac-Connach. But she deserves to be told the whole story. I should like to add my part to it, but I'm afraid I am going to have to ask you to excuse me. . . ."

Alex MacDuff, Monica noticed, was watching Ian very closely. Now he asked, "Walter, do you have your car here?"

"Yes," said Walter, and it seemed to Monica that he had acquired a new dignity; certainly he was exhibiting a new confidence in himself. Whatever the events of tonight, and even if they meant that he wasn't about to become the earl of Monbraithe in Ian's stead, Walter had come out on the plus side, she decided. In a way that she didn't yet fully understand, he had proved himself, and the teddy-bear illusion was dissipating. He was standing tall and straight, even holding himself in a different manner so that there seemed nothing flabby about him at all. No, this new Walter had the potential of being an attractive man, a Scot approaching middle age with his feet on the ground and, she suspected, quite a future ahead of him.

The doctor suggested, "Get Ian downstairs, will you? I'd appreciate it if you'd help, Mr. MacConnach. I shall follow you out to Monbraithe, but first I want to look Miss Winthrop over, to be sure that she's sound enough to make the trip back to the

States. Once you get Ian into the car, you can come back up here, Mr. MacConnach, and tell her all these things she's so eager to hear.''

Douglas nodded. Then he added, ''You're sure you don't want me to go along to the castle?''

''No. Angus can help at the other end. There now, Ian. Steady. Take it slowly.''

Monica closed her eyes tightly, almost feeling Ian's pain, too, even though she had a fair share of her own. What hurt the most was the deep feeling that she had been misused terribly by both Ian and Douglas.

She heard Ian swear softly, and it was Walter who said now, ''Steady there, man!'' She clenched her hands together, forcing herself not to open her eyes, not to look at Ian as he left the room.

After a moment a gentle voice at her side murmured, ''There, now. 'Tis not really all that bad, is it?''

She found that Alex MacDuff's pale gray eyes could be astonishingly warm and compassionate. Now her fear was that she would go completely to pieces if he were too kind to her.

He said, ''I can well imagine how you must be feeling, thinking that you were brought to Scotland as some sort of decoy, and that everything since has been arranged and plotted with you as an innocent victim. Yes,'' he continued, sensing her surprise, ''I do know a fair bit about it, my dear. I am very close to the principals involved, but at the moment 'tis as a physician that I'm approaching you. Later MacConnach, who is very competent about such things, can tell you everything you want to know. But for the present, young lady, I am going to examine you.''

This he did, calmly and adroitly. Finally he straightened up, to say with satisfaction, ''I am certain there's nothing too seriously amiss, I'm happy to tell you. Fortunately, Ian's reflexes remain excellent, despite the injuries he suffered last year. Thanks to him, the car didn't even brush you. The nasty shock and bruises you're feeling are the result of his having tossed you out of its path.

''Now let Douglas talk to you,'' Alex MacDuff suggested. ''Then I shall ask your friend Iris to come and keep you company while you take a very hot bath and, after that, you can take the sleeping pills I'm going to give you.''

Monica smiled up at him through a shimmer of tears. ''Thank you, Alex MacDuff,'' she said softly. ''You've very nearly restored my faith in Scotland.''

He smiled back and answered gently, ''I cannot blame you for losing it, at least for a time, Monica. But 'tis not Scotland that has been the culprit in all of this, not really. Rather, 'twas the rampage of a bundle of the sort of negative emotions that have been in the world since the beginning of time . . . or, at the least, since the beginning of man. Envy, greed— unfortunately those are 'commodities' common to all of us, international in scale. But so, though we sometimes tend to lose sight of the fact, are kindness and tolerance and love.''

Alex MacDuff hesitated, and she had the feeling he was about to say something more to her, but then he merely shook his head and smiled. ''Try to take things as easy as you can on your way back home. I know you've a job to do with the tour group, and responsibilities with it, but MacConnach will see to it that the major part of the burden is taken off your shoulders.

"Till we meet again," he said. And with that he left her.

CHAPTER TWENTY-THREE

DOUGLAS APPROACHED MONICA almost timidly. He pulled up a chair by the side of the bed and then seemed to sag with weariness, as he sat down on it. His face, too, was marked with a fatigue made pronounced, she realized, by the letdown after months of playing a role in which he didn't really belong.

It was strange to see Douglas like this. She felt a twinge of sympathy for him but managed to suppress it with very little effort. Douglas had used her; she couldn't forget it. Nor could she forget or forgive Ian, for it seemed to her that he had played upon her emotions in a truly unforgivable way. It was enough that she had been ''lured'' to Scotland. But Ian had been guilty of quite a different and far more devastating kind of luring, in taking her to his solicitor's apartment in Glasgow. Now, when she thought of his lovemaking, those traitorous sensual feelings came to arouse her once again; to her shame, for she despised herself for this sort of weakness. All of her New England background—a fair part of it puritanical, though in an era now long past, to be true—seemed to assert itself as she thought of Ian's treachery. She didn't at all like the effect such thoughts were having upon her.

She remembered "maiden ladies" whom she had known back home in Boston; there was a certain tight-lipped austerity about them, and they were quick to make it plain that they had very little use for men. Occasionally, delving deeper, she had learned that there had indeed been a man in the background of many of these women: a man who had abandoned them, or let them down in some other unspeakable way, just as Ian had done to her.

She tried to tell herself it was ridiculous to hate all men simply because of a Scottish laird who had blatantly used her to serve his own purpose. She thought of men like Gerald Strothers and almost wished that she had accepted his proposal of a few weeks back. Instead she had resigned from her job...and as a result had been free to take this fill-in position with Magic Carpets Unlimited.

Now she wondered how it might have been had the course of her personal history gone otherwise. If she had accepted Gerald, they might already be married or, at the least, planning a Christmastime wedding. She would be settling into an entirely different kind of life, slated to become a relatively proper Bostonian. In time the memories of Scotland, and a handsome man with dancing blue eyes, would have faded so that it no longer hurt to remember. She would, of course, never have discovered why Ian had failed to come to Prestwick that day; but now that she knew his reasons, might it not have been better to remain in ignorance?

This was not a question to which she could give a fair answer, she told herself glumly; certainly not yet, at least. Maybe time and distance would bring with them objectivity. Then she could hope to put everything that had happened in a clearer perspective, and for her own sake rid herself of some of the hate that seemed to be creeping into the very fiber of her being.

She sighed, and Douglas broke into her thoughts. "I cannot tell you how sorry I am."

"Spare yourself," Monica told him crisply.

He surveyed her morosely. "I know 'tis not the time to talk to you about anything personal," he conceded, "but I can't choose another opportunity, more's the pity, because with the morning you will be gone from Scotland. And I simply cannot let you go like this—"

"I hardly think you or anyone else could stop me," she informed him coldly.

"No," Douglas agreed, "just now I am sure that we could not. Perhaps someday I shall make a trip of my own to the States so that I can attempt to make you look at matters a bit differently than you are bound to look at them now, when you are so emotionally involved."

So emotionally involved indeed! This rankled, and she said, the words edged with ice, "Save yourself the expense, Douglas."

Ordinarily, he would have risen to such conversational bait and would have been quick with a retort, but he only shook his head sadly. "What can I say to you?" he asked her. "I might remind you of your own words; that's about all I can do."

"*My* words?"

"Yes," he nodded. "You told me you'd do anything within your power to establish his lairdship's innocence. Well, that, don't you see, is exactly what you have done, Monica. Without—"

"Without me," she said bluntly, "I am sure you would have found another little red herring to dangle along a trail. In the end, you would have caught your man. You always catch your man, don't you, Douglas?"

"We'd like to think we do, here in Scotland," he allowed. "Though I think you actually are referring to England's Scotland Yard, or else are conjuring up the ghost of Sherlock Holmes."

She surveyed him coldly. "I don't think it's exactly the moment for making jokes," she told him. "Not very good jokes, either."

"I wasn't trying to be funny, Monica," he protested. "If it seems that way, it's because I don't know what to say to you."

"Well," she suggested, "why don't you try to avoid being personal and tell me what happened tonight. That's all I want to know, and even Ian said it's information I have a right to hear."

"So you do," Douglas agreed. "After you've heard me out, though, please promise that you'll do what the doctor told you to do. Iris will come in, and then you are to take a hot bath and the sleeping drafts he prescribed for you—"

"Please, Douglas," she said. "You're stalling!"

"I suppose I am," he admitted. "I don't know quite how to begin. 'Tis a bit on the complicated side, the whole thing. I see that Walter left the whisky. Would you mind if I have a drink?"

"Help yourself."

He shrugged. "'Tis not much of an invitation, but I'll accept it." He went to the dresser, found a glass, poured, drank and then poured again. She watched in surprise, because she already had learned that usually, when it came to imbibing whisky or doing much of anything else, Douglas, while on the job at least, was very discreet.

"Now," he said, sitting down again, the second glass of whisky in his hand, "I will try to give you your facts—and be brief as possible about it."

"Thank you." There was definite irony in her tone.

"As you know," Douglas began, disregarding this, "the present laird's uncle, Terence MacGregor, was the oldest son in his particular branch of the family, and so when his father died he inherited the title. That is to say, he became the earl of Monbraithe."

"Yes," she broke in impatiently, "I know that. Must we have a course in the history of the Scottish nobility, Douglas?"

"I only wish to be sure that you fully understand the situation," Douglas said imperturbably. "Now, the second son—Ian MacGregor's father—went off to war and married a Frenchwoman. As you also know, I'm sure, 'twas quite a few years before she had a child, and then she died giving birth to him.

"The third son—Walter's father—had married quite early in life and had sired Walter. But the laws being as they are, this made no difference when it came to inheriting the title. However, when the third son was killed while still in military service, Walter actually was second in line for the title, for Ian had not yet been born. I think this is one reason why Jane MacGregor brought Walter to Monbraithe. By then, Terence's wife had left him. Jane became both housekeeper and hostess for him. She was ambitious, and more than a mite jealous. 'Tis said that over the years she never gave up hope of marrying Terence, but he wanted no part of such an alliance. As you've already heard, at one point he put her in her place about wearing the Jacobite medallion.''

''Yes,'' Monica said, ''and it seems to me that it was needlessly cruel of him.''

''That may or may not be,'' Douglas conceded. ''You must remember that well before this Ian's father had been killed in a hunting accident, and so Ian stood to inherit. As soon as Ian was born, Walter went down a peg in the line of succession, for that matter. As you may imagine, all of this made Jane very bitter. But not,'' Douglas added hastily, noting her expression, ''bitter enough to ensure by committing murder that Walter become the earl of Monbraithe. Also, Walter never has cared very much about the title himself—although he loves Monbraithe but strictly as a property. Walter, I would say, is a typical Scottish country gentleman. He loves to hunt, to fish, and he loves agriculture; he knows more than a bit about sheep raising and is intensely interested in it. In fact, I'm sure the present earl of Monbraithe would be the first to agree that his cousin is far more suited to run the estate than he is, quite regardless of who holds the title. But I am straying from the main point.''

Douglas finished his whisky and put the glass down, then continued, "Jane has fairly well solved her own problems, as I think Walter has probably told you. She has agreed to marry a man in Inverness, whom she has known for years. He is in a position to give her a great deal of what she wants, even though he doesn't have a title. Jane's forthcoming marriage, your Ian tells me, has already had a great effect on Walter—"

"He is not 'my Ian,'" she interrupted sharply.

"Very well," Douglas nodded, with a mildness that at once made her suspicious. "In any event, Walter is finally becoming free of his mother's domination. It is quite a heady feeling for him: for the first time in his life he is in a position of being able to breathe entirely for himself; and I do not think, at the moment, that he would remotely consider asking for anything more than that. I would say that there will be a new Walter MacGregor emerging, and he shows promise of becoming quite a man—"

"You can spare me the character analysis, Douglas," she interrupted again.

"Very well," Douglas said, but he looked at her reprovingly. "I suppose," he added, "that I cannot blame you for being touchy, but even so, Monica—"

"*Touchy!*" she fumed. "Douglas, for God's sake, you've gone around a whole range of mountains and you still haven't got to the point. *Who was it?*"

"Bobby Grier—the garage mechanic. He is the stepson, rather than the son of blood, of the lady who runs the gift shop at Loch Lomond."

Douglas reached into his pocket and brought forth

a somewhat crumpled pack of cigarettes. He lighted one rather absently, without bothering to offer the pack to her; which in itself was proof of his state of mind, for Douglas was usually scrupulously polite if nothing else.

He said, "I should have had some inkling before I did. I had thought of Brucie Grewar, to tell you the truth. I had even thought of Angus and Annie. But I did not think of the Griers. I had already realized there must be someone about with a dreadful lust for power, someone who was greedy to the point of near insanity, someone willing to kill for a title and estate and all the political power and prestige that would go with it.

"I even thought of Walter," Douglas confessed, "though from the beginning he didn't seem the right man. Nor did I entirely absolve the present laird. . . ."

"Ian?"

"Yes," Douglas nodded. "After all, his name had not been cleared, and at first glance he surely seemed to be the one to benefit the most from the old laird's death.

"Actually, I suppose I suspected Ian MacGregor to some extent until you came on the scene, though by then I'd become fairly convinced that he couldn't have been the guilty one. And once he'd talked to me I was completely on his side." Douglas snuffed out his cigarette and said very slowly, "He is quite a man, Ian MacGregor."

There was nothing she could find to answer this, though she sensed he was waiting for her to comment. At length he sighed. "Well, you see, when it comes to Bobby Grier, his family belong to the Mac-Gregor clan, as do the Grewars. Also, once I began to look into his background and learned a bit about his habits and the rest, I came to realize that he had been something of a political activist for quite a while. His mother filled me in a bit on that. She is a fine lady; she shares none of his convictions, and I knew she deplored the people he was associating with.

"Even so, the connection seemed so remote that I couldn't seriously consider Bobby Grier as having murdered the old laird with the thought of one day inheriting the title himself. At this point I began to look up the line of succession myself, and I came across facts that astonished me.

"When it was finally traced out, it became clear that, incredible though it may seem, if Ian and Walter both were dead, it would indeed be Bobby Grier who stood to inherit Monbraithe. And after him—equally incredible—Brucie Grewar, and then Angus!"

Monica shook her head. "It's archaic," she told Douglas. "The whole system is absolutely archaic!"

"Not really," he protested. "Perhaps, in this case, 'tis just a matter of the MacGregors not having been as prolific as they should have been in the past generation or so."

She glanced at him with quick suspicion, but he was quite expressionless. However, she knew Douglas! Although at the moment, she thought wryly, their respective senses of humor were poles apart. . . .

"You can imagine," Douglas said now, "what it did to the ego of someone like Bobby Grier when he realized there was a chance—even a slight chance—of his becoming the earl of Monbraithe. He was frank to tell us, when he became conscious shortly after being taken to hospital, that he could vividly imagine himself as the earl of Monbraithe, with the historic Jacobite medallion in his possession, actually starting a revolution that would bathe Scotland in blood. That is fanatic beyond the pale, to my mind, but Grier was entirely too paranoid to see what a fool he was. In his own distorted mind he was convinced that he was about to create a new throne.

"I feel a bit of a fool myself," Douglas continued, "because though I'd known that he was something of a radical politically, Bobby Grier still seemed harmless to me. He is an excellent mechanic, he loves cars, and he seemed reasonably content with his work and his life in general. A bit on the headstrong side at times; that's all I could have said might have been a warning.

"Also, there was a woman in his life—a pretty if somewhat stupid girl who works in Bert's inn, where Ian took you to lunch. She saw you both—"

"There was a girl polishing the bar as we passed the door," Monica remembered.

"Yes, that would have been Sally. 'Twas she who made the phone call from the inn that puzzled Angus Grewar so. 'Twas she, too, who contacted Bobby to tell him you were back again, and then he personally answered the call to the castle, to fix your car. He had Sally quite convinced that if she went along with him, she stood to become the next Lady Monbraithe. 'Twould be she who would be wearing the Jacobite medallion; he promised her that.''

"She's told you all this?'' Monica asked.

"Yes,'' Douglas said. "Some of our men took her into custody this afternoon. But it was vital that we keep word of her arrest secret from Bobby Grier, or he surely would not have kept his rendezvous in the hotel parking lot tonight.

"Initially, he hoped only to get the medallion away from you; he was blindly convinced that you had it. Then, of course, he discovered that Ian was to be on the scene, and so he had a twofold opportunity. There would be only Walter then between the title and himself, and he'd already planned to sabotage Walter's car, which Walter was about to have him fix.''

They had driven home from Glasgow in that car, with Bobby Grier at the wheel. Thinking of this, Monica began to shiver.

"He's a smooth talker, Bobby Grier is,'' Douglas went on thoughtfully. "And his Sally, as I've said, is not the brightest lass in the world. 'Twas simple enough for him to convince her there was no harm to his scheme; certainly he never outlined it to her fully. She never guessed that he contemplated murder, or she wouldn't have gone along with him. Yet she gave him the perfect opportunity when she told him of the quarrel that was taking place between Laird Terence and Ian at Bert's.

"Bobby had been plotting murder for quite a while. He had only to put his plan into action, and the full element of surprise was in his favor. First he stalked Ian and knocked him unconscious, then he shot the old laird. After that he carried Ian to the Bentley and set the car on its course, leaping out himself before it gained full momentum. He had gauged the whole thing very well; but then he really knows his mechanics. What he did took *both* mechanical knowledge and considerable strength. He has a full share of both, plus the kind of daring that, as far as I can see, only comes with a certain brand of insanity.

"Afterward Bobby had only to bide his time; his prime frustration was that the medallion remained missing. But I don't think he was convinced you had it until you came back to Scotland. Then you became a real obstacle to him. I doubt it was his intention to kill you, unless the time came when he felt he had to do so. In that event," Douglas said gravely, "it's unlikely he would have hesitated.

"I have yet to account to Ian MacGregor for what happened to you tonight," Douglas went on. "That will be something to face tomorrow, and I cannot say I look forward to it. I thought that because you knew of what was likely to happen you would not be in great danger. There was no element of surprise, and there was room and more for you to get out of the way of the car—"

"I know," she said. "And I panicked."

"I would not say that," Douglas protested.

"Ah, but I did. It was quite a different matter to handle when I heard that horrible roar of the engine and saw those huge glittering eyes coming toward me." She saw the expression on his face and added quickly, "Douglas, I'm not blaming you—at least not for that. I had volunteered to do it, and you had no reason to think it would turn out as it did because of my own... terror."

"I should have remembered that you've not had the sort of training given to people in my kind of work," he said bitterly.

"Well," she told him, "you did have trained people who were all around the place. You thought I would be protected."

"Yes," he said, "and then at the last instant I wondered how many loopholes I'd left. That's when I saw Walter—and believe me, that was quite a terrible moment! I began to wonder if I'd been entirely wrong and if if could have been Walter after all, behind everything. Later I found that Walter had come back to the hotel because he hoped to see you one more time. He told me there was something quite urgent that he wanted to tell you, but I've no idea what it was.

"To go back a bit to that day when you hired a car and drove to Loch Lomond," Douglas went on. "It wasn't entirely the long arm of coincidence when Bobby Grier saw you there."

"He drove in as I was leaving," she said.

"Yes. He was broke, as he is so often wont to be, and he'd gone out to ask his stepmother for the loan of a pound or two. Actually, he had planned this particular maneuver in advance. A great planner, Bobby is. He had stopped by the day before to get a radio she'd asked him to fix, and he was on the premises, unnoticed, when the tour group mobbed the shop.

He saw Mrs. Ewing buy that turquoise stole and give it to you.

"When he came back the next day, you were just leaving, and his curiosity was whetted a bit. He suspected you were an American, and he asked his stepmother about you whilst he was joshing her about the tidy sums she must be making from the tour groups. Mrs. Grier told me this herself. She thought he merely was curious about you because despite his relationship with Sally, Bobby has always had an eye for pretty girls. Of course, Mrs. Grier didn't know your name, but she confirmed that you were an American. She also mentioned that you'd asked about Castle Monbraithe: she thought nothing of it at the time; she told him only because she was a bit amused at your interest in a castellated mansion. But she did say that you seemed startled when she mentioned that the old laird had died and Ian MacGregor had inherited. 'Twas only idle chatter on Mrs. Grier's part, but it set Bobby to thinking.

"He soon managed to learn that there was only one tour still operating with an American girl working for it and that she had joined the company just recently because of some sort of switch. Bobby began to suspect you might be 'the American' the old laird had spoken to Ian about, after Ian had been seen with you at Prestonfield and other places last year.

"Bobby would have contacted you one way or another, of that we are sure," Douglas continued. "But of course when a call came in from Castle Monbraithe reporting car trouble it was an unexpected stroke of good fortune, for it enabled him to confirm your identity without doubt. Then Sally called him to report that even then you were at Bert's with the young laird, and Bobby was exultant. He bragged to Sally that it wouldn't be long before he could get the medallion for her, and he told her he was going to Monbraithe personally to fix your car. Sally twisted his message somehow—as I've said, she's not overly bright—and so she called back to the castle to assure them that Bobby was on his way.

"At that point Bobby really *was* on his way again—with matters culminating tonight. I shall have nightmares for years to come, I suppose, when I think how nearly the young laird came to making a target of himself. He began to get suspicious, you see, when I didn't come back to the room as soon as I'd said I would, and so he decided to investigate. He'd brought along slacks and a sweater, and he changed out of the kilt and managed to come downstairs without anyone spotting him. Then he came outside—at the precise instant the car started to bear down upon you! You know the rest. . . ."

"And so now," Monica said, "all the world will know of Ian's innocence, and he can get married and live safely ever after, and have lots of children so that there will be no danger in the future of the title slipping into the wrong hands."

Douglas glanced at her curiously. "Yes, I suppose that is so."

"And what of Walter?"

"Walter will make his way," Douglas assured her.

"Do you really think that if an attempt on Ian's life had been successful, Bobby Grier would have gone ahead with his plan to sabotage Walter's car?''

"Yes, I think so." Then he rose. "That fairly sums it up, I'd say. Tomorrow I shall be going with the group to Prestwick, of course. Then 'twill be back to Edinburgh for me to my usual work, which is certain to seem tame after this episode! I think you should know, though, that Laird MacGregor's friends will be highly pleased to know his name has been cleared completely. And I shall tell them, you may be sure, that it was due in a large part to the courage of a very lovely young American woman. I know what you think of us, Monica, but even so I shall tell them that. And I can only hope that sometime...."

Douglas in his own way was as miserable as she was, and it was very hard to keep her heart steeled against him. Tears filled her eyes as she whispered, "Douglas, please, no more. Not tonight."

"No," he agreed, "not tonight. You've already had more than your share to contend with."

CHAPTER TWENTY-FOUR

MONICA AWOKE to the sound of rain spattering the windowpanes. She looked out onto a landscape as gray and bleak as her own mood. Scotland's skies had opened, and she felt as if it were her own bitter tears they were shedding.

Iris, she saw, was already up and gone. She finished her packing and put her suitcases outside the door and was relieved to find Iris's luggage there, too. For a moment, noting the empty bed, she'd been afraid that her roommate had once again taken off, possibly for good this time.

She put the electric kettle on to boil and had just finished making a cup of instant coffee when Iris returned. She was wearing a plaid skirt and her Magic Carpets jacket, which had been little in evidence since the beginning of the tour.

Iris was actually smiling, and with her eyes sparkling, she said, "You're not going to believe this, love!"

"What am I not going to believe?" Monica queried.

"I'm going with you! To the States, can you imagine? I shall have only a week or so there, and then I shall have to come back, but even so it is a wild dream come true."

Spooning powdered creamer into the coffee, Monica asked, "How did this happen?"

"Douglas set it up," Iris told her. "He can be quite a miracle worker when the mood strikes him— and he does have connections! Seems he used them last night, despite the lateness of the hour, and arranged for me to make the trip with you. I always have an up-to-date passport, of course; it's a job essential."

Then she sobered and went on, "Douglas has confided a bit about himself, and he told me you suspected I might have been in on the whole...plot. I wasn't, you know, Monica. Nor is Douglas very happy about his own part in things. He seems quite troubled this morning."

"There's no need for him to be," Monica responded with a briskness she didn't feel. "It's over and done with. Now all I want to do is forget the whole thing."

"Both you and Mrs. Ewing," Iris agreed. "It was much too close for both of you. Was the earl of Monbraithe really involved in all of this?"

"Iris, please," Monica said wearily. "I don't want to talk about it, not now. I *can't* talk about it just now!"

"I know," Iris nodded, "and I shouldn't even be asking you. The fact of the matter is I suppose I've been glad of something to take my mind off my own troubles."

Monica waited, hesitating to question the other girl; but then Iris, pretending an indifference she obviously wasn't feeling, told her, "It really is over this

time, Monica. That's what he told me in Glasgow...
after we'd been to bed together, I might add. He saw
to it that we had one more session of lovemaking,
damn him!''

"Iris—"

"Ah," Iris continued, "I should have seen that
proverbial handwriting on the wall. I *did* see it, as a
matter of fact. I refused to read what it said, that's
all. Now, though, there is no turning back. He is going to emigrate to Canada with his family just after
the new year...and so automatically, I guess you
could say, I've been put out of his life.

"At first," Iris added, her eyes very dark, "I
wanted to kill myself! So help me, I even thought of
throwing myself into the Clyde.''

"Iris," Monica reproached her, shocked. "What
an absolute *waste* that would have been!''

"I am starting to think so," Iris admitted. "At the
time, though, I wouldn't have given you tuppence for
my miserable existence. But now...well, I think
Douglas has shown me that as long as one's alive
there is awlays the chance of something good ahead.
This trip to the States, for instance.... ''

Monica smiled. Perhaps, after all, one of her
dreams was coming true. Perhaps Iris and Douglas
were finally going to realize how right they were for
each other. Although it would be a long while before
she personally could get over what she still considered Douglas's deceit, she was beginning to think
there had been some valid reasons for his behavior.
He had, after all, been engaged in a highly dangerous
and important mission. The old cliché all's fair in

love and war flashed through her mind, and she supposed that this actually had been a kind of war, in its way.

Then her smile faded. Douglas had achieved victory; so had Ian. But she, as much as Bobby Grier, was on the side of the defeated.

Now Iris went to the door and opened it. "Bless them," she said, glancing out. "It isn't yet seven-thirty, but I think they've all of them put their bags out. They *are* a dear bunch of lambs!" She turned back to ask, "Is the water still hot enough for me to have a cup of tea?"

"Yes, I'm sure it is. I had it at a full boil."

Iris nodded. "Well, I shall just pop a teabag into a cup and let it go at that, without brewing this time. Not that I call it really brewing. . . . ."

Monica laughed. "I think you'd stage a whole ceremony every time you drink a cup of tea if you had the chance," she teased.

"That I would. There's nothing like a properly brewed 'cuppa,' as I shall show you one day when you come to visit me in London," Iris promised. "Monica, are you going to stay with Magic Carpets? I'm certain they'll offer you a permanent job. Douglas and I both plan to give you the highest possible recommendation."

"That's kind of you," Monica said evasively. "But. . . I really don't know."

"Haven't you liked the experience, love? Oh, I know you had a miserable time of it last night, but that's the sort of thing that wouldn't happen once in a million tours, thank God."

"I'm sure it wouldn't," she agreed evenly. "I don't know, Iris. I love to travel, to be sure, and in that sense it's a great kind of job...really an unrivaled opportunity to see something of the world. But I suppose what I'm afraid of is that they'll assign me to Scotland again, and then—well, then I'd have to give it up."

Iris nodded sagely, then asked unexpectedly, "Are you still in love with him, Monica? The earl of Monbraithe *is* the Scot in your life, isn't he? It doesn't take much to put two and two together, and when you were dancing with him last night I think everyone in the room realized—"

"Then they were entirely wrong," Monica cut her off flatly.

But Iris's question lingered in her mind as she dressed. *Was* she still in love with Ian? Or had the proof of his deception finally managed to kill her feelings for him?

Just now, she couldn't come up with an answer. This in part was because she was still numb emotionally. She was, in fact, moving around like a robot, and she wondered if some of her inertia could be attributed to the sleeping pills Alex MacDuff had given her. She was not accustomed to taking things like that, and no doubt about it, they'd had a powerful effect on her. She'd been grateful to sink into pure oblivion, but now she wished she'd rally. She didn't want to fall asleep on the bus to Prestwick, nor did she enjoy lagging around, feeling as if she were only halfway there.

She brushed her hair into a chestnut swirl that

curled around her shoulders, and she was especially careful with her makeup, because the events of last night had taken a toll on her. She needed a bit of extra cosmetic camouflage just now, she told herself, and added silently that later there would be more than enough time to decide whether or not she still loved Ian, or whether he truly had killed everything she'd felt for him. *Years* in which to think about it!

Iris said, "I hope you didn't pack your rain gear," and Monica was reminded of a similar comment made by Mrs. Ewing at the beginning of the trip, when they were approaching Prestwick for a landing. It seemed incredible to think that the time interval between then and now was such a brief one. She felt as if she'd lived a lifetime in the course of it.

As she sighed Iris asked, "How do you feel, love? You do look more than slightly peaked. Douglas said the doctor told him you're certain to have a fair assortment of bruises and quite a bump on your head."

"A fairly respectable egg," Monica agreed, touching it gingerly. "I ache a bit, but Dr. MacDuff left some pills for that, too. I'll take them once we're airborne; I wouldn't dare try them earlier, in case they knock me out like his sleeping pills did."

"Yes," Iris remarked, "you were out of it! I envied you, though. Sleep is still a stranger to me, but it will get better as time goes on."

This was quite an upbeat bit of philosophy coming from Iris, and Monica only wished that Douglas could hear it.

Iris was putting on a fuzzy red tam, and now she

picked up her own rain cape, in a plaid that matched her skirt. "Well," she suggested, "shall we be off?"

Monica nodded, but she felt strangely loath to leave the sanctuary of the little room. As anxious as she was to leave Scotland—there was no doubt in her mind at all about *that*—she shrank from the thought of facing all the others in the lobby because she didn't want to be fussed over.

Now it occurred to her that there was a slight possibility no one knew about her mishap last night. She had no idea of how she'd got from the parking lot up to her room. She did know that when she and Douglas had stepped outside the hotel, the whole area had been deserted—at least as far as anyone could see. Douglas's colleagues had been well hidden. So maybe. . . .

Iris, at the door, called impatiently, "Come along, love."

"All right," Monica nodded, conscious that Iris was watching her very closely as she crossed the room.

Then, as she reached the threshold, Iris said, "I should have told you sooner. Douglas says no one in the group knows what happened last night, and he suggests you'd be happier if we keep mum about it. They managed to spirit you upstairs through a back way, and fortunately the corridor was empty when they brought you in here. Does that help?"

Monica's smile was weak, but at least it was a smile. "Yes," she said, then added, "Did anyone ever tell you you're psychic?"

"Fey, it's called," Iris responded. "At least in

Ireland, and I'm Irish on my mother's side of the family. Don't tell Douglas—he likes to imagine I'm pure Sassenach all the way through. Gives him something to taunt me about.''

"Douglas isn't coming to the States, too, by any chance, is he?'' Monica asked now, wondering if Douglas, with his "connections," had managed to arrange that, also.

"No," Iris answered. "He told me he hopes to take a trip your way before very long, though. I wouldn't be surprised if you see him turn up in Boston on his next vacation.''

"And you with him?''

"Time will tell," Iris said cryptically.

The elevator whirred downstairs, marking, in its way, the end of a cycle. Love had come to her in a Scottish elevator, Monica thought moodily, and she felt she was leaving her entire past behind her as she stepped out into the lobby to face the tour group.

Emily Ewing and her friends were standing near the door, and at once she waved and beckoned.

Monica walked across to Mrs. Ewing. She'd grown fond of her, but the lady from Des Moines was very sharp. If anyone was apt to guess that something really had gone wrong with her, it would be Mrs. Ewing.

Just now, though, Mrs. Ewing had other things on her mind. "Isn't this amazing?" she exclaimed. "It was raining when we landed, and now it's pouring again as we're about to leave. Yet we've had good weather most of the time in between. I saw Mr. Mac-Connach a while ago, and he said that Scotland is crying because she hates to see us go!''

Monica smiled ruefully. "That sounds like Douglas!"

"I'm going to miss him," Mrs. Ewing admitted. "I've grown accustomed to that brogue of his, to say nothing of those Scottish good looks, even though he doesn't hold a candle to that lord of yours."

Monica stiffened, but Mrs. Ewing went on blithely, "I shall never forget his kissing my hand. It was like something out of a movie! My dear, haven't you and Iris had any breakfast?"

"Coffee and tea respectively," Monica told her, glad of the change in subject. "I don't want anything else just yet, and I don't imagine Iris does, either."

"We had some toast," Mrs. Ewing announced. Then she turned to answer a question one of the other women was asking her.

Monica was glad she was spared the necessity of making further small talk: it was becoming increasingly difficult to say very much of anything at all. She walked closer to the glass doors so that she could look out onto the parking lot, and she shuddered as the memory of last night's terrible moment came back to haunt her. It was as if the scene were being reenacted in front of her in the gray light of day.

She turned away quickly, only to become aware that Mrs. Ewing's eyes were upon her. With a sinking feeling she realized the woman was undoubtedly going to be asking her a few questions as soon as the opportunity presented itself. Well, the only thing to do would be to avoid sitting next to her, both on the bus to Prestwick and on the way back across the Atlantic.

Even as she wondered where Douglas was, he appeared from the direction of the coffee shop, and she realized that he at least hadn't gone without breakfast. He started toward her, but before he reached her someone said, "There are the buses," and she turned to see the big Mercedes buses pulling up in front of the entrance. The moment of departure had come, and now the knowledge that she was definitely leaving Scotland gave her an odd sort of wrench, quite at variance with the feelings she'd been expressing to herself.

Douglas and Iris at once went into action. "Is everyone quite *sure* that they have everything?" Iris asked. "You've not left so much as a toothbrush behind in your rooms?"

There was a chorus of "No!"

"Very well, then," Iris nodded. "I shall trust all of you."

The tour group began to file out the door, Monica bringing up the rear with Iris while Douglas busily ushered everyone aboard. Iris went to take charge of one bus, and Douglas indicated to Monica that she should come with him.

There was an intense kind of familiarity in taking her seat next to him up front; she watched him pick up his microphone with the feeling that she was reliving a dream. As he started in with the banter, he seemed to be in great form; yet when she looked at him closely she saw that his eyes were as deeply shadowed as her own, and when he wasn't smiling he looked downright haggard.

The engines revved and they started on their way. Rain slashed against the windows, and one man said,

"Well, I guess we aren't going to see much, but we can't complain. The weather's been great. Everything's been great!"

There was a chorus of agreement, then Douglas picked up the microphone again to boom, "And ye've been the best group I've ever had. I mean that, ladies and gentlemen."

There was a boisterous cheer and a round of hand clapping, but Monica, staring out the window, felt miles apart from all of it. The strange emotionless numbness was persisting.

Some time later, as they were driving along a slate gray street in the business section of a town, Mrs. Ewing, sitting just across the aisle from her, said, "This is Paisley, but it doesn't look like it, does it?"

"I beg your pardon?" Monica asked vaguely.

"Paisley," Mrs. Ewing repeated. "It's famous for its shawls. You know, my dear—paisley prints? The town doesn't look as I imagined it would, that's all. It's larger; it seems busy and quite industrial. I'd imagined something much more quaint."

"Oh," she responded, and was glad when Mrs. Ewing didn't elaborate further.

She didn't want to be aroused from the odd sort of dullness that had overtaken her to speak about paisley shawls or prints or much of anything else. She felt sure that at least a part of her inertia did stem from her reaction to Alex MacDuff's sleeping pills, which must have been decidedly potent. But then, she conceded, something potent certainly had been in order last night. She'd needed to be "out of it" for a while, and if anything she was grateful to the Scottish physician for having noted that and done something about it.

Also, there was an advantage to being emotionally numb on this last ride across Scotland. Had she been otherwise she would have been reminded too painfully of another rainy-day trip, a year ago, when she'd been counting the minutes until the bus reached Prestwick, because she was so sure that Ian would be waiting for her there. She had been equally certain that before she boarded the plane for America they would make plans that encompassed both their futures. There had been no doubt in her mind then that he loved her as she loved him; that the bond between them was as strong as a marriage could ever be. It defied reason, to be sure—even a year ago she would have admitted that, though now she was entirely convinced of it. She had been insane, *insane*. But a year ago the intensity of her feeling for Ian had been as valid as her hope for their future together.

Now her love had turned to ashes; everything connected with Ian had turned to ashes, he had betrayed her so completely. She reminded herself that she'd been right in the first place when she told herself she shouldn't have come back to Scotland. Her feelings had been proved out completely. One could seldom go back in life successfully, she found herself thinking; and suddenly she felt as if she were aching all over: aching from her bruises and aching emotionally, as well. And the emotional ache was much the harder of the two to take. Dr. MacDuff's medicine, she thought wryly, was finally wearing off.

Monica saw the airport's terminal buildings ahead,

and despite herself her heart lurched. An impossible thought sprang into her mind and would not be ousted. A year ago, true, Ian had not come to Prestwick, and this time he had told her flatly, both at Monbraithe and in Glasgow, that he wouldn't be coming to see her off. But was there a chance that what had happened last night might have changed his mind? Might he possibly be standing by the clock near the gift shop that sold Scottish souvenirs, as he had intended a year ago?

She chided herself for being all kinds of a fool, and after a moment she was sure she actually had muttered something aloud, because Douglas asked, "Are you all right?"

She nodded, and Douglas, his voice very low, said, "I'd hoped to be able to talk with you on the way over, but as you saw for yourself there wasn't the chance. They were all full of it this morning, and they had to be entertained. Not that I would mind ordinarily. And I was sincere when I said this is an especially good group. They are fine people."

"What am I supposed to do?" Monica asked crossly. "Take a bow for them?"

"Ah," Douglas said, "I can see I am still out of favor with you. I'd hoped that after mulling things over you were beginning to view everything that has happened in a slightly different light."

"Is there a different light?" she asked cynically.

"It wouldn't do me any good to say so, would it?" Douglas countered reasonably. "'Tis merely that all the way along you've clearly been engrossed in your own thoughts, and—"

"I was half asleep," she interrupted. "I did as the doctor prescribed last night, and I'm not used to sleeping pills. They're just now wearing off."

Douglas nodded. "I should have realized as much. Perhaps when I've got everyone sorted out there may still be time for us to have a cup of coffee or a drink before your plane takes off. We shall see."

"Perhaps," she said indifferently, and was aware of Douglas's frown. She relented to the point of saying, "It was kind of you to arrange for Iris to fly to the States with us. She needs a change of scene just now."

"Yes," Douglas responded, "I would say we all need a change of scene just now. Iris will be all right, though. Even I have to admit that the English sometimes tend to have more than a usual endowment of character—all that stiff-upper-lip bit, don't you know? We Scots are far more sentimental."

"Please," she protested.

"I shan't attempt to convince you," he promised, "but in time I hope you find it out for yourself, and then you can write me or phone me and say, 'Douglas, I was mistaken.'"

"I don't even know what you're talking about," she said flatly, and was relieved when Donald Ferguson brought the bus to a stop, and the passengers began to stir.

Donald had parked the bus as close to the entrance door as he could, but it still was going to be difficult not to get wet. Monica watched Douglas slip into a mackintosh that was reminiscent of the one Walter MacGregor had been wearing when she'd met him in George Square, though of a slightly lighter color.

Douglas helped the tour members off the bus one by one; he seemed to have an inexhaustible supply of good humor as he bantered with them. Then he and Monica sprinted toward the terminal building to be joined, a moment later, by Iris, who had been taking care of her own charges on the second bus.

Douglas said hastily, "We haven't much time to spare. Iris, don't let them all wander too far afield, will you? Tell them there are more duty-free shops once they get through immigration. I'd like to get them into the international area before we lose a couple of sheep at the last instant."

"I've warned my lot," Iris told him. "What a day—I'm chilled to the bone! I don't think I've ever come to Prestwick when it hasn't been raining."

"I could say the same about Heathrow," Douglas teased her.

Iris laughed. "Perhaps we're simply not lucky," she suggested. "Maybe if we banded together we could change all that. Two unlucky people, concentrating their forces...."

She had been joking, yet now she became aware of the potential significance of her words, and she colored deeply. "Really," she began, and Douglas burst out laughing at her discomfiture.

"We shall talk about that once you get back again," he told her.

Iris hesitated. "I shan't be coming to Scotland," she said then. "This is the last Scottish tour, remember, so I shall be flying into Heathrow, as it happens. Then there's a chance there will be another assignment for me."

"Where?" Douglas asked.

"There was talk that it might be Greece."

He smiled. "Perhaps we'll meet there," he said casually. "I shall see if there isn't some reason why I should make a trip to Greece myself!"

Listening to them, Monica felt as if she were in a world apart, especially when her eyes strayed toward the clock near the gift shop. But there was no tall sandy-haired man with blazing blue eyes standing near it. In fact, the area was vacant right now, as if fate had intervened to clear it out until she could be certain there was no doubt. Ian was definitely not about to appear.

"Oh, my God," Douglas broke into her thoughts, "a couple of them are starting upstairs to get something to eat. Intercept them, will you, Iris, and tell them they can get sandwiches or drinks or whatever they want in the international area. I really think we'd better move along through."

Iris went off at once, and with good-natured efficiency she soon had the tour group lined up and ready to pass through the portals that led from the main section of the airport into the international zone, which was open only to those who were leaving the country. It was a final point of departure—a very final point, Monica thought as she walked toward the doors herself, as slowly as she dared. Once she went through those doors, she knew, she could not return. Nor could a Scottish national pass through them in the first place, unless he was traveling abroad.

Now, at the last instant, she couldn't resist looking back over her shoulder, and this time there *was* someone standing near the clock: a short fat man wearing a rain cape and a deerstalker hat. Staring at him, Monica felt herself on the verge of hysteria and bit back a frantic laugh.

Douglas was at her elbow; in fact he was taking her arm and steering her through the door, when she realized that she'd stopped moving forward without even being aware of it. She forced herself to look up at him and ask, "Isn't this where we leave you?"

He shook his head. "No," he said. "I'm the only one permitted to go through with you people, to make quite sure that we've not lost any of you. Did you say goodbye to Donald, by the way?"

"No," she admitted, chagrined. "No, I didn't. Douglas, will you please...."

"Yes," he agreed, his face impassive. "Would there be anyone else you would be wanting me to take a message to, while I'm at it?"

Was he referring to Ian? She couldn't imagine who *else* he would be thinking of, and yet certainly Douglas of all people should realize that she wasn't about to send wishes of any sort to Ian, not now!

The line in front of them slowed as passports were checked and immigration forms turned in. Then they emerged into a vast waiting room that, as Douglas had promised, was lined with duty-free shops, as well as a bar and ample places to get snacks.

"May I get you a cup of coffee, or a drink?" Douglas offered.

She shook her head. "Thank you, no; I really don't want anything. They'll be besieging us with food and drink on the plane as soon as we're airborne."

The tour members had dispersed, bent on one last happy shopping fling, and Douglas said tolerantly, "They will be loading themselves up with Scotch, among other things. I should have suggested a brand or two. Monica...."

"Yes?"

"I am not at all happy with the way things are culminating for you here," he finished with a rueful smile. "'Tis not my business, perhaps, but over the space of a few days you and Iris and I—well, we've grown close to one another. A great deal has happened that has made me feel as if you are as dear as a sister."

"Thank you, Douglas," she said, and managed a smile. "Perhaps you'll invite me to the wedding."

"'Twill be a while," Douglas told her. "And frankly, I hope that Iris will be persuaded to stay hereabouts rather than to go off on a trek to Greece, where I may or may not be able to follow her. But 'tis you I am concerned about. I cannot help but think that I am partly responsible for the feeling you seem to have that Ian MacGregor has in some way...betrayed you."

"Please," Monica urged, "I'd rather not get into it."

"I'd rather that you could stay long enough to be a bit more sure of the facts," Douglas countered, "but I suppose that isn't possible. But you may want word from Scotland, Monica. If so, I want you to know that you will always have a friend here. Should you want to get in touch with me, write to me care of customs in Edinburgh. Your message will reach me wherever I happen to be, and you may be sure I'll get in touch with you promptly.''

Douglas paused, listening to a voice coming over the loudspeaker. Then he groaned, ''They're calling the flight,\and I've a feeling I've let myself lose track of some of the flock! Dear heaven, where are they all? Find Iris, will you, and then the two of you can help me round them up.''

The next few minutes were so busy that Monica didn't have time to think. Then finally everyone was in line, and as she joined them she looked up to find Douglas standing beside her. '' 'Tis the time to say farewell,'' he said. ''The best of everything, Monica, and we shall be meeting again.''

He bent to kiss her lightly on the lips, and inevitably tears came to fill her eyes. But even while she was wiping them away, Mrs. Ewing said at her elbow, ''Monica, hold this package for me for just a minute, will you? Oh, dear!''

Once again, Monica saw, Mrs. Ewing had been lavishly patronizing the gift shops. Now she fumbled, shopping bags slithered to the floor, and Monica quickly bent down to help try to bring order out of what had become sudden chaos.

''I should have consolidated,'' Mrs. Ewing apologized when they had both straightened up. With Percy Ewing's help they'd got her packages together to the point where they could be carried without courting disaster.

Her husband smiled. ''Emily,'' he chided, ''consolidating is something you'll never learn to do when it comes to either shopping or packing. If Emily were a thousand," he added, this to Monica, "she'd never be able to pass up something she thought might be a bargain, and all of these shops around here are having after-season sales. If all our friends and relatives in Des Moines wear the stuff Emily is bringing back to them, we'll have enough instant Scots around to make our own bagpipe parade!"

Monica laughed and blessed Mrs. Ewing for her impulse buying because the near catastrophe with the packages had actually been a welcome diversion. The line started forward again, and Mrs. Ewing, undaunted, said, "Well, we got our act together just in time, didn't we!"

Now they moved out of the waiting area, then down a corridor and around a corner. There, just before them, long tables had been set up, with both men and women in uniform seated at them.

Peering ahead, Mrs. Ewing exclaimed, "I've heard about this. They're going to frisk us!"

"Frisk us?" Monica echoed.

"Yes," Mrs. Ewing nodded. "I've been told they almost never do it when you're coming into a country, but depending upon what's going on—with smuggling, things like that—they often do when you're leaving."

Percy Ewing was also peering ahead. "Good God," he said, "they're going through the women's pocketbooks! If they try to get all the way through yours, Emily, we'll be here till tomorrow!"

"Fiddle on you, Percy," Mrs. Ewing told him, and he chuckled.

Monica wondered herself how long it would take

the customs officer assigned to the task to go through the contents of Mrs. Ewing's capacious handbag. She was fascinated as she watched his skilled fingers probing quickly with astonishing adroitness.

The handbag was returned to Mrs. Ewing, accompanied by a pleasant Scottish smile, and the lady from Des Moines beamed in turn. "You next, Monica," she said rather archly.

Monica had been watching Percy Ewing, who had already run the gauntlet at the table and now was being given a quick deft body search by a poker-faced uniformed man with a handlebar mustache that looked like something out of a Gay Nineties melodrama. She saw that Mrs. Ewing was being shepherded over to a uniformed woman who, with equal deftness, performed the same task. Watching, she found it impossible to repress a smile; she only wished she had a camera handy to record the shocked expression on Mrs. Ewing's face.

A voice laden with that all too familiar Scottish burr asked softly, "Would ye step forward please, miss?" and Monica was chagrined when she realized that, in her absorption with watching the Ewings, she had been holding up progress.

She stepped forward, still smiling at the thought of Mrs. Ewing's astonishment, and put her handbag on the desk without waiting to be asked. The uniformed attendant smiled back at her and opened it. His skillful fingers began searching, prying...and suddenly became suspended, as if they were power driven and the current had been turned off.

To her amazement, Monica saw that the customs

officer's face had become a mask. Now he asked coldly, "Where did ye get this, miss?"

She stared down at the object he was holding, disbelieving her own eyes. She was looking at a glittering medallion, in its center a magnificent amethyst that formed the core part of a thistle. Smaller diamond thistles edged the circle, and the medallion was suspended from a silvery chain.

Monica felt herself grow weak from shock. She had no doubt, no doubt at all, about what it was that she was seeing!

CHAPTER TWENTY-FIVE

A SHORT MAN IN UNIFORM stepped forward from a corner of the room, and the woman who had been examining Mrs. Ewing a moment earlier moved toward the table to stand next to Monica. She felt all at once as if she were surrounded by a sea of hostile faces, and she glanced around helplessly.

Iris had gone on ahead with the group from the first bus, she realized now, and she turned to verify the suspicion that she was, in fact, the last person in the whole line. Ahead of her Mr. and Mrs. Ewing were just rounding the door that led to the final approach to the plane, and she started to cry out their names, but the words stuck in her throat. She knew, without anyone telling her so, that it would do no good to call the Ewings. No good at all....

The short dark customs officer was watching her very closely, as if he suspected she might suddenly turn and make a run for it. Now he requested, "Will you step this way, please, miss?"

He was pointing toward a door she hadn't even noticed. A door, she knew, that would lead her away from the plane, going in entirely the wrong direction.

Fighting down a mounting panic, she said almost wildly, "Please! I don't know anything about this. I don't know where that necklace came from. I've had absolutely nothing to do with it!''

"Miss," the man repeated, "if ye'll come with me, please?''

"But I've a plane to catch!'' she protested.

He shook his head. "Ye should surely know that we cannot possibly let ye leave Scotland under the circumstances,'' he told her simply.

She stared at him, horrified. "You're acting as if you think I've *stolen* this,'' she said, pointing to the medallion.

"Miss,'' he ordered, very firm about it now, "if ye'll please come along? We can discuss the matter in a less public place.''

He was being polite enough, yet Monica had the distinct impression that unless she complied with his wishes she would be led away by force. The uniformed woman, now that she thought of it, looked strong enough to have a brown belt in karate at the least; and while the other customs officials were pretending to be busy with forms and papers, she was sure that in actuality they were taking in everything that was being said and would be prepared to render assistance at an instant's notice.

She was trapped and it was a terrible feeling. Making one last attempt, she pleaded, "Look. I have absolutely no *idea* how that necklace got into my handbag. I swear that to you!''

The little man sighed. "Please, miss,'' he said again.

Now it occurred to Monica that perhaps the reason they weren't whisking her away bodily was that she was a guest in their country, an American. "I think you'd better call the consul in Glasgow," she told him. "The American consul, that is. Or the ambassador in Edinburgh. Or someone."

"We shall, of course, get in touch with your country's representatives," she was assured.

The little man stepped forward, obviously having had enough of this, and he took Monica's left arm, while the woman moved up to take her right one. Their grip was light, just a touch really, but she could imagine how it would tighten should she try to get away, and tears of rage and frustration filled her eyes.

They whisked her through the door at the end of the room and along a corridor that led past a series of offices. When they came to yet another door the little man released her arm long enough to open it and then politely but firmly ushered her across the threshold.

She found herself standing in a very barren sort of room. It was furnished with a steel desk, filing cabinets and several straight-backed chairs that looked very uncomfortable. There was also a window with blinds but no curtains. The place was utterly bleak, instilling in her a sense of desolation that was close to overpowering under the circumstances, and she forced herself to say tightly, "Call the American consul, please."

"That we will, miss," the rather pompous little official assured her. "However, I think ye must understand that first we have no other choice but to arrest you."

"*Arrest* me!" The nightmare sound of the word penetrated and combined with the events of the previous night to make an emotional blow that sent her swaying.

"Sit down," the little man said quickly, pushing one of the chairs toward her.

The woman came forward to say, not unkindly, "There now, dear. If you've an explanation, we shall hear it, you may be sure. Don't go fainting on us!"

As if she had any choice, Monica thought weakly, her senses reeling. Dear God, what a finale this trip to Scotland was proving to have! She fought back tears that threatened to scald her eyes and thought of the tour group and Iris, who must be wondering now about what was delaying her. And she thought about Douglas. . . .

Douglas!

"Should you want to get in touch with me," he had said, "write to me care of customs in Edinburgh."

Customs. These were customs people detaining her now. Fighting back the nauseous giddiness that was threatening to overtake her, Monica said quickly, "One of your own men can vouch for me. Douglas MacConnach. Get Douglas MacConnach." And with that, everything went black.

CONSCIOUSNESS RETURNED SLOWLY, perhaps in part because she was not welcoming it. She opened her eyes to find herself in yet another bleak little room, lying on a cot that had certainly seen better days. It sagged, the springs creaked in protest when she moved, and the lumpy surface did nothing to ease her physical bruises, which really were causing some aches now. She hadn't had a chance to take the pain-relieving pills Alex MacDuff had prescribed for her.

She sat up slowly, to find the female customs officer sitting in a chair nearby, watching her.

"There now," the woman said, her manner friendly enough—almost maternal, in fact. "You're back with us again. Mr. MacConnach explained that you'd had a nasty accident last night. 'Tis a shame that this had to happen, too."

Monica forced herself to sit up, even though the movement made her head swim. "Where is Douglas?" she asked.

"With Mr. Buchanan," she was told. "We shall go back to them as soon as you're steady enough."

"I'm steady enough."

"I think not. I must insist that you rest for another fifteen minutes at least. Would you care for a drink of water?"

"No, thank you."

Monica sank back against the poor excuse of a pillow, compressing her lips in a thin line of pure bitterness. There was absolutely no use in trying to get up and leave the room; she realized that only too well. This placid-looking woman had been well trained, and despite the difference in their ages she could stop her in a minute.

She lay on the uncomfortable cot for what seemed an eternity, until the woman said, "Well, I should think we could get along now."

Monica swayed as she stood up, and the woman

offered her an arm for support in a gesture that was companionable enough. But she had no illusions about this sort of guidance; she was sure that the hand clasping her could become a vise as strong as steel were she to attempt to make the wrong move.

Nevertheless, a moment later she did make the attempt. It was only a short distance back to the other room, but on the threshold she stopped short, gasping audibly, and then turned with the urge to flee blindly—only to find her way blocked with solid efficiency.

There was a man sitting next to the metal desk, deep in conversation with the small man—presumably Mr. Buchanan—who sat behind it. At the sound of her footsteps he turned around, and she found herself looking into eyes as blue as the deep waters of a Scottish loch; and she learned in an instant the true meaning of degradation.

"You!" she cried, desperately trying to fight back tears that were a potent blend of distilled anger and the deepest sort of humiliation.

Ian got to his feet slowly, and she saw that his face was still shadowed with pain. He, too, had not been able to cast off the effects of last night's close-to-catastrophic happening.

"Monica," he began, "Mr. Buchanan has been telling me—"

"That they found the Jacobite medallion in my possession?" she finished coldly.

"Yes."

"I don't know how it got there, Ian," she said, forcing steadiness, "whether you believe that or not.

Last night I was told that the medallion had been returned and that it was back in its accustomed place at Castle Monbraithe. You know where I've been every minute since last night, so you certainly must know that I had no way of. . .of stealing it from you.'' Her voice broke. Struggling to get the final words out, she went on, ''It was planted on me, Ian.''

''Your lairdship—'' Mr. Buchanan began, but Ian raised an admonishing hand, his gesture close to imperious.

''Let Miss Winthrop speak, please,'' he commanded.

''That's very decent of you.'' Anger came to Monica's rescue to reinforce her strength. ''I've asked this before and I'll ask it again now: will you please insist that these people of yours call the American consul.''

''I've tried to tell Miss Winthrop that it really isn't necessary to involve the American consul,'' Mr. Buchanan interjected, and was stopped once again by a peremptory wave of Ian's hand.

''That's so,'' he said thoughtfully. ''As I see it, Monica, to involve your consul would put Mr. Buchanan in a bad light, and he's only done his duty; I think you'll have to agree to that. The Jacobite medallion *was* found in your possession and so you can hardly blame the customs people for detaining you.''

''I'm not blaming them,'' she responded, which was true enough. ''He and the others were only doing their job—Mr. Buchanan and the others, that is. I only wish they'd listened to me and let me catch my plane. They could have kept the blasted medallion; I'd be the last person in the world to want it, believe me!''

"Is that so?" Ian asked with a mildness she found deceptive under the circumstances. "You do remember the legend connected with it, don't you?"

"Please, Ian!" she protested wearily. "If I never hear another Scottish legend, I'll be grateful. Where is Douglas?"

Ian's eyebrows rose; the look he gave her was oddly penetrating. "There was no reason to keep MacConnach here once your tour flight had taken off," he told her. "He called me, and I was able to leave at once."

"How did you manage to get here so quickly?" she demanded. "By magic carpet?"

"No. By helicopter," was his succinct reply.

Frowning, she stared at him. Then he added, "However, MacConnach arranged a rental car for my use before he went back to Glasgow himself. We can leave for Monbraithe as soon as you're ready. You might wish to freshen up a bit first, I suppose."

Monica was well aware that her hair was disheveled and her makeup certainly streaked with an occasional tear that she hadn't been able to suppress. But she said stiffly, "Is Mr. Buchanan willing to have me leave here?"

Mr. Buchanan seemed to be startled by her question. "With his lairdship?" he asked. "Of course, miss." He reached for a small white envelope and handed it to Ian. "The medallion," he explained.

Without bothering to glance inside it, Ian tucked

the envelope into an inside pocket of his beautifully tailored beige tweed jacket. "Thank you," he said, as if this were any ordinary transaction, and then turned to Monica. "Shall we go along, then?" he suggested.

Monica felt a swift stab of resentment, yet she had no alternative but to follow him. This time their way led them out into the main rotunda of the airport terminal. She mumbled something about going to the rest room and once inside managed to restore at least partial order to her hair, as well as to wash her face and put on fresh lipstick; but at the moment she didn't really care how she looked.

She was sick at the thought of the reaction this whole incident must have provoked among the tour members, now high over the Atlantic. Did they know, did Iris know, that she'd been branded a thief? Further, it seemed abhorrent to think that Ian had actually come to Prestwick by helicopter to witness her shame, and the final blow to her ego was literally being released into his custody, as if she were a common criminal to whom his lairdship—for reasons she couldn't fathom—was making a grandiose gesture of forgiveness.

She wondered if he'd had to post some sort of bond in order to obtain her release, and she smarted at the thought of such a thing. On the other hand, she reflected bitterly, probably just being the earl of Monbraithe was enough to cause doors to be opened for him—even the door of the cell she might otherwise be occupying!

She looked to see if there was a back exit to the rest

room, but there wasn't. And that was just as well, she had to concede. Right now she had no place to run to; Ian's long reach would find her. But she could see no reason why Ian wanted to take her back to Monbraithe of all places—unless he intended to initiate a kind of inquisition of his own in an attempt to learn how she'd come to possess the medallion.

Well, she could give him no answers because she had none. Someone had set her up, that was for sure, and if she and Ian had any common bond left between them at all, it was that she wanted to find out who'd done this to her just as much as he did.

He was waiting for her, leaning against the wall, and as they started to walk toward the side entrance—where, he told her, their rental car would be waiting—she noticed he was moving very stiffly.

As if she'd questioned him, he explained, "Mac-Duff insisted I wear the damned brace for a few days, and I suppose he's right, but I feel as if someone's coated me in armor. How about you?"

"My spirit is hurting far more than my flesh is," Monica said tightly.

He shot her an inquiring glance but didn't answer. They came to the side door, and opening it, he said, "The rain's still coming down. But the car's just outside, I see. Pull up the hood on your raincoat so your hair won't get wet."

"I don't care whether it gets wet or not," she answered dully.

He shrugged. "Very well, then; let's make a run for it." At the moment, though, he clearly wasn't able to run, and she reached the car before he did, leaning her head against the back of the seat, her body aching and her mind reeling.

She saw him insert the key in the ignition switch, and she forced herself to focus on a single fact. "I know I'm not in any position to ask favors," she told him, "but I'm still going to request that you do just one thing for me."

"I can't promise that I'll be able to do anything for you, Monica."

"This really isn't much to ask of you," she persisted. "I don't want to go to Monbraithe with you, and I really don't see why you'd want to take me there. So all I'm asking is that you drop me off at a hotel either in Glasgow or somewhere else along the way."

"So that you can call the American consul?"

"That, among other things. As a visitor in your country I do have some rights, Ian. And you know as well as I do that I didn't steal your damned medallion."

"Yes," he agreed almost absently. "I'm certain that you didn't."

"Then you might have told the customs people so, don't you think?" she asked, her eyes sparking.

"I did, Monica. I was telling Mr. Buchanan that you couldn't possibly have stolen the medallion when you came back in the room."

"Then...?"

"He had no intention of holding you after that, of course."

"Yet he released me into your custody?"

"Not at all," Ian said. "I merely assured him that I would give you transportation."

She glared at him. "You mean that I could have left here by myself?"

"Yes." And as if he sensed she was about to try to get out of the car, he started it and drove with swift efficiency out onto the airport exit road.

Her voice low and charged with fury, she told him, "I'll never forgive you for this; I hope you realize that. You permitted my reputation to be ruined when you could very well have said something, done something—"

"You are jumping to conclusions," Ian countered, keeping his eyes on the road ahead as he spoke. "That's why I wanted to make certain you came to Monbraithe with me: we need the time and the place in which to. . . to talk things out. After that I'll take you to a hotel in Glasgow if you wish, or I'll even take you back to Prestwick and put you aboard a flight to the States, if that's the way you want it."

"That is the way I will want it," she assured him.

"Very well. We shall see," he responded, with a calm that was thoroughly infuriating.

They both lapsed into silence, a heavy silence. Ian seemed to have retreated into a mood that matched the weather, and Monica felt as if her nerves were coiled as tight as the springs in a clock.

The ride seemed eternal to her, but finally they came to Balloch, then struck the road that bordered Loch Lomond. She saw the lake in a new mood today: the pewter water was spattered with pelting rain, the wind ruffling it into a series of angry waves.

They came to the gate and she saw that it was open; obviously they were expected. Angus Grewar was not in evidence, but this was understandable in view of the weather. In any event, Ian must have told the old caretaker to open the gate and leave it open.

Ian, looking across at her, said with an almost gentle note in his voice, " 'Tis not the end of the world, Monica."

"That's a matter of opinion," she retorted, trying in vain to keep her voice even.

She looked ahead and saw the castle looming in front of them, huge and cold and forbidding. Ian parked the car directly in front of the entrance. "Unfortunately, they didn't make canopies to protect people from the rain in the old days," he remarked. "You will have to make a dash for it."

She did so, darting for the entrance. The massive front door swung open as if by magic.

Annie Grewar stood on the threshold. " 'Tis a pity it's so wet out, Miss Winthrop," she said, an unexpected bit of friendliness that caused Monica actually to falter. Then the old Scotswoman added, in the note of a longtime nursemaid addressing a beloved child, "Ian, Alex MacDuff will be most angry with you."

"Then he shall have to be," Ian said shortly.

"Angus has put a fire in the study," Annie went on, and Ian nodded.

He led the way through the grand hall and on through a beautifully carved wooden door into the room that, of all the many chambers at Castle Monbraithe, was by far the most familiar to Monica. There were lights turned on now, and logs blazed on the hearth, but this was the room where Ian had first held her in his arms; where she had first felt the full infusion of her love for him. She had seen it that night only in semidarkness, yet she knew the shape of everything. The long refectory table, the shelves with their books in jewel-toned bindings, the couch...all were blindingly familiar.

Ian said, "Will Scotch do for you?"

"Yes, please."

He poured from a decanter, then observed with a slight smile, "I see that Annie thought to bring along some ice." She heard the clink of cubes dropping into her glass; in a moment he was holding it out to her, and as she took it from him she hoped her fingers had sufficient strength left that she wouldn't drop it.

Unavoidably, she glanced up at his face and saw that it was stamped with the mark of exhaustion. He seemed very pale, and there was a tautness about his features. As he moved slightly she saw him wince with pain, and she swallowed hard.

"Why is Alex MacDuff going to be so angry with you?" she dared to ask him.

"Because he felt it important that I not move about too much," he admitted. "He doesn't want a recurrence of any of the problems with my back that followed the accident."

"Yet you went and took a helicopter to Prestwick and—"

"There are those moments when I do know where to assign my priorities, Monica," Ian said wearily.

"Even at the risk of your health?"

"I'm not risking my health. I may hurt for a while, but I will be quite all right...physically."

There was no doubting his emphasis on the word, and as their eyes met Monica felt herself seared.

She swallowed hard as the truth in all its totality came to engulf her. And she wondered how—no matter what he'd done, no matter what might happen to her as a result of it—she could have imagined ever feeling anything other than love for Ian. If she were never to see him again after today, she would love him at least to the end of her own world....

Still forcing her to meet his gaze, he said, "Monica, I swear this to you: I did not intend anything like this to happen to you. I had no idea the medallion would find its way into your handbag. I—"

He broke off, to go over and stand in front of the fireplace and look broodingly into the flames. Then he went to fill his glass again with Scotch, glancing in her own direction only to see that her glass was still almost full.

She watched him, puzzled. Ian had something to tell her; she was becoming increasingly certain of this. And it seemed obvious that it involved the medallion. Until this instant it hadn't occurred to her that he could be personally involved in the incident at Prestwick. Douglas MacConnach certainly had called him from the airport, yet Ian had felt his own presence at the scene was sufficiently important to go against his doctor's orders and leave Monbraithe. Why—unless he was very directly connected to what had happened to her.

He moved to sit on the end of the refectory table, and she studied his face, highlighted by the flickering firelight. She was beginning to realize that Ian was at his most aristocratic when he was feeling the need to camouflage what he really was thinking or reacting to. Which certainly was the case just now.

There was a hauteur about him that would have put off anyone who didn't know him well. But this time around she was not to be fooled by it.

She plunged. "You know how the medallion got into my handbag, don't you?"

He started visibly and took a moment before answering. Then the words came reluctantly. "Yes, I have a good idea of what must have happened. But I surely did not intend to have the medallion discovered in such a way."

"I don't understand," she said, and she certainly couldn't. Ever since she'd come back to Scotland she seemed to have been met with nothing but confusion; and this matter of the medallion seemed the most inexplicable thing of all.

He was watching her intently, and she rubbed her forehead, then said, "Very well. Someone certainly planted your family heirloom on me. I'm beginning to think that, though you're protesting your innocence, you know who it was. Would you care to enlighten me?"

"Mrs. Ewing," Ian said quietly. "It had to be Mrs. Ewing."

She stared at him, astonished: Mrs. Ewing was the last person in the world she would have connected with the Jacobite medallion. She shook her head, beginning to feel that she'd stumbled into a bad dream. "You can't be serious!" she accused him.

"But I am," he said, and to her astonishment she

saw his lips twitch. Then he smiled, and all at once she felt as if she were watching the blue waters of Loch Lomond dancing in the sunlight.

The sight did something to her. The sweetness of her love for him washed over her, and with it a sensation so tantalizing that it was all she could do to keep her distance from him. She could feel the core of a deep yearning that she well knew was only the start of the sort of game her body could play with her, and she was angry at such self-treason, angry with both Ian and herself.

She told him coldly, "It isn't very funny, you know. As long as I live I will never forget the humiliation of that scene at Prestwick—"

"I know," Ian interrupted, his soft Scottish burr playing havoc with her senses. "Ah, Monica, I know, and I am sorry. 'Tis not funny, of course. But. . . ."

He shook his head, as if in reproof at himself, and now he could suppress his amusement no longer. There were veritable ripples on her imaginary Loch Lomond as he said, "Were I not already in love I do believe I would fall in love with that woman, although she tells me she's old enough to be my grandmother!"

"Mrs. Ewing, of course?"

"Mrs. Ewing, of course. She does possess more than her share of your famous American ingenuity, plus as much daring as any Scot. I have to hand that to her!"

Monica sank into the nearest armchair, her legs suddenly too weak to be trusted. She said stiffly, "Would you mind telling me how Mrs. Ewing obtained your precious medallion in the first place?"

"I gave it to her," Ian said solemnly.

"You *gave* it to her?"

"Yes." He sobered, and there was a bleakness both to his face and to his voice as he explained, "Last night, when Alex MacDuff brought me back here, I was in a very grim frame of mind. For one thing, Alex ordered me into this damned back brace again, and he insisted he would put me in hospital for a fortnight if I didn't do as he said. Which meant, of course, that there'd be no chance I could get to Prestwick."

"You were intending to go to Prestwick?" she asked incredulously.

"Yes. It was my intention, certainly, to try to talk to you, although I didn't know whether you'd listen to me. You'd made plain your feelings for me and for Scotland and for everything else touching upon either one of us, and I couldn't blame you. I could only hope that you were speaking in the heat of anger and that once you'd cooled a bit you'd—well, perhaps you would change your mind. Yet I also knew that if you were to leave Scotland again with no word from me, I could scarcely expect you to reconsider later.

"Alex gave me some of his sleeping pills, but they didn't work for me," Ian continued. "All I could think of was the two of us, and how impossible our situation had become. I felt that once again I was being kept from you by what seemed a very cruel twist of fate, and yet I respect Alex's judgment. I had no wish at all to face months of confinement again, which is what he suggested might happen. That would only put me even farther away from you.

"So I decided to give you a message, a message I felt certain you would understand. You know the legend of the medallion; you know that according to tradition it must go next to the present earl's wife."

"What?"

"Monica, please—don't look like that!" Ian protested. "Hear me out before you come to any conclusions. There I was last night, unable to sleep, feeling as if my world truly was about to come to an end. I knew that I had only hours in which to do something, and yet I was unable to do very much of anything. And then I thought of the lady you'd introduced me to. She was such an obvious romantic. Luckily I remembered her name, and I telephoned her, even though it was an ungodly hour—"

"You telephoned Mrs. Ewing?"

"Yes," Ian said. "I asked her if she would come to Castle Monbraithe if my cousin Walter went to fetch her. She agreed to do so."

"She came *here*?"

"Yes," Ian nodded, "and I rather fancy that she quite relished it, too."

"I rather fancy that she did," Monica responded nastily.

The look that he gave her was a long and suspicious one, but he merely said, "In the wee hours of this morning Mrs. Ewing and I sat in front of the fire here and drank brandy and talked, mostly about you. She thinks the world and all of you, by the way. After a time I asked her if she would consider doing me a favor, one that involved you. She is a delightful woman and very much to the point. She told me that she'd do anything at all that would serve to bring the two of us together, because when she saw us dancing. . . ."

"Yes?"

"As I've mentioned," Ian said, "Mrs. Ewing is an incurable romantic."

"Ian. . . ."

Ian's jaw tightened. "Let me get the rest of this out, Monica. I told Mrs. Ewing about the Jacobite medallion and its history. I explained to her that it actually was behind the attack on her that had been meant for you, although I didn't go into all the details concerning last night's happenings. I said only that the culprit had been apprehended and so. . .so everyone was quite safe again."

For the first time this knowledge swept over Monica, bringing with it an entirely new rush of implications. It was true. Everyone *was* quite safe again. Now that Bobby Grier had been caught, Ian not only had cleared his name but was no longer in danger. . . .

"Mrs. Ewing was as intrigued as you would expect her to be," Ian continued. "So I asked her if she would take the Jacobite medallion with her, and once you were airborne if she would give it to you with a message from me. She promised she'd take care of everything. It didn't occur to me that she would set up an entirely different chain of events so that you wouldn't be able to leave Scotland at all until we'd. . .confronted each other again."

"I can't believe this," Monica said, "but she must have managed to slip the medallion into my handbag before we went through customs."

Now, thinking back, she remembered that moment when they'd been standing in line and Mrs. Ewing had lost her grip on her packages and scattered them all over the floor. In the flurry of picking them up. . . .

"It's incredible!" Monica said flatly.

Ian smiled. "Yes, it's clear that she must have decided to arrange something on her own that would keep you in Scotland until we could meet again. I know that what she did proved to be extremely embarrassing to you, but I still think it was quite wonderful of her, don't you?"

"No," Monica replied shortly.

His eyebrows rose. "No?"

"Mrs. Ewing is just as arbitrary in her way as you are in yours," she told him. "Obviously she never even gave a thought to the fact that she was ruining my reputation all the while she was trying to play Cupid."

"Come now, Monica," he protested, "that isn't so. I'll wager that by now Mrs. Ewing has told everyone on the plane what really happened. As for your position with Magic Carpets—if that's what is worrying you, I can assure you you'll have no problem there. The man who arranged the job for MacConnach is part owner of the firm and a good friend of mine. I can explain everything to him. You've no cause to worry."

"In other words," she said caustically, "once again you have managed to think everything through, and then to handle it in the high-handed manner of the true aristocrat, right?"

His jaw tightened again. "I'd call that a rather nasty crack."

"Perhaps it is," she conceded, "but I think it's justified. After all, you can rest in peace now, knowing the 'American' will go back to her country shortly so that you'll have no further obligations there. You will then be able to marry the lady whose father owns a distillery, and that will enable you to live here at the castle in the style to which you're accustomed. Then, as to your heirs. . . ."

"Please!" Ian protested, holding up his hand. "Stop a bit, will you? You're arranging my future entirely too fast for my comfort!"

"I think your future has been arranged for you, Ian."

"I take exception to that," he said. "In any event, you couldn't be more wrong. It is quite easy to understand why, though, because ever since you came back to Scotland I've given you a false impression about a number of things. That first day when you came here, I deliberately said what I said to you about marrying for money because I desperately wanted to drive you away, even though it nearly killed me to be forced into such a position. I don't think I will ever forget the look on your face. . . ."

"What about the announcement of your engagement, which is due to appear in the papers any day now?" she asked icily.

"There is no engagement," he said simply. "Ellen and I have never been engaged, nor will we ever be. She knows I love you; I have never pretended otherwise. She has been a very good friend. She *is* a very good friend. I note that when she comes here, though, Walter is hardly able to take his eyes off her, and she seems to be more than a bit receptive to him. Now that Jane is going to live in Inverness, it's my hope that Walter will be impelled to do some courting on his own. He and Ellen would be quite perfect for each other, as a matter of fact.

"As for Monbraithe," he added, "I've already told you I have no wish at all to live here and manage the place, and I've told Walter that I am going to turn the running of it over to him. He can raise sheep to his heart's content and even open the castle to tourists, if that's that he wants to do. It's entirely up to him."

"I see," she said slowly.

"Would you care to know what my own plans are?" he asked her.

"If you wish to tell them to me."

"Very well, then. As you know, I have a house in Edinburgh that I inherited from my father, and it is my intention to live there most of the time. The only reason I will ever feel inclined to come back to Castle Monbraithe, to be truthful, is that it's so close to Loch Lomond. . . and Loch Lomond will always remind me of you."

She couldn't meet his eyes.

"Further," he said, "I'm thinking of having a try at politics. There is a great deal to be done in Scotland, and I'd like to have my voice in the doing of it. I am for change, but moderate change, and I think it is incumbent upon a family such as mine to take an active part in things. It is essential for us to make our position clear. . . ."

He sighed. "I imagine you've had more than enough of Scottish politics," he acknowledged. "But along those lines, MacConnach told me very briefly on the phone of the risk you took last night on my behalf. I should have realized why you were out there in the parking lot, but stupidly I didn't. I only know that I was struck with horror when I saw you by the streetlight and then saw the car...."

She shuddered. "I'd rather not talk about that," she admitted.

"I can't blame you," he said gravely. "Nevertheless, I agree with MacConnach that it was your action, your courage, that led to the immediate clearance of my name. And I shall owe you a debt for that for the rest of my life."

She shook her head vehemently. "No," she protested, "you don't owe me anything! I don't *want* anything from you, Ian!"

She stopped short because he had recoiled as definitely as if she'd struck him, and in a terribly revealing moment she saw a side of Ian she'd never seen before. Before he managed to slip on that air of autocratic indifference he seemed to wear so easily, he looked absolutely stricken, his blue eyes mirroring an agony so intense that she felt herself cringe away from it.

Suddenly she had a vision of a small boy living in a castle with no one around at all who really cared for him. A boy who had never known his mother, and who would have to live forever with the horror of his father's death. Her own childhood had been filled with family and friends and laughter and lightness.

She had beautiful memories of her parents, memories that had sustained her through many very bad times in recent years. But Ian, she saw now, had nothing; nothing to cling to except his own pride and the strength of his own character.

She could only dimly appreciate his innate loneliness. And she could only marvel at the way he had opened himself up to her so quickly. Love had come to be planted like a seed between them and certainly, at first, had seemed destined to flourish into an entire garden of flowers. She could well imagine that Ian had never before given of himself so quickly, so completely—and so lightheartedly at the same time. Now she sensed that he'd never be that way again, and she wanted to cry for him.

Yes, she wanted to cry for him; but far more she wanted to love him. She wanted to live by his side for the rest of her life, to try to make up to him for all those cold bleak years when he'd been so much alone.

She started to speak, but it was hard, very hard, to find the right words. Before she could choose them he said quietly, "I'm so very sorry, Monica. I should have...known better. I should have known that I couldn't expect instant forgiveness from you, and that it was purely ridiculous for me to imagine you might ever be able to forget all the misery I've caused you."

He drew a deep breath, then went on, "I don't suppose I can hope to convince you that I stayed away from you only for your sake, not mine. That, too, was the reason I've tried to force you away from me since your return to Scotland. At moments, as you well know, I simply didn't have the strength to leave you alone, despite my best intentions; and that was wrong, also. But you see—'' and now there was no sunlight at all in his blue eyes ''—I had never really known what it was to love someone until I walked into that elevator in Edinburgh and found you there. In those few days that followed it seemed to me as if an impossible miracle had taken place. I felt as if the whole world had turned around. Then my uncle was killed and I was accused of killing him, and all the lights in my life seemed to have been plunged into darkness. I was in hell, and I couldn't take you there with me.''

Monica, her voice as quiet as his, said, ''There's no need for you to torment yourself, Ian.''

''No,'' he told her, ''let me finish. It's as well that you've been honest with me and I know where you stand. Were you to stay here today under false pretenses I don't think I could bear it when the time came for us to say another goodbye.''

He glanced across at her, and now there was no telltale emotion in his eyes; he looked supremely sure of himself. But watching him Monica knew she was only beginning to verify the suspicion she'd had about the facade he presented to the rest of the world.

He stood, and she held her breath as he started to walk slowly across the room to her, his stance stiff even for Ian at his most austere. She wanted to remind him of his doctor's orders, but she didn't. He'd spoken of priorities, and she knew what he meant.

And she also sensed instinctively that the most important moment of her entire life was at hand, and that she must be careful, very careful, of anything further she said to him, anything she did.

"Get up, will you," he asked as he came to stand in front of her, and she did so as if she were a puppet being pulled by an invisible string.

Ian took the envelope Mr. Buchanan had given him out of his pocket. From it he drew the shimmering chain with the diamond-and-amethyst medallion dangling from the end of it.

Before Monica fully realized what he was about to do, he placed the Jacobite medallion around her neck and fastened it. Then he stepped back to say softly, "There. 'Tis yours, you know. I meant for Mrs. Ewing simply to give it to you on the plane once you were aloft, as I've said. And I am deeply sorry that you were so mortified by what happened, though I don't think you should blame Mrs. Ewing for it. Her plans seem to have gone awry, to be sure, yet I am certain she was motivated by only the best of intentions...."

Monica wanted to tell Ian that she, too, was certain Mrs. Ewing had been motivated by only the best of intentions, but for the moment she had lost her voice. She could only stare at him, not realizing how blank her face was, so he had no way at all of judging her emotions.

He said, "'Tis a gift to you, Monica, and there are no strings attached to it. You may be sure it is entirely yours. I would never, I could never, give it to anyone else."

She tried to speak, and finally her words came out in a whisper. "You told me, Ian, that when you gave the medallion to Mrs. Ewing you also gave her a message for me."

"That's so," he admitted.

"Am I not to know what the message was?"

There was nothing at all inscrutable about Ian now. An emotion she couldn't quite define seemed to blaze across his face, and then he said, "Yes, I think you should know what the message was. I told her it was a symbol of my love to be worn by you until... until I was able to come to claim you as my bride. 'Twould have been a very short time, I assure you, though you may or may not believe that, too. But it doesn't matter what you believe, does it, Monica, because you've made it clear you want no part of sharing my life."

His voice taut with anger, he went on, biting off each word, "I fully admit that I don't understand you. I cannot fathom how someone could... could care enough for a person to risk her life as you did for me last night and yet be so willing to leave him forever at almost the next moment."

Her own anger sparked. "Did you think I had any alternative?" she asked him.

"It would seem to me that you did, yes."

"What was I supposed to do, Ian—ask you to marry me so that I could stay in Scotland? Was I supposed to curtsy low and appeal to his lairdship's mercy so—"

She was never to finish this sentence, because he drew her into his arms with a sound that sounded like a growl, and in another swirling instant his mouth had come to claim her lips, silencing her so effectively that she didn't even think of speech for the next few minutes. She could feel the rigid contours of the brace he was wearing, and it came to her that she should caution him—what, in God's name, would Alex MacDuff think of *this*—and then she knew that there would be time for caution later. Lots of time for it, just as there would be time forever for love.

He said, drawing back, "I will teach you to appeal to his lairdship's mercy!"

"Does his lairdship *have* any mercy?" she countered.

"That's to be discovered, isn't it?" he teased.

"And suppose I'm not willing to wait and find out?"

"Then you shall have to be thrown into the dungeon," he told her, "where in the small hours of the morning his lairdship will inevitably follow, if only to assuage his own guilt."

"I'll just bet!" Monica mocked him.

Ian laughed, a wonderfully free laugh, but in the next instant he sobered. "To go back a bit," he said quietly, "were I to ask you to share my life might I expect anything other than a negative answer?"

"That's a strange way to phrase a question," she accused.

"We Scots are both canny and cautious," he told her.

"We Americans like a bit more directness."

"Very well," he said. "Then I suppose I must ask, will...you marry me?"

His voice deepened on the last three words, and she saw him swallow hard. Unbidden tears brimmed as she stared up at him.

Brushing them away with a gentle finger, he said, "Is it a matter to cry about, Monica? I admit it is asking a great deal, because as you know, my life is in Scotland; but I wouldn't be at all adverse to spending time in the States, as well. You should know, too, that despite what I've said about the castle the reason I want Walter to take over here isn't that I'm one of those impoverished noblemen one hears so much about. My uncle was a very thrifty Scot; he didn't leave me penniless with only a title and a mountain of debts, which is what has happened to some. If the place in Edinburgh didn't suit you, we could actually live anywhere we wish. . . ."

She pressed a slender hand against his mouth. "Ian, please! Don't you know I'd spend my life on a rock with you, or anywhere else, if that's what you wanted?"

She caught her breath, because the smile he gave her was purely incredible. "How about in an elevator?" he suggested, and in another instant she was in his arms again, feeling this time as if she were drowning in the deep waters of Loch Lomond, and knowing that she never wanted to surface again.

After a time, he asked, "Will you want a wedding in the States? I'm not sure I can manage to wait that long to tell the entire world there's a new countess of Monbraithe."

She shook her head. "I want to be married in Scotland," she told him.

"Oh?"

"In St. Margaret's chapel in Edinburgh Castle," she said, "with just a very few people. Douglas and Iris and Walter and...and Ellen, perhaps. If it would be possible for us to be married there, of course."

"I would say," Ian answered, before he kissed her again, "that anything will be possible for us— wouldn't you agree?"

"Yes," she nodded. And then she forgot about everything but the rapture of being in his arms... until Angus Grewar finally came to bring more wood for the fire, which by then had long since evolved into glowing embers almost as bright as their love.

What readers say about SUPERROMANCE

Legacy of
PASSION
BY CATHERINE KAY

A love story begun long ago comes full circle...

Venice, 1819: Contessa Allegra di Rienzi, young, innocent, unhappily married. She gave her love to Lord Byron—scandalous, irresistible English poet. Their brief, tempestuous affair left her with a shattered heart, a few poignant mementos—and a daughter he never knew about.

Boston, today: Allegra Brent, modern, independent, restless. She learned the secret of her great-great-great-grandmother and journeyed to Venice to find the di Rienzi heirs. There she met the handsome, cynical, blood-stirring Conte Renaldo di Rienzi, and like her ancestor before her, recklessly, hopelessly lost her heart.

Harlequin Salutes... ANNE MATHER

The author whose romances have sold more than 90 million copies!

Harlequin is proud to salute Anne Mather with 6 of her bestselling Presents novels—

1 **Master of Falcon's Head** (#69)
2 **The Japanese Screen** (#77)
3 **Rachel Trevellyan** (#86)
4 **Mask of Scars** (#92)
5 **Dark Moonless Night** (#100)
6 **Witchstone** (#110)

Wherever paperback books are sold, or complete and mail the coupon below. ✻
